Life in the North

An Apocalyptic LitRPG

Book 1 of the System Apocalypse

by

Tao Wong

Copyright

Life in the North
Copyright © 2017 Tao Wong. All rights reserved.
Copyright © 2017 Sarah Anderson Cover Designer

A Starlit Publishing Book
Published by Starlit Publishing
PO Box 30035
High Park PO
Toronto, ON, Canada, M6P 3K0

www.starlitpublishing.com

Ebook ISBN: 9781775058724
Paperback ISBN: 9781775058731
Hardcover ISBN: 9781989458389

Books in
The System Apocalypse Universe

Main Storyline

Life in the North

Redeemer of the Dead

The Cost of Survival

Cities in Chains

Coast on Fire

World Unbound

Stars Awoken

Rebel Star

Stars Asunder

Broken Council

Forbidden Zone

System Finale

System Apocalypse - Relentless

A Fist Full of Credits

Dungeon World Drifter

Apocalypse Grit

System Apocalypse - Australia

Town Under

Flat Out

Bloody Oath

Anthologies & Shorts

System Apocalypse Short Story Anthology Volume 1

System Apocalypse Short Story Anthology Volume 2

Valentines in an Apocalypse

A New Script

Daily Jobs, Coffee and an Awfully Big Adventure

Adventures in Clothing

Questing for Titles

Blue Screens of Death

My Grandmother's Tea Club

The Great Black Sea

Growing Up – Apocalypse Style

A Game of Koopash (Newsletter exclusive)

Lana's story (Newsletter exclusive)

Debts and Dances (Newsletter exclusive)

A Tense Meeting (Newsletter exclusive)

Comic Series

The System Apocalypse Comics (7 Issues)

Table of Contents

Books in The System Apocalypse Universe 3

Chapter 1 9

Chapter 2 20

Chapter 3 30

Chapter 4 39

Chapter 5 51

Chapter 6 69

Chapter 7 88

Chapter 8 106

Chapter 9 124

Chapter 10 131

Chapter 11 150

Chapter 12 167

Chapter 13 183

Chapter 14 201

Chapter 15 208

Chapter 16 224

Chapter 17 243

Chapter 18 258

Chapter 19 273

Chapter 20 287

Chapter 21 301

Chapter 22 308

Chapter 23 318

Chapter 24 332

Chapter 25 338

Author's Note 345

About the Author 346

About the Publisher... 347

Glossary.. 350

    Erethran Honor Guard Skill Tree 350

    John's Skills 350

    Spells.. 352

    Equipment.. 353

Preview for Redeemer of the Dead.................................. 355

Preview for Adventures on Brad: A Healer's Gift............ 366

Chapter 1

Greetings citizen. As a peaceful and organised immersion into the Galactic Council has been declined (extensively and painfully we might add), your world has been declared a Dungeon World. Thank you. We were getting bored with the 12 that we had previously.

Please note that the process of developing a Dungeon World can be difficult for current inhabitants. We recommend leaving the planet till the process is completed in 373 days, 2 hours, 14 minutes and 12 seconds.

For those of you unable or unwilling to leave, do note that new Dungeons and wandering monsters will spawn intermittently throughout the integration process. All new Dungeons and zones will receive recommended minimum levels, however, during the transition period expect there to be significant volatility in the levels and types of monsters in each Dungeon and zone.

As a new Dungeon World, your planet has been designated a free-immigration location. Undeveloped worlds in the Galactic Council may take advantage of this new immigration policy. Please try not to greet all new visitors the same way as you did our Emissary, you humans could do with some friends.

As part of the transition, all sentient subjects will have access to new classes and skills as well as the traditional user interface adopted by the Galactic Council in 119 GC. Thank you for your co-operation and good luck! We look forward to meeting you soon.

Time to System initiation: 59 minutes 23 seconds

I groan, freeing my hand enough to swipe at the blue box in front of my face as I crank my eyes open. Weird dream. It's not as if I had drunk that much either, just a few shots of whiskey before I went to bed. Almost as soon as the box disappears, another appears, obscuring the small 2-person tent that I'm sleeping in.

Congratulations! You have been spawned in the Kluane National Park (Level 110+) zone.
You have received 7,500 XP (Delayed)

As per Dungeon World Development Schedule 124.3.2.1, inhabitants assigned to a region with a recommended Level 25 or more above the inhabitants' current Level will receive one Small perk.

As per Dungeon World Development Schedule 124.3.2.2, inhabitants assigned to a region with a recommended Level 50 or more above the inhabitants' current Level will receive one Medium perk.

As per Dungeon World Development Schedule 124.3.2.3, inhabitants assigned to a region with a recommended Level 75 or more above the inhabitants' current Level will receive one Large perk.

As per Dungeon World Development Schedule 124.3.2.4, inhabitants assigned to a region with a recommended Level 100 or more above the inhabitants' current Level will receive one Greater perk.

What the hell? I jerk forwards and almost fall immediately backwards, the sleeping bag tangling me up. I scramble out, pulling my 5' 8" frame into a sitting position as I swipe black hair out of my eyes to stare at the taunting blue message. Alright, I'm awake and this is not a dream.

This can't be happening, I mean, sure it's happening, but it can't be. It must be a dream, things like this didn't happen in real life. However, considering the rather realistic aches and pains that encompass my body from yesterday's hike, it's really not a dream. Still, this can't be happening.

When I reach out, attempting to touch the screen itself and for a moment, nothing happens until I move my hand when the screen seems to 'stick' to it, swinging with my hand. It's almost like a window in a touchscreen which makes no sense, since this is the real world and there's no tablet. Now that I'm concentrating, I can even feel how the screen has a slight tactile sensation to it, like touching plastic wrap stretched too tight except with the added tingle of static electricity. I stare at my hand and the window and then flick it away watching the window shrink. This makes no sense.

Just yesterday I had hiked up the King's Throne Peak with all my gear to overlook the lake. Early April in the Yukon means that the peak itself was still covered with snow but I'd packed for that, though the final couple of kilometers had been tougher than I had expected. Still, being out and about at least cleared my mind of the dismal state of my life after moving to Whitehorse. No job, barely enough money to pay next month's rent and having just broken up with my girlfriend, leaving on a Tuesday on my junker of a car was just what the doctor ordered. As bad as my life had been, I'm pretty sure I wasn't even close to breaking down, at least not enough to see things.

I shut my eyes, forcing them to stay shut for a count of three before I open them again. The blue box stays, taunting me with its reality. I can feel my breathing shorten, my thoughts splitting in a thousand different directions as I try to make sense of what's happening.

Stop.

I force my eyes close again and old training, old habits come into play. I bottle up the feelings of panic that encroach on my mind, force my scattered thoughts to stop swirling and compartmentalise my feelings. This is not the time or place for all this. I shove it all into a box and close the lid, pushing my emotions down until all there is a comforting, familiar, numbness.

A therapist once said my emotional detachment is a learned self-defence mechanism, one that was useful during my youth but somewhat unnecessary now that I'm an adult with more control over my surroundings. My girlfriend, my ex-girlfriend, just called me an emotionless dick. I've been taught better coping mechanisms but when push comes to shove, I go with what works. If there's an environment which I can't control, I'm going to call floating blue boxes in the real world one of them.

Calmer now, I open my eyes and re-read the information. First rule – what is, is. No more arguing or screaming or worrying about why or how or if I'm insane. What is, is. So. I have perks. And there's a system providing the perks and assigning levels. There's also going to be dungeons and monsters. I'm in a frigging MMO without a damn manual it looks like, which means that at least some of my misspent youth is going to be useful. I wonder what my dad would say. I push the familiar flash of anger down at the thought of him, focusing instead on my current problems.

My first requirement is information. Or better yet, a guide. I'm working on instinct here, going by what feels right rather than what I think is right since the thinking part of me is busy putting its fingers in its ears and going 'na-na-na-na-na'.

"Status?" I query and a new screen blooms.

Status Screen			
Name	John Lee	Class	None

Race	Human (Male)	Level	0
Titles			
None			
Health	100	Stamina	100
Mana	100		
Status			
Twisted ankle (-5% movement speed) Tendinitis (-10% Manual Agility)			
Attributes			
Strength	11	Agility	10
Constitution	11	Perception	14
Intelligence	16	Willpower	18
Charisma	8	Luck	7
Skills			
None			
Class Skills			
None			
Spells			
None			

Unassigned Attributes:

1 Small, 1 Medium, 1 Large, 1 Greater Perk

Would you like to assign these attributes? (Y/N)

The second window pops up almost immediately on top of the first. I want more time to look over my Status but the information seems mostly self-explanatory and it's better to get this over with. It's not as if I have a lot of time. Almost as soon as I think that, the Y depresses and a giant list of Perks flashes up.

Oh, I do **not** have time for this. I definitely don't have time to get stuck in character creation. Being stuck in a zone that is way out of my Level when the System initializes is a one-way ticket to chowville. The giant list of perks before me is way too much to even begin sorting through, especially with names that don't necessarily make sense. What the hell does Adaptive Coloring actually mean? Right, this system seems to work via thought, reacting to what I think so, perhaps I can sort by perk type – narrow it down to small perks for a guide or companion of some form?

Almost as soon as I think of it, the system flashes out and only the word Companion appears. I nod slightly to myself and further details appear, providing two options.

        AI   *Spirit*

I select AI but a new notice flashes up

AI Selection unavailable. *Minimum requirements of:*
Mark IV Processing Unit not met

I grunt. Yeah, no shit. I don't have a computer on me. Or... in me? No cyberpunk world for me. Not yet at least, though how cool would that be with a computer for a brain and metallic arms that don't hurt from being on the computer too much. Not the time for this, so I pick Spirit next and I acknowledge the query.

System Companion Spirit gained

Congratulations! World Fourth. As the fourth individual to gain a Companion Spirit, your companion is now (Linked). Linked Companions will grow and develop with you.

As I dismiss the notifications, I can see a light begin to glow to my right. I twist around, wondering who or what my new companion is going to be.

***

"Run, hide or fight. Ain't hard to make a choice boy-o."

Look, I'm no pervert. I didn't need a cute, beautiful fairy as my System Companion Spirit. Sure, a part of me hoped for it, I'm a red-blooded male who wouldn't mind staring at something pretty. Still, practically speaking, I would have settled for a Genderless automaton that was efficient and answered my questions with a minimum of lip. Instead, I get... him.

I stare at my new Companion and sigh mentally. Barely a foot tall, he's built like a linebacker with a full, curly brown beard. Brown hair, brown eyes and olive skin in a body-hugging orange jumpsuit that's tight in all the wrong places completes the ensemble. Ali my new companion has been here for all of 10 minutes giving me the lowdown and I'm already partly regretting my choice.

Partly, because for all of his berating, he's actually quite useful.

"Run," I finally decide, pulling apart the chocolate bar and taking another bite. No use fighting, nothing in the store that could scratch a Level 110 monster is going to be usable by me according to Ali and while there's no guarantee one of them will spawn immediately, even the lower level monsters that will make up its dinner would be too tough for me.

Hiding just delays things, so I have to get the hell out of the park which really, shouldn't be that hard. It took me half-a-day of hard hiking to get up this far in the mountain from the parking lot and the parking lot is just inside the new zone. At a good pace, I should be down in a few hours which if I understand things properly means there aren't that many monsters. Once I'm out, it seems Whitehorse has a Safe Zone, which means I can hunker down and figure out what the hell is going on.

"About damn time," grouses Ali. A wave of his hands and a series of new windows appear in front of me. Shortly after appearing he demanded full access to my System which has allowed him to manipulate the information I can see and receive. It's going a lot faster this way since he just pushes the information to me, letting me read through things while he does the deeper search. The new blue windows - System messages according to him - are his picks for medium and large perks respectively.

Prodigy: Subterfuge

You're a natural born spy. Intrepid would hire you immediately.
Effect: All Subterfuge skills are gained 100% quicker. +50% Skill Level increase for all Subterfuge skills.

"Why this?" I frown, poking at the Subterfuge side. I'm not exactly the spying kind, more direct in most of my interactions. I've never really felt the need to lie too much and I certainly don't see myself creeping around breaking into buildings.

"Stealth skills. It gives a direct bonus to all of them which means you'll gain them faster. A small perk would allow us to directly affect the base Stealth skill but at this level, we've got to go up to its main category." Ali replies and continues, "If you manage to survive, it'll probably be useful in the future anyway."

Quantum State Manipulator (QSM)

The QSM allows its bearer to phase-shift, placing himself adjacent to the current dimension.

Effect: While active, user is rendered invisible and undetectable to normal and magical means as long as the QSM is active. Solid objects may be passed through but will drain charge at a higher rate. Charge lasts 5 minutes under normal conditions.

"The QSM – how do I recharge it?"

"It uses a Type III Crystal Manipulator. The Crystal draws upon ambient and line specific…" Ali stares at my face for a moment before waving his hand. "It recharges automatically. It'll be fully charged in a day under normal conditions."

"No Level requirements on these?"

"None."

I picked Ali because he knows the System better than I do, so I can either accept what he's saying or I can do it myself. Put that way, there's really not much of a choice. It's what we talked about, though that Perk Subterfuge isn't really going to be that useful for me. On the other hand, any bonuses to staying out of sight would be great and the QSM would let me run away if I was found out. Which just left my Greater Perk.

Advanced Class: Erethran Honor Guard

The Erethran Honor Guard are Elite Members of the Erethran Armed Forces.

Class Abilities: +2 Per Level in Strength. +4 Per Level in Constitution and Agility. +3 Per Level in Intelligence and Willpower. Additional 3 Free Attributes per Level.

+90% Mental Resistance. +40% Elemental Resistance

May designate a Personal Weapon. Personal Weapon is Soulbound and upgradeable.

Honor Guard members may have up to 4 Hard Point Links before Essence Penalties apply.

Warning! Minimum Attribute Requirements for the Erethran Honor Guard Class not met. Class Skills Locked till minimum requirements met.

Advanced Class: Dragon Knight

Groomed before birth, Dragon Knights are the Elite Warriors of the Kingdom of Xylargh.

Class Abilities: +3 Per Level in Strength and Agility. + 4 Per Level in Constitution. +3 Per Level Intelligence and Willpower. + 1 in Charisma. Additional 2 Free Attributes per Level.

+80% Mental Resistance. +50% Elemental Resistance

Gain One Greater and One Lesser Elemental Affinity

Warning! Minimum Attribute Requirements for the Dragon Knight Class not met. Class Skills Locked till minimum requirements met.

"That's it?"

"No, you could get this too."

Class: Demi-God

You sexy looking human, you'll be a demi-god. Smart, strong, handsome. What more could you want?

Class Abilities: +100 to all Attributes

All Greater Affinities Gained

Super Sexiness Trait

"That's not a thing."

"It really ain't," smirking, Ali waves and the last screen dismisses. "You wanted a class that helps you survive? That means mental resistances. Otherwise, you'll be pissing those pretty little Pac-Man boxers the moment you see a Level 50 monster. You wanted an end-game? The Honor Guard are some mean motherfuckers. They combine magic and tech making them one of the most versatile groups around, and their Master class advancements are truly scary. The Dragon Knights fight Dragons. One on one and they sometimes even win. Oh, and neither, and I quote 'makes me into a monster'.

"If these are Advanced Classes, what other classes are there?" I prod at Ali, still hesitating. This seems like a big choice.

"Basic, Advance, Master, Heroic, Legendary," lists Ali and he shrugs. "I could get you a Master Class with your perk, but you'd be locked out of your Class Skills forever. You'd also take forever to level because of the higher minimum experience level gains. Instead, I've got you a rare Advanced Class - it'll give you a better base stat gain per level and you won't have to wait forever to gain access to your Class Skills. Getting a Basic Class, even a rarer Basic Class would be a waste of the Greater Perk. So, what's it going to be?"

As cool as punching a dragon in the face would be, I know which way I'm going the moment he called it up. I mentally select the Guard and light fills me. At first, it just forces me to squint but it begins to dig in, pushing into my body and mind, sending electric, hot claws into my cells. The pain is worse than anything I've felt and I've broken bones, shattered ribs and even managed to electrocute myself before. I know I'm screaming but the pain keeps coming, swarming over me and tearing at my mind, my control. Luckily, darkness claims me before my mind shatters.

Chapter 2

"You could have told me that was going to happen!" I shout at Ali who is hovering over my right shoulder as I rush the packing of my tent and gear.

"How was I supposed to know you'd bitch out and faint like a Goblin on his first date?" Ali smirks, contentedly floating alongside me and watching my back.

"You, I could, aaarrggghh!!!" I want to scream but I have to keep it contained as I continue packing. I have to push away that emotion and the fear that grips my guts, wanting to take control and force me to do nothing. We've lost over two hours already to my class change and the System is up and running. The fact was that the System was now in place and had saturated the Park with Mana, so much that spontaneous mutations were already cropping up all over the area, according to Ali. I needed to get out of here, preferably quietly and fast. On top of it all, the smoke trail down the mountain where the parking lot was located just said a lot of bad things about what happened to my car.

All in all, screaming was the least helpful reaction I could have at this point in time. Well, besides sitting around like a blithering idiot. "You could help you know."

"I am," Ali sighs and waves his hand outwards. "I'm watching your back."

I'd argue but at this point the bag is packed and it's time to go. I rip open another of my chocolate bars, chewing down on it as I slide the bag on and cinch up.

I spend a moment looking around the clearing again, a part of me registering the gorgeous view. Kathleen Lake sits in its glacial glory, waters rippling and throwing up waves as the wind howls around the snow-capped mountains that surround it. Pristine wilderness that could have been put on a postcard now shouts danger to me, forests hiding who knows what new monsters. Turning around, my eyes roam over the campsite to check there isn't anything else that I can do in my campsite and find nothing. The alpine underbrush around here is sparse, the trees small and stunted from having only a short summer to grow in, so I decide to bushwhack my way down the mountain rather than use the trail. Better to go slow and quietly than head down a trail straight into the waiting arms of whatever creature that decides to stake it out in this new world.

Thirty minutes in, I get a notification that I've received a skill called "Stealth". I can't say I'm surprised, sneaking was part of the plan Ali and I had come up with. Between my medium perk and being seriously under-leveled in a high Mana environment, the System is automatically generating additional bonuses to learning rates to help balance the risk/reward ratio. The moment the notification happens, a slight tingle travels through my body, the knowledge shifting the way I move, think and just analyse the surroundings.

The first sign of trouble that I encounter is the chittering. It's way too loud. I spot it next, a black shadow the size of a Doberman moving along the ground on six legs with antennae. Ants should not be that big. I freeze, then begin to back up slowly. Thank the gods it hasn't seen me.

"Oy, you big black beauty. Over here! Tasty morsel for your Queen. Yoo hooo!" a manically grinning Ali shouts above me, waving his arms to get attention.

"What the fuck!" There's no time to do anything beyond begin berating him since the ant, drawn to the little bugger's antics, turns to me and after a brief moment's hesitation charges directly at me. I bring my walking stick up and lunge forwards, hoping to spear it.

Yeah, not a fencer. Also, not a sword. The point skitters off harmlessly and the ant is on me, bowling me over and attempting to behead me with its mandibles.

I heave, bucking around before managing to throw it off me. Luckily, my backpack helps a little with that, the entire angle all kinds of wrong for lying flat. I even manage to get the ant to flip over underneath me when I throw it off. On top of the ant, I splay my body outwards before laying the walking pole across its neck, holding it in place with one arm while I desperately hunt for my survival knife. It takes a moment to find it on my belt and then it's just a few minutes of desperate stabbing before the creature stills.

I'm dirty, smelly and covered in ant guts. I don't give a shit about all of that as I stand up, absolutely furious. "What in the hundred hells was that?"

"Training." Ali shrugs unconcerned, "You needed to level up. That was a Level 1 Ant. No way you'd be able to find easier prey. Now you grabbing your loot?"

"You, you, you…" I splutter to a stop, turning to the ant instead and kicking it a few times to take out the accumulated frustration and fear. Adrenaline spent, I slump down beside the ant's body before I finally register what he said. "Loot?"

"Place your hand on the body and either think or say Loot."

I comply and blink at the pop-up that appears. I reach out, grabbing the loot that is displayed before grimacing. A hunk of ant meat.

"Put it in your inventory, stupid."

I've given up even questioning the insane things that are happening by now, forcing myself to just accept it all. When I think inventory, a grid of five by five appears. Putting my hand into the grid has the meat appear in it, filling a space. I wonder if it's stackable?

"Nice," I start reaching to undo my bag when I get called up short.

"Don't bother, only System generated items can go into the inventory," Ali comments as he continues to spin around me.

"Ugh. What a damn scam," I grumble, keeping my bag on as I stare at the rest of the ant body. I guess this new world doesn't have a dissolving corpse gimmick.

Level Up!

You have reached Level 2 as an Erethran Honor Guard. Stat Points automatically distributed. You have 3 Free Attributes to distribute. Class Skills locked.

Strange that the notification pops up only now. Then I pause, glancing to Ali who gives me a thumbs up. Ah, he's suppressing them till it makes sense to view them. I had been rather disappointed when I first woke up that the saved experience I had earlier hadn't leveled me up, even to Level 2 but Ali did explain that Advanced Classes had higher experience requirements. One look at my free stat points and I dump them all into Luck. Yeah, I know there might be smarter things to do with the points, things like maximising my Agility or perhaps my Strength to become all powerful.

Anyone who thinks that though hasn't lived my life. If my Luck stat really is that low, it'd explain a hell of a lot of things about my past. I wouldn't even be in the Yukon if my apartment hadn't burnt down a week after I lost my job as a programmer, which led to me coming up here with my then girlfriend. What a shitshow that had become with her too,. The damn insurance company wouldn't even accept my claims, which left me with nothing to my name beyond some meager savings. Rather than going home in shame to my father, I picked up and moved to a new Territory. I'd rather die than see my father like this. Now that I've got a chance to redirect some bad Karma or fate, I'm taking it.

"You know, it ain't that kind of lucky right boy-o?"

I am a bigger man than him. I am a bigger man than him. I am a bigger man than him. I give him the finger and head down, both of us getting serious again.

***

The rest of the day sees me climbing down cautiously, scooting around the rather ubiquitous giant creatures when I can and occasionally slaying them when I can't. The slaying wasn't my decision but after some hurried negotiation, Ali and I came to an agreement. He'd let me know of any low-level monsters we came across and I'd attack and kill them if I could do it safely. In return, he'd not force my hand – so long as I was actually making a good will effort. If I was in the army, I'd call him a drill sergeant. Since I'm not, I just call him an asshole.

Things only got really scary once. I walked under what I thought were a pair of trees and realised it was the legs of what I can only describe as a giant ogre. Thankfully, his first swipe missed and once I had him thinking I was running downhill, I activated the QSM and ran back uphill past him. I spent the next half-hour watching him rampage downhill, knocking down trees and smashing other monsters that got in his way. I'd never been more scared in my life, especially since the ogre's diet seemed to consist of anything fleshy.

On the other hand, I had him to thank for my highest level kill so far – a fox whose spine had been shattered by a fallen tree. The loot just consisted of more organ parts and its fur, but I'm not complaining about free experience and loot.

I'd like to say I spent the rest of the day struggling down the hill, heroically pushing past exhaustion and the fear, but by 3pm, I was done. Being on a constant adrenaline high, hiding and backing off continually had worn me down and I knew if I kept this up, I'd make a mistake. I wasn't making good time at all, having barely covered half the ground I needed to. When I found a small depression that was relatively well hidden I just gave up, pulling out my cellphone and trying to boot it up. It stays dead and I look at Ali.

"Don't bother. Electronics are always the first to go once ambient Mana reaches this point. If it's not shielded or made to work with Mana, it all shorts out," Ali explains.

"Fuck. All electronics?" I prod and he nods. Damn, that probably means most new vehicles are dead along with the Internet, cellphones and most modern conveniences. I rub my temple, putting the cellphone away and curl up, deciding to rest for a few minutes. I must have slept because the next thing I knew, it was 7 pm.

"Why us?" I queried Ali as I made dinner from my camping supplies.

"Unique snowflakes you humans. Perfectly unique with boundless potential," Ali, who has been keeping watch outside, answers without looking back to me.

"Enough sarcasm. Really, why us? Why now?"

"Sorry to say, there ain't no good reason. The ambient Mana flow finally reached a point where you could be added to the System."

"Alright, let's back off a second. What's Mana? I keep seeing it on my Status screen and you keep mentioning it but it explains nothing."

"I got a thousand explanations and none for you boy-o. Nanites that enter and control your body using quantum strings and ultra-dimensional energy. Or you could call it the ambient force of the universe, the singular force that makes up all the elements. It could be dark matter made from flesh or magic. It's all the same, just people prattling on without a clue," Ali shrugs. "It's what surrounds us, what makes the System work."

"Okay, then what's the System?"

"The blue boxes. The experience points. The loot. The Shop that lets you buy anything from anywhere or from the Shopkeepers who rent the place. It's the way we upgrade our world and ourselves. It's what constrains me to working with you and for you. It's everything. The System's your world, your universe now," exclaims Ali fatalistically.

"I thought the Galactic Council created it, I mean, their announcement…" I waved my hand to where the blue boxes were.

"The GC make something? About the only thing those bureaucrats could make is a pile of shit. And that's only because they'd been told where to sit. Those idiots only have the loosest control over the System and the galaxy's happier that way. Just leave it, kid, the System just is."

"Come on, you're not a little curious about what the System is? It rules our lives and…"

"Enough. Just stop already," Ali spins around, floating up to my face and glaring at me.

"I just want to know damn it!"

Congratulations! Quest Granted. **The System**
Find out what the System is.
Rewards: Knowledge is power. Or something.

The moment the quest appears, Ali lets out a groan and just floats away. I read it over and then dismiss it before I speak again. "What's your problem?"

"Nothing. Nothing at all," Ali just sits in the sky, floating with his legs crossed and refusing to face me.

"Ali."

"I hate that quest. It's the fucking turd-bucket of the galaxy. Everyone gets it, and everyone thinks they'll be the first one to solve it. And then you end up spending the next 80 years of your life sitting in a fucking library, debating with other fucking researchers over a Kricklik written article first published 2,000 years ago! And then, well, fuck..." as he speaks his voice gets louder and louder.

"I got it, I got it. You have issues. Can we please not bring the forest down on us?" I gesture with my palms down, trying to shush him.

Calming down slightly, Ali growls. "I ain't got issues. You need tissues."

Ummm.... Okay, moving along. Quests eh, I guess if the system continues to work the same way, then the quest tab is under...

Quests	
Unique	Get out of Kluane National Park alive
Party	None
System	Unravel the secrets of the System

"When did I get that quest?" I mutter to myself, staring at the first quest listed.

"Oh, I accepted that one for you while you were playing electric eel."

"You can accept quests for me!?" I stare at Ali. "How much control did I actually give you?"

"Not enough lucky boy," Ali smirks before he shrugs. "I'm your Companion. Can't do anything to hurt you and you were getting out of here anyway. Didn't matter if I accepted it or not."

"Fine, just let me know, will you? I don't like surprises like that," I close out the tab then stare at him a bit more. "What exactly is a Companion?"

"About frigging time. I'm a System Companion – Spirit Type to be exact. As a System-assigned Companion, I get access to your interface and certain aspects of the System that general users don't. We're linked so once you man up, I'll get more abilities too. At Level 2, I got access to information about the monsters that are in the System around us. Later on, I'll be able to provide you with more details, and at even higher levels, I'll be able to share my Elemental Affinity and even gain a body."

I nod in thanks to Ali and then fall silent, pondering what he said. Seems like having him as a Linked Companion was more powerful than I thought. Still, there was so much to learn. "There a Help file?"

A hand waves and in a moment, a giant blue box of text drops in front of me. I grunt and lean further back into the cave to begin reading. Hours later, I have a better understanding of the basics. The base attributes are pretty self-explanatory, though interestingly enough Stamina dictates not only my base Health but how fast I heal. Each point basically heals the same amount per minute. Intelligence dictates how large a Mana pool I have, while Willpower refreshes that pool on a per minute basis based on its statistical value. Of course, I don't really know how useful that is right now since I didn't have anything that uses Mana, but it's still good information.

Interestingly enough, Health wasn't just how physically healthy I was. It was actually a numerical value for how much damage the Mana embedded in my body would actually absorb, defraying damage done to me. It wouldn't stop instant death if I had a pick shoved through my brain, but it would actually reduce the force of the pick as it impacted me, if I had a large enough Health pool. Of course, that used up some of the embedded Mana, reducing my 'Health' at a more drastic rate. Such a strange thing, especially since this embedded Mana was completely different from the Mana that I could use for spells. As I fight off another yawn, I turn to poking at more information about the things I saw on the Status screen.

Class Skills were special skills, abilities that relied on Mana to produce their effects. They generally broke the law of physics, the amount dependent upon the skill itself. Some of the common examples make me think of action movies and anime - the ability to generate fire from my hands or get an armor-plated body seemed cool.

Spells, on the other hand, were just that, magical spells that used Mana to cast. The distinction between what was considered a skill and what was considered a spell seemed a bit arbitrary to me, but perhaps it will become clear when I actually get either one of them.

And Perks, well, Perks were things you gained for completing special quests or just being in the wrong place at the wrong time it seemed. Small or large advantages over your everyday non-perked person.

Now we had numbers, points to say who we are, what we are, what we're good or bad at supposedly. Would it have mattered when I was younger, to be able to point to a screen to say 'I'm not who you think I am', or would it have been the same? If my life had been governed before by this System, would I have tried to raise my Charisma or perhaps trained more to be stronger? Would I have failed less because I would have focused on things that I was good at already? Or would it not have mattered?

I sigh, rubbing at my eyes. There's so much left to read, so much left to learn about this strange new world. I want to read more but I can't fight off the exhaustion any longer, my eyes drifting shut.

Chapter 3

Congratulations. You survived an entire day! You humans really are an excellent bunch. Only 60% of you died yesterday. We are impressed. Have a cookie. And some experience. Remember, monster spawning will increase over the next week.

"60%!" I shut my eyes as my mind attempts to grasp the meaning of that number. 60% - over 4 billion dead. 60% - 6 in 10 people I've ever met are dead. 6 in 10… that means my family are dead since I'm alive. That last thought makes my breath catch, a yawning chasm of pain opening up. I've been avoiding thinking of them, of what this System means for the world but with this announcement, grief and rage and regret build. That chasm of pain and mixed emotions widen for a moment before it gets bunched away and put aside, compartmentalized. I don't have time to deal with this now, I have things to do, my own existence to keep alive.

"You know, crying is considered real manly in Kraska cultures. Of course, they're sort of like your earth crocodiles," Ali floats above me, watching me deal with my thoughts before he waves the notification away. "Let's go boy-o."

"Give me a moment," I mutter.

"You aren't really going to cry, are you?" Ali asks, spinning completely upside down in boredom.

"No, no I'm not," I state confidently. I can feel the grief if I focus but it, like most of my other emotions, is muted, like a heavy blanket thrown over a speaker. It's there, just hard to access. Enough for me to function, at least mostly. I can tell though, even now, the grief is mixing with that rolling sea of anger that I live in.

Anger…

"Ali, find me something to kill," I state dispassionately as I stand up and heft my bag. "Find me a lot of things to kill."

Ali for once doesn't give me lip, just doing as I request.

***

"It's dead," Ali speaks placatingly to me as I give the Ground Squirrel one last stab. I might have gone a bit overboard there – the animal is pretty much in pieces. Thank the gods the loot function doesn't take into account the body of the creature, giving my prize without the rather nasty stab wounds.

"Ali, how do I get a better weapon?" I stare at my knife and the creature. Luckily, I indulged my inner child when I picked it up and got a Bowie. Truthfully, it was way too much of a knife for camping but I had been on a Rambo kick when I bought it. Now, it's my one and only weapon. Well, that and a can of bear spray.

"System Shop. That'll be in a System generated safe haven, which currently is only in Whitehorse itself. You'll need to sell your loot to get it though, unless you get some System Credits which only sentients carry," Ali continues to explain. "Still need to work out your feelings?"

"Let's get out of here," I shake my head, the rage finally settling. I'm not sure what it says about me, that I took out my feelings on these creatures, but for now, I'm just going to avoid dwelling on that. It's mid-morning already and I've only managed to make a couple of kills so far. Hunting is getting more and more dangerous as even Earth creatures mutate at an increasing rate, out-leveling me and my pitiful knife.

"Alright boy-o, same deal as yesterday," Ali waves his hand down the path and I follow his directions.

***

Knife held out before me, I jump and swing downwards, the QSM deactivating at the last second as I plunge the knife into the Snowshoe Hare's head. I hope I hit something important since the hare is now the size of a horse but much broader. It rears its head and only a hastily grabbed piece of fur keeps me on it as I repeatedly plunge the blade into the back of its head and neck.

A minute later, sufficient damage is done for the Hare to fall over dead. A few moments ago, it finally managed to get me off its back by slamming itself into a nearby pine tree, breaking my shoulder and loosening my grip. As I lie on the ground, whimpering in pain I can't help but wonder why Ali was so insistent I fight the Hare. I give words to my thoughts while bones reform and pop back into place. Pulling myself to sit at the base of the tree and taking another chocolate bar out of my pack, I'm grateful that I always over-pack on the chocolate.

"Hare? I thought it was a Rabbit," Ali frowns, floating above the creature. "Damn. And here I wanted to say 'Nothing's up, Rabbit'. "

***

"Down!"

I drop to the ground and am smashed to the side as the creature hits my backpack. We're moving down the mountain at a good pace, Ali helping to keep me on my toes as monsters keep coming. I roll, coming up face-to-face with a rabid ball of fluff with way too many teeth. The walking stick goes in its maw, the creature biting down on the metal pole automatically. I keep shoving, pinning the creature to the ground as it begins to choke.

"Move!"

I jump, releasing the pole as another of the fluff monsters attacks me from the side, too focused as I am on killing the first. I lash out with my knife, cutting at the scratchy fur as I stumble backwards, desperately waving my weapon at it.

"To your right," Ali calls out and I look right, backhanding the third Tribble monster. The blow catches it and sends it spinning away, tumbling down the hill. The second monster takes my brief distraction as a sign to bite my leg and I scream in pain, stabbing down with my knife again and again till it releases me.

I push off, hobbling to where the first fluff monster continues to gag and cough and I kill it by stomping on the creature, repeatedly doing so till it stops moving.

"Behind you again," Ali calls out, bored now.

I spin, getting my arm up in time to let it chew on my forearm rather than my face and then proceed to stab it to death.

"Well, that's one way of killing monsters. Maybe try not to let them snack on you as much when fighting next time," Ali points out helpfully and I snarl at him, looting the balls of fluff. Really, fluff? That's my loot? Fluff? Then again, what was I expecting from balls of fluff. I dump it in my inventory, grimacing and get moving to the stream I recall being around here, limping my way to it.

I wash my clothing as best as I can in the stream, with Ali keeping watch above me. I work fast, getting rid of as much blood as I can without dampening my clothing too much. Wool or not, wet is wet and early April in Kluane means temperatures are only around 6 Celsius in the shade. As I clean myself, I ask Ali something that's been troubling me. "Ali, how come the monsters never attack you?"

"They can't see me," Ali answers.

I frown, "But that first time…"

"I can become visible with effort, but I can't sustain it for long, not yet at least," Ali pauses, turning to the East before he speaks. "Time to go pretty boy. Company's coming."

I get up hastily, shaking the water off my hands as I take off at a low jog South West, doing my best to keep as quiet as possible.

***

The sun has nearly set when I finally arrive at the car park. What should have been a half-day hike has turned into a two-day ordeal. I'm not surprised to see the burnt remnants of my vehicle, though the hissed word 'Salamander' gives me an idea of what could have caused the problem. Or it would if I knew what a Salamander was.

"Giant lizard with a Greater Affinity to Fire magic. Breathes fire actually, some think it's a lesser variant of a Dragon," Ali explains. "Good news and bad news too."

"Explain," I murmur softly, eyeing the clearing for monsters.

"Bad news – it's headed to your Haines Junction," Ali motions to the rather obvious tracks. When I don't bite at his silence, he sighs and explains the good news, "Its presence is likely to drive away most of the monsters from its path. Makes it safer to follow after. If it doesn't double back."

Great. Just great. I'm going to be following a giant, fire-breathing lizard on its way to the closest source of civilization that I know of and hope it doesn't notice me. At least it ain't called Godzilla.

***

I'm not much of a gamer, but my ex was and I'd picked up enough of the lingo to know the term 'kill stealing'. I would almost feel guilty, ending the life of these Lightning Elk and gaining some minuscule amount of experience from it, but considering they are either mangled or suffering from significant burns, I'll call it a humanitarian act. Beyond those acts of mercy, I resolutely ignore the roasted, half-eaten corpses that make up the majority of the herd and the Salamander's most recent meal.

Level Up!

You have reached Level 3 as an Erethran Honor Guard. Stat Points automatically distributed. You have 3 Free Attributes to distribute. Class Skills Locked

The locked skill draws a grimace from me but considering the ridiculous Stat increases, I can live with it. Since I have a brief moment, I pull up my Status Screen to review it.

Status Screen			
Name	John Lee	Class	Erethran Honor Guard
Race	Human (Male)	Level	3
Titles			
None			
Health	190	Stamina	190
Mana	220		
Status			
Normal			
Attributes			
Strength	15 (50)	Agility	18 (70)

Constitution	19 (75)	Perception	12
Intelligence	22 (60)	Willpower	24 (60)
Charisma	8 (16)	Luck	10
Skills			
Stealth	6	Wilderness Survival	3
Unarmed Combat	2	Knife Proficiency	5
Athletics	3	Observe	4
Cooking	1	Sense Danger	2
Class Skills			
None (2 Locked)			
Spells			
None			
Perks			
Spirit Companion	Level 3	Prodigy (Subterfuge)	N/A

Unassigned Attributes:

Would you like to assign these attributes?

3 Stat Points

(Y/N)

"Whoa! Where did all those skills come from?" Seeing my Status Screen for the first time in days makes an eyebrow go up.

"You've been gaining them all along, I've just been hiding the notifications for now," Ali shrugs, doing an aerial handstand as he waits for me.

"What! Why?" I growl at the little man, eyes narrowing.

"It'd be a distraction. It's not as if you'd have done anything differently, would you? The skills gained from the System get added straight to your muscle memory and mind, so it's not as if you haven't been gaining from it as it stands. The rest is just numbers," Ali sniffs. "Numbers mean jack shit if you aren't doing anything. Best not to obsess."

What he says reminds me of a conversation I had with a school counselor once. IQ means nothing if you don't study he would always say. Hearing Ali mention something so similar, I can't help but glare at him. "Next time, give me a summary every night, will you? I'd at least like to know what's happening."

Ali sighs, acting all put upon as I get moving, adjusting the screen so that it's mostly transparent. I continue studying it, trusting the little man to keep me informed. As annoying as he is, he's a good lookout.

"Ali, the maths doesn't make sense."

"You got a few points from all that running and hiding you've been doing. And once you got a class, your Stats back paid into your Hit Points," Ali states as if it's the simplest thing in the world. To him perhaps, but it'd have been nice to know that could happen. The Help Guide he'd provided had given some understanding of things, but there was obviously still a lot that I didn't understand. "Don't expect any more though, you've leveled up to a point that unless you became a professional athlete, you're better off spending your time leveling."

I nod at his words and then try to decide on what to do with my free points but realise I have no clue, all of the minimums are so far away they might as well be on the moon. With a quick calculation, I'd need at least 18 levels to get just my Strength up to my Class level if I didn't put any points into it. Instead, I leave the points unallocated for now. Maybe I'll figure out what exactly I need later.

"Ali, question about messages. They seem to change in tone, from businesslike to well, kinda dickish."

"Ah, well the base System messages are what you see mostly, the businesslike ones you mention. However, the GC has control of the messages too, so occasionally they take a hand especially if it's something that interests one of their observers," Ali explains.

"Observers?" I grunt, eyeing him and then the surroundings.

"Yeah, but you'd have to do something really big to get their notice. Don't worry about it, not as if you can do anything," Ali points out and I nod. I still find myself hunching my shoulders in a bit - Big Brother is watching.

***

A couple of hours later, I pause and pull out my compass. A quick reckoning of the path ahead and I look to Ali who nods confirmation to what I've guessed. The Salamander has changed course, moving away from the Junction.

Scarily enough, the Salamander is going to be one of the least powerful regular monsters that will inhabit the park from now on, using the overgrown and leveled up native fauna for its food source. Thankfully, the Salamander is dumb, a creature of pure instinct that roams the park and its surroundings.

Readjusting my backpack, I pick up the pace. Hopefully, there's a car or some other vehicle I can borrow that'll get me to Whitehorse. At the very least, there will be survivors who I can join.

Chapter 4

Crossing out the Park nets me a simple message and a reward. Nowhere close to getting enough for another Level Up but every little bit counts.

Quest Complete!
You have survived Kluane National Park and even managed to keep all your limbs!
5,000 XP Awarded

As I near Haines Junction, I try to recall what little I know of it. Town population of around 800, so there should have been at least a few hundred survivors left, if the numbers hold true. The smoke that I see rising from the center of the one road town has me worried, so I take my time, diverting into local houses that make up the approach to the few buildings that mark the town center. I find a car and even keys but nothing works, the car's too new. Damn System.

I luck out when I do so, coming across food and clothing that I can use along with a real weapon at last – an abandoned .56 caliber rifle and a box of bullets. The rifle itself is trigger locked but thankfully, the trigger lock key is easy to find hanging on a nail right across the case. Thank the gods for human laziness.

Signs of struggle are everywhere including a few over-turned cars, pools of blood and smashed windows. Disturbingly, I find no bodies, though perhaps the survivors have collected them all for burial. At least, I hope that's the case, though with the way many of the animals I've met have expanded their diets, I don't hold much hope.

Armed with the new weapon, I venture closer to the town center. Never know what could be awaiting me, though I'm praying that Frosty's is still standing. I could definitely make do with their milkshake, burger and fries.

Beyond one derogatory comment about the peashooter I picked up, Ali has been uncharacteristically quiet. A somewhat unfair observation perhaps – when it's time to be serious, the Spirit is actually rather professional, if a bit much of a know it all.

The first indication of trouble is the overgrown misshapen head that I spot as I creep closer. Looking like a cross between a Neanderthal and Big Foot, the 14-foot tall creature seems to be happily munching on its dinner. Things get even worse when I realise that that's the kid, as the mother, unclothed and very female, strides over and drags her kid back to the center of the town. Ali frowns, staring at them and then a glowing green bar floats above their heads along with a short descriptor.

Ogre Youth (Level 12)
Ogre Matron (Level 21)

I breathe deeply, quelling my pounding heart before I creep forwards further. Something about the meal the kid was holding nags me. I have to know, and when I do get close enough to see, I suddenly wish I didn't. I've found the villagers, or what's left of them. Surrounding a cookfire, there's a good baker's dozen of the adult Ogres, mostly in the Level 20 ranges, lounging after a truly epic feast. Playing in the bone pile is a pair of children, sword-fighting with the thighbones of the former residents of Haines. The only consolation I have is that it looks like the villagers managed to kill a couple of the Ogres by the bodies that are laid aside with care.

I come to my senses when I realise my hands are aching, clutching the rifle so hard all the blood has gone from my fingers. Crawling back into hiding, I force myself to breathe deeply and take control of my emotions. Every time I begin to do so, I recall the small bones that I saw, the half-eaten face and another child, crying and wondering why no one ever came to help. I draw a deep shuddering breath, my hands shaking and unshed tears in my eyes.

"There's nothing we can do John. It's time to go," Ali murmurs consolingly.

"I'm going to kill them. Kill them all," I hiss as rage burns within me, overflowing from its confines and wrapping me in its familiar embrace.

"Not a chance. Even that kid could take you down with a single hit. Give it up, we'll come back another time," Ali insists.

"I. Don't. Care." I snarl, standing up and moving as the anger consumes me. I'm not sure where, but I can't keep still any longer.

"You can't do this. As a group, they'd be a challenge for monsters five times their strength!"

Suddenly, I can feel the anger cool, turning ice cold as a mad plan forms.

***

The plan has three parts. Each part insanely dangerous. To complete the first part, I dump 2 points into Agility and another into Constitution to raise my Stamina. I'm going to need to be fast and fit for this.

Most monsters keep away from Haines Junction, the presence of the Ogres is sufficient deterrent. The ones that don't are quickly dispatched and added to the fire, their bodies butchered just like the humans'. That works to my advantage as I get my plan ready. It takes a couple of days to pull what I need together, days that I barely sleep or eat in as I work at a feverish pace. Twice, I'm almost found out. I spend nearly two hours the first time, hiding beneath a truck waiting for the Ogre pair to move on. The second time, I have to use the QSM and duck pass the converging group to hide. I can tell they are beginning to suspect something, their actions getting more and more agitated as the days go by but they can't find me even if they start huddling closer together and patrolling more.

Preparations finally complete in the Junction itself, I hide my supplies and take only the bare minimum that I need. The gun, two magazines full of bullets and enough food and water for a few days.

When I finally find my objective, I can't help but feel my face split into a humorless grin. I can feel the tightness in my chest, the speeding up heartbeat and the dump of adrenaline as I sign my likely death warrant. It's all secondary though, secondary to the rage that fills my being. I've had enough of hiding and sneaking and fearing for my life. Enough of this System that has driven friends and family to death, wiping out 60% of humanity's population.

If I was going to die, at least I'll do it trying to strike back. The last thought is punctuated by the crack of my rifle, the shot spinning hundreds of yards to smash into the unsuspecting Salamander. I work the bolt, firing again to lock its attention on me. When it turns and begins to lumber towards me, I take off.

I lure the creature to Haines Junction for hours, running as fast as I can and when it finally begins to catch up, I use the QSM to disappear. I husband the use of the QSM, bolting as far as possible and hiding, sneaking away to give myself more distance before I attract its attention again by firing at it. It could go faster but I need the QSM to last me so I often take breaks when the Salamander roots around, searching for me. After a while, I expand the range I shoot from, firing from over half a kilometre away and mostly missing even if it is the size of a barn. Hurting it really isn't the point anyway.

Only twice do I nearly die. Once is near the start, when a sudden surge in speed has it almost catch me. Only a last-minute barrel roll gets me out of the way in time, leaving me with a small wound before I activate the QSM and run like hell to a hiding spot. The second time, the Salamander launches a series of fireballs into the sky, landing them all around me. Fun fact about being in another dimension – I might be able to ignore most physical structures but energy – specifically heat energy - crosses over. By the time I get away from the fire, I feel half-cooked and my flashing health bar in the corner of my vision matches. After that, I keep further away from the creature and only give it brief glimpses of me when I need to pull it closer.

By the time I reach the Junction, I'm nearly out of bullets. The Ogres are lined up, watching the incoming enraged monster. I breathe a sigh of relief when I see them, part 2 of the plan required that the Ogres be willing to fight. When they catch sight of me, they roar and one tries to step forward, only to be chivied back into line by the others. I grin, stopping a good hundred yards from them and wave cheekily at them before turning back to the incoming monster.

"Ali watch them," I growl out, slipping the rifle from my shoulder one last time and lining up a shot on the Salamander. This time around, I need to hurt it enough to draw it all the way, which means I need to make the shot. I draw a few deep breaths, trying to get my thundering heart to calm and my breathing to slow. Already past the boundary of its 'natural' region, the Salamander will need a little more encouragement.

The first shot misses and I snarl, wishing I had spent more time at the range. I always said I would, but somehow never did. Too busy procrastinating. The second shot hits and the explosion is everything I wish it to be. The abandoned propane tank lights up behind the Salamander, too far away to do any real damage but scaring it slightly. Already annoyed with me, the creature charges forward, smart enough to put the sounds of the gunshot and the annoyances it's been facing for the last few hours together.

Bullets out, I toss the rifle to the side and hope I can retrieve it later. Rather than run immediately, I watch the Salamander charge me, waiting. Emboldened by the fact that I've finally stopped running, the Salamander picks up speed and when it is a bare hundred yards away I turn and sprint for the Ogres.

The Ogres are pissed, but without ranged weapons of their own, there's little they can do to stop as I bring their end right to them. Just before I reach them, I trigger the QSM and let the club that's swung at me pass through my body as I duck through their lines. A last, spiteful move makes me release the QSM long enough to plunge my knife into a creature's back and then I take off, leaving the monsters to do their thing. As much as they'd like to chase after me, staying together to fight the Salamander is more important.

A safe distance away, I watch the battle unfold in hiding. It's vicious and not nearly as one-sided as I would have expected. The Ogres hold their own against the Salamander at first, their oversized leader triggering some form of ability that wreathes its club in green as it smashes down on the Salamander. The blow does real damage which the other Ogres are quick to take advantage of, pummelling the dazed Salamander. At first, I almost think the Salamander might die without doing any damage.

That is until its entire body starts glowing red and it releases a cloud of red steam all around it. The Salamander seems to boil its own blood and release it, scalding the surrounding attackers and driving them back. After that, the Salamander bites down on a female Ogre, ripping her arm from her body. The rest of the battle just gets bloody and nasty but half-way through, I realise something is wrong. It takes me a moment to realise what though.

"The kids aren't here!" I snarl out towards Ali who is watching the fight with amusement, somehow having conjured up a bag of popcorn. He stops eating long enough to point before going back to ignoring me.

I follow his directions, sneaking from one building to another to find the children being guarded by the Ogre Youth. My eyes narrow, considering what to do, before I return to the main event. I smile grimly, the battle nearly over by the time I'm done, the badly injured Salamander roasting the last Ogre with its breath.

How do you like being cooked? A part of me is worried about the hateful glee that I'm exhibiting, but it's a very small part. Once the Salamander is done finishing off the last of the main Ogres, I make sure it finishes the job, leading it by taunting it further to the children.

Part 2 complete, I smile humorlessly as the Salamander munches down on the Ogre Youth before I hurry away. I could end it here, revenge taken for the residents of the Junction. However, the rage is not quenched, my anger still needing a final outlet. The Salamander was a monster and it needed to die.

Part 3 was very simple in theory. In fact, I had made a big bet that it'd be the Salamander that was still alive at the end of the battle since I had built my little toy with it in mind. I'd hidden the weapon close on-hand and was grateful the Ogres weren't familiar with human technology or too inquisitive as I find it untouched. Grabbing the shopping cart by its handles I wheel the contraption around to see the Salamander.

I cross my fingers, hoping this works and then shove, sending the entire cart hurtling towards the monster. It doesn't understand what's happening, but it does understand me running away which sends it chasing after me again, obviously wanting to finish me off at last.

Surprisingly, the first bump when it hits the Salamander head-on doesn't set the entire thing off. The second, when its hind foot lands on the cart, does. The cart is packed in layers. The innermost layer, which took serious effort, contains a bottle of home-brewed nitroglycerin. The bottle is sealed tight, packed with cotton around it to ensure that casual bumping doesn't set it off. Around that, I packed half-filled gasoline cans interspersed with hair spray. On the outside, I had a thin layer of nails, screws and nuts. This was my improvised bomb and what took the majority of my time to put together.

When it goes off, the improvised shrapnel does most of the damage as expected. The Salamander might be resistant to high heat and perhaps even partly resistant to the concussive force of the explosions, but there isn't much it can do about the shrapnel that rips up from its foot and into its body.

Of course, I mostly figure that part out later. When the explosion happens, all I remember is sharp pain and the concussive force of the explosion throwing me forwards before blackness takes me.

***

When I wake up, I find Ali hovering over me with a worried look on his face. It disappears the moment I open my eyes, the unimpressed grump pulling back to his usual station. A slight twitch of his hand is all I see before my vision is filled with blue.

Congratulations!

You have been instrumental in the destruction of the Ogre Village (Newbie). Even down to the children. Who is the monster now?

+13,000 XP

Congratulations!

You have helped kill a Salamander (Level 108). You really shouldn't play with bombs, next time they might go off at the wrong time.

+27,000 XP (XP apportioned according to damage done)

"Uhhh... Ali. Did the System just warn me off?" I eye the blue screen worriedly. Did Big Brother actually pay attention to what I did? Could they influence things if I tried something similar? Then again, I wasn't exactly planning on doing this again. Half-remembered YouTube videos and chemistry classes were not the way to build bombs.

"Seems like it, doesn't it?" Ali replies as I dismiss that notification to keep going through the field of blue.

Title Gained

For killing a monster over 100 levels higher than you, you have been awarded the title 'Monster's Bane'. All damage dealt to monsters of a higher Level than you +15%

Congratulations!
For achieving your first title, you receive a bonus +5,000 XP.

Level Up! * 4

You have reached Level 7 as an Erethran Honor Guard. Stat Points automatically distributed. You have 15 Free Attributes to distribute.
Class Skills Locked.

My vision finally clear of the field of blue, I peruse my Status bars and other notifications slowly. Health is still below half and the little additional status icons tell me I'm concussed and exhausted. No shit. Still, no rest for the wicked as I push myself onto my feet, after which I proceed to vomit.

"That's just nasty." Ali sniffs and waits for me to mostly finish before continuing, "Now move it buttercup. Carrion creatures are coming soon and you need to finish looting."

I grimace but get moving slowly, doing my best to not lose my breakfast again. Or is it lunch now? Dinner? Gods, I really don't know and my head hurts way too much for me to care. Still, no complaints— I'm alive which is not what I was expecting. In fact, I'm pretty sure I wasn't actually thinking straight these last few days. Who the hell lures a mini-dragon into a deathmatch with a group of Ogres that just wiped out a village by themselves and builds a bomb by hand?

The Salamander gets me a Salamander Fire Sac, its skin and more meat. Surprisingly, when I open my inventory to put the items away I realise that it's increased in size again.

"Ali... am I seeing things?" I frown, staring at the new 6 by 6 grid.

"Nope, inventory space increases every 5 levels," Ali explains and eyes it. "Lucky for you."

I can't help but agree since otherwise I'd have to toss some of this away. While items of the same type stacked, unique items needed their own slot and the different kinds of meat were all considered unique. Either way, lucky me. I grab the loot from the Salamander and dump it in my inventory, moving on. The children Ogres get me some Ogre skins while the adults are a disappointment at first, giving me an assortment of crude weapons, oversized armour, Ogre hide and 5,000 Credits in total. The Credits go straight into my inventory as a notification, which helps since I've started leaving older loot like the Ant meat aside. When I finally get to the Ogre Chief, I carefully bend down to grab the club it dropped and almost drop it again when the notification pops up.

Enchanted Oversized Club of Smashing

Base Damage: 38

Enchantment: Ignores 20% of Target Armour

Damn. My knife only did a base damage of 4 to start. Of course, as the guide explained, damage after base was based off the targets' armor and where and how you hit. Better kinds of armor absorb more damage, though armor has a tendency to get damaged as it absorbs more and more punishment. In addition, melee weapons had additional damage modifiers that included your strength, which in the Ogre's case was probably significant.

I can barely carry the damn oversized club and the fact that I can even heft it at all breaks all kinds of physics rules, which is why I just leave it on the ground as I reach out to loot the Chieftain next. He gets me another Ogre hide, 7,000 Credits and a golden key. When my hand closes around the key to put it in the inventory, I get another blue screen.

Key to the City

Would you like to take control of Haines Junction? (Y/N)

"What the hell?" I shout to Ali and immediately regret it, my head spinning. Ali zooms over to join me, staring at my screen and being silent while I recover. For a moment, as my head spins, I wonder if he's gotten bigger. Then I get distracted again by him talking.

"Mary's sweet spot," Ali breathes, pointing to the key. "That's why those Ogre's weren't running. They bought the city."

"Explanation, damn it," I reply.

"Ugh… okay. Yeah. Your cities aren't real cities, not at least according to the System. You want to own it, you need to buy the rights to the city. That's what the Ogre's did. They must have pooled their resources, bought the rights from the System and a portal here. Must have cost them a fortune even to get a dump like this," Ali explains quickly, spinning in an agitated circle. I guess that made the Ogres pioneers. Dead, roasted and eaten cannibalistic pioneers.

"Whatever," angrily, I decline the System's offer. Damn System, thinking what we built isn't real. Ali's exclamation of surprise at my actions is cut short by another prompt.

Control over city declined.
No other sentient found in domain.
Would you like to resell the rights to Haines Junction? (Y/N)

I giggle slightly, as I point at Ali, "Not sentient!"

"Dance on a stick. I don't count because I'm linked to you boy-o," Ali retorts even as the key disappears from my hand.

Rights to Haines Junction sold for 10% of cost. 200,000 System Credits credited to account.
As a one-time offer, would you like to spend your System Credits now? (Y/N)

This time, I don't get to choose as Ali does it for me.

Chapter 5

One moment I'm standing amongst the burnt, savaged remnants of the Ogre clan aching in pain and fighting off waves of dizziness and silliness. The next I'm fully healthy in a high-tech retail store that has a thing for yellow. I raise my eyebrow at the color choice, having thought it'd be all blue, but yellow it is, from the walls to the waiting chairs to the counter top where a yellow lizardman waits.

"You're big!" I shout as I see Ali. Unlike his normal foot tall experience, this Ali is a towering 7 feet. Thankfully, he's still clad in his usual orange jumpsuit, which I have to admit, sets off his mocha-colored skin very well.

"This is my real size," Ali grouses and points to me. "You just can't contain my awesomeness."

"Awesomeness?" My jaw almost drops at his choice of words.

"I get bored. Your world has a lot of interesting entertainment forms," Ali says dismissively as he strides over to the waiting lizard. "Malik! You old scoundrel. Have I got a deal for you!"

I stare at the lizardman and my Companion as he begins to pull stuff from my inventory, already getting into an argument over pricing. Better him than me but what the hell should I do? For that matter, why the hell was I healthy?

"Perhaps the Master would like to peruse our wares?" comes a soft voice down by my elbow, making me spin around and throw a strike at it. I catch a glimpse of the speaker, a bipedal fox before it slips under my blow with careless ease.

"Sorry! I'm really sorry. I just, you know, apocalypse!" I apologize profusely.

"Not at all Master, completely normal. It's this servant's fault for startling you," the young fox's grin widens as he gestures to a doorway I didn't see before. "The wares Master?"

"Yeah, I guess I could…" I follow its lead. I am rich after all, or at least, I think I am. "By the way, I was injured beforehand but now I'm feeling fine."

"Ah, part of the transfer process. Galactic Council policy dictates that all purchases be done by individuals in their full health. You will be returned in the same form as you were before though," the Fox explains easily as he leads me to the doorway. The room that we enter is in cool yellow, so large that I can't see the end of it. Inside, the room is dominated by a floating spaceship, reminiscent of the one that Superman came to Earth in from the classic movie. In front of it is a single screen, floating.

Mark VIII Regulus (200,000 Credits)
Single passenger spaceship originally capable of achieving hyperspace travel. Comes equipped with the 3rd Generation Link Laser and 2 Ares Launcher Bays. More… Would you like to purchase this? (Y/N)

My hand unconsciously twitches and moves upward. A ship to get the hell out of here and leave as the System suggested. An escape from the blood and insanity that is my life now, a way to be free of the fear. It's everything that I could want. A slight shift in stance draws my attention to the Fox and my eyes narrow. There's something about the way he's holding himself, something in his eye.

Son of a bitch. They're playing me. Once again, anger rushes through me and I have to work hard on relaxing, on tamping my emotions down. I roll my neck and resolutely hit no. The Fox says nothing, which is lucky for him.

After a brief moment, a giant list of products appear. A tight smile appears on my face before I speak, glancing over to the Fox, "Be a good boy. Get me a chair and some coffee and any chocolate you have on-hand. I'm going to be a while."

The Fox slinks off and I start browsing. Time to make this more manageable.

"Remove all items costing over 200,000 Credits." The list shrinks for a moment before repopulating. I grunt, not surprised. Let's see, what next...

"List only Human specialty items." This time, the list almost completely disappears except for 3. I guess we're too new for a bunch of specialty products.

Human Genome Treatments

Genome Treatments are individually tailored for each client. Each treatment's goal is to fix and optimise the client's base genetic code, removing errors due to aging and radiation. Optional improvements to the treatment include the removal of less than optimal genetic code and the addition of best practise genes.

Base Cost: 10,000 Credits

Removal of Genes: 2,500 Credits

Insertion of Genes: 2,500 Credits

"This won't make me sexless or something strange, will it?" I question the returned Fox, somewhat puzzled at the words 'optimal'. After all, an alien race's definition of optimal might include making us hermaphrodites or adding back our tail.

"No. The Genome Treatment is specifically catered to humanity including your race's societal hangups," the Fox replies, back to its cool professionalism. I grunt and grab the window, swinging it to the side to leave open. Definitely getting that.

The Basics of Mana Manipulation for Humans

Using System Patented technology, the knowledge of basic Mana manipulation will be downloaded directly into your mind. Mana manipulation is a requirement for basic magic skills.
Cost: 5,000 Credits.

Interesting. Playing on a hunch, I pull out a comparison.

The Basics of Mana Manipulation

Using System Patented technology, the knowledge of basic Mana manipulation will be downloaded directly into your mental storage unit. Mana manipulation is a requirement for basic magic skills.
Cost: 1,000 Credits.

"Care to explain?" I turn to the Fox who looks perfectly relaxed with this information. He points to the cheaper option first.

"This is the System created option that is purchasable by any being that is part of the System. However, as it is developed for use for the entire System's inhabitants, it does not guarantee assimilation of the knowledge and in extreme cases may cause harm. In all but the most edge cases, only the most basic information is imparted.

"The second option has been specifically tailored by one of our Craftsmen to ensure that full assimilation of the knowledge will occur. We stand by the product 100% and this product has been particularly successful in your world. Certain gifted individuals have been able to glean a higher base level of skill from purchasing this product."

"What's the chance for the average human to get the skill from this?" I point to the System skill.

"32%"

"And me?"

"98%"

"That's what I figured," I grunt and swipe the System skill window over to join the Genome Treatment. Seven Levels in, my Intelligence is way above base human. Never mind the fact that I was never considered dumb. I turn back to the shopping windows, eyeing the last specialty item.

Thrasher's Guide to Surviving the Apocalypse on Earth

This guide imparts basic information about the System, the current apocalypse and future plans. Included are explanations of common skills, magic, technology, Safe Points, the Shop and more.

Cost: 50 Credits

Eyeing that one dubiously, I create a second section for 'Maybe's'. I have a feeling Ali has more information than a 50 Credit Guide, but it never hurts to ask. Next up, my class "List information purchasable about the Erethran Honor Guard."

A giant list detailing the Honor Guard's training, history, customs, battle tactics, gear, current organisational structure and more appears, most of it in the 20-50 credit range and I grab them all. Interestingly enough, there's even information about Secret and Hidden Missions available for sale, though those I avoid. The Guard is going to be pissed off enough with me as it stands I assume, I really don't need them to get uppity just because I bought some insider knowledge from the System.

Moving on to Basic Skills. I eye the wide range of skills for a second then narrow them down to combat skills for now. The usual series of Unarmed, Bladed, Blunt, Polearms, Archery, Rifles, Pistols and more are there. I could learn to drive a tank if I wanted! A part of me giggles at the idea, though I quickly dismiss it. For one thing, I don't even think there's a single tank in the entirety of the Yukon even before the apocalypse. Now, it'd just be a hunk of metal.

No, better to focus on things I do need. I grab the skills for unarmed combat, adding it to the 'To Buy' pile and then add the rifles and pistols along with bladed weaponry to the 'Maybe' pile. I'll have to figure out the kinds of weapons I'm buying before I get to that.

I pull up the Class Skills selection and wince. Even the cheapest Class Skill starts at the tens of thousands of Credits and they don't particularly look that good. I definitely need to balance my desire for a cool skill with the fact that I need weapons, transportation and skills. Still, I highlight a few and swing them into the 'To-Buy' column.

I grin, finishing up the coffee and then waving the empty cup at the Fox, pulling open the chocolate bars. Oh, right - a quick search reveals a whole series of chocolate bar options and I indulge, picking up a stack of Swiss chocolate. Right, next! A weapon would be great, but I need to remember that I need to allocate money for armor and a mode of transportation. It's only another 160 kilometres or so to Whitehorse but on foot, that would be an easy couple of weeks. That's if I don't account for the various monsters that are likely hanging around.

Best find out how much transportation costs first then. The resulting list makes me wince. Even a basic bike is a few thousand Credits and a compact is over ten thousand Credits with fuelling requirements for gasoline. Anything more advanced and the prices start jumping higher, though a glance at the details shows why. Many of the more advanced vehicles power themselves directly off collected Mana. Armor is likely going to get expensive too. In fact, it'd probably be more expensive than any weapon I buy if humanity's own history is anything to go by.

I snarl in annoyance, staring at the vehicles. There's got to be a way to do this...

***

"Where the hell are you? You better not have bought anything!" Ali slams the door open, looking around desperately for me, obviously finally remembering he wasn't here alone. He rushes over and points a finger at me, snarling; "I look away for one second!"

I snort, feet up in the air and staring at the windows floating in front of me in all their blue glory. A thought and they minimize before Ali can read them, instead pulling out a new window.

"Oh, shut it. I've already got someone better." I point to the window and he spins, staring at the accusing window.

Sixth Generation Lambda Class AI Companion

Resulting from the combination of a Delta and Epsilon class AI, this Sixth Generation Lamba Class Companion is still in its infancy but with its base code can be expected to process significant levels of data and manage the operation of up to 3 Rank D machines or 1 Rank C machine.

Rank: C

Requires: Minimum Rank D Hardware for Installation

Furiously reading, Ali's eyes widen and he sputters for a second, "You, you, you replaced me with a hunk of code!" He's shouting at the end, his face completely red. "You ungrateful meatball, you undeserving maggot eating swine-licking sheep-loving…"

He sputters to a stop as I am bent over, giggling at him. I try at first to control myself, but when his ranting comes to a stop, I fall from the chair and just whoop it up. Every time I think I have a handle on my emotions, I catch a sight of Ali's long-suffering face and I collapse again. Even the Fox is slightly amused from the way its tail is waving around.

I don't know how long it takes me to get control of my emotions but it's a while. When I do, I point a finger at Ali, "Some Companion you are. These hucksters nearly got me."

Ali's eyes narrow and I sigh, calling forth the spaceship. Ali looks at it, the window flickering as he reads more details and grunts. "Yeah, that's a piece of shit. 3 generations out of date, no missiles included, no armor and they've ripped out the original space drive for a hunk of crap that might or might not get you into hyperspace and you certainly need to refuel after every jump. They didn't even frigging fuel it."

The Fox just stands there, with a smile that wouldn't melt ice cream on its face, as we speak. These guys have no shame. Which is why I'm going to be happy to let Ali do the haggling later on and take them to the cleaners.

"Alright, enough fun and games. How'd you do?" I gesture back the way he came from.

"I will get you back," Ali mutters before answering me. "Pretty good. The Salamander Sac's the first to come from Earth, so you got a premium so it sold for $23,187 Credits. The Ogre Hides mostly went cheaply except for the kids. Those are premium, softer you know…"

He shuts up as I hold up my hand, not really needing a detailed list of his exploits. He grumbles for a moment about ungrateful children before answering, "38,632 Credits for all of it."

"That gives us 250,632 Credits yes? And correct me if I'm wrong, but we can buy and apply these in any order we need, yes?"

"Yeah…"

"Good. Here's what I'm thinking," I gesture back to the newly pulled up windows, getting ready to argue with the Spirit.

***

"You can stop anytime pretty boy," Ali grouses as I continue to stare at my reflection. I just flash him a grin, touch the helmet again and make it retreat into a simple metal collar around my neck. The one-piece jumpsuit that I wear is all in black and leaves nothing to the imagination, but that's okay since it is also armor.

Pretty boy is an actual truth for once. The Genome Treatment seems to have, amongst other things, made me actually good looking. My chin has strengthened; my features become slightly more symmetrical and elongated, blending my Chinese origins with other races. I look closer to Keanu Reeves than myself in some ways. Some things I've kept such as my black hair and eyes but additional minor changes have occurred all across my body, including an extra four inches of height and a significant amount of muscle. Lines that had started cropping up in the last few years, small enough that only I'd notice, have disappeared, wiping away another decade and making me look to be in my early 20's again. The facial changes were particularly unnerving but thankfully, I seem to have sub-consciously adjusted to all the changes relatively well. I guess the mental resistance training that came with my class is helping me - either that or the System is just altering my mind to let me get on with my life.

Surprisingly, beyond the surface changes, I don't feel a significant change in the performance of my body. When questioned, Ali explained it as a side effect of my Level and Class – I've long ago exceeded peak human genetics so the Genome Treatment could only provide minor additional adjustments. Something about creating denser muscle fibres, a higher level of red blood cells, increased grey matter and more, most of which I tuned out.

Mostly, what I've focused on are the mental changes. As part of the Genome Treatment, it seemed that a chemical flush was required which has left me feeling more stable, my emotions a bit more under control. There's still residual anger and guilt for surviving, but for now, I'm functional again without the rather severe neurological chemical imbalance I had. Of course, seeing how my mental resistances was handling the outward physical changes with aplomb, I wonder exactly how close I would have been to a breakdown without the class. For a former office worker, I'd done a hell of a lot of running, hiding and killing over the last week.

It doesn't really matter; I am still here and the 'what ifs' could go on forever. It is what it is. Still, I curiously pull up my Status Screen to see the changes.

Status Screen			
Name	John Lee	Class	Erethran Honor Guard
Race	Human (Male)	Level	7
Titles			
Monster's Bane			
Health	390	Stamina	390
Mana	360		

Status			
Normal			
Attributes			
Strength	27 (50)	Agility	38 (70)
Constitution	39 (75)	Perception	14
Intelligence	36 (60)	Willpower	36 (60)
Charisma	14	Luck	10
Skills			
Stealth	6	Wilderness Survival	3
Unarmed Combat	2	Knife Proficiency	5
Athletics	5	Observe	5
Cooking	1	Sense Danger	4
Jury-rigging	2	Explosives	1
Class Skills			
None (4 Locked)			
Spells			
None			
Perks			
Spirit Companion	Level 3	Prodigy (Subterfuge)	N/A

Unassigned Attributes:
12 Stat Points
Would you like to assign these attributes? (Y/N)

"Didn't your mother tell you not to rub it so much," Ali grumbles and I come back to the present and pull my hand down from rubbing my head. There's not even a scar, but if I focus, I can feel the installed neural link in my mind become active. I could almost swear I can feel it sitting in my brain, but that I know is purely psychosomatic. Once again, I call up the detail window of the link.

Tier IV Neural Link

Neural link may support up to 5 connections.

Current connections: Omnitron III Class II Personal Assault Vehicle

Software Installed: Rich'lki Firewall Class IV, Omnitron III Class IV Controller

Dismissing the window, I walk over to my Personal Assault Vehicle (PAV), stroking the handlebars. The PAV looks like a road bike on steroids in this configuration, pure black with sleek lined armor plates. That's not the only thing though; with a thought the PAV can break apart and attach itself to me, acting as power armor. That's right – I have bike mecha. It almost makes up for all the stupid, crazy shit that I've gone through. Almost.

I can't help but call up the details of the mecha again, just to gloat a little.

Omnitron III Class II Personal Assault Vehicle (Sabre)

Core: Class II Omnitron Mana Engine

CPU: Class D Xylik Core CPU

Armor Rating: Tier IV

Hard Points: 4 (1 Used for Quantum State Manipulator Integrator)

Soft Points: 3 (1 Used for Neural Link)

Requires: Neural Link for Advanced Configuration

Battery Capacity: 120/120

Attribute Bonuses: +20 Strength, +7 Agility, +10 Perception

Ali had even been helpful – working with me to tweak my initial choice of the Ares version of this product to the Omnitron. The Omnitron was more heavily armed and armored normally but suffered from a smaller Mana engine. Instead, at Ali's suggestion we had sacrificed the installed weaponry and the better armor for an upgraded Mana engine. The result was a bare bones product that had no bells and whistles but could be upgraded significantly and that has a significant recharge rate.

To keep costs down, we also went with ablative armoring. The way armor worked in this new world, you could either choose super-tough armor that would shatter if it ever was breached or ablative armor that crumpled and reduced but was useable even after getting damaged. Of course, Tier IV armor was still extremely strong by pre-Earth standards. In fact, most of the monsters I've fought directly wouldn't even leave a scratch on it. I'm obviously not counting the Salamander since I never really fought it - just ran away a lot.

The only upgrade we had purchased for the bike was the integrator to the QSM, which by itself had cost a quarter against the price of Sabre. Yeah, I named it. Sue me. I would say I was surprised at how expensive the upgrade was, but considering how ridiculously useful the QSM had turned out to be, I was willing to pay for it.

Of course, that left us with much-reduced funds for my personal weapon. In the end, we had settled on 2 different weapons. The first was attached via a handy holster to Sabre with some minor modifications. It looked for the most part like a regular semi-automatic hunting rifle with a faux wooden stock, just with a slightly bulkier than normal stock. Of course, it wasn't:

Ferlix Type II Beam Rifle (Modified)

Base Damage: 38

Battery Capacity: 21/21

Recharge rate: 1 per hour per GMU (currently 12)

I had to bug Ali to get an explanation of the recharge rate, which he finally did explain in detail, way too much detail in fact. He even pulled up graphs and charts with maps of both the solar system and galaxy. Truth be told, I tuned out after the first 5 minutes. It all boiled down to this – the Galactic Council had instituted a series of measurements based off the 'base' Mana available in the ambient surroundings in the capital. This was a single Galactic Mana Unit or GMU. All Mana engines were rated based on their ability to absorb and charge a Mana battery based off a single GMU. However, in Dungeon Worlds and zones with higher levels, the recharge rates would increase as there was just more GMUs. Mana batteries could be recharged directly but it was a specialised skillset since an improperly charged Mana battery would explode.

My close-range weapon had resulted in a lively debate. Ali had wanted me to purchase a pistol – that man was a gun nut – while I wanted a sword. He had only relented when I pointed out that I needed a weapon that didn't run out of charges in the middle of a fight, otherwise I'd be completely hosed. He's still sulking over losing that argument.

I'd started with a simple hand-and-a-half for my sword and watched it change the moment I made it my personal weapon. Initially, it had a light pattern where the fuller was on the blade, a green inlay on its hilt and a flared guard. It was simple but pretty for a weapon, but choosing it as my personal weapon stripped it of its ornamentation. Now, the sword was sleeker, all traces of ornamentation gone. The only beauty it had now was in its stark simplicity of purpose – this was a weapon meant to kill and kill well.

Tier II Sword (Soulbound Personal Weapon of an Erethran Honor Guard)

Base Damage: 48

Durability: N/A (Personal Weapon)

Special Abilities: None

The sword had grown even sharper and while it could still break, I had only to dismiss it and call it back for it to reappear in its original state.

Preparations complete, all the basic knowledge absorbed, there was but the skills left to do. I finally step away and nod to the Fox, ready for him to begin. As soon as I nodded, I felt the shift. This was even more marked than the previous purchase of knowledge like the world had stopped and then restarted with a lurch. Windows bloom soon after.

Unarmed Combat Skill Gained (Level 6)

Blade Mastery Skill Gained (Level 6)

PAV Combat Skill Gained (Level 4)

Energy Rifles Skill Gained (Level 3)

Meditation Skill Gained (Level 5)

Mana Manipulation Skill Gained (Level 1)

Minor Healing Spell Gained

Even as I finish dismissing the windows, another notice appears.

The System Quest Update

The journey to understanding the origins of the System and Mana has many beginnings, but all roads lead to the understanding of Mana. You have taken your first step in understanding the System.

Requirement: Learn Mana Manipulation

Reward: 500 XP

"Huh," I grin, dismissing the quest update. My business done, my funds drained, I find myself back in the real world.

The smell of burnt flesh and spilt guts return along with the pain. No longer under the System's care, all the damage I had received comes back with interest. Knowing it was coming does little to stop me from dropping to my knees in pain, head swimming. It's only with great focus am I able to cast my Minor Healing Spell, fixing the damage as I recast it again and again. Ali stays silent through this, waiting for me to become mostly functional before he speaks, "Alright, let's get this show on the road!"

"No." I shake my head, shrugging my shoulders as I walk over to my bike. I sit on it, triggering the change in my mind and feeling the armor crawl and attach itself to me.

"Oooh, we going to farm some carrion?"

"Not exactly," I walk towards the town center while looking for potential threats.

"Stop that! We're not playing 20 questions here. What the hell are you up to boy-o?" Ali grouses, flying after me.

"Being human."

***

I shoot the last oversized coyote that crawled out to see if it could get dinner and loot it before turning back to the pyre I had made. I probably should have done something about the other monster corpses, but I didn't give a damn about them. The citizens of the town though, they deserved something better. Even in power armor, the chopping and hauling had taken me hours especially as I had to stop every once in a while and kill a few wandering monsters.

I don't have words for when I'm done, even though I've tried to find the words these past few hours. In the end, all I have is this, "I'm sorry."

As I turn away, calling Sabre back to its bike form, I hear from behind me a rough voice.

God lay dead in heaven;
Angels sang the hymn of the end;
Purple winds went moaning,
Their wings drip-dripping
With blood
That fell upon the earth.
It, groaning thing,
Turned black and sank.
Then from the far caverns
Of dead sins
Came monsters, livid with desire.
They fought,
Wrangled over the world,
A morsel.
But of all sadness this was sad —
A woman's arms tried to shield
The head of a sleeping man
From the jaws of the final beast. [1]

I twist around, staring up at Ali who shrugs. "It seemed appropriate"

Yeah, it did.

---

[1] "God Lay Dead in Heaven," Stephen Crane

Hidden Quest Completed!

You have laid to rest the bodies of the fallen and avenged their death against all odds. The System might be callous, but you are not.

Reward: 5,000 XP, Title Gained: Redeemer of the Dead. Reputation change with certain factions.

"And fuck you too, System," I whisper and gesture the notification away. It's time to go home.

Chapter 6

"Ali, I'm not wrong, right? You're bigger?" Gunning the engine, I shoot down the road, weaving around newly created potholes and debris. Looks like monsters don't have any civic pride, the way they destroy common roadways. It's been hours since I've left Haine's Junction and so far, Sabre's doing a great job of getting me back to civilization quickly.

"More than big enough or so the lady's say," Ali smirks.

"You're a Spirit. You don't even have a gender," I growl back, leaning into the curve as we shoot past a startled Moose. Holy shit, that thing was the size of a bus!

"Now that's heteronormative thinking. It's thinking like that that has kept half of your population down for the entirety of your history," starts Ali.

"I hate you," I grouse, tuning out Ali. I had a serious question about his abilities, but every single time!!!

I'm purposely tuning him out so when he screams "Down", it takes me a moment to realise he's serious and react. It almost costs me my life as I duck down, sending the entire vehicle into a spin. Missing me by inches, a dragon pulls up from its dive, screeching its anger as batlike wings and purple scales glisten in the sunlight. I feel the pressure, the aura of fear that surrounds it as it closes on me, trying to lock my muscles together and make me prey.

My resistances kick-in, even as I focus on getting control of my bike. Realising it's a lost cause, I trigger the change, the entire bike coming apart beneath me as I take a death-grip on the handlebars. It's a good thing that the overalls I'm wearing have light armor plates stitched in or else I'd have some terrible road rash.

The transformation takes seconds, armor plates sliding to protect my arms and legs, liquid metal filling in gaps at the joints while the bike's wheels attach to the back with the exhaust, creating a bulky backpack section. My actual hiking backpack and its contents get strewn all over the road during the change. As I slide along the ground, I dig in my bottom foot and come up to a crouched position in a display of agility, co-ordination and strength no normal human could ever exhibit.

When I do manage to slow down and look up, I get a chance to actually see the information Ali has pulled for me.

Shadow Drake (Level 74)
HP: 14,780 / 14,780

Christ on a pogo stick! There's no way I'm winning this fight. A mental command triggers the QSM and I bolt for it, heading into the surrounding forest to hide.

Ali comes back to my hiding spot hours later after the sun has finally set and risen again, pointing upwards. "We're clear. It's gone."

I breathe a sigh of relief, my hands trembling slightly from the accumulated adrenaline finally subsiding. I rest my head on my arms, forcing myself to breathe slower, pushing the fear back down after a moment. That Drake had been tenacious, unwilling to leave even after it lost track of me. If I hadn't the QSM to lose it initially, I would have been Drake chow. I was lucky, so damn lucky…

Once I have control of myself again, I take a quick glance at the inbuilt compass in my helmet and I take off towards Whitehorse through the forest, figuring I'll eventually meet up with the road. Best to give it a few more hours before I risk the road again.

Ali seems unusually quiet for a few minutes as I sneak through the forest, just floating beside me and not even humming an annoying tune. "I am bigger. Told you, as you grow stronger, so do I and I'll eventually be able to manifest a real body."

"You said at Level 2 you gained the ability to sense the System monster's around us. How did the Drake get so damn close?" I gripe at him.

"Shadow Drake. Stealth abilities affect my ability to sense them through the System since the System dictates the skills themselves," Ali explains and I make a mental note to start paying more attention myself. It seems like I can't just rely on him.

"What'd you get for the other levels?"

"More access to the System. It's why the information I've been displaying has been getting more and more accurate. I've also extended the range of my spot function and I can manifest longer too." Ali explains, "If you hit Level 10, my affinity will be something you can gain, if you spend some time practising it."

I nod, happy. Finally, some real information.

***

After a few hours of walking off the road, I get back on it and head in at speed. Most of the rest of the journey to Whitehorse goes by relatively peacefully and fast. The closer I get to the city, the lower the level of monsters. In fact, the latest monster that I deal with is a giant brown bear whose level sits at a measly 35. At Ali's insistence, I kill it and loot it. Poor thing stood no chance as I just sniped it to death from a distance. I don't get a Level and I feel somewhat bad about leaving the rest of the meat to rot, but I just don't have the ability to carry the non-System generated body.

Something to think about for the future – getting some form of inter-dimensional storage.

When I get within a kilometer of the Takhini cut-off, a bare 20 minutes away by bike to Whitehorse, Ali starts jabbering. "Pedal to the metal boy-o, unless you want a re-run of the Junction."

I snarl, gunning the bike. Sabre roars, the Mana battery ticking down as I pull more power than the engine can recharge. Not the time to worry about it. I can't see the problem till I take the last corner, easing off the throttle enough to let me ascertain the situation.

Troll (Level 32)

HP: 1673/1842

The Troll is the aggressor here, all 13 feet of gangly, warty green skin facing off directly against a diminutive Japanese woman who wields a polearm-like weapon. Even as I pull to a stop behind them, she slips a strike, spins the blade to slice open the Troll's arm and then reverses the cut immediately to slash open its throat. As she makes the last strike, a white glow seems to envelop the blade itself, making the second cut pass through the Troll's body much easier. She has the Troll outclassed in sheer speed and skill, but it doesn't seem to matter as the Troll is already regenerating the damage, old and new wounds closing. Unlike the Troll, the woman isn't regenerating damage and blood drips from the scalp wound she has already received.

Mikito Sato (Level 27)

HP: 282/420

As interesting as the fight is, the giant Huskies that dart in and out to annoy and distract the Troll are more so. Those creatures are nearly the size of a small pony each, varying in color and size by only a small amount. Controlling their actions with barked orders are a pair of redheaded humans, their owners I presume.

Richard Pearson (Level 24)
HP: 210 / 210

Lana Pearson (Level 24)
HP: 230/230

Further behind are a crowd of non-combatants, children and more. I don't pay attention to them as I struggle to get the rifle out of its holster. I curse myself for not practising drawing the weapon when I had the time, fumbling the motion and costing precious seconds. Mikito misses a dodge, blood from her wound blinding her for a crucial second and it is all the Troll needs to smash her down. The killing blow is delayed at the cost of a Husky's body, thrown at its raised arm and then my rifle is free.

I aim high, figuring a missed shot will stay missed that way and pull the trigger. The first shot catches it on the shoulder, burning and then cauterising the flesh as the beam weapon punches a hole through it. The Troll hunches down, making a smaller target as it then sprints towards me on all fours.

Rather than run, I line up a proper shot, this one smashes the left collarbone and keeps going, right through its body to dig into the earth behind it. The Troll crashes to the ground, momentum keeping it rolling to me. When it recovers, it launches itself in a straight lunge that I meet with a boot to its face. Unfortunately, I forgot about that bitch physics which still has some control over our lives.

Instead of throwing the Troll back, I'm the one who goes flying backwards and into the ground. I take the fall and roll, a part of me marvelling at the fact that I can even do this kind of crazy acrobatics, the other, larger and smarter part, snapping another shot off at the Troll.

This one completely misses, but it does make the Troll pause long enough to let me stand up. Again, I make a mistake, forgetting how long the creature's arms are and it smashes the rifle aside, nearly taking my head with it except for a quick reflexive jerk backwards. My arms throb, but none of its claws get through the armor. Seeing me disarmed, it launches itself forward with little care.

***

Too bad an Erethran Honor Guard (stolen class and all) is never truly unarmed. I pivot and drop, letting instinct guide me as my sword appears in my hands and I let the Troll disembowel itself. I'm already stepping out from its shadow, a downward slice severing tendons in the back of the knee before my hands join together at the hilt for a hard block that disarms the Troll. Literally.

The Troll's strike with its remaining arm is dodged and then help arrives, the Huskies bearing down on the wounded creature. I take the time to help lop off its other arm while the Huskies and Mikito keep it busy before I retrieve my rifle to end the fight and start blasting away at it. I grin behind my helmet, watching it fry and die.

Troll (Level 37) Slain

+3700 XP

"Whoa! That was amazing," Richard walks up and claps me on the shoulder. Danger over, I pull my helmet off and nod back to him, reeling internally at how easy that was. I mean, sure I screwed up a bit, but that thing was significantly stronger than me in terms of Levels. Yet, I have a feeling with just a little more experience I could have kicked its ass all by my lonesome.

"Richard! Hilda needs some help," Lana calls out, bent over the injured husky. As I look over, my eyes lock on the buxom redhead whose green blouse is slightly parted, leaning over the dog and my breath catches for a moment. Good lord, she's gorgeous. Pulling my gaze away, I look at the dog on the ground, spotting its low health. Hmmm...

"Let me try something..." I walk over, calling forth the memory of the spell that I've gained and place my hands on the creature, ignoring its labored breathing. I chant Minor Healing in my mind, my hand glowing from the Mana that infuses it before spilling out onto the husky to begin the recovery process. I have to wait for a minute each time before I can recast the spell, but I eventually prop her health above the two-third mark. In between waiting, I loot the Troll gaining some Troll Blood and hide, being the slayer and the only one able to do so. I also check out the non-combatants who number just under 8, a split of 6 adults and 2 kids. With nothing better to do after all that, I review my spell again.

Minor Healing

Effect: Heals 20 Health per casting. Target must be in contact during healing. Cooldown 60 seconds.

Cost: 20 Mana

"Thank you!" Lana clutches the newly recovered dog, pushing her head into its fur as the dog returns the favor with long licks.

"How did you learn that? And how come your bike is still working?" Richard is eyeing me with pure lust and jealousy after the first healing. I look back up, noting the family resemblance, the light smile that twists their lips, the striking features that they both have. Richard is pretty damn good looking too, though it's an ephemeral charisma that draws the eye to him when he speaks. He's clad in a plaid shirt and jeans with a light summer jacket on his body, a shotgun held casually on his arm.

"Bought it in the Shop," I casually mention. Best not to mention Sabre is a mecha for now, a working bike these days is wonder enough.

"The Shop?" Lana butts in while Mikito stays silent, watching over the group. I look over and nod to the other fighter in this group and she just stares at me. Right then, not the friendliest one that one.

"Place where you can sell the Loot drops. There's one in Whitehorse," I pause, then hold up a hand to forestall more questions. "Let's get moving, we can talk when we're safe. Then I'll answer your questions."

The trio nod grimly, being reminded of the problems of standing around in the wild. I gesture over the children and one of the mums to get on the bike, remotely starting it and setting it to move along at a slow pace next to us.

Now that I've got them moving in the right direction I put my helmet back on and speak into it, obscuring my voice, "Ali, keep an eye out. Let me know if there's any danger, will you?"

"Not introducing me? Ashamed of me, are you?" Ali grumbles, floating next to me.

"Just cautious. They seem nice enough people, but those dogs are huge," I eye the hounds who trot beside us, even the one that got smashed around by the Troll. Seems like those things heal faster than we do which is saying something. I guess I wasted a bunch of my Mana for nothing.

"Beast companions. Bet you a hundred Credits those two have a Beast Tamer Class," Ali points to the Pearsons. I open my mouth to ask more when Richard drops back to speak to me and I pop my visor open to stay polite.

"Thanks again. I'm Richard, that's my sister Lana and the lady over there's Mikito," Richard gestures in turn to the combatants before proceeding to point at the other non-combatants who stay in the center of our little group and naming them. Truth be told, I forget their names as fast as he says it, I've always been terrible with names and with Ali around, I don't even have to try.

"John," I offer my hand for a quick shake before I begin probing for their story. It seems he needs to talk since it doesn't take long to get the details of what happened to them. When the System turned on, both Richard and Lana had been offered classes as Beast Tamers as their recommended small perk. They'd ignored the option at first, but after dealing with their first monster, a giant Squirrel it seems, they'd accepted. That had caused their mushing team to transform into the current pack that ranges around us and gave them a linked connection to their pets.

Mikito had been with her husband at the Takhini Hot Springs, hoping to get pregnant under the Northern Lights but things ended in tragedy. Neither of the Pearsons have been able to get the story of her Naginata out of her as yet, but whatever it was, it wasn't pretty as the woman seemed to throw herself at the monsters they'd encountered at the drop of a hat. The rest of the non-combatants they'd picked up, neighbours and others, independently moved to Whitehorse in hopes of safety.

"How come they don't have classes?" I point to the group in the center, letting my head swivel around for new threats.

"They do. Karl's a Farmer, Jorge is an Industrialist and so on, they're just not fighters," Richard shrugs and then mutters. "Neither am I really but you know…"

"Yeah, I do." We both fall silent then, finishing the walk in our own thoughts. Being drawn into a fight or die situation has not been easy, not for any of us. I stare forwards as we walk, my mind turning to Whitehorse. We can rest when we arrive, the Safe Zone a place where we can find some peace. Maybe put down our weapons, stop killing. Find some sanity in this crazy new world.

***

When we finally catch sight of Two Mile Hill in Whitehorse, the entire group lets out a little cheer. Walking through the industrial park and suburbs had been depressing, even if we hadn't ventured from the highway to check out the abandoned buildings. Closer to the town, the zone level had dropped all the way to the mid-20s, so it was pretty safe as far as an apocalypse goes. No more flying drakes at least. However, the signs of struggle and death were all around us as we traveled and once again I was reminded that not everyone received or took a combat class - or had a chance to take one.

The cheers die off as we note another party coming down Two Mile Hill from the community center on bicycles. To our right sat the massive white and blue building that made up the community centre, seeming to cast an oppressive gloom around it. The Canada Games Centre is something we are going to have to keep an eye on as from what Ali could tell, the Mana flows were pooling quite deeply which would result in more monsters being drawn in. In time, if it isn't cleared out, it'll turn into a proper monster lair and after that, a full dungeon. Thankfully, that's a problem for another time and another person.

I drop the visor in the helmet to pull up basic magnification to start collecting information of the other group. The group consists of a pair of what look like extras from the Lord of the Rings; elves, a dragonman wannabe, a mini-Giant in full plate and what have to be a pair of casters by their long flowing robes. That's right, the entire group looks like a LARP party on steroids, though with Level's from low to mid 30's which makes them a serious threat.

"Ali, what's up with their levels?" I mutter into my helmet.

"Mmm… Whitehorse probably saw a lot more spawning in the initial period. You're all getting bonus experience at the start, so if they've been working together and killing the monsters around here, levelling is pretty easy. Though, I'll admit - it's still pretty high," Ali intones, eyeing the group as well.

I groan after a moment as I get a better look at the casters, the pair of them having the least amount of changes from their pre-Apocalypse visages. No acne makes the pair of teenagers look significantly better but it's definitely them. I pull my helmet off completely to run a hand through my hair, shoulders hunching slightly. Lana, buxom Lana whose company is definitely more interesting than her brother Richard's, shoots me a worried look from my side.

"I kind of know them," I start throwing a prayer to whatever gods there are who might be listening.

There probably is, and his name is Murphy because the bicycle-riding group swerves our way and I get a chance to read all their System names including the female Elf.

Luthien Celbrindal (Level 32)
HP: 420/420

"Fuck me sideways. I swear, I should have put more points into Luck," I roll my neck, attempting to get rid of the tension that's suddenly built up. Mikito hefts her naginata, getting ready for battle and I realise even the dogs are rumbling. "Not that kind of trouble people. I think. It's personal."

Lana gestures and Richard and the rest of the group come to a stop, obviously waiting for me to explain, "That's my ex incoming. Bad breakup and all. I left the city to get away from her…"

"You're scared of a girl?" Ali chortles at the same time Lana speaks. "You ran from relationship issues into the apocalypse?"

"No, I just don't want to deal with the she-bitch," I protest, waving them to be silent. Lana looks puzzled for a moment before gesturing for Richard to keep moving. That annoying redhead is trying to hide a grin, something that Ali doesn't even bother with as he's rolling in the air laughing his ass off.

"Halt! Who goes there," the Giant calls out as we near.

"A bad role-player," I say beneath my breath, letting Richard take the lead in the discussion as I attempt to fade into the background. Introductions are quickly made with Richard relaying a short version of their trip.

While Richard does the speaking, I eyeball the group and their weaponry. The swords, bows and maces are well used and while the group might seem friendly, they're all keeping hands near their weapons. They seem to have stuck to the fantasy motif, which doesn't surprise me at all – her role-playing group were all about D&D.

"How'd you get the bike working?" his Status bar says Tim and it takes me a moment to place him. Right! He was a mechanic before all this shit happened. Now he's a half-dragon, half-man mixture, seven feet tall carrying a battleaxe clad in chainmail. I guess some interests don't go away.

"Well?" He pushes and I realise everyone is waiting for me to answer, even the Pearsons and Mikito.

"I bought it from the Shop," I say, leaning against the vehicle and oh so casually having my hand near the stock of my rifle. Not that I expect to have to shoot anybody but Tim's just a little too happy to see a working bike.

"There's a Shop out there?" Luthien the she-bitch butts in. I have to admit, the Elf look works for her - tall, thin and blonde is what she was before, but the additional pointy ears and tight leather pants and armor certainly accentuates everything. Looking good was never her problem though, lying, cheating, manipulating, that was another matter.

"No. I got access due to some… special circumstances," I pause, trying to figure out the best way to get around this. "It was in Haines Junction…"

"You were there? Did you see a man named Perry?" The other Elf speaks up, pushing forwards in the group surrounding me now.

"No. The town, it's gone," I look down, not really wanting to be the one to pass on this news. "Ogres took it over, killed them all. The Ogres were killed by a Salamander and when I looted them, I got a chance to use the Shop. That's where I got the bike and my weapons," that should do it. Just enough truth without going into detail about my part in it.

I watch the Elf, Jeff, crumple at the news and turn away. The others give him some space but Luthien and the last mage, Kevin, just stare at me. In the end, it's Kevin who speaks, "Is that you John?"

"Yes," I answer him and as he opens his mouth to speak, I wave him away. "Glad to see you all alive," I mouth, my brain turning on automatic as the roiling pit of anger and disgust thrums through me. I shake my head and swing my feet over the bike and get ready to leave.

"John..." Luthien says.

I ignore her, kicking the bike into gear and pulling away from the group, forcing one of the teenagers to jump aside or get run over. Yeah, I'm running away. I still can't be in the same place with her, not right now. I grit my teeth, pushing aside the emotions again as I head down Two Mile Hill into downtown Whitehorse. I guess my peaceful return to normalcy just got shot out the window.

"*So, John... figure I should let you know this now,*" Ali speaks to me. Wait, into me! "*Yeah, we've got a mental connection so you can stop talking into the air like a crazy person.*"

How do I do this...?

"*If that constipated look on your face is anything to go by, you're trying it right? You got to think at me first, then I'll hear it. It's not mind reading,*" Ali says.

"*Like this asshole?*"

"Perfect! Of course, no one can hear me so I won't do the 'duh I'm stupid stare' like you," Ali adds.

"Asshole," I mutter into my helmet.

Once I'm down the hill, I take 4th Street, passing the burnt-out shell of the McDonald's and more abandoned commercial buildings on both sides of me. In a minute, I have to slow down to a crawl as the number of people increases significantly and none of them are obeying traffic laws anymore. Not too surprising, since the number of working vehicles can be counted on one finger. Though, it looks like bicycles have made a giant comeback, with riders swerving in and around pedestrians with little care. I guess when your health regenerates within minutes, even bruises and broken bones become less important. The humans all move jerkily, flickers of anger or fear crossing faces when a movement is too fast or something catches them unaware. Shoulders are hunched, others have eyes wide and staring and these are the good ones - the ones willing to come out from hiding.

It takes me a moment to realise what is nagging me about everyone — there's not a single pair of spectacles to be seen. Like my own on-going ailments, it looks like the increased regeneration rate from the System removes minor issues like that. More interestingly, I spot two pairs of high-level individuals with rifles patrolling the streets, each black-skinned, silver-haired Elves in a tunic uniform ensemble of more black and silver. Shacking up with Luthien, I know immediately these guys aren't your typical Elves - they're Dark Elves, the evil version of the Elves. At least in bad fantasy lore. Surprisingly, their presence doesn't seem to generate much interest from the humans around, most seem to be scurrying back and forth on their own errands.

At École Elementary School, it's my turn to be shocked as I spot a working truck amongst the people on the street, engine running as people hurry around it and into the sea of tents on the school grounds. The sound of the diesel engine cranking over is loud as a group of First Nation hunters unload a Moose from the back. Like most of our native fauna, this one seems to have tripled in size at least from the sheer quantity of meat that they are pulling off and handing down into the school.

I pull my bike over near them and one of the First Nations' elders who is directing the unloading looks to me with caution, a hand unconsciously tightening on the rifle butt. He's old school with a permanent squint from being outdoors all the time and lines across his tanned face. Dressed in a rawhide vest, plaid shirt and jeans, he could be out for a Sunday afternoon stroll in Whitehorse if not for the blood that covers his clothing. I'm sure I've seen him around town before at one of the many public functions but for the life of me, where and when eludes me. I raise my hand in greeting and I can see him look towards my bike in consideration.

"You hunt that yourself?" I let the surprise and admiration creep into my voice. Even a glance at their Status Bars shows me their average Level is in the single digits.

"Yup. Took half our bullets too but we still have some." The warning is clear, though I just chuckle and raise both my hands clear of my own rifle.

"Don't want no trouble. Just a little information as I just got in. People gathering in the school?" I gesture to École and get a nod in confirmation.

"So, what's that?" I point towards the biggest change in the city, the towering 8 storey, shining metal building that dominates the town and is probably smack centre in Main St. Whitehorse was a picturesque town, one made of short rectangular buildings, wide roads and occasional gestures to its pioneer past. There was even an ordinance that kept buildings beneath 30 feet, so the Blade Runner escapee of a building was not normal.

A spit is my initial answer before the elder continues, "Building appeared 3 days after the monsters. Some asshole who says he owns the town now lives there."

"That's where the Shop is boy-o. Someone purchased the rights to town, give me a second and I'll see what I can dig up," Ali says, going back to staring into space.

Realising I've still got my helmet on, I pull it off and set it on the handlebars. "Mind if I ask a few more questions?"

The elder sighs and after getting me to add myself to the chain, proceeds to answer. Lifting and tossing the meat is cheap for the information that I want. The moment my foot crosses the line into the school, I get a new window, one that I've never seen before.

You Have Entered a Safe Zone (École Whitehorse Elementary School)

Mana flows in this area are stabilised. No monster spawning will happen.

This Safe Space includes:

A School (+10% Skill Progression)

I soon learn that the guards are the town owners and they have been dealing with most of the spawning monsters, patrolling the main thoroughfares. Both École Whitehorse Elementary and FH Collins were Safe Zones and where nearly everyone was crashing these days since it was the only way to guarantee a monster didn't just spawn in the middle of the night under your bed. Space was a premium though and hygiene levels had dropped since both electricity and water wasn't working anymore. This explained the rather rank smell of unwashed bodies. Then again, I was not complaining - I hadn't washed in days either.

The meat was for the general stew pot as the regular truck delivery had never made it and a ton of food had spoiled when the electricity died. It was only some quick thinking that had the stores barricaded, with food being served in the cafeteria. The hunters were doing their best to supplement, but with nearly five thousand mouths to feed, they weren't keeping up and everyone was on short rations now.

While I'm speaking the others catch up and the non-combatants and kids are quickly ushered in by a welcoming committee of delighted looking residents. In the background, I can hear questions being asked about where they came from and of any confirmed deaths. I guess knowing one way or the other is better than not. Richard and the other fighters are dragged away by my ex and her group, a quick glare by me keeping them away for now at least.

Unloaded, the men hop up onto the truck looking grim. The only other working truck they'd found had never come back from a recent trip so they need to get hunting immediately. However, hunting monsters bigger and tougher than you are with our basic hunting rifles could not be easy.

"Jim," I call to the elder and he turns back to me from speaking with his group about their next hunting grounds, obviously irritated by my interruption. Hopefully, this will help, "Ran into a bear along the ride-in. I had to kill it and leave the meat. It's about 45 minutes drive from here on the way to Haines Junction. Might be a bit rotten, it's been a few hours but…"

"Where?" His eyes narrow, already considering it. Free meat that doesn't require them to fight is too good to pass up.

"I'll show you," I head back to the bike and then stop as two guards appear in front of me, their faces impassive. "Hi there."

"Lord Roxley would like to have a word," the taller of the two Dark Elves speaks, his hand casually resting on his sword hilt.

"Really now," I can feel my lips widen and my balance shift before Ali practically shouts into my ear. "Don't be an idiot! If he wants to, he can ban you from the Shop!"

That would be bad. "I guess I'm coming with you."

Jim glares at the guards but says nothing, nodding to me to show he understands my predicament. On a whim, I grab the rifle from the holster and hand it to the man. "Shoots just like the real thing, except no recoil. You've got 21 shots in there. Try not to break it, will you? I expect it back."

Jim grunts, checking the rifle out as his friends look on in surprise.

"So, Ali, you got the locator beacon on that turned on, right?"

"Definitely. Still stupid, but these hicks won't be able to figure out how to turn it off," Ali smirks.

"Let's go see your boss then," I flash the pair a wide grin that doesn't reach my eyes as I get onto the bike and wave them to lead me. This should prove interesting at the very least.

Chapter 7

On closer inspection, the building that the Shop is housed in is sheathed in some form of reflective silvery material. Spreading upwards in a rectangular block, it dominates the cityscape, jarring in its alienness. As we approach, the door slides open and we enter the foyer which is all black marble and more silver highlights. The moment we do, a System message appears.

You Have Entered a Safe Zone (City Centre)
Mana flows in this area are stabilised. No monster spawning will happen.
This Safe Space includes:
Village of Whitehorse City Centre
The Shop

"Village?" Yeah, the city's small but that's a bit of a demotion. I guess the System is only counting System recognised housing.

"Getting a map now John, I'll overlay with your human maps in a bit so you can see things properly when you put on the helmet," Ali speaks, eyeing the building we walk in. "Of course, if you got those cyber-eyes, I could just shoot it through to you but you just got whiny about wanting to keep your meat eyes."

So not the right time. I sigh and rub my temples, wondering for the thousandth time whether there was something in the Shop that'd let me neuter Spirits. Or at least gag them.

We enter the elevators and shoot up to the top floor, the motion completely imperceptible. Heck, the only reason I know we're on the top floor is due to the 360-degree view that the transparent walls afford me.

"Lord Graxan Roxley, Baron of the Seven Seas, Hunter of Drakyl, Master of the Sword and the Black Flame, Corinthian of the Second Order and acclaimed Dancing Master of the 196th Ball," the guard announces as we step from the elevator. At my side, Ali translates in his usual helpful manner "Dark Elf, Baron, killed over a hundred demons, blade master and special fire mage, likes to cuddle with men aggressively and is a pretty, pretty dancer."

The guard, unaware, continues his introductions. "My Lord, the Adventurer John Lee, Monster Bane and Redeemer of the Dead."

Interesting. So, my Titles actually mean something it seems. While I'm being announced, I take the time to watch Lord Roxley. The man (Elf?) is tall, a good 6' 6" of lithe grace and purple hair that reaches his back. Pointy ears, black skin and purple eyes dominate an angular face atop a military cut swing jacket that's all in black with hints of purple. Resting easy on his right hip is a sword and across from it on his left a pistol. He exudes easy confidence and charm and a part of me wants to go up and grab his trim butt and see how kissable he really is.

Mental Influence Resisted

The flashing note brings my lustful thoughts to a halt and Ali floats next to me, nodding at my glance, "Yup. He's putting out a low-level bubble of charisma. Looks like a mixture of pheromones, good genes and subtle body mimicking behavior." He pauses and then continues, "Still, feel free to jump his bones. I'll watch and tape it."

"How come his Status Bar is just a bunch of question marks after his name?" I ignore Ali's assertions, though a part of me still wouldn't mind. It's not as if I haven't dabbled before but maybe another day.

"Can't access his information. Something's blocking me," Ali says.

"Welcome to the Village of Whitehorse Adventurer," Lord Roxley says.

"Thank you," I stand around, trying to figure out what the hell is going on. Why me? The way we were announced tells me something formal is going on here, but what beats me like a white guy the day before the welfare check arrives.

"I must say, I had not expected one so... inexperienced, for one so titled," Roxley smiles and this one is not at all friendly.

"Yeah. I got... lucky," okay, downplay might be the better bet here perhaps. Or at the least, close to the vest.

"There is no Luck with the System," Roxley states and the way he says it, it seems like it's a quote. He gestures to a pair of lounging chairs and I walk over to join him, waiting for him to sit before doing so myself. Some courtesies I know, though who knows if they use the same forms.

"I will not keep you long. I'm sure you wish to use my Shop and see what has transpired in your city. Still, I would feel it remiss if I did not speak with you beforehand, to ensure that certain matters are clear," Roxley leans forward, meeting my eyes and waiting for a nod before continuing, "I am the System registered owner of this Village. I have every intention of growing it to its fullest and adding this region to my Clan's holdings.

"To ensure that, I've already hired many of your compatriots in the village. I understand you even met up with some of them and were instrumental in bringing some survivors back. For that, you have my thanks"

Quest Completed: The Safety of Many

Reward: 2,000 Credits per Each Survivor (22,000 Credits Received); 500XP per Survivor (5,500XP Received)

Type: Repeatable

Level Up!

You have reached Level 8 as an Erethran Honor Guard. Stat Points automatically distributed. You have 18 Free Attributes to distribute.

"Ah, congratulations!" Roxley smiles slightly as he watches me even as I will away the windows. He then stands and walks away to a sideboard, getting us a couple of drinks. "In my culture, each Level is celebrated."

"Ali, how the hell does he know what's going on?"

"At a guess boy-o? He's got a System Companion too. From his eye, I'd say it's an AI. Or you know, he could be reading you like a crystal," Ali shrugs. "I've stopped a dozen probes into our information on the System already, and I only managed to stop them from reading us completely. He definitely has your basic stats at least. Well, hello there… Got to go. Try not to get killed."

With those last words, Ali is gone. What the hell?

"To Strength!" Handing me the glass of dark blue liquid, Roxley toasts. I echo his cheer, sipping on the drink tentatively first. It's sweet and smooth, almost like drinking a good mead. On that thought, I pull the drink away from my lips as memories of waking up on a beach, pantless intrude. Good times with Luthien… I push those thoughts away too. Not now.

"I will of course reward you similarly for any others you may find and for other relevant information," Roxley says.

"Ummm…" I pause, considering and then fill him in on Haines Junction giving him the abbreviated version I gave the others. His eyes narrow a bit but he doesn't interrupt me, just thanking me for the information.

"Well Adventurer Lee, this has been enlightening. I expect I shall be seeing more of you, one so titled after such a short period is certain to do much," Roxley states, offering me his hand. I take it, feeling a shiver pass through my body on contact, which I push away. When he lets go of my hand, he inclines his head to the door and I take the dismissal, following the guards out. They deposit me a few floors down into the Shop.

***

Interestingly, when I arrive and place my hand on the crystal that will transport me to the Shop, I get a System window asking me to choose which one. I also have a default option and after brief consideration, I decide to go with it. Ali seems to know them and I do too, a bit. Who knows - the others' Shops might be even worse.

The Shop itself hasn't changed much in the time that I've gone, which isn't surprising. The two within greet me with cool professionalism until they realise that Ali isn't here. Then the professionalism thaws a little bit, probably in anticipation of fleecing me.

Too bad I don't have much for them to buy or sell. I push them a bit on the last few pieces of Ogre loot I hadn't been able to contain in my inventory the first time around and the few pieces of extra loot I've picked up then but don't bother haggling too much. Better to let them have a good deal now to build up some goodwill for when I bring Ali and more loot back in the future.

That done, I take a deep breath. I've been putting this off for a bit, making excuses for why I couldn't do it in Haines Junction, promising that I'd do it once I was in Whitehorse. Now, faced with the ability to check on the Status of my family, I find myself hesitating. Believing they are dead and knowing are two different things. I bite my lip and then finally pay the cheap, cheap price to the System for information on my family.

I close my eyes, hands clenched before me as I hold back the tears by sheer force of will. I make myself look up and breathe, push my will onto my body and by that, my emotions. I knew the answer before I paid, I knew this was the likely result. I knew it, but the pain still chokes me up for a moment. I cycle my breath for what seems like hours but is probably just a few minutes before I stuff the grief away again. Another time - I'll deal with it another time.

I came down here for another reason though, one that came to mind when I stepped into the school. I pull up information on these Safe Zones, browsing for information. A quick perusal and a few questions get me the answers that I need. Any building purchased from the System is considered a Safe Zone, the System automatically stabilising the flow of Mana in that location. Locations within a city are generally more expensive as the City Owner tax all prices but in return, if 80% of all land that lay within a city's boundary was part of the System, the entire city would be considered a Safe Zone.

Once again, I can't help but feel the entire System is a scam. It seems engineered to force people into using it – destroying sensitive electronics with Mana, creating Safe Zones only when a building is purchased, even the inventory items. If Steve Jobs was still alive, he probably would be jerking off to the System Help Guide.

I pull up the listings for the schools and then the other buildings that have been bought in short order. Not many at all, most owned by Roxley himself, with the only exceptions an armoury, an alchemist and another house. The house is registered as owned by Nicodemus of the Raven's Circle, which puzzles me for a second before I recall the Giant. Ah right, Nicodemus / Nick, he was the accountant and GM wasn't he? That must be where the 'Raven's Circle'' was headquartering themselves.

Out of curiosity, I make another query of the System and grimace. Of course, it'd work that way. Unless a fee was paid to register a designated heir, all buildings owned by an individual upon death would revert to the System. Yeah, keeping Roxley alive was in our best for now - he literally kept the monsters at bay by being alive.

I make a note to mention this to someone at some point before finally pulling up my own residence.

89 Alsek Rd.

Current Ownership: None
Current Occupant: John Lee, Adventurer
Cost: 20,000 Credits (50% discount for previous occupancy status)
Current Assigned Purpose: None

I'd rented a 1 bedroom suite beneath a house, but it looks like the System has decided I live in the entire location. I eye the Credits that I have left and I bite my lips for a moment. Easy come, easy go.

Congratulations!

You have purchased 89 Alsek Rd. You now own the building and may assign a purpose and upgrade the building. Upgrades may be purchased at the residence itself or at the Shop. Please note that all buildings have a minimum maintenance cost and if not met, will be returned to the System Pool.
22,000 Credits Deducted

Even after the Apocalypse, there are taxes.

***

Coming out of the City Centre, I come across a group of teenagers trying to bikejack Sabre. Something a little cruel rises up in me and I just stand there, grinning as one hunts for the keys and ignition, another attempts to pry up the seat with a crowbar, while the last fiddles with where the engine is, trying to discern how to get it started. The crowbar slips, putting its edge into his friend's shoulder but not even leaving a scratch on the bike.

Next to me, the pair of guards who escorted me move to do something about this but I wave them down. They look at me incredulously at first but soon find as much cruel amusement as I do in the children's futile efforts. In fact, we start betting on how long it'll take before the group give up. They take 5 and 8 minutes, I take 10.

Teenage stupidity and stubbornness win me 50 Credits each after the ten-minute mark passes. By this point, the kid with the crowbar is whaling on the seat in an attempt to get the bike to do something, anything. Tier IV Armor might not be much to the System, but in old Earth standards, I might as well be driving a tank.

Having made an easy 100 Credits, I send the command to Sabre to turn on. The kids jump and finally spot us and I give them a slight nod before touching the band around my neck to call forth the helmet. As the helmet folds up around my face, they jump back and then as one, scatter.

Kids.

Strange. What started out as a cruel prank has actually lightened my spirits, at least a little. Feeling happier than I have been in a while, I raise my hand in goodbye to the guards and head home.

***

As I cross the bridge that separates downtown Whitehorse from the Riverdale subdivision, I note that the river seems to have risen higher. I wonder how the dam is doing but now is not the time. Instead, I gun it, passing F.H. Collins on the right where another tent city has sprung up on its grounds, covering every single piece of protected land in canvas and humans. The greenery on the left has me keeping a close eye out and I'm not the only one as the series of guards posted at the school attest. I hit the roundabout and more guards stand outside the Super A, making my lips twist in distaste.

Passing empty ranch houses on my left and right as I cross through the suburb, the entire place feels like a ghost town with not a single person present. Broken doors, shattered windows and blood marks tell a desperate, bloody story. Cars are abandoned in driveways everywhere, previously snow-covered lawns now brown and grey with a lack of care.

I pull Sabre to a stop in front of my house as I come to the end of the street at the T-junction, staring at my house with its double garage doors beneath the open-air deck, the two-storey white residence connected directly to the garage itself. Wind ruffles my hair, bringing the smell of pine from the trees that cling to the clay-cliff face behind the house. The main entrance doorway has been broken into, both doors off their hinges and the usual white coat of paint marred by a single dark red streak at the door. The bushes that make up our fence look to be doing fine, adapted as they are to a Northern spring. I glance to the right, noting the stand-alone workshop has its door rolled open, the contents stolen with only a few scattered items left. To the side, I see the fence which blocks off the garden and abuts the hill in the back is at least still in good condition.

The moment I turn onto the driveway and pass the lot threshold, I get a System message.

Welcome to 89 Alsek Rd.

Current Ownership: John Lee, Adventurer

Current Occupants: None

Current Assigned Purpose: None

Structural Integrity: 94% (More...)

Would you like to assign a purpose?

Interesting, purpose? I mentally select yes, curious to see what it speaks of. The list of purposes come up, most of them greyed out but the top two – Residence and Safe House. A quick verification shows the first gives a bonus to resting and offers more upgradeable options in terms of add-on facilities. The second, a reduced cost for security upgrades for the entire lot. My hand hovers for a moment, trying to decide between the two. The Safe House option would allow me to build walls, cameras and other security measures fast but the Residence, with add-on facilities, could really make use of the workshop.

Really though, I should ask Randy first before I make any further decisions. I dismiss the pop-up and draw my sword, heading in through the broken door. Best to see if there are any unpleasant surprises awaiting me inside.

There are, just none alive. The large pool of blood and the blood splatters around the room tell the tale of Randy's likely fate. The body is gone, hopefully taken care of by one of the citizens, but I really wouldn't bet on it. The tang of rotten, clotted blood fills the house, mitigated by the open doorway but I sigh, making a note that this will need to be cleaned soon.

I make my way to the garage and open the doors, rolling the bike in securely before making way to my own suite beneath the stairs. The door here is broken too, but nothing seems taken. Then again, it's not as if I had a lot to take. A couch and my laptop dominate the small living room while in my bedroom, my king-sized indulgence lies unmade. Everything looks exactly the way I left it, and for a moment, I have this surreal feeling that everything I've experienced was just a bad dream.

I lean against the doorjamb, mind spinning as I finally realise I'm home. I'm safe - mostly. Monsters can't spawn in here and Ali would warn me of anything that spawned close by. A tightness in my chest that I've carried for days releases slightly, just a little bit, and I find myself smiling.

I run a hand through my hair, feeling the stickiness from not having a proper wash and shake the feelings off. First things first, grab a change of clothing and then it'd be time to check out the rain barrels at the back for a quick wash. I grab a shirt and pair of jeans and then pause, laughing to myself.

"Leave you alone for 5 minutes and you go completely nuts eh?" Ali snorts, floating next to me as he surveys my old home.

"Ali! You son-of-a-bitch! Where did you go?" I grouse, throwing the useless clothing aside. Adding a bunch of inches in height was great, except for the fact that none of my old clothing would fit me. I head upstairs for Randy's closet, after all, he isn't going to need it anymore and he was always a big man.

"Got an invite from a shiny pair of bits. Rox-boy had an AI Companion who invited me over to chat," Ali chuckles, shaking his head. "Figured you could handle yourself for a few minutes. Decent buy on this place, but you got fleeced at the Shop."

I grunt, picking through and finding some clothes that I figure will work. I head to the back, beginning to strip before I raise an eyebrow at the Spirit who shakes his head negatively. Good, no monsters.

"Talk," I say and begin the process of bathing in the garden. It's not great, but it's certainly better than nothing and while I couldn't necessarily smell myself after days of stewing in my own stink, I'm sure others could. Not to mention that the simple act of being clean is bliss in itself.

"Hmmm... where to start. First, don't fuck with the Elf. He'd eat you, me, your friends, the entire city and then wonder when the main course would be. He's got at least an Advanced-class in the high levels, or, and I'd lay good money on this, a Master class. Very little chance he's got a Heroic class otherwise he wouldn't be hanging out in a dump like this. Second, he's in a rush. I don't think X-124 knew I picked that up, but again, we're outclassed here. Third, he's the reason why the Raven's Circle is so high-level. He's been giving out quests like candy in an attempt to get as many survivors in town as possible," Ali says.

I finish dunking myself in the water and pause long enough to ask "Why?"

"Mmmm, City prerequisites. Once we get the buildings bought up, he'd be able to upgrade to a Town that gives us a series of new building options. There's a minimum citizen requirement for that though, and of course, you guys are his tax base."

I grunt at that and then nod. Makes sense. I pull up the house's menu and flick it to him as I get dressed, sliding the high-tech jumpsuit on first before more normal clothing. Thank the gods the jumpsuit had an auto-clean feature on itself, otherwise, I'd refuse to wear it again. "Recommendations?"

"You're asking? Shit, did he drug you?" Ali teases as he spins it around and points to the Residence option. "No choice. If you intend to stay, this is it."

I nod, happy that we concur and make the selection. Sorry Randy, guess I'm taking over your place. If you are alive, I'll apologise in person. That done, I also make a quick payment on a rush basis to bring the integrity of the location back to 100%, which fixes all the doors. It's amusing watching the System take care of it as the doors shimmer and then reappear, fixed and brand new. Much more convenient than doing it myself.

"Where to now boy-o?" Ali asks.

"Got to get my rifle back." I make sure the doors are locked before I roll the bike out, the sun still shining with its cheerful brightness. I grimace, pulling up a clock and realise it's nearly time for dinner. Damn midnight sun.

**

"Jim!" I wave to the Elder, having parked the bike around the corner from the school on 5th street. Not as many people roaming by and while it's out of sight for me, Ali can sense it and I can easily call it to me through the Neuro Link. The helmet I stow in its band form around my neck, finally giving up on acting like it's a normal helmet.

"Ah, John," he comes over to shake my hand before he unslings the rifle from his shoulder and hands it back to me a tad reluctantly. "That is a powerful weapon."

"Yup and…" I shut up, my brain kicking in before I finish the sentence, *if you get me a pouch of tobacco and your daughter, it's yours.* Not appropriate.

"And…?" Jim says.

"Uh… there's a basic version of one like it for around 500 Credits in the Shop. If you skip getting the upgrades, it's pretty decent," I reply, quickly backpedalling.

At the mention of the System, Jim's lips tighten, "The rifle came in handy. We had to fight off this three-legged, furred creature that was eating the bear. Couldn't save all the bear meat, but it more than made up for it."

"Good! What'd you get for the loot?" I grin at him, curious.

"…" Jim pauses, speaking slowly. "Loot?"

"Shit. No one told you about that?" I wince, wondering how much they must have missed.

"Not as if you knew either noob," Ali points out helpfully.

"Put your hand on your next kill, or whoever does the kill, and think 'Loot.' The System will let you grab some items that can be sold for Credits in the Shop," I explain and then add. "You can still use the meat that's left, it just gives you a small portion of the creature. That's how I skinned the bear."

Every time I mention the System, Jim scowls. I can understand not liking the world we are in or the damn scam that it is, but the way he acts, it's pure spite. It's not as if the System cares if we loot a body or not. "Try it the next time. You'll need to get new weapons soon, unless you want to try killing things with spears when you run out of bullets."

Jim's grimace is enough to let me know I've gotten through to him. I nod a goodbye saying, "Alright, I guess I should try some of this food…"

He nods back, gesturing me into the building itself and I head over, surveying the grounds for more familiar faces. In the school, only a small walkway is available as people sit, squat and rest, marking out where they will be sleeping tonight. A few questions have me directed to the cafeteria, most watching me with wary or curious eyes.

The serving tables are set-up in the cafeteria itself, people streaming in and out as they get food before most of them leave for less crowded environs, the close-packed quantities of unwashed humanity a bit much on the senses. Everything is dirty, dishevelled and demoralised; many just sitting down without a goal. No electricity means no easy entertainment or ability to use a million, billion electronic distractions that we have come to rely on, and until more buildings are purchased, Safe Zones are at a premium.

I stand in line and wait my turn, eyeing the portions doled out. The stew is mostly water with some slivers of meat and vegetables in it. Considering I lost my backpack and all my rations to a dragon and that someone had already raided my house, I don't have many other options at present. I'll have to look into purchasing some food from the Shop the next time, but for tonight, this works.

A part of me wants to be among the throng, unwashed and demoralised as they are. The press of flesh, the closeness of people is something that I hadn't realised I missed until I met up with Richard and his crew. It's not easy for most, shifting from a peaceful lifestyle to dealing with the System and its monsters and I can see more than one person being comforted as they suddenly break down crying or just stop, staring into space. I'm mostly a stranger here, having only arrived a few months ago so I have no true ties to the community, unlike many here who have lost friends, family and co-workers in days. Whitehorse has always been a small town, so everyone has lost someone.

I grab the bannock, flashing the server a smile and getting a blush back, before I go looking for butter, with no success. Stew and bannock it is then, and I head for the doors, hoping for some fresh air. I catch more than one glance, a few looks filled with hope, which is quickly dashed. Outside, I find an empty spot and continue people watching as I mull over the future.

What happens to us now? Traditionally, the First Nations hunted for their meat but with such a large group that probably won't help in the long run, not to mention that many of the hunting grounds are at least an hour away. We're lucky this is mid-April, giving us the option of getting more plants into the ground, but there is no way for us to actually plant all the food the town will need. No more food from the south means the winter will be brutal, unless we can find another source of supplies. We need the System and all the ability to buy and sell in the Shop - which means not pissing off Lord Roxley.

It's not a nice conclusion, especially since it seems like he's just another vulture dropping onto the still twitching corpse of Earth, but it is what it is. I wonder how many of these others are seeing that, thinking that far ahead? For that matter, why am I? I've never been much for this kind of thinking before.

"Ali, those increases in Intelligence. Are those things making me plan and think further ahead?"

"Yeah, sort of," Ali shrugs, turning away from trying to look down a nearby lady's blouse. "It's a bit hard to pinpoint the changes, but sort of. When you increase your Level or your base stats, there are two effects. The first is, of course, an increase in your Mana pool, which the System adjusts for you. The second is a change in your brain, allowing you to process and understand data better and then eventually process that data into information to put things together into concrete ideas and plans, especially in unexpected ways. That's the physical side, the thing that makes you, you."

"So, what, I'm smarter than Einstein now?"

"Ein... who? Look, you weren't a complete Goblin before. But you've also mostly been fighting and running so your increases have been focused in that area. You're faster and smarter at fighting, not at solving world peace.

However, there's also side benefits like your ability to plan and think about things, at comprehending information."

I grunt, mopping up the last of the food. That's frightening, that the System - that Mana is changing me so directly. It's also just as scary thinking what someone who specialises or puts all their points into Intelligence would be like. What else is the System changing without me knowing? The more I learn about the System, the less I like it.

As I stand, I realise that the group of children playing in the corner are doing so with some mini-ponies masquerading as dogs. On a whim, I walk over, depositing the bowl in a nearby tray. Lana gives me a hug when she spots me, Mikito offering me a slight nod. Richard seems to be missing, but that's okay as I view the two ladies in turn, both of them having obviously found a washbasin somewhere to clean up the worse of the dirt and blood. Mikito looks at first glance to be doing fine, stoic and calm, but little signs show she's on the edge. Fingers trembling ever so slightly, a twist in the mouth when no one is looking.

Lana looks to be doing better, more subdued by the generally gloomy atmosphere here but certainly not as broken. She has also changed into new clothing and the top she's found is just a little too small, ensuring that more than one man has enjoyed looking at her generous assets. I have to work hard on not staring myself, reminding myself that I'm not a teenager anymore. No matter what my damn hormones are saying.

"How are you guys doing?" I gesture around before we return to watching the pair of dogs give rides to the kids. Parents watch on, some disinterestedly, some with deep concern but none make a move to stop it. I watch for a moment then I pull some chocolate from my stash, waving over some of the smaller ones and handing out the chocolate. It looks like they could do with the calories and after the initial rush, the children return to playing with the dogs. In the meantime, the girls stay silent.

"We found a place to stay but it's... umm... crowded," Lana answers once we are alone again and Mikito nods firmly. "Richard's taken the dogs to Collin's, we're hoping there's more space there. Where are you staying?

"In my house," I say.

"That's not safe!" Lana hisses, turning to me. "I know you've been out in the woods yourself, but it really isn't safe. You never know when a monster could spawn."

"Oh," realising my mistake, I quickly explain. "I bought it from the System so it is a Safe Zone. Still, won't stop them from breaking in, but I'll have enough warning especially since the doors and windows are fixed."

"Mmmm...."

"Is that where you bathed?" Mikito speaks up from her seat.

"In a way. Randy, ummm, the former owner, he had rain barrels that were still filled up in the back," I explain.

Mikito smiles and shares a look with Lana before they each take hold of one of my arms, gripping them firmly. "John..."

And that's how I ended up with three new guests and a half-dozen mini-pony dogs. At least the dogs make a great alarm system.

Chapter 8

In.

Out.

In.

Out.

The world centers on my breathing and then nothing, a complete absence of thought fading in and out at times. I still have a long way to go, even with the purchased skill but as my alarm goes off, I realise I've been at it for half-an-hour now. Much better than what I could have done before the purchase.

It's strange that such a simple thing helps me feel so much better, more balanced and calm. A part of me still wants to poke and prod at the System, about the why's and wherefores, but it's easy to push aside now, to focus on what is. Those questions can be answered in due time, but for now, there are things to do. Like breakfast.

***

"I love you." I come down after a rain barrel bath, rifle clutched in one hand to grab the cup of offered coffee. "If that's bacon, I'm marrying you."

Lana laughs, shaking her head and poking me with the spatula as she stands in the kitchen cooking up breakfast using my spare camping stove in a plain black borrowed shirt. The house looks cleaner, more put together with the bloodstains removed and furniture put aright. It must be my guests since after being forced to invite them home, I spent the rest of the night hidden away in my room going over the various upgrade options of my new residence. Spending so much time alone recently and being a natural introvert meant the rush of humanity drained all my social batteries.

"It's the end of the world, not my taste," Lana retorts and points to a seat. "Sit and eat."

I comply happily, digging in before I have to ask, "Where did this come from?"

"Richard. He visited the Shop this morning while you were asleep and traded in our loot for some groceries. We gave most of what we got to the others, but we kept some essentials," Lana answers me.

"Where are they?" I look around and note that both Mikito and Richard aren't around.

"Hunting. Richard got an invite to join in and Mikito insisted on going. They took the dogs with them and joined up with a few others to work the area around Long Lake. Seems like you can put together parties in town and share experience that way," she explains. "I'm going to see what I can do to help at the schools. What's your plan?"

"Nothing," I smile slightly, shrugging. "I was thinking of taking it a bit easy, maybe spend a little time looking over the rest of the house and resting."

Lana purses her lips, looking at me for a moment but does not comment further. After a moment, she finishes the last of her coffee before she heads off to the room the girls shared to get dressed. Dressed for sure, since when she walks around the counter, I realise she's not wearing pants. My jaw must have dropped because she grins back at me mischievously and explains in a purr that she doesn't have anything to wear.

Ali just wolf-whistles and helpfully points out that she's probably coming on to me and proceeds to provide me full graphic advice on what to do. I tune him out again, and when Lana does come back out wearing the same worn jeans as the day before, I almost wonder if what she said was the full truth. Either way, not the problem at this moment. She waves goodbye to me, heading out and I sit back, staring around me.

The next hour has me puttering around the house, cleaning up the dishes and the stovetop, sorting out the remaining mess upstairs and my suite and then the workshop. When I find myself trying to turn on the water to water the plants, I realise I'm just trying to find work to do. Anything to get my mind off that gnawing pit of grief that is still bottled up in my body. I walk over to my bookcase, staring at my old friends and shake my head, knowing that's not going to work either.

Fuck.

I close my eyes, leaning on the bookcase and realise that make-work isn't going to cut it. I either have to deal with my emotions, all the things that I've been putting off... Or I need to be out there, fighting. That's when I don't think. Out there, with the monsters, I can't afford to do it.

I grim humorlessly, staring at my hand. Stupid. Such a stupid idea. But there might be more survivors who need help, more people trying to get back to town. Maybe I could do a little good too.

***

First step is to swing by the old hospital near the school and then take the road down to check out the scattered homes on this side of the river. There's not a lot of people who live past the hospital, but with the increased number of monsters down this way, anyone who did live here might have been trapped. Anyway, it won't take me longer than a half-hour. Other than a single, unwary crab-like monster that I kill, Ali and I find no sign of surviving humans and I don't feel the need to go hunting here. The quest and the potential lives I might save are more important, at least for now.

After that, I leave Riverdale itself, the goal is to make it to Porter Creek and the other suburbs to do a final check. There are more people out during the day, even the threat of on-going sudden death can't beat pure boredom. In Rotary and Shipyards Park on the river, I note people working the fields over, breaking up the earth to begin planting. I'd barely glanced at Rotary Park on the way to Riverdale last night, figuring the churned earth was just another apocalyptic change.

Once I leave downtown, it's a faster ride to the suburbs. I don't even bother slowing down to shoot at the monsters I see on my way there, but a part of me knows my haste is wasted. If there are survivors, they could have made their way in from these nearby suburbs on foot easily enough or someone like the circle would have escorted them in. Still, I'll feel better making sure.

Surprisingly, I come across a few holdouts; families and individuals who refuse to leave their residences from sheer pride or stupidity. By the sounds of it, I'm not the only one who has tried to convince the holdouts to move, so I leave them to it, just making notes of where they are. I'll leave these idiots for someone else to deal with. Unfortunately, by the time I finish my circuit, other than a few simple kills, I've not found a single survivor to bring back and I've wasted half the day already.

It's strange, driving through abandoned houses and spotting the occasional dead and rotting body, the smell carrying through the wind. I know I should feel something for them. Pity. Sympathy. Grief. Something. I don't though, just this hollow emptiness where the feelings should be. Pushing aside my own emotions over my own loss has left me with this emptiness, this coldness. Why should I cry for someone I didn't know when I haven't for those that I do? I can't change the fact that they are dead, can't make them come back alive. Dead is dead and there's no point wasting any further thought on them. It's cold and heartless, but it's reality. What is, is.

The only good news I have is that you can flash-cook monster meat with a burst from my rifle. Having forgotten to bring lunch, this was a happy solution, if not particularly tasty. Still, food is food and it means I can move on to phase 2 of the plan.

If everything that is easy to reach by bicycle is taken care of, then I just need to range wider. Until I'm able to find a more general solution to the transportation problem though, closer is better since I can only carry one other with me. That means that the Lorne Mountain Community and eventually Carcross are the way to go. Decision made, I swing back out to Klondike Highway and gun it.

The Klondike has never been very well kept and it's not much better now. Already, I can see potholes and depressions occurring and I wonder how many years it'll be before the entire highway is useless, permafrost and lack of maintenance returning the Yukon back to its pristine state. Idle thoughts as I scan the forests on either side, a part of me for the first time really seeing my surroundings again. It's a beautiful place, but the human can only take wonder for so long before it makes it mundane. Now, having to watch out for monsters that Ali might miss, I see it all again.

Forests that go on for as long as the eye can see, lakes a beautiful glacier green, snow-capped mountains in the backdrop. It's no wonder we had a constant flow of tourists, a veritable horde of Southerners descending each summer in search of the untouched beauty of nature, that pioneer charm that city life in the south has been stripped of.

It's all a lie of course. Among the trees are the occasional residence, the lodges and bed-and-breakfasts that catered to the tourists. All nestled away in the forest as they attempted to convince their guests they were part of the wilderness, all the while providing the benefits of electricity, the Internet and running water. Now the lodges and B&B's lie empty, their occupants either dead or fled. No one wants to return to the pioneer days really, even the First Nation communities demand their rights to modern conveniences like running water, working schools and electricity. It's no wonder – the wilderness is dirty, smelly and deadly.

Morbid thoughts are pushed aside as Ali bids me to pull over.

"So, remember how you mentioned you wanted to work on some of your skills?" Ali enquires, sweet as can be.

"Yeah…" I reply warily.

"Good. Transform the bike and grab your sword. There's a nest of Ants about 800 meters in. Chop chop time," Ali grins.

Even as I do as he says, I can't help but ask, "Why the sword?"

"That's your personal weapon. And you couldn't stop talking about how cool the Guard was in your videos," Ali says.

"Okay," I nod firmly, not bothering to hide my path through the woods. We still haven't left the low zones yet, so this should be a good test.

***

The Erethran Honor Guard are feared for their combat abilities for a number of reasons. To start with, unlike many other groups, they don't specialise in Tech or Magic, mixing and matching to suit the individual preferences of the Guard members. Unfortunately, I have only a single spell right now and it's not one that I will likely need to use. The other reason they are feared is due to their Class Skill, their ability to enhance their Personal Weapons, transforming even the simplest weapon into something truly deadly. I can't do that either. To be frank, and Ali can be Sally, I wouldn't even qualify to join them.

However, if I ever want to make full use of my class, I need to start training the way they train. One thing that was very clear from the downloaded footage is that they make use of their personal weapons in a very unique way due to the fact the weapons are Soulbound. It's entirely different from any fighting technique used by humanity too, which is why all I can do now is experiment.

Of course, first I have to find the damn Ants. "Ali, are you sure its 800 meters?"

I don't need an answer since the Ants give me one, springing their ambush as I walk blindly into it. The first rushes out from behind a bush, closely followed by another. All around me, I can hear Ants. Ants the size of bulldogs come boiling out.

I drop into a reverse lunge, letting the Ant skewer itself on my blade. Instead of taking the time to extract the blade, I let go and I shift to my back-stretched supporting leg, ramming an elbow into the Ant behind me. I hear carapace shatter and spot another Ant jump towards my face, its black mandibles nearly on me. I raise my hand in a cut, calling the Soulbound sword into my hand. My control is slow, my commands hesitant and the sword appears half-way through the creature in a weird explosion of light, destroying the sword itself and the Ant and pelting me in heat and broken metal. It's bad enough that I get a small damage alert from Sabre itself as the explosion tears apart some of the armor.

Ooops. Thrown onto my back from the attack, another Ant clamps itself onto my leg and another one attempts to bite through the armor in my torso. The first actually hurts a bit, its mandibles exerting pressure enough that I decide to take care of it with a swift jerking motion of my leg. I ignore the second Ant, its attacks are insufficient to penetrate the thicker armor around my torso.

Time to get back to practising. A single failure is no reason to quit. I flip myself back onto my feet, the Ant in my middle dislodged from its futile attempts and I recall the sword to plunge it into its back. More and more Ants swarm me and I start moving, lashing out with punches and kicks in my mecha, calling and recalling the sword at intervals. It's a bit of a curb stomp really. The Ants can barely do any damage to me individually and I never stay still long enough for them to pile on, the added speed and strength that Sabre provides me allowing me to over-power even when a five Ant team that had me held down for a moment.

It takes a long time for me to kill them all off though and when I'm done, I must have ranged over a hundred meters, smashing, stabbing and killing. Ali watches, popcorn in hand with an occasional warning or an even rarer useful piece of advice. Once I've recovered, I begin the slow process of looting the bodies.

"Any progress?" I grumble, touching another body and flicking the loot into my inventory. There's got to be an easier way of doing this.

"Of course not. You think it's that easy to get a new skill? Or increase your current skill level?" Ali snorts, shaking his head. "It takes years for Mastery to occur and you're on the steepest part of the slope. Gains will take forever. This? This was a warm-up."

I grunt and get back to looting the corpses, each Ant removed of its chitinous outer shell and a slab of meat. Occasionally, I get even some mandibles, though god knows what that's for. The entire looting process takes longer than the fight and I wonder if it's even worth bringing the bodies back. Ants, even giant Ants, don't really have a lot of meat on their bodies.

No, better to get a move on if I want to actually make it to Mount Lorne at the very least. The community is isolated enough that I might find a survivor or two.

***

It's not even 5 minutes later when Ali announces, "We're entering a higher-level zone soon, figure average level in the low-to-mid 20's."

Even before I can acknowledge it, Ali continues; "We've got trouble. There are 8 Hakarta warriors in a building to the left at the t-intersection."

"Hakarta?"

"Large, aggressive green-skinned individuals with tusks who come from a warrior culture. Often hire themselves out as shock troops. Closest analogue are Orcs," Ali explains hurriedly to me.

"About time," I grin slightly beneath my helmet. What kind of fantasy world would it be without Orcs? As I spot the two-storey log building that dominates the Carcross cut-off, I note a slight glint in the bottom window. Instinct makes me start leaning to the side and I feel the beam punch through my shoulder, my body spasming around the damage. I'm sliding off the bike into a controlled crash, the pain too sudden for my body to catch up with it.

As momentum keeps me rolling on the ground, another blast kicks up the asphalt. Pain radiates through me, my shoulder a complete mess with a hole burnt right through it. I manage to trigger the Quantum State Manipulator (the QSM) just before a third shot passes through where I would have been, pain tearing through me again from the energy that passes through the dimensions. I finally come to a stop about ten feet and another dimension from my bike. I'm invisible and in another dimension so the

Hakarta aren't shooting at me anymore as I just lie on the road, dealing with my injuries.

After a time, I manage to gain sufficient control to cast my only spell, patching my wound such that I'm able to stand. When I turn to look at the building, the Hakarta are coming out in a group of five, their movements with that polished training you see in movies. Ali's right, they are extremely muscular, green and tusky. At a glance, they'd be perfect Orcs – if Orcs wore body armour and carried beam rifles.

"What the hell Ali! They have rifles. Why didn't you warn me?" I snarl as I stagger over to where my bike is, pain from the shoulder wound slowly fading.

"I did! They're Hakarta, of course they have rifles!" snaps Ali, affronted.

"Orcs don't have rifles. They're Orcs!" I snarl, casting one last heal on my shoulder. It's not fully patched, but it's workable for now.

"I said the closest analogue is Orcs. I didn't say they were Orcs, I said they were Hakarta!" Ali says.

"Fuck it. Later. I need you to distract them so I can drop out and trigger the change," I point away from me, bending down to the bike. I'm so not leaving Sabre here for them.

"Now he wants me to get shot," Ali flies off, grumbling all the while. "Yohooo! Big, green and dumb, think you can hit me?"

The Hakarta react with speed, tasked to deal with him, aiming and firing in a single swift motion. I turn off the QSM and trigger the change immediately, yanking the armor on. Unfortunately, a simple distraction isn't good enough and the Hakarta covering my bike opens fire. Luckily, this one is caught mostly on the armor that slides over me. It still makes me jerk in reaction, sending me sprawling and I have to trigger the QSM once more as I roll away, the armor sufficiently equipped to come with me thankfully.

"Move! They've got a quantum grenade," Ali shouts urgently and I bolt for it. The grenade hits the ground where I was and explodes, picking me up and throwing me forwards. It feels like a hundred burning needles have shoved themselves throughout my body and damage reports from the mecha suit start streaming in. I crawl my way away to the treeline and push myself till I'm a good distance away before I allow myself to breathe.

Thankfully, the Hakarta aren't pursuing at speed so I have time to catch my breath. Ali keeps an eye out for me as I recover and check over the damage reports. Thankfully, nothing is broken irretrievably but a number of systems have re-routed to secondary circuits to deal with the existing damage.

"Still doing a sweep, they've got a scanner. Looks to be only a Mark V though, so you've got about 5 minutes before they're in range. Run or fight boy-o," Ali calls out.

Run or fight. I'm injured, in pain and outnumbered. They've got training, experience and levels on me. Good sense says run.

"Let's kill them," I snarl, retrieving my rifle and checking it for damage. Stupid, but if I wanted to be smart, I'd be home. Two can play this game.

***

Bad news for the Hakarta. Their scanner works great, but if I'm no longer using the QSM it has nothing to pick up on. Curled up and ready to ambush them with Ali providing real-time updates on their positions, I get ready to take my revenge.

"Coming around the tree in 5, 4, 3…" intones Ali.

The Hakarta step around and I take my shot. The first shot goes for the scanner itself, blasting the valuable equipment into so much junk. Of course, the Hakarta holding it has it up to his chest so he gets shot too, though it doesn't look like a killing wound.

I roll back into cover under the tree and keep rolling, letting the gradient of the hill get me out of the way of the return fire. A quantum grenade arrives soon afterwards, but this one does no damage as I'm still phased into this reality and the ancillary explosive damage in this reality is insufficient to breach Sabre's armor at this distance.

I trigger the QSM the moment it's safe and leg it to a nearby tree, spinning around and waiting. The Hakarta are aggressive, coming around my original sniping position and getting ready to finish me off. They are disciplined and smart, moving fast with each member having their own field of fire. Me, I just shoot the green bastard who is facing me straight in the face. As the others begin to swing around to finish me, I fire again before rolling behind cover and triggering the QSM.

Two more times. That's as many times as I can use the QSM, if I keep my time in the other state short. I make sure I do, booting it not away from them but directly to them. When I get close enough, I drop back into reality, my rifle pointing straight at the third Hakarta. I take a moment before I pull the trigger. The blast catches it in the side of the neck, blowing his head clean off but I don't have time to watch. There are 2 more left from the initial party, one wounded, and I need to finish them. I drop the rifle, swinging my right hand in an overhand chop direct into the arms of another Hakarta who is turning to bring his weapon to bear. Too big for close range combat, he never gets it to me in time before I disarm him and then behead him with the sword I call into being.

The last Hakarta doesn't bother with his rifle, instead tackling me. I lose grip of my sword as I fall. Thankfully the shock absorbers in Sabre remove most of the damage and I get an arm in the way of the plunging knife, redirecting its force sufficiently that it doesn't skewer me, it just leaves a deep cut in the top of my shoulder armor. I grip him close with my arm then and recall my blade with my free hand before pummeling him with my pommel. His helmet stands the first few blows well enough but eventually shatters. A few more strikes leaves the Hakarta lifeless above me, at which point I push the creature off.

5 down. I cast another Minor Healing to staunch the bleeding in my injured shoulder where I've re-opened the wound and then proceed to loot the bodies. Surprisingly, the first body I loot gives me access to all their weapons and armor. I guess fighting humanoids who actually buy their equipment from the System is extremely profitable. I can't help but grin, grabbing everything possible and dumping it into my inventory. By the time I'm done looting the bodies, I've received 5 Beam Rifles (Type IV), 5 Tier V personal body armor (3 significantly damaged), personal arms for each Hakarta and 3 Plasma Grenades along with 432 Credits.

"Ali, scout the building will you?" I begin to make my way back, wondering if I could somehow lure at least a few others out.

"Sir, yes Sir!" mouths Ali but I ignore it. Got to let the Spirit get his shots in, otherwise, it's impossible to work with him. Thankfully, he still does his job.

"3 left. They are set-up in the center room of the ground floor. Looks like the leader and a couple more grunts, guarding the entrances to the room," Ali reports back in a few minutes. I've set-up a short distance away, watching the building from the tree line across the highway. I nod at his words, getting a little more detail about the layout before working out the new plan.

Letting Ali keep an eye on them, I walk boldly up to the door and open it. I spin out of the way just in case, but no bombs or shots go off. A quick peek shows me it's still clear and I walk up to the next door, pulling and priming a grenade. Once at the door, I gently depress the door handle and then quickly toss the grenade in, hunkering around the corner even as the Hakarta open fire, tearing chunks out of the door and even catching me a glancing blow.

The explosion is significantly more powerful than I expected, tearing drywall apart like tissue and dumping me on my ass as more damage messages scroll through in the bottom left of my vision. I roll around, trying to get my rifle to bear and realise I might as well not bother, the lifeless and mangled bodies of the three telling its own tale. Battle over, Ali lets the important notifications creep into my view.

Level Up! * 2

You have reached Level 10 as an Erethran Honor Guard. Stat Points automatically distributed. You have 21 Free Attribute Points to distribute.

Twice in a single battle? I knew I was getting clobbered by running rather than fighting, and the first ten levels are the easiest to gain, but still, twice? No wonder the others had gained levels so fast. Those free attribute points were really starting to creep up there. I'd have to make a decision soon since they weren't doing me any good just sitting unallocated.

***

I spend a few minutes putting out fires to ensure the building doesn't burn down, beginning to realise how lucky I am. After I loot the bodies, I then drag them out of the house and stack them to the side. No reason to let them rot in the building after all. This time, looting the bodies gets me some scrap, a few personal weapons and their System Credits. Note to self, plasma grenades should not be used unless I really need them. I make a final sweep of the building, finding some minor conveniences including what looks to be a Mana-charged stove, food stores and high-tech sleeping bags. As I put them into my inventory, I can't help but think that Lana would love the stove.

Other than the bodies, there's only a single glowing crystal in the remnants of the room I dragged the bodies from which I eye askance.

"Ali...?"

"Control crystal for the fort," Ali explains.

"What fort?"

"The one you're standing in of course," Ali says.

"This is a restaurant and grocery store, not a fort!" though it looks like the Hakarta have cleared out most of the grocery items and started putting together a proper base of operations.

"System designated fort. Created at locations of importance outside of a city, generally a building that commands significant views or a strategic location. Considering we're about 45 minutes out from Whitehorse on the only major highway in? I'd say both. Now, go on and touch the crystal," Ali replies wearily.

Would you like to take Command of the Carcross Cut-off Fort?
(Y/N)

Congratulations! You are now Commander of the Carcross Cut-off Fort
Population: 1/1
Assigned Guards: 0/20
Structural Integrity: 68/100

Upgrades: None

First Fort Won!

Bonus +3000 Experience Awarded

"So, what now?" I frown, staring at the upgrade option.

"Nothing, now we leave. Next sentient who comes in will take the place, but at least you'll get a notification," Ali says, sounding bored.

"But…" Just leaving this place right after I won it is frustrating, but he's right. It's not as if I'm going to guard it, I still have to get to Mount Lorne and Carcross. I grit my teeth and stomp out, assuaging my feelings by pulling out my new status sheet.

Status Screen			
Name	John Lee	Class	Erethran Honor Guard
Race	Human (Male)	Level	10
Titles			
Monster's Bane, Redeemer of the Dead			
Health	510	Stamina	510
Mana	450		
Status			
Normal			
Attributes			
Strength	33 (50)	Agility	50 (70)
Constitution	51 (75)	Perception	14
Intelligence	45 (60)	Willpower	45 (60)
Charisma	14	Luck	10
Skills			

Stealth	6	Wilderness Survival	3
Unarmed Combat	6	Knife Proficiency	5
Athletics	5	Observe	5
Cooking	1	Sense Danger	4
Jury-rigging	2	Explosives	1
Blade Mastery	6	PAV Combatics	4
Energy Rifles	3	Meditation	5
Mana Manipulation	1		
Class Skills			
None (5 Locked)			
Spells			
Minor Healing			
Perks			
Spirit Companion	Level 3	Prodigy (Subterfuge)	N/A

Damn, that's a big difference from when I started. I'm not even remotely within human normal anymore, with reaction times and strength that are off the charts. I don't even feel the weight of my armor or seem to run out of stamina doing normal things. At this rate, there are only a few more levels before I finally unlock my Class skills and after seeing Mikito use hers, I really can't wait. On the other hand, it feels like I'm not utilising the changes in my body properly, my actions themselves jittery in the extreme. I wonder if it's my low Perception – I'm not able to properly perceive what I need to do and what I'm doing, especially with the way my body is moving.

"Ali? Recommendations?" I enquire, waving to the Stat Screen as I get ready, the slight hitch and a barely audible grinding making me grimace as Sabre switches form. Damn, but I'm going to have to get this fixed.

"Perception. Maybe you'd get a hint or two next time before you get shot," Ali answers immediately.

I grimace but have to agree. I dump half my points into it and then, on a whim, I put another 3 into Luck. It's such a nebulous stat, but from what I understand, it affects minor things in the System in my favor. A shot that does more damage than it would normally, maybe more or better System assisted Loot drops. It should also reduce the likelihood that someone with high Luck bends the System to their favor. More Luck doesn't seem to hurt anyway.

The moment I confirm it, the world shifts. It's so startling I begin to lose control of Sabre and even as I realise that, I correct it. It happens faster than an eyeblink, perception, understanding and reaction. Oh my, this is going to be fun.

Chapter 9

"Ali, information dump time. How come the System designated the Cut-off as a fort if no one bought it before?" I enquire as I ride down the winding mountain road. On both sides is untouched, unclaimed wilderness as far as the eye can see. Only occasionally is there a road that swings out to a lone farm or suburb, but each time Ali just shakes his head slightly, indicating a lack of human life.

"The building was there and it was a strategic spot. Seems like the System decided it was worthy of being picked," Ali shrugs, disinterested in the conversation.

I'm not as easy to put off, "But why? I thought we had to buy locations."

"Settlements certainly. However, forts aren't the same – they are freestanding fortifications. You are limited to guard, security and observation upgrades, which generally limit what you can do drastically. Of course, you can always buy other upgrades like an armory and the like, but it's always more expensive." Ali says.

"Didn't look like much of a fort to me, just a normal building," I point out.

"Sure, that's because no one has upgraded it yet. Get some walls built or buy the upgrades and it'll start looking like a real fort," Ali replies.

"Wait, we can build walls? Won't the System ignore them?" After all, it's ignored most of our other buildings.

"Nope. You guys are all System-claimed now, so what you do from now on matters to the System," says Ali.

No use getting angry over this, but I can't help but feel it. The System this, the System that. It makes decisions and discards everything that we ever did before it came, remaking us and our world without care. I find myself grinding my teeth and force myself to breathe out as I push the anger aside.

In control once more, I ask lightly, keeping my voice calm. Or at least I think it's calm, "That mean those non-fighter classes we found, they could fix up the cars?"

Ali nods, "Sure, if they use System registered materials, no reason it wouldn't work. You'd either have to salvage or work the materials from start or buy from the Shop, and if they wanted Mana engines and batteries, they'd have to get their skills up."

Good news. I lean into the next turn, falling silent for now as I scan for more trouble. Even driving at speed, I see more than I used to - my increased perceptions able to take notice of more. I spot our local, non-transformed wildlife – squirrels, ground squirrels, a fox, occasional birds. I also spot a few transformed and new animals, but none that are a danger to me so I don't stop. I came out to check for survivors after all, not kill monsters.

Mount Lorne is a bust, the various small residences and communities that cluster around the community centre empty. They leave another mystery though – unlike many of the houses in Riverdale, many show signs of an organised exit. Doors closed, windows shut, no damaged or broken buildings to be seen and no blood. It is almost as if they evacuated somewhere else, those that weren't attacked immediately at least. Did they make it into Whitehorse already? A puzzle for sure, but not one that I can solve right now.

I look up the time and note it's 7pm already, glad that my helmet and Sabre came with a clock. The longer spring hours in the North throw me for a curve, daylight lingering till 10pm these days. If you'd asked me, I would have guessed it was no later than 4pm. A dangerous little trick the North likes to play, making inexperienced backpackers push themselves till late at night, unaware of how long they have exerted themselves.

It's another twenty minutes to Carcross at speed, but I take it a little slower and get there in half-an-hour. As I begin to pass the world's smallest desert on my left, Ali pops back into life, finishing up the game of cards he has been playing to talk to me. "Humans. Lots of humans. At least a few hundred."

I grin at his words, relaxing. Thank the gods, not every small community was being wiped off the map. I slow down anyway since I figure whoever is there is going to be jumpy and I'm glad I do because I'm so not ready for what I see.

***

Just before I get to the town, I run into a barrier made up of cars, trucks and stacked furniture that reaches all across the road and down to my right as far as I can see, probably all the way to the river. The town itself is built adjacent to the river, spreading out from near the bridge and along the West side of the highway. From what I can see, where they have run out of cars and furniture, they have dug a trench on one side and just piled the extra earth on the other, shoring the entire thing up with occasional felled trees. Quite a feat if they have it all the way down to the river since it's at least a good kilometer away.

I slow down and creep up to the barrier, waiting to be challenged. I don't have to wait long.

"Who's there?" A voice shouts in the slightly slurred accent of one of the First Nations. Tagish probably, considering we're in Carcross.

"John Lee. I'm here from Whitehorse," I shout back, touching my helmet to make it disappear. I hear a gasp behind the barrier even from this distance. I guess the disappearing helmet trick is still kind of new.

"You human?" the voice continues to question.

"Yes!" I grimace, shaking my head at the question. I can hear the arguments behind the barrier as someone else points out that that's a stupid question. A hurried discussion happens even as they send one of their own to get someone in charge.

"Who's the Greatest Hockey Player ever?" This time, at least, the question makes sense.

"Gretzky of course." I snort, shaking my head. "Look, I don't mean any harm, I just came to see what I could do to help."

"Right, sorry about that. Just come up slow now. We got guns," my unseen conversation partner says. I comply readily enough, riding my bike closer and then am forced to wait till they pull the makeshift gate aside to ride in.

Inside the barrier, Carcross had not changed much. A single lonesome gas station connected to the motel and gift shop is a short distance away on the left, while to the right, the Tagish First Nation's office building, a church and a variety of other residences spread out to the river that the entire community nestles against. Surprisingly, everything looks pretty normal, though there are guards standing around me and further afield, all of them looking around with that wary expression I've come to recognise of people under siege. The guards on closer inspection are low-leveled, all in the single digits and have a new appellation next to each of them – Warrior, Riflemen, Guard and more.

"Ali, what's with the new information?"

"New information that I can display. Not super useful all the time, and I'm translating it as best I can from what the System gives me, but there you go," Ali replies, gesturing to the Status bars.

"Evening. Sorry about the reception, but we've had to be careful," an older brunette woman with a pixie haircut walks up to me and interrupts any further conversation with Ali. She's dressed in a pair of jeans and plaid shirt and could be generously called hefty, though she moves her weight with grace and carries a giant hammer over her shoulder with ease. The Status bar over her head reads Melissa O'Keefe, Level 38 Protector. "I'm Melissa."

"John," I take the proffered hand and watch as a crowd begins to gather, coming from the gas station and the office building, consisting mostly of children and teenagers. "This place is… impressive."

"Thanks. If you don't mind, there are a few people who'd like to talk to you," Melissa says and waves me to the Tagish First Nation's offices. I park Sabre there once I can and after a moment's hesitation, I grab the rifle from its holster on the bike. Looks like everyone is armed in this town.

The meeting hall is buzzing, people moving with purpose. Random snatches of conversation that I overhear give a sense of organisation, of people working towards a common goal, something that was missing in Whitehorse. Surprisingly, I notice that everyone here has a few levels, a vast change from the majority in Whitehorse. I don't get to linger though as I'm directed towards a boardroom where three others await – a gaunt, tall teenage Wizard, a matronly First Nation Shaman elder and a local member of the Royal Canadian Mounted Police (RCMP) still in his uniform.

The last makes me pause, a part of me wondering about the lack of RCMP members in Whitehorse. I'd have thought they'd be on the front lines of this. I frown, and then push the thought aside. Something to look into when I'm back if I really was that curious. In the meantime, introductions seem to have been made for me, but I've missed it. Ah well, not as if I need to remember their names, what with Ali providing their Status bars.

Interestingly enough, the kid is the highest Level at 36, the constable is a Level 34 Guardian and the elder only a Level 8 Shaman.

"So, Mr. Lee, you came from Whitehorse," Constable Mike Gadsby says, his heavy Francophone accent taking me a moment to decipher. "Can you tell us about the state of the city? We have had no word."

I nod and settle into a chair, getting ready for a long talk. We start out with Whitehorse and then I get a briefing on Carcross before we range back to the System. Once they realise I'm a fount of information, the kid takes over the conversation, sending probing and insightful questions my way. More than once Ali has to provide me with the answers to questions that the kid raises.

When the first message came, quite a few of the residents of Carcross had congregated at the RCMP's office. That meant that when monsters spawned, there was much less ground to cover, allowing the RCMP to organise and protect them. In the meantime, it seemed the kid - Jason Cope - had convinced his Mum, Ms. O'Keefe, that he knew what he was talking about and then dragged her along on a monster hunt to 'power-level' themselves, picking on the various lower leveled monsters that cropped up. Working together with their neighbors, they quickly managed to not only level, but work out the Party System and proceed to sweep the surroundings repeatedly, keeping the residents safe and gaining experience constantly. When an initial monster horde had rushed the crowd, it was only the timely intervention by the O'Keefe's that managed to keep the casualties to the minimum.

In the meantime, I learnt about the Party System in more detail. Seems it was both obvious and annoying, much like most of the System. I could make a party at any time with anyone I wanted, though I could only have one party. A party shared experience to some extent, but only if party members actively helped during a fight. The actual division of experience varied depending on the contribution offered and included damage done, healing or buffs provided or just general support. It seemed that disparate levels in the party meant that people gained experience in different ways and the System actually registered groups that moved together as unofficial parties, whether we wanted it to or not.

In addition, the other thing I picked up was that it was quite viable to increase Levels outside of fighting if you were a non-fighter based class. Leveling in those cases focused on the development of their Class Skills, with increases in Class Skills providing experience that then increased their overall Levels. In addition, it seemed non-fighter characters seemed to gain quests at a much faster rate, which were mostly focused on developing those skills. It was one of the reasons for the levels I had seen as everyone worked on developing their skills and completing quests in Carcross to grow stronger. They had people working on the various loot drops right now, making makeshift armor, weapons and even cooking using the materials. Amazingly enough, bodies that were worked by the proper Class could even generate additional materials over and above what the System gave. While they couldn't keep the city itself safe from random spawning, everyone had leveled up enough that your average monster mutation was less of a danger.

We talk for hours; the ubiquitous meat stew and bannock being brought in while we continue the conversation. They probe me for more information continuously, pausing only when they learn of my time in Haines Junction to relay the news of the tragedy. By the time they've finished pumping me, it's past midnight and darkness has finally fallen. I'm offered a place to stay, which I take gratefully, happy to let someone else keep an eye out for potential trouble while I rest.

Chapter 10

"Interesting," I look around the automotive shop that's been turned into a community workshop, various residents already hard at work at their respective stations this early in the morning. I'm sipping on the coffee that's been offered to me, eyeing what the crafters are up to. 4 of the workbenches seem to be devoted to armor making, 2 working on various insect carapaces and another 2 on leather. Another pair of benches seem to be creating makeshift melee weapons while the last is the most interesting, a broken-down energy rifle laid out next to a normal gunpowder rifle. Soldering irons and electronic equipment are arranged next to it.

"That's mine," Perry, my guide, waves to the bench I'm eyeing. "I've been focusing on trying to replicate their laser guns, but haven't had any luck. Got a Level in Energy Weapons at least when I took it apart."

Ali snorts, floating above the disassembled weapon, "It's like watching a monkey try to build a spaceship with a stick."

"You probably need a few more levels," I reply diplomatically. I'm still impressed, all things considered, and I shake Perry's hand as I take my leave.

"Good. You're still here," Jason runs up to me, his gangly frame doing the weirdest run I've ever seen. He must have dumped all his stats into Willpower and Intelligence; he definitely isn't doing anything for his Agility. Behind him, moving much slower is Gadsby who looks like he could use a couple more cups of coffee.

"Long night?" I enquire.

"Rough. We had another breakthrough – lost a couple more to a spiked creature that rolled right over our trenches," Gadsby replies, grimacing. "It's why we need to talk to you. We need to visit this Shop of yours. We need to make this a Safe Zone, get better weapons and supplies."

I feel a flash of guilt at that, remembering the weapons and armor I took off the Orcs. I pause for a second, a selfish, small ignoble part of me not wanting to give them the guns. I need money for better weapons, for better defenses, to fix Sabre for myself if I want to continue this stupidity of running around outside of town. Unfortunately, so do they.

"Nope. No way, not happening," Ali floats in front of me and stares me in my face. "First rule of the System – no one gets anything for free."

"People are going to die if we don't help them," I think back.

"I'll deal with this you bleeding heart Qwixly," Ali spins around and waves. "Alright you crazy humans. My man here picked up a few guns, some armor and some Ant carapaces that you fashionable humans could easily use."

"What the hell!" Gadsby pulls out a gun, pointing it at Ali. Jason just stands there staring before blurting out. "It's a fairy!"

"Fuck you. Price just went up. I'm no fairy," Ali glares at Jason, ignoring the gun completely.

After that start, Gadsby and Ali get down to haggling. Jason, on the other hand, pulls me aside to get a debrief on Ali, which I refuse to elaborate upon beyond the basics of the System. After a moment, I realise the two hagglers aren't going to stop their haggling anytime soon.

"You mentioned that you send sweeper units to deal with the monsters out there?" I enquire of Jason, absently pulling out a chocolate bar from my inventory and breaking off a piece. I sigh and toss the other half to a kid that has magically appeared next to me, eyes wide.

"Yeah, why?" Jason frowns, moving to adjust his glasses that he no longer wears. He paws at his face for a moment before giving up.

"I'm not in the mood to listen to those two. I'd rather go kill something," I answer and walk over to a corner, dumping out the weaponry and armour from my inventory. Once done, I repeat, "Let's go."

Jason blinks and then looks over to the two, "I'm not really supposed to go past the barrier without my mum or Gadsby."

I just look at him, letting the teenager hear what he just said. After a moment, he grins wide. "Yeah, let's do it."

***

Four hours later, we're back for lunch, chatting happily. Hunting without Sabre and Ali is an interesting experience, one that makes me glad for my advantages. Once outside the barrier, Jason starts sneaking and I follow his lead. We spend most of the time hunting for trouble to get into and twice, he moves away from a fight. In reflection, I think we could have taken them but with no armor and no backup, our margin of error is much higher. When we do attack, it's from hiding and with overwhelming force, working to kill the creatures as quickly and efficiently as possible. It's also my first experience with a formal party and being able to watch Jason's Mana pool go down while he casts spells is quite an interesting experience. I kind of have to say though, I'm truly jealous at the ease that he wields his magic, changing from homing darts of blue energy to ice blasts and ivy chains without a thought. Of course, I could do without the waving hands and twisting fingers, but everyone has their own process. Truth be told, out there, he does most of the damage and I'm just there as part of the mop-up operation.

The moment we cross the barrier, we run into the fiercest resistance yet – Ms. O'Keefe. I idly note that at least a few of the guards have acquired new weapons that look very familiar.

"Young man, where were you?" she stands there, tapping her foot with one hand casually on the hammer. I call a tactical retreat, waving goodbye to them both and making sure not to meet Ms. O'Keefe's eyes as I head for the restaurant where lunch is being served, ignoring the beseeching looks for support sent my way.

Ali floats back up to me soon after, glowing from having a good haggling session it seems; "Alright, we traded the guns and armor for 10,000 Credits on an IOU basis. They need to keep what Credits they have, so we got a better deal. I figure we can collect it in a month if they survive.

"Also, you're going to take the old lady with you into Whitehorse and carry whatever you can of their loot in your inventory. We help them buy and sell and cart her back here too."

Quest Received – Help Carcross

Help Carcross make their first successful visit to the Shop in Whitehorse. You will need to get Elder Andrea Badger to Whitehorse and back.
Reward: 2,000 XP

Nice. Maybe I should let him talk more. "When?"
"Right after you finish stuffing your face," Ali says.

***

The ride in is surprisingly comfortable and quiet. I don't slow down, not for anything and Ali keeps us informed of any potential problems so I know when to really speed up. Elder Badger just laughs when we do speed up, obviously the old woman enjoys going fast. I don't tell her of the dangers Ali informs me of, but I can feel my shoulders relax. My grip loosens slightly when we finally get within the lower zone around Whitehorse again. Some of the monsters that prowled the mountains and forests would not have been fun to fight.

In Whitehorse, I slow down for safety's sake and for the Elder to take it in. Not much seems to have changed from a few days ago, with only guards and the occasional hunters moving around, other than just in the Safe Zones. It is a stark contrast and again, I wonder what the major differences are. It almost seems that not having a Safe Zone forced the people of Carcross to step-up, to either face the challenge or die.

Dropping Ali and the Elder at the city centre, I decline to join them. Ali has full access to my inventory in the Shop, so there's no point in going in directly. Instead, I ride the elevator to see Roxley himself to turn in my quest. Interestingly enough, Ali still can't provide any further information even with his higher Level. I guess we're still not up to snuff.

"So, there's a settlement of humans in this Carcross, numbering hundreds. But you only brought back one – who isn't even going to stay. Is that right?" Lord Roxley stares at me with those soulful black eyes under long delicate eyelashes.

"Yes."

"And you wish to be rewarded for this," Roxley continues and I admire the way his lips twist as he speaks, the barest hint of a smile. "Even if your quest is for bringing survivors back to my city?"

"Mmmm… yes?" I pause, seeing his point.

"Well, I really can't do that," Roxley shrugs his shoulders, which are surprisingly broad for such a willowy frame, muscles rippling beneath his silver and black tunic.

I shoot him a rather pitiful glare, one lacking any real heat. He is right after all – the citizens of Carcross aren't actually contributing to his city. Not that the citizens of Whitehorse are contributing either, but that's a different thing entirely. Still… "I'm sure this information is worth something. And eventually, some might come."

"Eventually is not now." Roxley picks up a glass, sipping on it and adds, "Did you Level Up while you were gone? You seem… broader."

"Yes, thank you," I answer back, wondering if he's going to offer me a drink again.

"Well, I can't really reward you for the citizens you didn't bring back, but the information is valuable…" Roxley runs a finger along the edge of the glass before smiling. "Yes, this will do."

Quest Completed!

Bring News of the Survivors
Reward: 2,000 XP and 1,000 Credits

Roxley watches me for a moment before realising I'm not leveling up and then he flicks his hand, dismissing me. I shrug and head off, the Credits better than nothing.

Now what? A quick stop in the Shop shows that Ali and the Elder are really going at it, so I leave to head out. When I walk out, I see Sabre and realise that someone needs some loving. Right, Ali mentioned there was an Armourer in town. Let's see what they can do about poor old Sabre then. I follow the small map in my helmet to the building and stare at it, frowning.

It looks like your typical concrete and metal warehouse, no different than any other building in the industrial park. Well, no different except for the sign out front saying 'Don't shoot the proprietor'.

I walk in, wondering what the sign is about. I tap the button, withdrawing the helmet and walk into the building. I look around for a moment, eyes adjusting to the darkness and then I pull my sword, jumping a good foot back as I choke on a scream.

I'm not scared of giant spiders. I'm not scared of giant spiders. I'm not scared of giant spiders. Squatting in a web that crosses above a workshop counter in front of me, a giant black and gold spider sits chittering and working on a dismantled energy pistol. The spider looks up as I wave my sword around and for a moment, seems to even sigh; "Please put sword down."

I inhale and then exhale again before finally making the blade disappear. Right. That's what the sign was for. "Sorry! Sorry!"

"No shot. Good. All good. You work?" the creature chitters and sets down the pieces it's been working on.

"Yes. I have a damaged Omnitron III Class II Personal Assault Vehicle that needs fixing," I mutter, staring at the creature. My feelings slowly start to settle, adrenaline dropping as my instinctive response slowly subsides. Right, giant spider can talk and is sentient and is the mechanic.

"I open. Bring in. I look," the spider chitters.

Damn, without Ali around, I can't read its name. "Sure."

When Sabre is rolled in, the spider flows out from its web and begins to crawl around, clicking to itself and poking at damage areas. It twists to me halfway and at its prodding, I engage the transformation sequence. Ten minutes later, it comes to get me.

"Damaged. Not bad. Superficial mostly. Some electrical. 5 hours. 2,700 Credits," the spider chitters and I shiver.

"Ummm…" I stare at it, realising I'm out of moves. I have no idea if he (it?) is quoting high or low, though if it's a mechanic, then it's probably on the higher end. So, umm… "That seems high."

The creature chitters and I swear, it's laughing at me. "2,700 Credits I fix. System fix, more."

"Fine. Fix it," I grumble.

The creature flicks a bunch of things in the air and then a moment later, a text window shows up confirming our agreement. Easy come, easy go.

Time to find something else to do then. 5 hours… there was another building wasn't there? An alchemist? I just hope it's not another giant insect creature staffing it.

***

It takes me nearly half an hour to walk back to Main St, which makes me think I should really plan my trips without my bike better. Still, the alchemist shop is much closer to what I'd expect even if it is set in the middle of Whitehorse's quaint, 1960s strip of shops.

"Welcome!"

The chipper greeting makes me smile and I look for the greeter. It takes me a moment to find her. "Hi there."

"Oooh, can I try that again? Welcome to Sally's Alchemical and Magical Emporium," the gnome, because really, that's what she looks like, announces. 4 feet tall, bright purple hair that comes all the way down to her tiny, shapely ass and clad in a smock, Sally bounces with pent up energy. "Was that better?"

"Yeah, better." I can't help but return her smile, looking around the insides. The shop is filled with rows upon rows of potions and bottled ingredients, a weird mixture of a spice shop and liquor dispensary. "So, what do you sell?"

"Alchemical and magical ingredients galore. If you name it, I have it. Well, except for Tier I, II and III ingredients right now, and I'm missing some Tier III ingredients too for strength potions, but otherwise, I got it all!" Sally nods emphatically, waving her hands around.

I ponder what I recall of magical potions and give it a shot, "So, you have some health potions?"

She nods emphatically, walking over to a corner and pointing at an array of bottles. The first shelf consists of bottles in different tints of orange, the second in purple and the third in blue. "They are all Tier III to V. I even have a few Tier II potions, but those aren't on display."

Seeing my hesitation, Sally smiles and continues on, "I bet you haven't seen these before have you. These are potion regeneration, body regeneration and straight healing potions in order. The first heals using the ingredients inherent in the potion itself, the second boosts the recovery rate of your body and uses your body's physical resources. The last and most expensive tap into ambient Mana and the System generates direct healing of your body, much like a healing spell."

Beneath each potion, the Credit costs display. The cheapest starts at 50 for the body recovery potions and rise from there, going up to a staggering 2000 Credits. Considering these are consumables, I can see my Credits burning through at an astronomical rate. And these aren't even the good stuff "How much do they heal?"

Sally pauses and then admits, "I'm not entirely sure for the regeneration potions. I haven't had any human customers yet, so the effects might vary.

The potion regenerators should be anywhere from 20 to 50 health for the lower end. The body regenerators have always been dependent on the individual, but should be between 2-4% increase on the low-end again. As for the System Health Potions, well, those are regulated and will heal you a minimum of 25 and increase in increments of 25 per size and tier."

I might not be Ali, but I can sniff out a deal myself, "So, you need a guinea pig don't you."

Sally's eyes widen and then a playful grin crosses her face, "Well, that depends. I'm sure those Raven Circle humans would be happy to work with me too."

Unlike Ali, I don't live for the haggling, but I do well enough to get a bottle of each of the potions for only 50 Credits. Of course, I have to promise to actually use it within the next day and report back, but I don't expect that to be a problem.

Soon afterwards, Ali and the Elder make their way out of the Shop with the Elder heading off to speak with some others at the school. I escort her most of the way there but not before she drags a promise for me to pick her up the next morning. Seems like she has a lot to discuss. After that, Ali and I take a walk back to grab Sabre, stopping long enough at the river to get in some target practice before we pick her up and head home. I also learn the mechanic's name at the same time, though I can't even attempt to speak it. We settle on Xev.

What a strange couple of days, I can't help but think as I drive home. It certainly turned out very differently from what I had expected or planned for. Then again, at least it provided sufficient distraction.

***

My head twists slightly as the slap comes in, moving in what seems to be slow motion. I turn to let the blow slide along my face, cheek feeling just the lightest of brushes as Lana clutches her hand. "What the hell! Are you made out of rocks?"

"I'm sorry. Didn't realise not showing up was a problem," I say, smiling slightly at the buxom redhead. Good lord, where the hell did she find that fragrance? I rub at my nose covertly, trying to get rid of it. She smells divine but that's so not the right thing to be thinking as she glowers at me.

She shakes her head, "Don't you dare disappear again."

I raise an eyebrow at her, a part of me wondering when I managed to get myself a wife before I speak, "Yeah, sorry. I'll make sure to leave a note next time I head out. I just figured that I should take a look for some more survivors since I have the only working bike."

Gorgeous blue eyes narrow at my words and then she draws a deep breath, taking visible control of her emotions. She rubs at her eyes, head down before she speaks, "It was a good idea, John, it's just…"

"Yeah," I hesitantly reach out and give her a hug before looking around the empty house. "It's late, isn't it? Where's Mikito and your brother?"

"Out," replies Lana, waving her hand out to where the school is. "Seems like the hunters are busy bonding."

I nod at her words then grin, "Got a gift for you. Come on."

In the kitchen, I pull up my inventory and note that Ali's swapped out the food stores from the Hakarta for human appropriate ready-meals. Good — I wasn't entirely sure I was ready to try eating whatever it was that the Hakarta ate. I pull the stove out and lay it on the counter with a flourish, spoiled only by the confusion on Lana's face.

"It's a stove that is fuelled by Mana," I explain.

At that, she grins and hurries over to poke and prod at it. I say my goodbyes, wanting to get washed up. In my suite, I find myself standing in front of the bathroom half-naked by sheer habit. Gah! It is a chilly day today, barely above 5 Celsius. I have no desire to go outside and take a bath from the rain barrel but even I can smell myself.

Well, I do have some money…

89 Alsek Rd. (Residence)

Current Ownership: John Lee, Adventurer

Current Occupants: 4

Upgrades: None

I concentrate on the Upgrades, curious to see what is available:

Upgrades Available

Grounds

Structure

Add-On Buildings

A quick perusal shows that add-on buildings, even the existing workshop is well out of my price range. Grounds are particularly interesting, especially the ability to add some much-needed security options like a wall. On the other hand, if we can make the entire city a Safe Zone, I wouldn't have to worry about the occasional random spawning or mutation. Upgrading the Grounds would also mean I have to worry less about the mess the dogs are making of the front lawn as they guard the house. Lastly, I'd really, really like to get something a bit more interesting than a stone wall – those force fields mentioned in here would be amazing.

After playing with the other options, I pull the one that I'm most interested in.

Structural Upgrades Available for 89 Alsek Rd.

Security

Structural

Utilities

Décor

Miscellaneous

I'd love to look at Security a bit more. I'm sure there are fun things to have but funds are limited and Utilities make more sense. I pull it up and after scanning the information available, I find what I want - an atmospheric hydro generation machine that connects directly to our existing plumbing, providing both drinkable water and showers. Cheap too at less than 2,000 Credits after I add the upgrades to make it possible to produce hot water.

Nothing seems to happen after I confirm the prompt and for a moment, I wonder if anything actually happened. A quick check shows that the upgrade is there, but then I notice the rather annoying notation that the generator would need a few hours to fill the tanks.

Well, that sucks.

I sigh and head back upstairs, holding my towel and rifle in one hand. Cold bath it is. In the kitchen, Lana is hard at work making a meal and I pause long enough to let her know about the recent changes. She stops chopping up her vegetables, staring at me in silence and I have to repeat what I say before she acknowledges it. Guess she was concentrating pretty hard on finishing dinner.

Cold. The water in the rain barrel is cold. I shiver, toweling off quickly and glad that this is my last cold bath. When I get inside, my towel wrapped around my waist, Lana calls me over before I can get dressed.

"One second, let me get dressed," I reply but she snorts and waves me over.

"Food's ready now. Just sit down. I have something to talk to you about," Lana gestures to the table and after a moment's hesitation, I comply. The lady can cook after all. Whatever she has to say, it gets set aside as we delve a bit deeper into what I was up to, Lana asking a few probing questions about Carcross and the fort.

"That's pretty interesting." She smiles slightly, turning her glass of plain water in hand as she peers at me over its rim. "It seems they've gone down a more community model of development, where everyone is working together." At my nod, she continues, "Won't work here though. Too many people."

I raise an eyebrow and she waves her hand, speaking, "Barter and community systems like that break down over time due to the lack of personal bonds between all participants. It's fine when the community is small, but in a larger community, there is nothing to stop free riders from derailing the system."

Seeing my raised eyebrow, Lana explains, "Business major with a minor in Economics. Richard dealt with customers, I dealt with the books. We both took care of the dogs, of course."

"Doesn't explain why people aren't doing anything though," I grumble as I remember the large swaths of people just sitting around the schools.

"They are, you just don't see it," Lana explains and then shrugs. "What we have is a lot of manpower, but no resources. Most of what we had before doesn't work and though some have Skills, they don't have the tools or resources to actually do anything. The only people with any Credits are the hunters and most of their money is being devoted to upgrading weapons and themselves."

I grunt, acknowledging her point, "Kind of hard not to, what with death being the alternative if you are one of the hunters."

"Oh, it's understandable but it's not true for all," she points to the sink and continues. "You just spent what? A few thousand Credits on getting hot water? What if you had used that money to buy a basic toolkit and passed on some of the materials like those Ant carapaces? They'd be able to start training their skills just like Carcross."

I grimace, wondering what it is with people making me feel like a selfish idiot. I risked my life for the guns, for the Credits. Shouldn't I deserve something for it? Still, I hadn't even thought about her point either.

"Nope. Not happening toots," Ali focuses and begins visible, floating next to me. Lana reacts poorly, screaming and falling off her chair to which Ali giggles a bit over. It takes a few minutes to get her to calm down and to explain who he is before we can return to the conversation.

"It's all puppy dogs and rainbows, but we're not giving away shit for free. First rule of living in the System, it's all about me," Ali waggles a finger at her.

"Did I say anything about charity? It doesn't work, not in the long run," Lana replies bitingly, glaring back at the foot and a half tall brown man.

"So, what are you thinking?" Ali says.

"Microloans," Lana replies promptly.

"Ooooh... I like you. John, keep this one. She's got great tits and a brain!"

I roll my eyes at that and Lana, after realising that she can't actually hit the Spirit, starts expounding on her point. I check out at that point, going to get dressed. I did not survive the Apocalypse to listen to economic theory or whatever the heck they are discussing now. I'd rather watch paint dry.

Problem is, staring around my suite I realise I'm at the same point as I was before I left. Not a lot to do these days and I can feel the edges of my emotions, my worries worrying at me. I should really spend some time, think and feel. I take a deep breath, closing my eyes and trying to open the boxes and realise that I don't really know where to start. I shut the boxes tight, but it's not as if I have a key, that I can just switch off the blocking and it comes back to me. I prod at it cautiously and realise I'm not sure how to do this, not without tearing the entire thing down and I can't, won't, do that. Too much, too fast.

I flex my hands, staring into space and then take a deep breath, exhaling. Alright, find something to do.

***

Outside in the backyard, I shoo the dogs aside and begin. It's strange trying to practise a fighting form that doesn't really require you to hold on to a sword. It's entirely different from the memories and skills I've purchased from the Shop, so much so that the forms that I practise don't really seem appropriate. Without an enemy to work with, it seems strange to attempt to swing the sword and make it disappear and appear at unseen enemies. Eventually, I settle on splitting my practise in two parts – firstly, on recreating one of the fights of an actual Erethan Honor Guard to mimic as a form and secondly, on practising calling forth the weapon and making it disappear at speed, switching hands as I do so.

When Ali and Lana are done, they come to the backyard and Ali just starts laughing while Lana has the grace to at least attempt to hide her giggles.

I know exactly what I look like, a crazed man spinning and swinging around his hands, only occasionally catching and grabbing the weapon that appears out of thin air. Calling a Soulbound weapon into being when still is easy. However, calling a weapon requires me to specify the exact location and it can only be within a certain distance from my body so I have to understand not only where my hand is going to be but how long it'll take for the sword to appear. Add the fact that I can start moving in all 3 directions and things start getting complicated.

Overall, it's been a frustrating couple of hours so when Ali asks to speak with me alone, I'm more than happy to comply. Rather than elaborate on what he and Lana were cooking up, other than the fact that he'd be using some of my Credits, he instead wants to talk about magic.

***

"We're Level 10 now. That means I can share my Elemental Affinity with you, if you'd like to learn it," Ali speaks, hesitant for once.

"More magic? Of course!" I grin, dismissing the sword and looking excitedly at Ali. Nice. I've been wanting to get a new spell from the Shop, but this would be even better.

"An elemental affinity," corrects Ali.

"What's the difference?" I ask him, eager to learn and a bit annoyed at the pedantry.

"Magic as you currently wield it is just using Mana to have the System create the effect for you. That's why you had to get Mana Manipulation before you could learn your healing spell. Each spell is like a ready meal and the Mana you put into it is the energy you need to cook it," Ali says.

"Yeah, still not seeing the difference."

"If you'd just shut up for a moment," Ali says and then continues, "Using Mana isn't the only way to use magic though. Spirits like myself are made of the elements, the forces that dictate the world. It's like gravity – just because there's a spell that can affect gravity doesn't mean there wasn't gravity before the System came along. An Elemental Affinity means you have a connection, an access point to manipulate that element directly without learning spells. You don't need to use Mana anymore to do it, though most do."

I raise an eyebrow at the last and Ali shrugs, "It's easier. Imposing your will on the elements directly is like shifting a car with your bare hands. You can do it if you're strong enough, but isn't it easier to just use a lever? Mana is the lever in this case."

"Okay. Sounds great. Let's do it," I continue on, wondering what is up with him.

"Chill John. Not all Elements work well with others and creating an affinity with one element might mean you lose access to others. Maybe all of them, if the conflict is too great. And there's no way to tell for sure," Ali explains. "It really depends on the individual."

"What's your affinity?"

"Electromagnetic force."

"Umm…" I pause, staring at Ali. Well, electricity then – which explains Ali's preference for energy weapons and his coveralls. Still, "Lightning?"

Ali rolls his eyes at that, just giving up and walking away with his hands in the air shouting, "God damn corporeals. I say electromagnetic force and. Every. Single. Time. It's Lightning Bolts or Electric Shocks. Get some fucking education."

I blink, watching the Spirit walk away and then just disappear. I scratch my head, wondering what the hell has gotten into him. Fuck. Well, that ended just dandy. I sigh, staring at the sky and then stretch, walking back to the gardens.

Fine. Fuck him. I'll just keep training then.

Chapter 11

The next morning, I'm up well before Lana. At Ali's insistence, we head out to 'get some mats' for Lana in the surrounding low-level region. Clad in Sabre, running and bouncing through the woods at Ali's directions against these low-level animals is actually quite relaxing. None of them can actually do damage to me inside my armor so I can practise my burgeoning style to my heart's content.

The guards at F.H. Collins are rather surprised when I start bringing back my kills, dropping off the various mutated animals for the cookpot. Ground squirrels, a couple of wolverines, various hares, a pair of foxes, marmots and shrews are all the recognisable animals, even if they are at the minimum the size of a big dog. Then there are groups of creatures that I've never seen before, creatures with 3 legs or 7, with a dozen eyes or none, furred, scaled, sometimes both or with carapaces. Interestingly enough, I begin to notice that the plants are beginning to transform too, growing thicker and wider as well as adding defenses to protect themselves. Even our usual pines mutate, the sap becoming thicker and stickier – I found one particularly unlucky hare stuck to a pine, unable to move with the sap beginning to congeal around it and liquefy its flesh. Seems like the peaceful, easygoing hikes of pre-System life are gone.

On my last trip in, a female guard walks up to me. Tall, wide, with dirty blonde hair, she could easily be put in a pioneer dress and get away with it. She clomps her way to me to prove it, giving off the vibe of tough competence. The remainder of her RCMP uniform speaks of previous experience. That and her Level of 14.

"Thank you. This is going to help a lot. Though I'm not sure that's edible," Amelia Olmstead gestures to the most recent carcass that I have dropped off. It's spiky, a lurid blue and missing its claws, and it seems to have a weird rubbery thing around its face for its eyes.

"It should be," I glance at Ali who gives a nod back. "Seems like the System makes sure that most animals are now edible to each other. If you avoid the poison sacs – and I've got those out already."

Amelia falls silent digesting the information. I take the chance to ask something that's been bugging me, "So, what happened to the emergency services personnel? You're the first RCMP member I've seen in Whitehorse."

Her eyes darken at that and she looks down, her words a whisper; "Most of the others are dead. There was a monster a few days after it started, this rock thing. We tried to kill it, but guns didn't hurt it much and hitting it just didn't do anything. We... I... " she stops, forcing back a sob.

I bite my lip and put a hand on her shoulder for a moment and she doesn't push it away, shivering before she looks up at me, eyes filled with unshed tears. "I hate this world."

"Don't we all," I agree with her, though a part of me wonders. It's kind of been fun, especially the fighting. At least when I'm fighting, I don't have to think and there's a thrill to it, a rush that makes me feel well and truly alive.

Amelia smiles at me again, pulling away from my arm and then bends down, grabbing the blue creature by its tail and hefting it. "Thank you again."

I nod and watch her walk off for a moment before heading back to the house to enjoy the luxury of a warm shower. Ali goes to Lana's room to 'report on our excursion' but the glint in his eye makes me think he has other motivations. I consider going after him, only to deal with him of course, but I dismiss the idea after a moment. It's not as if he can't go spy on her when

I'm asleep either after all. Seriously, how can a sexless spirit be such a pervert?

Shower done, it's time for me to meditate again. No skipping more than one day of this, otherwise, I'm sure I'm going to have problems. Strange that such a simple thing is so important to my stability. I spend over an hour, sitting and breathing and find that by the time I'm done, Lana has left with my materials and nearly all my Credits.

"You know, I'm not entirely comfortable with this taking my stuff without my permission thing you've got going on here," I eye Ali and he snorts, waggling his finger at me.

"Spirit Companion. Can't do anything that could harm you," he reminds me.

"Yeah, I recall an Ant. And a bee. And that weird plant thing," I reply.

"The first two were for your own good. You needed to Level," Ali points out.

"And the last?"

"It was hilarious?" Ali grins and then holds his hand up horizontally, flapping it side to side. "Rules are a little shaky on non-lethal amusements."

I stare at him, not sure if he's joking or just telling the truth. I sigh after a moment, rolling my eyes and head out after finishing the meal Lana set aside for me. Time to finish my escort quest and make some more money. It seems some things hold true - money or Credits, they never last long.

***

Unfortunately, my plan of a nice and easy ride back followed by more hunting, is interrupted by those annoying things called humans. In this case, it's Jim with my escort standing together waiting. At their insistence, I'm brought into another boardroom to have a chat. Really. Boardrooms? More of them?

When I get in, there is quite a bit of a crowd. There is Jim and Badger – sorry, no laughing, it's a traditional name – sitting together on the left and in the center, a cluster of six boomers, four men and two women arrayed facing the door and me. In addition, both Richard and Mikito are here along with Nicodemus and *that woman* clustered together on the right with some of the other hunters. Interesting, the fact that all the boomers have a non-combat class with Class levels ranging from a Level 8 Minion to a Level 12 Dealmaker.

***

"Mr. Lee, thank you for coming. We understand you've been very busy and we were hoping we could have some words with you about your recent actions," the man in the middle, slimy and overweight, breaks the silence. Mr. Slimy and overweight looks really familiar...

"You're the ex-Mayor, right?"

"I am the duly-elected Mayor of Whitehorse, yes;" Fred Curteneau says, leaning forwards with a smile on his face that makes me need another bath. "The Council and I would be grateful for any help you could provide."

"Boy, this looks real fun, doesn't it?" Ali asks rhetorically to me as he yawns, lounging on a bean bag and floating next to me.

Out of the corner of my eye, I spot Luthien smile at Fred's words, absently running a finger along her cheek. Next to her, Nic just stays silent while I spot Mikito waggling her fingers at what is likely her Status Screen. At least someone's getting some use out of this time.

"Of course," I reply, deciding not to commit to anything. This isn't going to be good either way, but let's see how this plays out.

"Well, let's start with your report on Haines Junction. I understand you informed one of the Raven Circle members that it has been destroyed entirely?"

"Yes. A group of Ogres had entered the town and killed all the residents," I pause then continue, trying to tread lightly here. "They were killed off after that and I managed to bury what bodies I could find."

"And you somehow gained access to the Shop in Haines Junction and purchased a working motorcycle at that time?" short and florid next to the Mayor whines.

"Yes," my eyes narrow at the unsubtle accusation.

"How… convenient," shorty continues to whine. I ignore his name for now though I wonder why anyone would take the class 'Minion'. If they don't want to introduce themselves, that's fine. I'll give them a name myself.

"It was, wasn't it?" Within me, I can feel a little bit of anger pulsing through me, attempting to escape the restrictions I've placed on it and my other emotions. Anger – the one emotion I always had trouble handling. Love, compassion, sadness, I could always contain those. Anger somehow had a way of bubbling up, escaping, drowning me in it. Perhaps as another ex had pointed out, I just had too much anger to contain.

"Elder Badger says you're quite knowledgeable about the System that's imposed itself on us. That you have a short fairy friend that aids you?" the Mayor continues and I nod slightly, grumbling mentally at Ali for making himself known. Not that he'd be hidden forever, but I really hadn't wanted him to show himself immediately. "Could you elaborate on that?"

I pause, considering my options for a moment and then shrug, "I managed to acquire a Level 1 System Spirit Companion very soon after all this started. He's sort of like a giant help desk with a personality. Of course, most of what he's told me is covered in Thrasher's Guide in the Shop."

At my side Ali snorts, flicking his hand.

Skill Acquired

Dissembling (Level 1)

The truth is such a bendable thing in your hands.

The Mayor nods at my words and there's some quick discussion about the revelation of the guide with a single pointed question letting them know how much it costs. I'd send them the Guide myself but I'm restricted. On the other hand, 50 Credits isn't that hard to get especially if the Hunters pooled their resources. Christ on a pogo stick, what have they been up to?

Minion looks like he's eaten a lemon, his face all screwed up as he speaks, "Show us this fairy."

"Mmmm… unfortunately, my Spirit Companion is an independent entity. I can't make him do what he doesn't want," I shrug and glance to where Ali laughs at my description of him.

"So, you have little control over your Companion?" Minion sneers.

"More or less," I can feel my lips pulling into a smile, one that holds no humor in it. To my side, I can see Luthien begin whispering to Nic. She knows what that smile means.

"Mr. Lee, would you tell us about your interactions with Lord Roxley?" Fred takes control of the discussion again, dismissing the other thread of enquiry.

"I've seen him twice. He gave me a quest to find other survivors the first time and the second, I went to complete part of a quest by informing him of Carcross," I reply, watching their reactions.

"You let that invader know about Carcross?" this time, a grey-haired, flower-wearing old woman hisses at me. "Why would you do that?"

"Quest."

"You betrayed us for a quest!?!" she leans forward, glaring at me and I decide to call her Battleaxe. Minion is nodding in agreement, joining the glares while the rest of the group stay silent. Interestingly enough, Ms. Badger doesn't seem as concerned.

"Betrayed? I didn't realise there were sides," I snap back, then draw a breath trying to push the anger down.

"He invaded us, stole our town and declared that he owns it!" she smacks her hand down on the table, half-standing now as she snarls. "He's an invader. He took our lands! How can there not be sides!"

"He's also the one who bought the schools and has been sending his guards to deal with the nastier monsters. Seems he's doing as much good as he has done bad," I point out.

Battleaxe is about to start shouting when Fred cuts her off. "Miranda, not now. This is a discussion for later. Mr. Lee, we'd like it if you perhaps worked with us, perhaps reporting in on your activities? We didn't know about Carcross until Elder Badger herself walked in."

Struck by a thought, I look up to my Companion, *"Ali, why aren't I getting a quest like you did with the Elder?"*

"It's a matter of importance, hierarchy and levels. If you don't have a high enough Level or status, the System only recognises quests that are important. Getting the Elder here and back? Important. Making reports on a daily basis? So not important to the System," Ali replies.

While I listen to him, I pretty much ignore the group who are just glaring at me as I stare into space. I hear Fred clear his throat but I ignore him as I think about it. Importance… Okay, let's see if we can actually get something out of this then, "Why should I?"

"We are the Council of Whitehorse, your government!" Minion barks, glaring at me.

"Yeah, and you guys do civic planning and ummm… whatever it is you do." Alright, so I'm not actually all that knowledgeable about local government responsibilities. "I'm still asking why."

"Young man, certainly you can see the advantages of working together in such a time. We humans need to stick together," this time, it's the other old lady speaking in an English accent. She's very average, other than being in her 60s I'm not even sure I'd remember her if I saw her again so I mentally name her DA for Downtown Abbey.

"That still doesn't say why you need me to report back," I say.

"You are being very confrontational. It's such a small thing…" DA continues to speak, taking the lead for the moment.

"He started it," I point to Minion and he bristles.

"This is a waste of time," snaps Minion and I widen my smile. Well, if I'm not getting a quest, we're both in agreement there.

"Are you refusing to help us, Mr. Lee?" Fred speaks now, his voice growing stern.

"I'm refusing to dance without knowing the song," I say.

"We cannot make plans without knowing the status of the world around us. You seem to have acquired transportation, are actively exploring the lands around us and have a knowledgeable Companion. We just ask that you provide us information that might benefit the community when you come across it," the Mayor snaps back.

Quest Received

Report to the Council of Whitehorse any information of importance.
Rewards: XP Reward Varies
Accept: Y/N

I watch everyone around me jerk as I mentally accept the quest and they get their own notifications. A quick confirmation with Ali leads me to talk, drawing everyone's attention; "Okay, lesson 1 then. Simply put, you guys can't create quests unless it's important. However, if you do designate an activity that is important enough, the System will generate the quest for you. This holds true until you guys Level up. A lot."

I leave out the part of hierarchy, no need to rub it in their face that they actually aren't officially part of anything. At least, not as far as the System is concerned.

"Second thing, you want information? There's a fort out at the Carcross Cut-off. Found a bunch of Space Orcs there wielding energy rifles. I've got control of the fort now, but it looks like forts can be created or designated all around the city as buildings of strategic importance. It's also in a zone that's significantly tougher than the surroundings, so I'd recommend not going there yet for the majority of you guys." In the corner of my eye, I see Ali create ultra tiny pop-ups of XP rewards before making them disappear as I speak.

"Third? You guys need to get on the entire buying up buildings in Whitehorse. I'm not sure why Roxley isn't buying more, but as residents, we get a discount. Buying a place makes it a Safe Zone as you guys probably know, but what you might not have realised is that if you get 80% of the buildings in the Whitehorse city zone claimed, the entire city becomes a Safe Zone.

"That what you're thinking of for information?" I smile widely, knowing that it is.

"That... that will do," the Mayor just blinks at the series of notification windows popping up in front of him as I get my quest rewards. I smirk mentally, noting how it has derailed the rest of their enquiry. Right, time to get out of here before they remember they had anything else to ask me. "Good. Ms. Badger, let's go."

I turn and start walking away before Luthien finally speaks up. "What are you planning to do, John?"

"What I've always done isn't it? Whatever the hell I want," I shoot back and walk out.

***

"John..." Ali is floating beside me as I walk to Sabre, leaving Ms. Badger to catch up. Ah good old Chinese culture, not even able to think of her as Andrea in my mind since she's an old person. "Not saying I'm a people-person, but what the hell?"

"I don't like those guys," I say.

"No shit."

"They're idiots. They want to start a fight that they can't win with Roxley. Hell, they had the Shop from day 1 and could have gotten knowledge of the System pretty fucking easily, but they're so affronted by Roxley that they refuse to talk to him or go into the Shop and use it properly. Luthien and her friends obviously know about it, but somehow, they haven't mentioned shit. Or perhaps they haven't been listening. They let Jim and his people run around not knowing about looting for over a week!

"They're so fucking incompetent and then they fucking start accusing me of whatever the fuck it is they were accusing me of. They can go fuck themselves." I can feel the

frustration that's been building up inside me want a release as I snarl out at Ali mentally, "*I get it, we need to work together. They don't have money to pay me, don't have any resources and are desperate. They could have asked nicely, but they decided not to. So, fuck them, I'll be damned if I let them drag me into their petty games. My life, my rules. I'll help them the way I want to and for the rest of it, they can fuck themselves.*"

Ali backs off a bit as I bite his head off, a hand held out placatingly. I draw a deep breath, forcing some calm over me and hit the button on my helmet as the Elder comes out, hiding my face as I straddle Sabre. Time to get this shit done.

***

The ride back is held mostly in silence. This time around, my inventory isn't stuffed to the gills with cheap materials, so I'm guessing the Elder hasn't really done as much buying as I thought she would. Then again, I have no idea how many Credits she managed to get. We only stop once, pausing long enough in the fort for me to show it to her. We switch ownership briefly to allow her to gain the experience before I take control again. She doesn't protest when I do it, which is good. I'm not sure what I need a fort for, but I bled for it.

Back at Carcross, the moment I roll in, the quest completes.

Level Up!

You have reached Level 11 as an Erethran Honor Guard. Stat Points automatically distributed. You have 11 Free Attribute Points to distribute.

Finally. Unfortunately, from now on Level Up's are going to slow down again with experience requirements for each Level twice as much as previously. I'm still far behind most of the combatants in Whitehorse, at least in terms of absolute levels, which is not surprising. From what we've worked out, it'll take me roughly twice the amount of experience to go up a level compared to those who started with a Basic Class.

The Elder heads into the Tagish Centre almost immediately, leaving me to sit on my bike in the middle of the road wondering what next. Beyond curt nods, no one pays attention to me. Everyone is obviously caught up in their own work and I realise, for all the favors I've done, I don't belong here.

I feel a wry twist crossing my face, a half-remembered piece of advice coming to me - do good, but never expect gratitude. I give myself a mental shrug and turn the bike around, waving the guards to open the door. Right, there's another town to check out anyway, just about 20 minutes down the road - Tagish. Ali tells me no one from Carcross has tried to make contact that far as they've needed to keep their fighters close on-hand. It'll only take me a few minutes and if I find even a couple of survivors who want to head into Whitehorse, I'll earn more Credits than hunting.

I take the Highway down, though really, it's a 2-lane road that's pitted and potted. The scenery is gorgeous and dramatic as usual, towering cliffs next to the road and straight drops with untouched forests and mountainous vistas in the distance; all bisected by the glacial Tagish river that can be spotted once in a while. Occasional birds flap in the distance, some looking larger than normal, along with something that I can only describe as a short-nosed pterodactyl.

At Crag Lake, Ali starts telling me to slow down and I spot the group soon after. There are about a score or so of humans walking together and eyeing the scenery for potential trouble, mostly adults with a small scattering of children. They look rough, beaten and scared and there is more than one injured among them. As I approach, the leaders in the front level guns at me and I stop a good distance away. It's only when I drop my helmet and show my human face that they actually relax.

These are the survivors from Tagish, everyone that is left. They've left a trail of bodies behind them, those who never grouped up in time, those who died defending the group and the fallen from the initial monster attacks. The entire group looks like they would shatter in a stiff breeze and it's only the insistence of the leaders that have kept them moving.

I channel my healing magic and do what I can for those that need healing, offering up the bike to the young to speed up the group as I walk. It's not the best option for defense, but since Sabre can self-balance, it's the fastest option. I keep my rifle with me as we make the trek to Carcross, my head swiveling for potential dangers as the occasional sob is choked off behind me.

It's a strange thing, escorting such a large group on foot. The first time we are attacked, it's by a spine monster that rises from the cliff face, its presence hidden by simple camouflage. It starts the ball rolling by firing spines into the group from its back, each spine over a foot long and dirt brown. We lose another human that time, a spine impaling her chest and heart. I'm wounded too, in my shoulder, from the initial barrage as I move to put myself in front of the kids on my bike. Killing it was not the easiest with a single hand to maneuver my rifle. Luckily, the fact that I'm doing the most damage drags its attention to me so we spend a few minutes shooting at each other from the cover of rocks, away from the main group. Damn but sneak attacks suck.

The second and third time, Ali warns us well in advance and I'm able to intercept the danger. The first is a crazed wolverine, so fast and vicious I end up having to fight it in close range since I couldn't manage a killing shot at distance. As fast as the wolverine is, it doesn't have a sword and lopping off its paws is sufficient to end the fight. The third time, I fight my first slime monster, a gelatinous greenish-purple creature that rolls along the forest floor leaving a trail of slimy destruction behind it and which sits at Level 42. It's only Ali's coaching on where to shoot that lets me defeat it – seems like the creature uses a diffused nervous system with a small number of clusters that must be destroyed, otherwise, it's pretty much immune to most damage. Unfortunately for it, slime doesn't work well against beam weapons and being able to attack from a distance forces the creature to chase me around in a futile attempt to hurt me. The slime gets me a slime nervous system core as loot, a spongy mass that makes up its central nervous system. According to Ali, it's quite prized as a material for bioware implants.

Other than the occasional fights, the rest of the journey blurs into one long, tedious and mentally wearing half-day. Every time there is a monster close enough to be a danger, I head out with Ali to deal with it. It's possible I'm being paranoid and that many of those monsters would never have known or cared about the group, but it's better to be safe than sorry. Each time, I collect the loot but leave the bodies, mentally making a promise again about finding a storage solution in the Shop when I get back and have enough Credits.

"Ali, what's up with the monsters? We're in a zone 40 plus area, but we've only seen one major monster," I ask the Spirit in my mind as I walk alongside the children.

"A few things. We're just starting the transition, so higher level monsters aren't that populous yet. The Council normally grabs a few high-level monsters at a time, dumps them into a Dungeon World like this and basically lets them breed. In a year, this place will be crawling with monsters," Ali says. "Also, don't forget – monsters need to eat. A high-level zone also means a higher number of low-level monsters, most of which are created from mutations of local animals. Of course, the mutations might actually come up with something really interesting too, but that's normally in the later half of the transition."

I nod slowly, reviewing what he said; "So, if we kill off a bunch of high-level monsters now, does that mean we can lower the level of the area?"

"Yes, no, maybe?" Ali shrugs. "Depends on how major a change it is and what the Council decides. It might lower the level here or the Council could just grab more monsters to add directly if they think the zone needs it."

"Why create a Dungeon World in the first place?" I ask.

"Resources and power. The best way to get both is via the System, which requires fighting like what we've been doing. The Dungeon Worlds allow the Council to ship off the dangerous activity of resource gathering and leveling out of their backyard, basically creating farmland. Not to say that there aren't dungeons in other worlds, but Dungeon Worlds are purely dedicated to it."

***

When we get back to Carcross proper, most of the survivors are just grateful to be somewhere relatively safe. Only two want to actually go to Whitehorse, but 2 is more than I can carry. That's another thing that I need to fix at some point, though I'm loath to trade in Sabre. Perhaps a sidecar? Elder Badger has picked up the parts needed to rebuild a few trucks as Ali points out, but it's not going to help me right now. Well, nothing to be done about it right now so I just plan to do a pair of speed runs, blazing through the turns at speeds that leave monsters that want to fight me at odds.

That is until I'm on my way back after the first run. Increased Perception lets me spot the problem a few moments before I hit it, the spider silk strand so thin I don't see it till then. I don't bother attempting to stop as I'll never make it, instead I engage Sabre's transformation so that I can keep hold of Sabre when I hit the strands.

I end up spinning through the air, skipping along the pavement and only coming to a stop after smashing through a couple of trees by the side of the road. I groan piteously, a flashing notification letting me know I'm stunned.

In the distance, Ali is bouncing up and down and letting me know of the incoming monsters now that they've revealed themselves. Not that I can pay much attention to them as I struggle to bring my thoughts into focus. I swallow the pooling blood in my mouth, realising I bit my tongue somewhere along the way as well as adding a concussion to my list of ailments. I slowly push myself up, reaching to detach my rifle and realising it is not even there.

Shit.

I look around for it but doing so makes my head spin and I have to focus on casting a Minor Heal on myself instead. It takes precious seconds to cast the spell in the state that I am in and by the time I do so, the Spiders are on me.

Except these aren't really spiders like Xev - they are a weird hybrid spider-wolf creature. Spider legs and their bulbous body carry the creature forward as it is clad in dark black fur, a snarling canine head with all too sharp teeth bearing down on me. Calling forth the only weapon that I have, I lunge forwards and skewer the first monster. Unfortunately, it doesn't kill the creature and it tosses me aside with ease, sending me spinning into the ground again. I stumble up and recall my sword immediately to swing to the left, catching another of the creature on its front legs.

After that, things get really hectic. Even partly healed, the mild concussion keeps me off-balance, though not nearly as off-balance as the creatures circling me, attacking one after the other. It takes only a few hectic minutes of swinging before I realise this isn't a fight I can win, not injured and outnumbered like I am. Their bites scratch at and damage the armor bit by bit and they work like wolves, wearing me down for the final strike. I can't win this, so I trigger the QSM and run away. It's a lurching, scrambling run that I'm glad no one but me can see.

When I get far enough away that Ali says they have given up looking for me, I start casting Minor Heal to fix the majority of the damage and down all the potions that I have. What's not great is that I need to use my entire Mana pool and Sabre's pretty battered too. Structural integrity's down to 48% and from what Ali tells me, my rifle is broken.

Not a good day. No Mana, no rifle and creatures that Ali can't spot automatically makes the way into Carcross dangerous. I groan, staring out into the distance and remember my promise to bring the other lady out. Fuck. Better to be safe than sorry though, I can't afford to test those spider-wolf hybrids again. I just hope Ali is right and the slime's nervous system is something that's wanted because I'm going to need Xev to fix Sabre.

Worst part? I didn't even get a damn level from all that.

Chapter 12

"Wexlix Spiders," Mikito repeats after Ali, wagging her chopsticks in my face as we sit around having dinner together for the first time. Seems like both Richard and Mikito decided to stay with Lana and I, instead of going out again tonight. We are having fried noodles for dinner, all working with the chopsticks that I keep in my drawer, chatting about our days. Both Richard and Mikito were both a bit surprised to be greeted by Ali at first but after the initial shock, they've taken it in stride. I guess a small, floating brown man in overalls who isn't attempting to kill them is not a problem. "Mixed wolf and spider?"

I nod firmly, rotating a shoulder again. I know it's healed, my health bar says it's full but my mind insists there's still pain. "Tough bastards. Broke my rifle too while fighting them and I damaged Sabre significantly. Zev says it'll take her at least a few days to fix it, some of the parts aren't actually available till tomorrow."

I'm already missing Sabre, having to walk all the way back on foot was less than optimal, stopping only long enough to let Sally know the results of the potions and let Jim and thus the Council know of the fate of Tagish. Unfortunately, I had to give nearly every single Credit I had to Zev to fix the major mechanical issues. I'll just have to deal with the fact that the armor isn't going to be fully up to snuff for a bit.

"Nasty," Richard shakes his head and uses his fork to spear more noodles. "Things are quieting down around here, most of the really bad monsters seem to have been dealt with by the guards by now. Mikito and I spent most of today just hunting for the pot. Seems like the mana mutations have also increased the speed these animals grow and populate, otherwise we'd be in trouble trying to feed everybody."

I nod at his words, glad to have caught up with them. Now that the hunters knew how to loot properly, they were able to generate actual Credits from the System. Right now, everyone was putting a small portion of their earned funds into a pool so that the Council could purchase the community garden from the System with the goal of creating and stabilising the city's food sources. On top of that, Lana reports that the initial batch of materials I gave has mostly been used up and either resold to the System or given to the hunters as protection. The levels of the crafters were increasing and some were even talking about getting the hunters to sell their materials direct to them so that they could process the materials and sell it all at a higher price to the System. Looks like we are slowly getting an economy into place, but we're miles away from creating a Safe Zone for the entire city.

"You tired of running around alone yet?" Lana asks, finished with her meal already. I'm not exactly sure where she put it either – one moment there's a full bowl of food, the next it is empty and she's eyeing her brother's. He surreptitiously moves his own bowl closer to him and away from her.

"I was the only one who had a vehicle," I point out defensively and Lana shoots a look over at Mikito and Richard. The two look at one another and then sigh.

"You haven't asked us what we've been doing with our Credits," Richard says.

"Didn't think it was any of my business," I reply and then exchange a nod with a departing family. While we were gone, it seems Lana had let it become known that we had a working hot shower and become hygiene central – for a modest fee. Between those who wanted a hot shower rather than washing in the glacial river and the workers on the concrete wall that Ali and Lana had arranged to start building in front of the house, my once peaceful abode is a busy little haven. Still, it leveled up the construction workers' skills and gained me a System recognised set of defenses so I'd call it a win overall.

"We bought a Mana engine and a Mana battery from the Shop. We're installing it in a truck now, should be ready in a day or two," Richard shares and points a finger at me. "Raven's Circle actually has a truck of their own too, as of today."

"How much did it cost?" I enquire, curious.

"6,000," Mikito replies, finishing up her noodles and holding the bowl out for more from Lana. Lana complies, filling it up while I blink. Not as bad as I thought, but still, yeesh.

"So, you don't have to play Lone Ranger anymore," Lana follows up, blue eyes narrowed at me. "If you're willing to wait a day."

I nod slightly at her words, recalling the fight earlier today. She's right – if I hadn't been able to slide into the next dimension, I'd be dead right about now. Then again, I'd be dead many times over without the QSM. "Be good to have some company. Most times, I've been finding people in groups anyway so this could be helpful."

Richard nods and Mikito inclines her head before returning to her food, "You planning on hunting tomorrow then?"

"A bit. There's a conversation I need to finish first though," I give Ali a very pointed glance before continuing, "and then I might need to do some training. After that, yeah, hunting. Need to earn my keep."

"There are reports that the eagles are mutating, the ones near the cliffs? I'm thinking I might see if I can tame one of them. I could use the help though," Richard says.

"Sure," I glance past them out to the backyard where the puppy-ponies sit. Most look worse for wear, scars indicating where previous injuries have accumulated. Interestingly enough, Lana has added a mutated red fox to the group who lounges in the sun by itself, watching the gamboling Huskies with a lazy eye. Surprisingly, they all seem to get along quite well – a side effect I'd guess of being pets now.

I smile quietly as they nod back to me and then I look down, staring at my right hand as it holds the chopsticks. I put them down quickly and slip my hands under the table, not wanting them to see the trembling. Yeah, okay, company would certainly be nice.

***

The next morning after my shower, I turn to Ali, "Alright, care to explain?"

"Well, a man and a woman really love one another…"

"Ali!"

"Electromagnetic force – it's one of the fundamental forces of nature," Ali sighs and waves. "It does include electricity, but it also involves things like light, magnetism, hell, even friction. You'll gain an affinity for it, so you'll be able to manipulate it in small doses."

"Ah… well, let's do this then," I shrug. I'm not sure I understand the full uses of this, but there's no point in worrying till I can actually use it.

For a moment Ali just stares at me before he grumbles, floating up and putting a hand to my forehead. The next thing I know, I'm lying on the bed with the worst headache I've ever had.

"What the hell! You could have warned me!" I shout at Ali and then immediately regret it.

"I figured you'd faint again anyway," Ali smirks, looking me up and down and then sighing. "Good news or bad news?"

"Just talk. Quietly," I hold my head in my hands, already casting a Minor Heal. Instead of speaking, Ali just flicks up the notification.

Elemental Affinity Gained (Electromagnetic Force)

Affinity: Very Poor

Congratulations!

For gaining your first Elemental Affinity, you have been rewarded 2,000 Experience Points.

"You suck at this. Seriously. You're barely above the grade that the System recognises and that's because I had to get in there and shove," Ali shakes his head. "You won't ever be able to use this fully, but at least you aren't blocked off other affinities either."

I groan, clutching my head. Minor Heal doesn't seem to help, so I keep my eyes shut and focus on the most important thing that Ali said. This headache – it's all his fault.

An hour later, I'm able to open my eyes without ice picks being jammed into them. At that point, Ali makes me start training. Makes, as in nags me till I agree to actually spend some time exploring this new ability. The exploration itself is relatively simple, a form of guided meditation. Surprisingly, the spirit's actually serious and there's not even a single joke about my too tender feelings or the like.

It's a frustrating couple of hours, the feeling that he's speaking about is at first not at all graspable and then when I finally manage to sense it for the first time, if only briefly. It takes until nearly the end of the session when I begin to really feel it, to be in the moment and sense the forces flowing through me and around me. It's only for a second when I finally manage to grasp the senses. I realise it's all around me, the shifting of forces. For a moment, it's like I live in the Matrix except instead of ones and zeroes, it's a humming stream of energy that encompasses everything.

I definitely need to work on this.

***

Unfortunately, as much as I'd like to play with my new toy, I've got plans for the rest of the day. As I join both Mikito and Richard outside the house, we start walking towards the bridge and the Millennium Trail. Walking through the neighborhood, I can see the beginning of decay throughout the subdivision. Destroyed windows, uncollected autumn leaves, dry and brown lawns and discarded garbage that hasn't been picked up, snow run-off that isn't taken care of, even the occasional unwashed blood splatter. No one is here to clean up or take care of the homes and it shows; even the occasional whiff of rotten meat reminds me of the compost bins that haven't been collected.

When we leave Riverdale itself to cross the bridge, I note that the ice still hasn't left the river though the fishermen are out. Interestingly, a new addition to the fishing groups are the hunters who stand with guns at rest, watching over the fishermen. I guess even the fish have gotten more dangerous. We pass by the S.S. Klondike as we come off the bridge and I pause, staring at it for a moment, an idle thought passing through my mind. I push it aside though; the white sternwheeler has been laid up for years.

As we continue the walk, Richard waves to the puppies, bringing them back to him and he absently ruffles their fur as he walks.

"You ever try riding one?" I enquire and Richard chuckles, shaking his head.

"No, I like my own feet. I'm really not much of a rider anyway," Richard answers, as I start eyeing the clay cliff faces that surround the downtown, trying to spot the eagles who nest there. It's only a few more minutes before we realise we're not the only ones who have heard about the mutating eagles – Raven's Circle is here.

"Ah fuck…" I mutter and Mikito flashes me a quick sympathetic glance. Richard just snorts and takes a few quick steps to bring himself in front.

"Afternoon everyone," Richard flashes a big charming grin, looking utterly relaxed while surrounded by four dogs each the size of a pony.

"Afternoon Richard," Nicodemus replies, walking forwards and engulfing Richard's hand in his. The red-haired giant seems to have gotten bigger I swear, now topping over nine feet at a guess and with muscles that go on for days. I'm kind of jealous – I've bulked out a bit, but nowhere near his extent. I've got more of a gymnast figure while he does the man mountain thing. "You guys here to deal with the eagles too?"

"Actually, I was hoping to tame one or two of them," Richard explains and Nicodemus nods at that.

While those two talk, Luthien and Kevin make their way around the group to talk to me. I brace myself internally, wondering what these two want.

"John…" Luthien doesn't stop at a normal distance, instead approaching close enough to reach up and put a hand on my chest. I step back smoothly, noting her new level and her class as a Sorceress.

"Yes?" I keep my voice level, even if my words are curt.

"I just wanted to make sure you're okay. You've been avoiding me," Luthien continues.

"I've had things to do, Anne," I pause and shrug. "And I'm doing fine."

She looks at me with sympathy, just the barest flash of anger at the use of her real name as she continues, "What happened to your bike?"

"Being repaired," I tell the truth, not particularly caring if she knows.

"Oh, John! Do you need some Credits? I'm sure we could spare some," she tosses a glance at Kevin who nods agreeably.

Tired of this, I wave my hand, "Anne, just, go away."

"Why are you being so rude?" she pouts at me now, switching tactics.

"Because I know you. Perhaps a bit late, but I know you," I turn from her and start walking to Nic and Richard when Kevin grabs my arm and glares at me.

"Don't speak to her like that. I'm willing to put up with some shit because of what we did, but…"

I shut him up by punching him hard enough to break his nose and when he lets go of my arm, I kick him away from me. I stop then, though his friends already have swords drawn and a bow pointed at me. Impressive. Luthien doesn't do anything though, running over to her boyfriend.

"Don't touch me. Either of you. Don't come near me, don't talk to me, just don't. I want nothing to do with you people," my voice comes out in a whisper, rage that rushed into me the moment he touched me barely contained.

Richard looks between us all, a hand held out to his side to the puppies while Nicodemus waves his guys down. I stalk away from them, giving them my back as I try to calm down. Damn. I played into her hand again. Now they are the ones who are the injured parties.

A short while later, Richard comes up to me and points so I follow him up the trail, Mikito trailing along behind. The first minute of walking is done in silence before Richard finally breaks it, "Are you going to explain why Mikito and I nearly got killed just now?"

I shake my head, knowing that the Circle probably wouldn't have killed them. Or me, for that matter. Still, it's nice they were willing to back me up, even though we barely know each other. My hand still trembles at my side from the adrenaline and I fight to keep my voice steady as I answer him, "Anne – Luthien's – my ex. You know that. What you don't know is that we were a couple for years, though every summer she'd travel up here for work. Didn't think much about it, but when I lost my job in Vancouver and my place burnt down, she suggested we move up here together permanently. A new start. So, I did. Uprooted my life and left my friends and family to be with her. Except she and Kevin had been cheating on me this whole time and I finally clued in.

"You know the stupidest thing? I realised I stopped caring about her a long time ago. Stopped loving her, but every time we'd talk about something serious, she'd redirect it. I'm not even sure she ever loved me either, I was just another trophy, another admirer. But mostly," I draw a deep breath before continuing, "mostly, I just want it done and over with. I'm done being manipulated by her, and if the only way to do that is to avoid her, so be it. I won't get drawn into her web again. Not if I can help it."

By the time I'm done, we're nearly at the top of the short hill and looking towards the trees that the eagles normally nest in. Not surprisingly, the eagles haven't stuck around while we hiked to their nest which leads to a more interesting question. "Richard, what exactly was the plan here?"

"Well, if we can net one of them, I can dominate it and make it a pet if I can enforce my will on it. Tame it if you will," Richard explains.

"Great. But they aren't coming back till we're gone so...?"

Richard pauses, staring up at the empty tree and then looks back at me and then Mikito, "Oh, right. I didn't really think about that."

175

***

I exhale slowly, carefully, and pull the trigger. When the shot finally comes, it's a surprise that makes me lose a few precious seconds, the tubular shotgun that Richard lent me going off with a hiss rather than a bang. The other eagle that I wasn't aiming at takes off while I recover, making it well out of range before I can even try to take a shot. I stand swiftly and walk over to my netted target as it struggles, attempting to free itself from the slowly constricting metallic net that covers its body.

The bald eagle is definitely mutated. For one thing, it's about six feet tall and on top of that, I'm pretty sure there's something wrong with its wings – the way the air ripples around them now and when it was landing seems to indicate something more is going on. Thankfully, the netting and gun were bought from the Shop especially for Beast Tamers looking to capture new pets so it can't get out.

I can see Richard and Mikito scrambling up the cliff now that I've taken my shot. The other bald eagle that fled is circling high above me; it's unmutated form watching what we are doing to its sibling. I'd feel sorry for it but I just spent the last three hours squatting in a crudely built camouflaged dugout, hiding from it and its brother till they returned to their nests. Seems like neither Mikito nor Richard had bothered to learn any Stealth skills as yet, something we'll have to fix if we are to work together.

When Richard does make it up, what he does next is truly mystical. He squats down next to the eagle, meets its eyes and they engage in a staring contest. That goes on for nearly ten minutes before he finally breaks away and starts untying his new pet. Yup, real mystical.

With most of the day spent getting Richard a new pet, one that he quickly names Orel, we don't have a huge amount of time to hunt. With that in consideration, we decide to head straight along the river, moving across the trails that line Miles Canyon in search of prey. Richard sends Orel in the air and keeps the Huskies ranging in front of us. Ali's almost superfluous in the beginning with Richard's pets in play, Orel sending us in the direction of potential prey and the Huskies running them down. The dogs are well trained though, often just hounding the monsters till we arrive so that we can finish them off and get the experience as a group. Otherwise, Richard would just be getting all the experience.

We don't get very far, even with all three of us having a high enough Constitution that we're moving at a brisk walk the whole time. We still have to fight and kill the monsters and we stop every single time to firstly loot and then butcher the monsters to let a Husky bring the butchered carcass back. It's an efficient method of transportation, though it does mean that we run out of puppies after a while. Ali takes over guiding us to the prey that Orel spots from above and he even drags us off to deal with some monsters that the eagle misses. Without his pets in play, Richard isn't as useful so both Mikito and I get a chance to shine, fighting the monsters in close combat. Sad to say, it is quite obvious quite quickly who is better at that - and it's not me. Unfortunately, once we kill a few of the monsters, we realise we still have to wait for a puppy to get back which means we still have to wait anyway. As frustrating as it is, we're all conscious enough of the food situation back in Whitehorse that no one even voices the option of leaving the carcasses behind.

The fights themselves are interesting as it's clear that Mikito and Richard have worked out a system to deal with monsters. Richard stays back, opening fire immediately with his shotgun-ish weapon in battle, using a somewhat more traditional shell and ball bearing load out. According to him, other than nets, he's also got shells for instaset glue, explosives, electricity and even a grappling hook. Seems like if you could think about it, you could buy a shell for his weapon in the Shop.

Mikito on the other hand still uses her naginata, wielding it in close combat and taking on the monsters directly. Since we last fought together, she has gained a new Skill that causes the head of her weapon to glow red hot with each strike, sizzling through flesh and bone. I wonder if we could use the blade as a hot plate for cooking but I'm too scared and too smart to ask. In battle, the quiet Japanese woman becomes a focused whirlwind-of-death, sliding past attacks with ease and crippling creatures with swift, accurate strikes before moving to the next monster while Richard finishes off the cripple.

For the first few battles, I watch them fight without taking part. I watch how Richard focuses on commanding the dogs when they are around and how the dogs work with Mikito to take down the monsters they face. Once I get the gist of the idea, I step in and try to help and let's just say, I'm more of a hindrance than help. I'm in the wrong place for Mikito's strikes, I pre-empt the attacks by the dogs forcing the monsters to move in the wrong direction, I even dodged straight into one of the animals in an attempt to get away from an attack. I'm all wrong for a party fight like this.

Who'd have thought that the fact that you could hurt your friends would make such a difference in combat? Mixing up melee and ranged fighters in a swirling arena of blades and teeth seems to require a lot more co-ordination than I'd have expected. Damn movies, making it seems so easy.

When we get back to my house, we agree to postpone dealing with the Spiders for at least a day. Better to stay close to town and work on our teamwork. It would be tragic to be shot in the back by a friend in the middle of combat against the Spiders. Or elbow a party member in the face. Or cut one of the puppies. Purely as an example.

***

In the evening, when the others have broken off to do their own thing, I join Lana in washing the dishes. She has her hair in a bun, wearing a tight blouse and jeans, the bright evening sunlight highlighting her hair and cute button nose. For a moment, I just admire her from the side before I forcefully remind myself of an earlier promise.

"Lana, can you tell me about the town?" I begin.

"Huh?" Lana turns to me, puzzled by the generic question. I quickly clarify, "How are the people? The microloan programs? What's the City Council managing to do and what are they failing at?"

"Oh... not asking for much are you," she smiles at me before handing me another plate to dry. "I really miss dishwashers you know. Where do we start? Things are getting... better. People are moving around more, focusing on what they can do. Even if it's nothing more than taking apart a door and putting it up again. Now that they know they can level and do something to improve themselves, it's helping. We've got a few people working as lumberjacks, fishers, carpenters. All of that. We still don't have enough guards and things are still dangerous, but people are I guess, getting used to the world.

"The loans are working well, we're getting more and more of the hunters to sell the materials to us. Profits are abysmal, but the training is more important. Once they level their Skills up and produce better quality items, the amount we'll make will improve. A few of the workers have even reported getting specific quests, pieces that they need to make.

"The Council... well, they're organising the guards and the food. Until your announcement, they were really focused on the food situation so they had the farmers organised at the parks and the garden. Now, I think they're looking at the housing situation more closely and are trying to work out who is still alive and what buildings to buy next.

"The problem at the end of the day is money, John. Credits. No one has enough and as much as people want to help, there's only so much they are willing to give."

She falls silent, the spiel coming to an end. The bright, bubbly personality is gone, the worried sister and citizen making a showing. "We just don't have enough, not for everyone. Those that don't hunt are rationed, those that do get double portions and often supplement with the Credits they earn from looting. That makes everyone else angry, especially the citizens who don't have a class that automatically gives them a way to earn Credits. Teachers, doctors, scholars - those classes can level their Skills but they are dependent on an economy that we just don't have. Worst, we've got people who are still in shock and people are still disappearing. The hunters report a few bodies every day in the river…"

Lana has stopped washing, her hands clutched around a plate. I hesitate before closing a hand around hers, squeezing it and she looks up at me, unshed tears in her eyes, "I don't know how you do it. The hunters, even Mikito and Richard aren't willing to go as far out as you did. You just drove all the way to Carcross as if the monsters didn't matter, that it was just another day before this shit happened. And the rest of us, we're just trying to get through another day."

I blink for a moment, staring out the window at the lounging puppies and fox as I attempt to answer her, "I… I guess I'm just too stupid to know better."

"Don't you feel anything? Didn't you lose anyone?" she pulls her hand away from me to stare at my face, searching it.

"I…," I struggle for a moment, trying to figure out how to explain my own complicated life. "I did. I think. But…" how to explain my relationship with them, the dearth of love and the parade of nannies and then later, boarding school. How I barely saw my father through my youth, and even less as an adult while my mother had left when I was born. I've never even met her. Of all of them, only my sister had ever been close to me and even we had drifted apart as she grew older. How to explain the irrational grief for something that I never really had, the way I learnt to tune it all out just to get through another day. Better not to. "It's over. I can't do anything for them even if they were alive, not from here."

She shakes her head, sitting back down at the dining room table. I watch her for a moment as she collects herself, uncomfortable in the silence so I get back to washing the dishes. I'm nearly done when she speaks again, her voice soft. "We have thousands of people, and nearly half of them are combat classes but so few dare to go out. It's too much, too dangerous and we keep losing people, here and there. The hunting groups get smaller, the food gets less and people get more and more scared."

I frown, shaking my head and I stare into the distance. Shit, that doesn't sound great. In an MMO, in a game, there'd be noob training grounds, places where people could start fighting monsters that were level appropriate. Maybe go out on quests and kill 10 rats or something.

Here though, we're stuck in the real world and even the zone around Whitehorse is in the 10's to 20's. Sure, there are monsters that are lower leveled, in fact, the vast majority are low-level mutations but now that it's been over a week and a half since the System came into play, even the mutations aren't in single digits anymore.

I can't blame them, can't blame the citizens for not wanting to go out. We aren't used to this, fighting and killing. I'm not used to this - but I can't sit around either. Caught up in our own dark thoughts, the two of us sit quietly as the evening comes to a close, sharing some chocolate.

Chapter 13

In the morning, as we pass by the school, I spot the Constable heading out.

Amelia Olmstead (Level 14 Guardian)

HP: 410/410

"Still Level 14 eh?" I mutter and wave to the Constable. My companions look at me, wondering what I'm up to as Amelia trudges over, looking exhausted.

"Amelia, that your weapon?" I point to her beam rifle and Ali snorts, muttering something about how you couldn't call that a weapon. I ignore him as she nods, thankful the little bastard is not visible or audible.

"Good. Come on, we're going hunting," I jerk my thumb to the trail that heads out to Long Lake, our current hunting ground.

"What? No! I just got off a shift," she protests.

"Yeah, but you're tough. A few hours, come on," I reach out and grab her arm and start dragging her along the trail. She tries to yank her arm out of my grip and finds she's unable to, while I continue to speak. "Look, Amelia, you want to get stronger, right? Protect people and all that jazz?"

"All that jazz? What are you? A '50 crooner?" Ali next to me snorts.

"I... well... yes," answering me, Amelia forgets about fighting me.

"Good, then come on. Only way to level up in this crazy ass world is to go all murder happy," I suddenly chuckle and the three others stare at me as I begin to giggle, doing my best to explain. "Constable. Murder happy."

"Baka!" Mikito mutters, stomping pass me as I continue to giggle and pull Amelia along while she keeps casting very worried glances at me. She can't escape my grip and after a while stops trying to, which is good since I wasn't really going to drag her the entire way. Only so much forcing I'm willing to do.

Amelia does well, though, by the time we pass the third hour, she's nearly falling off her feet. I let her go then, smirking as I watch her glowing Status. Yeah, Level up as promised. We escort her back of course and help drag the meat with us and when some guards hear about what we did, they quickly ask us to help out. For the next few hours, we cycle back and forth dropping off new low-level volunteers in our party, occasionally lending out weapons for them to use. Mostly we do our best to ensure they stay safe, though my Minor Heal spell comes into use more than once. After a quick discussion, we get an on-going agreement where we keep most of the Loot drops except three from the escorted parties. We leave them with a little since that'll give them something to sell and buy in the Shop and at least helps pay for our time a bit.

Over the next few days, we spend most of the day playing escort for new guards and hunters, helping them slowly level up and learn to fight the monsters. With the three of us on-hand, we can keep even the Level 1's safe, which means we focus on bringing those volunteers with us as much as possible, giving them a quick level up. It's slow going though - most of them don't have the stamina that we have, at least until they get their first few levels. In the evenings though, Mikito, Richard and I spend time hunting by ourselves and learning how to fight together. It's also when we can make the most money as we target bigger and nastier monsters.

Standing in the Shop, it feels like it has been ages since I've been in. I know exactly what I want to purchase this time, which is good because I don't have that much to spend. Unfortunately, while fighting weaker monsters is great for our teamwork and the cooking pot, it doesn't do much for our wallets.

To start, I pull up information about electromechanical force. The costs for simple, college level knowledge about the force is quite low, only a couple of hundred Credits. However, costs keep going up after that in leaps and bounds and there's even a notation that leads me to information about the elemental affinity itself. My jaw drops at the price though – a million Credits!?! Definitely buying the basic physics understanding of electromechanical force, I'll leave the understanding of the affinity aside for when I'm rolling in riches. As it stands, I can, if I work really hard, actually feel the force for a brief 10-second window.

Since I'm thinking of spells, I spend a few minutes perusing the spell lists. I've been feeling rather naked without a ranged offensive option, though the only spell I can afford is something called 'Mana Dart'. Not exactly thrilling and the details on the spell itself are less than inspiring.

Mana Dart
Effect: Creates a dart out of pure Mana, which can be directed to damage a target. Does 10 damage. Cooldown 10 seconds
Cost: 25 Mana

I could flick my finger at a monster and do more damage! Okay, probably an exaggeration and I guess it is a beginner offensive spell, which makes it one more offensive spell than I have and it's ranged too. Still not thrilled but it's better than nothing.

Noting that Ali is finally coming to a conclusion in his haggling from the tone of their voices, I skip over to what I came here to buy – a sidearm. I scan through the various options, finally selecting one that meets all my criteria.

185

Silversmith Mark II Beam Pistol (Upgradeable)

Base Damage: 18

Battery Capacity: 24 / 24

Recharge Rate: 2 per hour per GMU

Cost: 1,400 Credits

It's not a great damage dealer, but the Silversmith can be upgraded, which means that I'll actually be able to use it in the future. It's a good backup short-ranged weapon at least. As Ali concludes his haggling, he flicks the total over to me and I let out a low whistle. He might scream, shout and throw a tantrum, but his results are impressive. I still don't have enough money to buy a Class Skill, not with the way my funds keep draining but at least now I've got more offensive weaponry.

Breakfast is somber in the morning. This is our first real test as a group, the Wexlix Spiders are significantly more dangerous than anything we've dealt with so far. On the other hand, the half a dozen or so that I spotted shouldn't be impossible. I've got my new pistol strapped to my thigh and I'm somewhat comfortable with it now after spending the previous evening practicing. I'm no crack shot, but I can hit a barn door at twenty paces.

Just as we're about to leave, Lana moves to give Richard a particularly hard hug and whispers into his ear. Richard nods firmly while Mikito escapes from the culturally inappropriate touching by virtue of using her naginata. The two of them headed out, Lana corners me and pokes a finger into my chest, "Don't you dare let my brother get injured, do you hear me?"

I nod, a slight smile twisting my lips, "Did you tell him to abandon us if it got too dangerous?"

She snorts, obviously not finding me amusing right now, "No. I told him not to die."

Impulsively, I give her a hug and whisper, "I promise to send him running first if things get bad."

Lana's stiff at first but relaxes after a moment, pleasant squishiness reminding me suddenly that it's been a while since I've actually touched another human being in this way. I release her quickly, flash her a smile and beat a hasty retreat. I'll deal with that later, it's time to go kill some monsters. A little trickle of anger runs through me, a vicious streak that demands I take revenge.

***

The Huskies sit in the back of the brand new dark blue truck that Mikito and Richard have acquired. It's huge and monstrous but strangely silent, the Mana engine and battery not making a single sound as they run. It's an incongruity that clashes with my understanding of how things should be that I struggle with, even with Sabre. Still, the good news is that Sabre runs smoothly even if it does look like it's seen better days.

Of course, Xev was less than impressed considering I had just gotten it fixed and had rather firmly told me to be careful. You'd think she'd enjoy the extra business, but I guess having your work wrecked in the space of a day was a bit frustrating. I'm definitely going to have to see about getting on her good side soon though since she's the only Master-class Armorer in town. It'll take months if not years for the rest of the humans to catch up with her and till then, it's either her or the System.

Idle thoughts as we drive down the Highway, heading to fight the Spiders. We stop only long enough to switch the fort out between all of us, Mikito and Richard gaining the experience bonuses before I take it back. I should make a note to bring Lana out while it's still in our control. Easy experience for her and there's no reason not to. In fact, I bet we could run a train of people through here to give them the experience and get them a significant way to their first level.

When we start getting close to the original ambush point, we pull the truck over and disembark. I trigger the change and feel Sabre slide all over me, locking into place and giving me a sense of invulnerability and safety. My smile widens and it's only the barking of the dogs that brings my attention back to our task. I've missed this.

"Mecha!" Mikito is pointing at my newly power armored clad form, her jaw on the ground. Oh shit, I forgot to tell them.

"Yeah…"

"Fuck man! How come you didn't tell us about this?" Richard swears, eyeing my armor-clad form.

"Ummm… I forgot? I've been trying to keep this quiet. Don't want it stolen and what not, you know," I shrug uncomfortably, feeling a bit like a jerk. They are working with me after all, they deserve to know some things.

Ali is laughing his ass off, invisible as usual. "Real smooth boy-o."

Richard continues to glare at me before he visibly shakes himself and lets it go and walks over to inspect Sabre. "Damn, but that's cool. Like, really cool. How much did it cost you?"

When I name the number, their jaws drop again. They just stare at Sabre and me and then Richard barks a laugh, "What's your class? Moneybags?"

"No," I begin to protest and then realise he's teasing me.

"You are going to let me test this out," Richard points his finger at me and Mikito nods firmly at that. For the first time, there's a look of wonder and glee on Mikito's face, the first I've ever seen. Mostly, she's this quiet, reserved, perfect little Japanese girl until she fights, then she's just death on two feet. But now, now she seems almost happy. It's gone in a moment and her face closes down again. Thankfully, the PAV can resize to a certain extent though I'm not sure it'd fit Mikito. Still, we can give it a shot.

"Of course. Just, keep this quiet, will you?" At confirming nods from both of them, I breathe a little sigh of relief. Not sure if it matters, but keeping a few aces up my sleeve still seems like a good idea. "So, we follow the plan?"

Once I get their acknowledgment, I draw a deep breath and head into the woods first with Mikito and Richard following a good distance behind. Small radios clipped to their body and installed into my helmet lets us keep in contact at a distance while I scout out the Spiders. It'd taken nearly a full day for Richard to learn Stealth, Mikito only needing a half-day but neither had very good levels yet, which is why I'm in front.

Getting all the way to the ambush point takes nearly an hour of slow, careful moving. I can't rely on Ali's abilities so I have to look for them myself. When I do spot the first Spider, it's lying in the treetops among its webs, just waiting for prey, occasionally shifting its head to sniff at the air and twitch its furry ears. The creature is still weird looking, a strange mixture of a wolf's head on top of a spider's furred body.

Wexlix Spider Adult (Level 34)

HP: 780 / 780

The moment I spot it, I start scanning the ground and I begin to see the thin threads of Spider-silk laid around the base of trees ahead of me, ready to catch and hold unsuspecting prey. There's no way in, not without triggering a trap or alerting the watching Spider so I call a halt to Richard and Mikito over the radio before hunkering down.

"Ali, you can still spot them using your eyes, can't you? And they can't see you right?" I think to my Companion and he nods, flying forwards. It's nice that he actually can be serious when he needs to be.

It takes nearly an hour before the Spirit returns to my position, floating above me and wiping at non-existent cobwebs. "Yeah, you're fucked."

Okay, mostly serious.

***

"Details Ali," I mutter in exasperation. We're far enough away that the Wexlix Spider guard can't hear me, especially while I'm in my helmet but I still curse myself out. No need to talk when I can just think at my orange-clad Companion.

"Right, remember how you fought 5 of them and got your ass kicked? Well, there's about a dozen adults and half a dozen youngsters. And a Spider that's about half again the size of the biggest one whom I'm guessing is the Alpha," Ali says. "Oh, and I found your rifle. It's in the middle of the road, in enough pieces I'm not sure even Zev can fix it."

I crawl back carefully, making my way over to my party members before letting them know the bad news. They fall silent at my news, the numbers well above what we had initially expected to fight. As much as I want to get my revenge and pick up the young lady for the quest, this is way too challenging for us right now. I'm doing this for, well, money and a distraction. Getting killed is definitely not on the cards.

"Time to leave?" I suggest.

Mikito shakes her head, anger flaring in her eyes at even a mention of running away. I'm somehow not surprised; I've never seen her decide not to fight.

"Mikito..." Richard begins.

"No. They will kill others. We are here. We kill youkai," she insists and clutches her naginata to her.

Richard frowns, looking at the determined widow and then me. I groan slightly, shaking my head. "Mikito, this is insane. There's more of them than there are of us."

"We fight. I fight," she points to herself, standing up and I growl, grabbing her arm and pulling her down. She isn't able to fight my strength and has to sit, though she glares at me till I let her go.

"This is a bad idea," I say and Mikito looks at me, and then Richard who looks between the two of us.

"Boy-o, one thing to note. The longer we wait, the harder this is going to get," Ali chimes in next to me, pointing backwards. "These guys have an Alpha which means they're breeding. Longer you wait, the more there are."

I grunt, shaking my head and then relay the information. Richard draws a deep breath and Mikito looks triumphant. Shit. Still, there's no reason we couldn't get a few more hands - but really? Who would we ask? Most of the others are too low level or just not equipped enough and the only other option is Raven's Circle. You know what, fuck that shit. "Okay, fine."

"How are we doing this then?" Richard says. I frown and then stare back, thinking about our options before I start speaking.

***

What do you do when you've got to fight a force that outnumbers you? Fight them piecemeal, of course. Seems like not all the Spiders will leave to attack immediately, at least from my experience. If my rather limited encounter of experience holds true, all we need to do is make sure we attack and pull back, drawing them to us and killing them in small bursts. It's why I'm back at my original scouting position while Mikito and Richard have drawn the truck further up the road, only a short run from where I am.

Can't hit it with my pistol or the Mana Dart from this range, so I get ready to trigger the Quantum State Manipulator. When I do activate the device this time, I can feel the QSM extend its field, enveloping my body and shifting me to another dimension I guess. I can feel the effects, the field that wraps all around me and the energy that floats through me, around me. For a moment, I just stand there in surprise, taking it all in.

"You can feel it, now can't you? It's our affinity," smirks Ali.

"Yeah..." purchased knowledge comes flooding in now that I think about it. I stand there for a second, trying to understand what I already do - which is as strange and confusing as it sounds before I shake my head. Something to look into later, I got things to kill. Later. Always later.

I ignore the need for Stealth, just making sure my escape route is clear of spider webs before I grin, focusing on the creature as I trigger the QSM off. Time to test out my new spell. The moment I phase back in, I cast the spell, sacrificing mana so that the floating blue bolt of energy can form in the air. I gesture with my hand and the dart flies straight out, slamming into the creature's eye, blinding and angering it. The Wexlix Spider howls in anger and a moment later a reply comes from its pack mates.

Ali stays behind, floating in the air and counting, "1, 2, 3... and that's 5 adults and 3 of the juveniles. Best run fast boy-o!"

No need to tell me twice as I bolt for it. Good news is that I'm able to stay ahead of them, though I have to duck and roll once when a Spider shoots its web at me. Other than that, I manage to make it back to the road without much trouble, the Spiders only 20 feet behind me. I run straight towards the truck and my team, spinning around with my pistol in hand to snap off a shot. The creatures burst out of the foliage even as I turn around, clustered in a clump of skittering spider legs and howling wolf heads.

Richard on top of the truck opens fire, launching an explosive shell into one side of the group and then another, tossing Spider bodies around like so much confetti. Even as they begin to recover, I add to the carnage with my pistol, targeting the injured to end their lives quickly. As much damage as the explosives do to the ones that they hit, there's too many for Richard to stop and the remaining Spiders flow across the gaping holes in the asphalt and around their dead or dying friends.

Mikito and the four Huskies are there to meet them, both sides clashing in a maelstrom of fang, fur, claws and metal. Mikito slides past the lunging bite her first opponent makes, the blade of her naginata leaving a scorched wound across its body as she dodges, engaging the second almost immediately. Her blade flashes, blocking and cutting at legs as she dances between the two adult Spiders.

The Huskies each take on the rest individually, pouncing forwards to bite at a leg before scrambling back. The juvenile Spiders are out-weighed by their opponents and seem to be getting the worst of it, but an adult Spider slams into the black and white puppy that attacks it, a leg rising and pinning the dog to the ground. Before it can attack again, I turn my pistol on the creature, burning a hole in its neck. It distracts the creature for a brief moment, long enough for Orel to swoop down and pin the Spider into the ground, claws piercing the body. Orel doesn't stop there though as it flaps its wings, the elemental blades of wind that surround them shifting the air to help it lift the creature off the ground.

I stop paying attention to Orel as I take off to help Mikito, swinging my sword at a back leg that comes into range. It causes the Spider to lurch, giving Mikito a chance to open its chest up. The rest of the fight is actually relatively short, Richard and the puppies work to stall their opponents till Mikito and I finish off ours. Once that is done, we use overwhelming numbers to kill the remaining Spiders, massacring them with ease.

I exhale, staring around at the various Spider corpses and a part of the tension I've been carrying since Mikito first insisted on this fight dissipates. Yeah, we can do this.

As I move to cast my Minor Healing spell on the injured dog, Ali shouts, "Incoming!". The dog that I was about to touch lunges forward, putting itself between me and the launched webbing. The injured dog staggers and the web stream continues, sticking its body to the asphalt. Another dog is caught in the sticky web attack and restricted but everyone else manages to get away unscathed. Behind the flying webs, the remainder of the Spiders come rushing out from the undergrowth, baying their need to extract revenge. At the back of the group, a truly massive Wexlix Spider looms, its fur dark grey and its eyes glowing red.

Wexlix Spider Alpha (Level 42 – Boss)
HP: 3280/3280

"RUN!" I shout to my friends, grabbing a plasma grenade from my inventory and tossing it into the incoming horde. A rainy day has definitely come and my only regret is that I don't have time to get a second one out. Mikito ignores my order, flashing forwards as she activates her Charge skill and then goes into a slide underneath one of the creatures, her naginata held upwards to disembowel it.

On the truck, Richard curses the woman and unloads a round of normal shots before he begins to return the favor by using an instaglue shell on one of the closer Spiders, eyes flicking down to where his target just shot. "They webbed the tires!"

The explosion of the plasma grenade is less intense in the open, heat and flames rushing out in a sphere of super-heated air that bowls the Spiders and my companions over. Sabre's extra weight and its gifted strength helped keep me on my feet, while I spot Mikito slowly stagger upright, leaning on her polearm, having been partially shielded by the body of the fighter she had been fighting under. I take the extra time that I'm given to sprint forward and behead a juvenile Spider as our enemies recover. Screeching its anger, Orel returns to the battle from the skies and picks up another adult into the air, circling to gain altitude immediately as she gets ready to drop her opponent. The remainder of the adults, including the boss, recover quickly and I see little choice but to wade into the middle of them to distract the creatures before they can focus on my companions.

There are too many though, too many for me to distract completely. The injured black and white husky has its throat torn out, unable to avoid its fate as it struggles to free itself from the webbing. Another has its side pierced by a Spider leg, the creature rearing over it to finish it off. Richard screams in anger, unloading shot after shot into the Spider, and manages to punch a hole through the creature's chest where it collapses on his pet.

I only catch glimpses of all this as I turn and attack in the middle of the Spider horde. A leg slams into my shoulder, spinning me around and I take the momentum to slice off another foot that comes towards me. I no longer have time to think, reacting purely by instinct as fangs and claws come at me from all directions. Ali pops into existence occasionally throughout the fight, adding to the confusion as attacks pass through his incorporeal figure, buying me slivers of time.

As I fight, I catch a glimpse of Mikito. Her face is one of intense concentration and rage, lips pulled back even as blood drips from a cut down the side of her face. Her skin red as if she's been standing in the sun too long, portions of her long black hair burnt off. The naginata twirls in a dance of light and fire, slicing first one, a second, and then a third leg off before burying itself in the throat of her opponent, all in the time it takes for me to exhale. Even as she finishes it off, she instinctively steps away from a lunging bite that comes from her side, swinging the butt of her polearm into its throat.

A mistimed block ends up with a Wexlix Spider's mouth around my right arm, attempting to crush and rend. Hundreds of pounds of pressure come to bear and even under the armor, I can feel my bones begin to crack. I release the blade from that hand and transfer it to my left, angling my cut to slash open the throat that is so invitingly positioned.

Even as blood gushes and the creature flops forward, pulling me off balance, another blow catches me from behind and I am sent sliding along the asphalt. Before I can recover, a leg pierces through the armor into my abdomen, pinning me face down on the ground. I scream into my helmet, activating the QSM to fade out from the pinning leg and scramble away to see my attacker.

Wexlix Spider Alpha (Level 42 – Boss)
_HP: 2430/3280_

I know the creature wasn't directly in the blast of the plasma grenade, but I know it was close. I groan mentally, backing up as much as I can to give myself space, mind racing. Blood drips down from my wound even as Sabre reacts to the damage, applying pressure through electronic sheathing around my stomach, slowing the bleeding. Adrenaline is keeping most of the pain away for the moment, but I know if I stop now, it'll come back with a vengeance.

No time to treat the wound properly as the Alpha gets over its confusion at the disappearance of its original prey and it skitters to the truck and Richard, who stands on it. I don't let it as I take a few running steps and leap into the air, calling the sword into both hands as I angle to land on the creature's back. Just before I do, I release the field and come back fully to this reality, sword landing first into its back.

The blade sinks in deep, cutting through coarse fur and muscle into vulnerable organs beneath as I land with one knee bent, the other splayed behind me as I try to keep my balance. Or at least, I hope vulnerable organs. I twist the blade with both hands, then as the creature bucks I fall flat and take a grip on the open wound. I dig my hands into its back, crushing flesh as I attempt to stay on the monster.

While I keep the Boss distracted, my companions take the fight to the remaining Spiders. Orel returns after having dropped its latest prey, this time landing on and staying on top of another wolf to peck it to death, its beak tearing into the creature's neck and spine. Richard has switched to slugs, each shot tearing a hole into the Spiders he targets, creating distracting, painful openings for the Huskies to finish the monsters off. Mikito seems to have lost her naginata in the body of a Spider, switching to fighting with a pair of glowing curved short swords that she wields with finesse and speed.

197

The Alpha, unable to buck me off, spins towards the truck again and launches itself at Richard without warning. Only battle hardened instinct alerts Richard, making him throw himself off at the last second. He's unable to escape completely and the creature's fangs clamp down and rip off his foot as he dodges. For a brief moment, Lana's face flashes before my eyes as I see Richard almost lose his life and that centre of peace that I fight in shatters. Rage comes in its place, the same cold angry focus that I felt when I saw Haines Junction. My world narrows down to one goal and one goal only – ending this thing before it hurts anyone else. As the Alpha attempts to stabilise himself on the truck, I shove my left arm all the way into the wound to my shoulder, grabbing at whatever organ I can find.

The Alpha rears up, howling in surprise and rage as I dig around its abdomen and grasp hold of something slimy but tough. My position fixed, I call my sword to my right hand and begin thrusting it into the abdomen, twisting and repeating the attack again and again. When the creature slams itself into the truck to throw me off, I don't dismiss the sword but instead throw my weight behind it, letting the creature's own momentum widen the wound.

I don't know how long it takes, my world taken over by my need to end this creature, to kill it and all its kind. I vaguely recall a tree shattering around us in the eternity of bucking and stabbing. When the Alpha stops moving, having collapsed on the ground, I find myself a hundred yards from the original scene of battle in the woods, alone. Hovering over me, Ali is silent and worried. Extracting my arm from its innards is a disgusting, revolting process and once again, I really wish there was a magic dissolving corpse option.

Free of the creature, I drop to my knees and focus, working on rebuilding my self-control. The aftershocks arrive soon after, my entire body shaking and I have to pull my helmet off when I begin to throw up, pain dragging me to my feet as my stomach wound makes itself known. When the smell finally hits me, I begin retching again, my stomach clamping around my open wound and making me fall over to my side in pain.

"Boy-o?" Ali whispers worriedly, after I finally stop shivering and whimpering, long enough to cast a Minor Heal on myself. My body's System-assisted regeneration helps too, patching together my body even as I damage it by throwing up.

"I'm okay. I'm okay," I close my eyes, the fury driven away by the pain. I work on my self-control, rebuilding my walls as I put the anger aside. "The others?"

"Safe. Injured but safe," Ali replies and I nod. I slowly push myself up and hurry over to my companions to provide them with a little bit of healing. Mikito has already bandaged Richard's leg, the man caring less about his foot than the corpse of his dog. For a moment, I feel regret that I've not taken the time to learn their names and resolve to do better as I watch Richard grieve. Richard holds the corpse close, sobbing into it even as the other dogs snuffle around them, letting loose occasional howls of grief. All I can do is cast Minor Healing on both of them, helping to speed up the process.

Ali floats over to me, his usual sardonic smile back on his face as he waggles his fingers to throw up a pair of notifications, "Congrats boy-o. Your first Boss kill."

Congratulations! Wexlix Spider Alpha – Boss Slain
+11,700 XP

Level Up!

You have reached Level 12 as an Erethran Honor Guard. Stat Points automatically distributed. You have 14 Free Attribute Points to distribute.

When I finish reading, I cast another healing on Mikito before turning back to Ali who has continued speaking after I'm done, "That could have been worse. Looks like easy mode is over though if Boss monsters are beginning to appear."

"You mentioned that earlier. Care to clarify?" I ask for clarification. Better to not make assumptions.

"Boss monsters are leaders of a group of monsters, always the strongest son-of-a-bitch. Their presence generally increases the breeding and mutation rates of their followers." Ali shakes his head. "Good thing you killed it, Wexlix Spiders are nasty predators and could easily have made this entire region a lot harder to deal with. Of course, there are worse things out there."

I look around the carnage, the dead body of Richard's pet and our injuries and shiver at his words, looking out into the wilderness. If what he's saying is true, then out there, there might be more monster hordes breeding. Monsters that we know nothing about, growing unchecked till the horde comes crashing down on us in an unstoppable wave. Ali sees my reaction and just nods soberly. We're running out of time.

Chapter 14

I stay silent while we loot the bodies and get Richard back into the truck along with the rest of the animals. I stay silent when, at Ali's urging, Mikito and I head into the webbed forest and find the eggs, collecting them all for sale. I stay silent through the entire drive back till we drop Richard off with Ali at the Shop.

Once Richard disappears, I turn to Mikito and snarl, "What the hell were you thinking!?" She looks right back at me impassively and I continue, raising a finger. "I said run. That was a fucking plasma grenade. If you had been any closer, you'd have died. Hell, it's pure luck you didn't die. Richard stayed back because you fucking didn't run and he nearly died for it. I nearly died."

She looks to the side, not meeting my gaze and I growl, raising a finger. "Don't ever fucking do that again. If I say run, run. If Richard says run, you run. If you don't listen to us when we fight, you'll get one of us killed."

Mikito looks up for a moment, meeting my eyes briefly before looking down again, her hand clutching the naginata tightly. She jerks her head slightly at my words and then without saying a further word walks to the crystal and touches it, disappearing into the Shop. I scowl, shivering with rage at that crazy woman. Fuck!

A small part of me knows that it's not just her that I'm angry at. I'm angry at me, for agreeing to it and I'm angry at the System. I thought I had begun to get a hang of it, thought I had an idea of what to expect. But each time, things just keep getting worse and worse - more monsters, higher level monsters, Boss monsters. Monster hordes next.

"Adventurer Lee is it not?" the voice is urbane and cultured and sends a shiver down my spine. I turn and spot Roxley and once again, I am struck by just how pretty he is. Delicate features that still hint at the strength of his body, a commanding aura that attracts attention. I blink when I realise I've probably been staring longer than I should have.

"Yes, sir," I reply immediately and then pause, considering what to call him. Lord just seems pretentious but it is what he is.

"And where is your Companion?" Roxley looks around, smiling slightly as he speaks.

"... with a friend. They're selling our loot," I say and then I realise something. "Oh, I have some things you might want to know."

"Do tell," Roxley says.

"Yeah," I pause, trying to decide if should hold out for some reward. However, after a moment I decide against it. He's been pretty generous so far and goodwill can often be better currency than actual currency. Old friends are important. "Well, firstly, did you know that there's a fort at Carcross Cut-off? I kinda own it now, but yeah, there's one there. Also, there are Boss monsters now."

"Really. A fort?" Roxley smiles slightly, looking at me as I stare at him. "Well, you have been fast at picking up property have you not."

"Yeah, I guess so," I reply and shrug, my lips twisting into a slight smile.

"Well, I'm sure there's a story there but I was just about to go for lunch," Roxley says and nods to me. "Adventurer Lee."

"Lord Roxley," I reply automatically, trying to get my brain back into gear. Switching from anger to fear to lust in a short span of time seems to have short-circuited it. Or maybe that's just my consciousness.

As he walks to the doors, he stops and then smiles slightly, "Perhaps you'd care to join me while you wait for your friends? You can tell me more about the fort and these Boss monsters then."

"Ummm…" I reply and then realise my stomach is growling, letting me know that running around fighting, killing and healing does require a large number of calories. "Sure."

***

Lunch itself is amazing. I stare at the plates, scraping the last of the dessert up with the spork that seems to be utensil of choice here and sigh, leaning back contentedly. Roxley is smiling slightly as he watches me. "It is good to see that our civilizations share certain taste."

I blink then nod, sitting up, "Yes."

"I am surprised that you had no trouble with the Urike tentacles though, I understood that North Americans were pickier," Roxley says and I know exactly the dish he was speaking of. It looked like a lurid, purple mess of suction cups and twitching meat.

"Ah, I'm a CBC. Canadian Born Chinese. My father was very traditional and I grew up eating, well, everything," I explain and smile slightly, remembering pig brain soup and snake blood shakes. Yeah, trips back to his hometown were always fun and I quickly learnt to just eat.

"I see," Roxley gets this faraway look for a second before those dark eyes of his snap back to me. "A melting pot of cultures then. Interesting."

I just nod to his words, sipping at the water that is laid out for me at my request. Over lunch, Roxley had extracted the story about the fort and the Wexlix Spiders from me, though he seemed significantly more troubled by the Hakarta than the Spiders. Then again, I guess the Boss monsters were something he knew to expect.

Gods, I hate being behind the curve, knowing less than everyone else. It reminds me of every time I was put into a new school as a kid - never knowing where everything is, always bumping into existing friendships and missing all the cues that everyone else who had a shared history got. Don't date this person. Don't talk to this one. That teacher was particularly stern.

"Adventurer Lee?" Roxley says again and I blink, coming back to the present.

"Sorry!"

"As pleasant as this was, perhaps we could continue this at another time? I have other matters to attend to," Roxley says as he stands, pushing away from the table and I stand quickly too.

"Thank you," I offer him my hand and he stares at it bemusedly before taking it, shaking once and letting go before he walks away.

Once more at the doorway, he turns to look at me and says, "I shall have my Companion contact yours to continue this then," before sweeping out. I stare at him for a second, blinking and walking down to the Shop. Well, that was interesting.

***

"Boss monsters?" squeaks Minion, staring at us.

"As we said, they're more powerful leaders of the normal monsters. They increase the speed the monsters under them breed and mutate," Richard repeats, standing on his own two feet. I glance down at them again, marvelling at the Shop. It hadn't even been that expensive to have them regenerate his foot for him, all things considered, and we'd made enough that I had Xev fix up Sabre fully.

"Yes, thank you very much, Mr. Pearson, for informing us," Fred says, waving Minion down. Minion subsides like the good little minion that he is, glaring at us and I can't help but smirk. "This is disturbing news. The Council will have to discuss what we should do about it."

I blink, staring at him. Do about it? Do what? There's not a lot that I can think of that we can do beyond what we're doing now. Maybe work a little harder to level up, get tougher, get a militia together, maybe get some defenses? Okay, maybe there are things that can be done.

"In the interim, will your group continue to locate and attack these creatures for the Council?" Fred says, leaning forward. "Your actions will provide immediate relief for the city while we work on other options."

Quest Received (Repeatable) - *Kill the Boss monsters around Whitehorse*
Boss monsters are appearing around Whitehorse. To reduce the danger of a monster horde, you must kill the Boss monsters before they grow too strong. To succeed, kill 4 Boss monsters.
Rewards: 20,000 XP

I blink, staring at the quest as does Richard, who flicks his hand to the side, waving the screen away most likely. Arse. Perhaps if we stick to around Whitehorse itself, the Bosses will be more manageable. In fact, put that way, it'd be an easy way to game the System. I feel my shoulders loosen a little as I rationalise things, the recollection of the creature pinning me to the ground still fresh.

Richard is speaking again and I sigh, turning my attention back. Not that I expect I'll hear anything useful but you never know.

***

Lana, not surprisingly, wasn't particularly happy with us when she heard our story. She glared at all of us before walking away, leaving us staring at the half-made meal and wondering if dinner would be served. We sit around awkwardly, wondering if she'll be back for nearly 15 minutes before we give up and Mikito takes over the cooking.

"John," Richard says, as I stare to where his sister left.

"Yeah?" I glance back at him guiltily, hoping he didn't realise what I was thinking.

"We were talking and we were wondering, would it be possible to turn the lights on if you had the Credits?"

"Definitely. Just depends on how, but it's not actually at all expensive. Just need a Mana engine and battery for the generator and that's not too expensive. About five hundred Credits," I answer him and then shrug. "Don't have the money right now though."

"Yeah, about that," Richard waves his hand and I blink at the transfer notification. "Call it rent."

"Uhh… sure," I accept it and then put it straight to buying the generator, smiling slightly as I feel the shift around us. I walk over to the light switch, testing it out before popping back down. "That'll be useful."

Richard nods, smiling slightly. It's still light enough that we won't need it right now, but at least we have electricity again, even if all our electronics are broken. Oooh, maybe we could get someone to fix up a TV.

Mikito waves to us, bringing us back to reality as she drops our plates in front of us. I nod to her in thanks and so does Richard before we get down to the serious business of eating.

"Are we doing this? Hunting the Bosses?" Richard asks and I blink, the forkful of meat halfway to my lips. I frown, popping it in and chewing as I look to Ali who shrugs back at me. Going out, hunting and visiting Carcross, fighting. It was fun sort-of and necessary but after today, the threat is all too real. If there was anyone else…

"It's not a great quest," I offer and Richard nods. Mikito stays silent, probably because we all know what she'd recommend. "But if we're out hunting anyway, I guess it can't hurt to have it."

Richard nods and I go back to my meal. I guess that's settled then.

Chapter 15

Rather than head out immediately, we spend the next day hunting around town, bringing new people out with us to gain some experience and meat. It's interesting, working with the lower levels and after a quick discussion, the three of us split into two groups. Richard and his puppies lead one group of newbies, Mikito and I another. It helps us cover more ground, bring in more food and train up more newbies in the same time frame. Of course, we barely get any experience but after yesterday, the change of pace is rather relaxing. I can't wander around in Sabre, but with Mikito and I around, the monsters we meet are more than easy to deal with if they get out of hand.

We keep each group with us for about half the day, every time we get back, most of the members have leveled up at least twice. It'll be a while before we can get most of them to decent levels, but as I understand it, even the normal hunting groups are beginning to bring one or two of the more advanced newbies with them.

The problem mostly is that of equipment. If we could get some of these groups outfitted properly, they could start hunting on their own. Unfortunately, till they have better equipment that they own themselves, they have to rely on us. However, that's a raw deal for them too since we take most of the Loot afterwards as payment for our time. It's still a lot less than what we'd earn if we were working ourselves but it's better than nothing.

As evening comes, I make my way to the Shop. My original rifle is unfortunately too broken to use so I have to buy a new one. My share of the Loot drop and the Boss fight should cover it I hope.

Ferlix Type II Twinned-Beam Rifle (Modified)

Base Damage: 57
Battery Capacity: 17/17

Recharge rate: 1 per hour per GMU (currently 12)

Yeah, the battery capacity is a bit lower but the base damage is significantly higher. I've also been able to salvage the Mana battery from the other rifle so I can just swap it out as necessary, if I need to. Let's hope it doesn't come to that of course. As I walk out and straddle Sabre, I sigh as I stare at my Credit balance. Damn world. Credits fly out as fast as I earn them, fixing Sabre, getting new weapons, healing myself, learning new Skills. The list is endless and the only way to earn, at least for me, is to go out and risk my life. Again and again. I draw a deep breath and let it out slowly. Right, what is, is.

***

"Where's Richard?" I ask, pulling up a seat next to Lana and Mikito.

"Mmm... with one of his 'friends' I believe," Lana's lip quirk slightly, waving her hand to the front door. "He's gotten quite popular as I understand it."

I nod slightly, recalling the way the majority of his group had been made of women. I guess his increasing Charisma score had certain side benefits. After a moment's hesitation, I bury myself in dinner, murmuring words of praise to Lana. Conversation quickly devolves to the inanities of life, mostly led by Lana since Mikito and I know what we did.

"The Council sent Jim and his group into the dam today and they swept the area for monsters. They can't afford to buy it right now, but with some work, they believe they can at least get the emergency release valves set to fully open so that the dam isn't a threat," Lana explains and I nod. Huh. I didn't even realise that was a problem but I'm glad someone looked into it.

As a kid runs up to me, I exhale and reach out, pulling a snack-sized chocolate from my inventory and handing it to her. She grins, gives me a quick hug and runs off and I find both Lana and Mikito eyeing me.

"Bad," Mikito points a finger at me and I shrug. Hey, I like chocolate - and the kid probably doesn't get much in terms of treats these days.

When we finish up, Mikito takes over the dish washing and Lana grabs my arm, pulling me to the backyard. She tosses the remainder bones out where a brief scuffle settles who gets the scraps before she turns to me, waist length red hair swaying above her bottom.

"John, you're headed out with my brother again tomorrow aren't you?" Lana says and I nod in confirmation. Her lips purse as she visibly struggles with what to say next, arms crossed underneath her bosom. Eventually, she lets out a little huff, "I can't stop you. Or him. If I told him no, he'd just go. Just, watch over him, will you? He's my little brother and he's, well, he's stupid."

I grunt, scratching at my head as she says that and then glance back inside to where Mikito washes the dishes silently, "I'll try, but..."

"I know. I know it's not safe. Just be careful, please. He came back without a foot. And Jim, he loses someone every few days. Just yesterday they lost half a hunting party," Lana says and hugs herself tighter. "I can't... if I lose him..."

I nod and then after a brief moment's hesitation I walk over and give her a hug. She is stiff at first and then relaxes into my arms, just letting me hug her as she shivers. I push aside the tightness in my own chest, my own fear and loss, for a moment. I can deal with my own issues later.

***

The next morning, I spot Richard as he drives up with the truck. He whistles and the puppies dash out from the back, looking to start clambering onto the truck bed. Time to go hunting.

"Why am I here again?" I whisper to Richard as I survey the boardroom a few days later. He grimaces and kicks me under the table and I exhale forcefully, leaning back. Fine. He's right.

"We cannot keep adding citizens to our population. As it stands, non-combatant personnel are receiving a daily allocation of 1,400 calories, which is significantly below what is recommended and we'll need to drop that to 1,000 calories next week once the last of the perishables are used up. Even worse, a significant portion of that comes via protein intake as that is our most reliable food source," Miranda states, leaning forwards and eyeballing both Richard and myself. Mikito has run off, citing the need to continue training new combat classers and she even managed to drag Lana with her this time. That means the two of us have to take the brunt of the meeting. "Until we get our first harvest in, we just don't have enough vegetables and fruits."

"Are you saying we should leave them in the wild?" Norman speaks from the corner, peering at Miranda over steepled fingers.

"Well, we can't take them here," Miranda states again and adds, "unless the hunters are willing to give up a larger percentage of their earnings, we just don't have the resources."

Jim shakes his head as the other hunters start speaking up behind him, a low-voiced grumble that he cuts off, "We're already contributing over 30% of our Credits. We need the Credits to get better equipment and better skills."

"How about the Raven's Circle and Richard's group?" Minion adds, staring at Nic and Richard. "As far as I know they don't contribute to the city at all."

"That is not true," Nicodemus rumbles. Even talking softly, it comes out as almost a shout as the half-Giant continues, "We provide 10% of all our earnings. It is smaller in percentage, but as we fight more powerful enemies, in total the Circle provide more Credits than any other group."

"And we spend every other day currently training up your combat classers so that they can gain some levels and become useful," Richard adds, tapping his fingers on the ground. "We've already had one full hunting party graduate and they now add to the food supply and Credits."

"Yet you don't supply the city with any Credits at all," Minion presses.

"We need that money to upgrade ourselves! You've requested that the Circle and us hunt down the Bosses, how the hell are we supposed to do that without better equipment?" Richard states, glaring at him. "The last time we met one, we nearly died. You can't expect us to fight, train your people and look for others while giving up all our Credits. The Circle doesn't do any training at all!"

"That's because we are busy hunting the Boss monsters," snaps Nicodemus. "We aren't waiting to level up like you guys."

Fred speaks up, looking from group to group, "Please, let's not get personal. We are all here to work together for the city." As the participants all settle down, he adds. "Now, I know we are asking a lot from our premier parties, but as Miranda has stated, we desperately need more food. 1,000 calories is insufficient. We are here to work together on this matter."

"How about asking Roxley?" I ask. I can feel my stomach clench at the idea of reducing food to the population even more. As it stands, those of us who have combat classes and are fighting are already looking significantly healthier than the general populace. I can just imagine what it'd be like if we had to put them on starvation diets and the kind of unrest it would cause.

"Well…" Fred pauses, looking around.

"Why would he help?" says Minion and I see a few heads nod.

"Well, for one thing, he's taxing anything we buy in the Shop right now. If there's a tax, there should be services," I say and then shrug. "He's also not going to want us to starve to death."

"I don't like it," mutters one of the councilors, a pinched-face portly gentlemen. "He's an interloper."

"He's taxing us already whether or not you like it. We should be talking to him about this, not excluding him from these meetings," I shoot back, glaring at them.

"That would give his government legitimacy," Minion snaps and shakes his head. "We won't do it."

"Then people will starve," I say, crossing my arms and stare at him.

Voices rise again, some people calling for us to talk to Roxley, others like Minion refusing to do so. In the end, Fred has to hammer his hand on the table repeatedly to get us to shut up. "Enough. Mr. Lee has put forward that we speak with Lord Roxley about the food situation. Do we have a seconder?"

Richard backs me up quickly but we lose the vote and I growl, shaking my head. Idiots. The fight starts again about how we're going to fund the purchase of additional foodstuff from the Shop, everyone refusing to give up a little bit of the pie.

I fall silent, watching as Fred wheedles, cajoles and pleads with everyone, finally getting the Circle to agree to help out with training and reducing the time we spend on it, to twice a week. It'll give us more time to hunt and earn money, but that means we take a 10% contribution. I'm still not happy about this, but what can you do? Until the local economy recovers, we're reliant on the System to provide the carbohydrates and vegetables needed for survival.

Once that particular argument is over, another one begins around what next to buy in terms of buildings. I grunt, shaking my head and sink further into the chair. This part I really hate so I only pay partial attention, letting the arguments wash over me.

**

"John?" Richard says again and I blink, realizing I've been zoned out for a while. He sighs, shaking his head and stands up. Everyone else has left and I grunt, standing with him. "You know, you really should pay more attention."

"Yeah, yeah," I say and wave my hands. "It's all bullshit really. They need to be talking to Roxley."

"I know, John, but you've got to admit, it sticks in the craw that he's the Lord of the city just because he bought it from the System," Richard points out as we walk out of the school boardroom.

I nod at his words, letting my eyes wander over the inhabitants of the school and trying not to wrinkle my nose too much. Washing in the river is both dangerous and cold and so few people go down often enough. With so many crowded into the hallways, the smell lingers. As we walk through, we attract quite a bit of whispered attention. More than one woman shoots Richard an admiring glance, flashing smiles at him that he returns.

"Richard," a young lady, probably no more than 18 and wearing a pair of tight pants comes up to him, placing a hand on his chest. "Will you be coming by tonight? Or I can come over…"

"Tonight? I'm ummm… busy," Richard says as he stops.

"That's okay, I'm willing to share," she smiles at him again and then runs a hand through her hair. "I can meet you at your house…"

Richard looks at her for a moment, eyes raking her body and then he nods jerkily, "Sure…" She grins, going on tiptoes and kissing him on the lips before dropping down and moving away. Richard stares at her sway away before looking at me and my raised eyebrow. "Hey, it's the end of the world. And she's… nice."

"Uh huh," I mutter and wave him on.

He chuckles, looking at me and shaking his head. "If you didn't glower at everyone all the time, you might have some better luck."

"No time, Richard," I mutter, waving out. "We've got monsters to kill, skills to train and people to help."

"Still no reason not to have fun," Richard says.

I just grunt in answer. He's right and yet, the idea of engaging in those kinds of conversations, of talking to someone and building a connection, of even just having those kinds of interactions, makes me twitch. I just don't have the energy or desire to do so, not right now. Sex might be nice, but there's so much to do. Maybe later, when I have time.

As we exit the school, we glance around. No Mikito yet, so we're on our own. Richard grins slightly at that, waving goodbye to me to work his emotions out. I watch him leave and watch again as he's surrounded in moments by others and I shake my head. Well, he's got his own thing to do.

I've got monsters to hunt. I've wasted enough hours listening to inane chatter. Time to go do something useful, work out some anger and some of this energy. I still need more Credits, especially if I want to buy some of the things I've been eyeing. I send a mental call for Ali, pulling him back from wherever he is and getting on Sabre. Perhaps I'll try the area around Fox Lake today.

***

"Down!" I shout, bringing my rifle to bear. Mikito ducks, giving me the opening I am looking for and I let her rip, tearing a hole in the lizard creature she is fighting. Mikito stands up, spinning the naginata as she does to get momentum and slams the blade into the creature's side, forming a new wound and moving forwards to target their leader. I move to the left, breaking from the Circle in hopes of getting a shot. To my side, three of the puppies are nipping at the creature that Richard glued to the ground, tearing into its legs as Richard unloads shot after shot into the lizardman.

"Right boy-o," snaps Ali and I duck and spin, bringing my rifle to target the third lizardman that rises from the ground, snarling at me. I blast it in its face and watch the creature stagger back before I put one last shot into it and wince as a notification shows that I've got 2 shots left.

"Left!" Ali shouts and I spin, calling my sword into being and letting the creature run itself onto it. My momentum lets me tear the sword halfway through it before I finish and then I boot the dying lizardman away, making the sword disappear as I let it go and grab my rifle looking for more trouble.

Even before I can bring my rifle to bear, a pair of dogs tear into the last remaining lizardman that has shown itself and I breathe a sigh of relief. I look around, breathing fast and as always, glad that the helmet filters the smells of combat away from me, and find nothing.

"We're good!" Richard calls out and I let out a low exhalation as Mikito relaxes too, bending down to begin looting. As an official party, we don't have assigned bodies to loot so Mikito and I just loot everything while Richard and his puppies keep watch.

"Damn invaders," Richard mutters, staring at the lizards. I can't help but wonder if they were sentient like the Ogres. If they had come on purpose or were just caught up in the transfer. Perhaps they were here because they had sold themselves to the System like Ali. The System was unforgiving in such cases but it always had a use for you.

Once we finish, we get moving again with Richard driving and Mikito in the back while I range ahead. We're headed to one of the smaller communities today, hoping to find some survivors. I don't hold much hope for that but we've got to try.

An hour later we finally reach the series of rundown houses that make up this community. I look around at the shattered doors and windows and even one torn down wall and I shake my head slightly. Small communities are hardest hit - too remote to make it to Whitehorse by foot, too few to mount a proper defense against larger predators, no access to the Shop. This is the third community we've visited in the last week and once again, it looks like no one is around.

Richard whistles and the puppies move out, searching while Ali turns around, scanning. If there are living humans around, they most likely learnt a Stealth ability of some form, which means Ali's System scanning might not bring them up. Thus, the puppies.

They spread out and after a few minutes, the black Husky called Shadow, barks. I blink, swinging my head in the direction of the noise. It only takes a few moments for Richard to discern what is going on and then we are moving, weapons drawn and on foot to follow the puppy into the forest. Looks like we might actually find someone.

Two hours of pushing through the forest and one brief encounter later, we are halfway up a mountain and coming close to a stream. I frown, tilting my head to the side as I catch a whiff of something and one of the puppies is barking at it. A brief investigation indicates that humans are living around here and they need more fibre in their diet.

Our first indication that something is out there is the voice, calling out to us, "Stop or I'll shoot!"

We freeze and look around, Mikito crouching low as the puppies let out a low snarl. They hold though at Richard's command and after a moment I spot the barrel of the rifle poking out at us and the head of the man behind it. Balding, white and squinting, the weapon he's using is probably a .56 calibre.

"Easy there friend," Richard calls out behind me and I can hear the smile in his voice. "We're not here to harm you. We're actually here to bring you to Whitehorse where everyone's gathering and it's safer."

"I ain't trusting you," the man waggles the rifle barrel again. Even as he speaks, Ali darts past him into the cave, invisible to the naked eye. "You guys just get going. I'm fine here."

"Well, we won't force you. But perhaps you can ask your friends?" Richard continues and I mentally sigh. Yeah, he's not the only holdout we've run into - people who are too distrustful, too scared to come. We can't force them, but sometimes, I think we should.

"Ain't no one else here. Now you best get going, you're drawing attention," the man answers again curtly.

"*John, he's not alone. There's a pair of women in here and a couple of children. You better get in here,*" Ali sends to me and I frown beneath my helmet.

I step forward, hands held out to my side, "Look, we got it. We do have some food to spare though, so if you let me just drop it off, we'll be on our way. Got some ready meals that you could use and even some chocolate."

I can see Mikito tense at that, crouching lower as she eyes the rifle. Richard behind me falls silent, watching me walk forward even as the gun barks and a stone shatters next to me.

"I said stop!" the voice goes higher, sounding a bit more panicked.

"Yeah, sorry, sorry. Thought I'd make it easier for you. One second," I bend down, pulling some of my ready-meals from my inventory and placing them on the ground. "Here, just going to grab the chocolate…" I mutter and as I see him relax slightly, I move.

Before the System, I hated running. I was never good at it and my knee always ached when I ran on pavement. Too short, too slow, too untrained to really be good at it. Now though, now I can move. I cover the forty feet that separates us in less than a blink, his reflexive shot missing me. He doesn't get a second as I grab the rifle, pulling it aside and then wrap my fist around his shirt and lift him from the concealed entrance with one hand. He gurgles as I hold him up and he tries to kick me. Rather than block it, I slam him into the cliff and make my sword appear in my other hand, holding it against his neck.

"Mikito, Richard. He's not alone. Check the cave," I bark, staring at him. I idly slap his hand aside as he attempts to go for the knife at his side. "Stop it."

I keep an eye on the man and the surroundings idly while the noise of the two moving into the cave ahead of me comes. After a moment, Richard starts cursing and then cuts himself off. I blink, frowning and then Ali comes floating back up to me.

"What's going on Ali?" I ask the Spirit.

"Goblin-shit here thought to play king of the mountain. Unfortunately, it looks like his subjects didn't agree and he's been, well, lording it over them,"

Ali spits to the side as he glares at the man. The man in turns looks at me speaking to thin air and his eyes widen further.

"Do I want details?" I say softly, a tightness in my stomach.

"No," Ali says and I nod. I look at the man, considering if I should kill him now or leave it for his subjects...

Mikito walks out, looks to me and then without a word, flicks her naginata at the man. It catches just above my arm, slicing through the lower half of his jaw. I reflexively jerk and then throw the man away, glaring at her as I shake the blood off. She doesn't even spot me doing so as she's headed back in.

"Fuck..." I snarl, considering going in or not but as Richard comes out, he shakes his head. Right, not our place for now. Staring at the twitching body, my lips twist and I really wish he was still alive. No. Better this way. Drawing a deep breath, I walk away from the cave entrance to keep an eye out. Fuck. The world ends and people go all Lord of the Flies.

It takes hours before Mikito comes out with the other survivors, hours for us to make our way back to the vehicles. We have to deal with one predator in-between, drawn to the smell of blood and Richard has to send the puppies and me out to deal with threats on our walk back. Mikito stays next to the women, helping them along as Richard plays close-quarter guard.

It's more hours before we get back to Whitehorse and all through the journey, silence is all we get from the kids. When I tried to offer them some chocolate, they flinch from me. There is a look in their eyes, a knowledge that should never be there that makes me wince and the rage boil in my stomach.

When we get back to Whitehorse, we drop the survivors off with the Council. Richard explains while Mikito stays close by, the women unwilling to let her go as yet. I watch from my seat, unable to do anything, feeling useless.

Finding survivors was supposed to be a good thing, a victory. I don't feel particularly victorious right now.

***

"You're my group?" I stare at the small number of wannabe-combat classers who are part of my team today. I look them up and down, the short Filipino father, the pair of gym junkies who look tough but haven't even leveled yet and the single lady of the group with a cat t-shirt and short blonde hair. I get nods from them all and I flick my gaze over the weapons they carry, a mixture of loaned rifles and scavenged bats and axes.

"Right, those of you with rifles. You know how to shoot right?" I make sure and get confirming nods from the two gym rats and the lady. The Filipino just shakes his head and I grimace, pointing a finger at him. "Keep your finger off the trigger. Don't raise the gun until you get a clear shot. That means no one in your way." Turning to the girl, I pull my rifle off my shoulder and hand it to her. "Doesn't have kickback. I expect it back."

She nods gratefully and I notice one of the guys shift on his feet, opening his mouth to say something and then deciding against it. Good.

"Rules are simple. I'm in front, you guys are behind. We're going to head through Long Lakes and hunt for low-level monsters for you to fight. While we are out, I expect you to be working on moving silently and quietly - and when we're done today, I expect you to continue practising that. The Stealth skill will keep you alive if you ever have to hunt. Stay behind me, listen to me or Ali and wait for me to give you the go-ahead to attack. If I say run, you run back to the last point I told you to wait or the school. Got it?" I wait for confirming nods before I turn and head in, rolling my shoulders in an attempt to get rid of my tension. I really don't want to be doing this, not today, but we promised.

The first few hours are the usual, slow going and boring for me, though not for the newbies. They scream, throw up, run and on one occasion nearly shoot one another as we deal with the low-level monsters around here. Mostly, the throwing up is when I make them butcher the carcasses and put the bodies in their bags to carry, getting more than one dirty look since I don't help.

We're coming up to the three-quarter mark of their training session when I turn to them. "Right, time to pay up. If you don't know how, think about sharing the inventory to me." It takes a few seconds before the first few trade offers are made, but one of the gym rats crosses his arms, shaking his head. "What is it?"

"No. You didn't do shit. You just walked around with us, let us do all the killing and then you're going to take our stuff. No way," gym rat says and I look up at his Status bar, reading the information.

"Okay, then Peter. You can go now," I state and wave him away as I confirm acceptance of the other trades. His friend hesitates, looking between the two of us. "You too, if you don't want to pay."

"What do you mean, go?" Peter bristles.

"Go. Leave. Head home," I wave again, grinning at him savagely. "Take a walk through the woods."

"Fine, I will," Peter turns and then takes a few steps back from where we came. He frowns, pauses and then looks around. We're a few hills past Whitehorse and since we've been following Ali's directions, we've been off-trail from the very beginning. He twists around uncertainly, staring as he tries to figure out which way to go.

I ignore him, turning to the two who have paid me, "Right. So, we're going to keep going for another hour..."

"Hey man, you can't leave Peter out here," his friend says, already sending over his own payment. I accept before shrugging.

"All of you knew the deal before we came out. He wants to break it, he can figure out how to get home himself," I state and then nod. "Right, this way."

As we start walking, Peter follows and I turn to him pointing in the direction we came from. "You're not following us. Go."

"You can't stop me!" Peter smirks. Patience gone, I cross the distance between us and shove him ever so slightly. He flies backwards a few feet, rolling over his shoulders before coming to a stop. He coughs a bit and I idly note he's lost a few hit points while he struggles up.

"You want to play games? I can play games. Keep following me and I'll break both your legs and leave you here," I snap and point a finger at him.

"You can't..." the Filipino man looks at me, shaking his head. "That's not right."

"Neither is him stiffing me. He wants to be an ass, so can I," I snap. "Except I've been going out, fighting while you lot have sat around so I'm a much better asshole than you guys."

Peter's friend has rushed over to him, whispering to the man. Peter shudders in anger, pulling himself up but his friend pushes against him, whispering again. To the side, the lady has moved away to watch, the rifle slung down low and not pointed at anyone. Eventually, Peter sends me a notification and I look it over, accepting the loot.

"This way then." I point again and start walking, Ali watching the group for me. Fucking little shits.

Chapter 16

Life falls into a routine. One day training, one day hunting and another looking for survivors. The city slowly comes back to life, though I guess you can't really call us a city - more a small town now. Either way, the news of the Boss monster fight spreads quickly and everyone begins to work harder. It's strange that the constant harrying attacks of the spawning monsters did nothing but the potential that we might actually face a horde of monsters galvanises the population. They begin to take an active interest in their life again, attempting to Level themselves, to build themselves up. Roxley hires builders from within the community and they begin to construct stonewalls at the three natural choke points that surround the city.

We've not made much more progress in finding other human settlements. The few further settlements north of us that we've journeyed to have had scattered survivors, the vast majority hiding in cracks and dodging monsters as best they can. None refuse our offer of moving down to Whitehorse, which makes Roxley happy at least.

Roxley comes through on the second invitation and I found that speaking with him was easy. He never had any expectations and he gave as good as he got, providing me with information about the System and how it affected the wider world around us. Afterwards, we retired to his private workout room where he deigned to give me a few pointers on my sword technique. Somehow, celebratory dinners and after-dinner training sessions with the sword become a routine thing after each successful rescue.

One of the survivors actually becomes the fourth in our small party, a female mage named Rachel Martin. If it weren't for the scar that cuts down the left side of her face, her dark hair, high cheekbones and dark brown eyes would have the boys clustering around her. Unfortunately, the scar and her refusal to have it removed at the Shop along with a hundred-yard stare seems to keep all but the bravest young men away. It's Mikito who insists she joins us, making a point that Rachel's safer with us than going out alone, as she threatened. Truth be told, after our first day out, I'm glad to have her on our side. She specializes in earth magic, combining moving sheaths of earth with warping the greenery around us to create effective barriers and weapons.

As for myself, I can't help but feel frustrated at my lack of progress after nearly a month of training. I have barely made any progress with expanding my understanding of my Elemental Affinity, only snatching a few minutes here and there to work on my connection. I can now find it within 5 minutes of intense concentration, which is a big improvement, but until I can actually grasp the connection instinctively, I can't even begin to work on additional spells.

I have improved my overall Mana Manipulation though, even if it has come at the cost of my pride and self-esteem. I probably could have progressed that faster if I could stand to deal with the teacher, who Lana found for me, for longer than 20 minutes at a time. Unfortunately, even with the death of the world, hipsters have managed to survive. The only good thing I can say about the man-bun wielding mage, Aiden, is that he's not part of the Raven's Circle. Sadly, he's still the best option to learn from since he somehow has a better understanding of how to manipulate Mana than anyone else in the community.

In fact, working with Manbun, I've been able to improve my Mana Dart and Minor Healing spells to send a second dart and heal more respectively, though neither are spells I'd care to use in the middle of a fight. As a backup, I've also picked up a single area effect spell, though it drains a ton of my Mana. I haven't had to actually use it in a do-or-die situation, though my one test with a grouping of yellow gremlin-like creatures was more than satisfactory. Satisfactory for me anyway – Rachel proceeded to show me what a real mage could do a moment later by pinpoint attacking the remaining creatures with a single Earth Spike spell.

So much has changed, but I'm still stuck, just a short distance away from finally unlocking my Class Skills. We're no closer to figuring out how to speed up my acquisition of a new title, but at least we should have a lock-on the level minimum for being a Guild Leader soon.

Status Screen			
Name	John Lee	Class	Erethran Honor Guard
Race	Human (Male)	Level	14
Titles			
Monster's Bane, Redeemer of the Dead			
Health	710	Stamina	710
Mana	570		
Status			
Normal			
Attributes			
Strength	48 (50)	Agility	66 (70)
Constitution	71 (75)	Perception	24
Intelligence	57 (60)	Willpower	57 (60)
Charisma	14	Luck	13
Skills			
Stealth	6	Wilderness Survival	4
Unarmed Combat	6	Knife Proficiency	5
Athletics	5	Observe	5
Cooking	1	Sense Danger	5
Jury-rigging	2	Explosives	1
Blade Mastery	7	PAV Combatics	5
Energy Rifles	4	Meditation	5

Mana Manipulation	2	Energy Pistols	3
Dissembling	2	Erethran Blade Mastery	1
Lip Reading	1		
Class Skills			
None (7 Locked)			
Spells			
Improved Minor Healing (I)			
Improved Mana Dart (I)			
Lightning Strike			
Perks			
Spirit Companion	Level 14	Prodigy (Subterfuge)	N/A

The last skill still makes me smile slightly. I'd accidentally stumbled onto it while waiting for Richard to arrive one morning. Increased perception meant I could easily see Lana's lips while she and Mikito were talking, and I might have been staring a little too much. It still made me feel strange to have gained such a skill, but it has come in use more than once when I've been dragged into the City Council deliberations.

We've managed to kill over a half dozen Boss monsters, but it never gets easier. No matter how much we level, it's never enough. Monsters slowly increase outside of our immediate vicinity, forcing us to range further and further in search of the Boss monsters, leaving us exposed. Multi-day trips are now not uncommon and the strain is beginning to wear on all of us.

As Lana said long ago, it's all about Credits. There's not enough of them, especially when the only decent source of income is monster slaying. As much as I want to be out hunting today, the first order of business is a damn City Council meeting. Thankfully, the Council has gotten its act together for the most part, though I still worry about their interaction – or lack thereof – with Roxley. We could do so much more if they'd just work with him instead of trying to make everything work around him. Unfortunately, the fact that we managed to get past the food shortage seems to have bolstered their belief that they can manage without interacting with Roxley. Frustratingly, he doesn't seem to want to push the issue either, content to rake in his taxes from the Shop and leaving us to self-govern ourselves.

If we get out in time, we've got a supply run to finish to Carcross. The town finally managed to pool enough Credits together to buy it from the System a few days ago but Shop supplies still have to come through Whitehorse. At least until they save enough to purchase permanent Shop access in the town itself.

Walking out of my room, I nod to my party as we gather around the kitchen table, as is our custom. Bacon, eggs and pancakes in large quantities litter the table – a side effect of our increased constitution is an increased calorie consumption. Even now, with food supplies stabilized, I notice most combat classers don't eat in the cafeteria. Putting away as much food as we do gets more than one dirty look. Flashing the team a quick smile, I take a moment to review their Status Bars.

Mikito Sato (Level 30 Samurai)
HP: 470/470

Richard Pearson (Level 27 Beast tamer)
HP: 210 / 210

Lana Pearson (Level 25 Beast tamer)
HP: 230/230

Rachel Martin (Level 26 Mage)

HP: 220/220

We've slowed down significantly in terms of gaining Levels - our other responsibilities and the need to actually work on our skills means we aren't fighting as much as we could be. It doesn't help that we barely get any experience from fighting monsters around Whitehorse anymore - it's only creatures in higher zones that are worth anything. On the other hand, we did get Lana to come out on a few hunting trips with us which has resulted in small increases in her level. Richard found the trick to that one by pointing out that her pets were fast becoming pudgy little creatures through lack of proper exercise.

Fighting at higher levels has required a change in tactics and gears though. All of my party members are now clad in real armor, lightweight bodysuits like the one I wear, but with even more armor plating. It doesn't hinder their movements and gives them a layer of added protection with the goal of getting them even better armor eventually. So far, Mikito has refused to buy a helmet like the other two, saying it restricts her field of vision too much.

Breakfast is an efficient, if friendly affair, conversation held to the minimum, as we get ready for our days. Lana is fast becoming a player in the local scene, though so far, her presence on the City Council has not been requested. I still can't pin down if she's happy or upset by this, but as she manages both my residence, her loan business and the pooled resources of the group, she has significant say in the city anyway.

We take our trucks and Sabre into town via Alsek and Lewes, the trip giving us full view of the school and the suburbs. In the last month, the houses near ours have started acquiring residents even though we're not in the most convenient location. I guess Lana's ranging pets help keep the overall incident of random spawnings down. Each ranch style residence is packed, anywhere from twelve to fifteen people living in each house, but they are the lucky ones. With the municipal water system back in play, the residences have basic hygiene facilities and are significantly less crowded than the schools. At night, volunteers keep an eye out for more spawnings in shifts, a post-apocalyptic neighborhood watch.

The unlucky or unmotivated remainder still live on the school grounds, under guard by volunteer fighters and Roxley's men, cramped in classrooms, hallways, gyms and offices. Mana-fueled stoves have been supplied to the main cook areas, though individual camp stoves can still be seen in use on occasion.

As we cross the bridge, the work on the park-turned-farm ahead of us continues. The first Mana-fueled harvest has already been taken in and the next crop has been started, the farmers weeding and watering. As we drive by, I can see smiles of joy crossing more than one face on the workers. Everything grows faster and more aggressively under the System and the last harvest was amazing. In fact, as I understand it, they expect an even better harvest next time.

Pulling up to the building that the City Council has taken over right opposite Roxley's building, I watch as Mikito and Richard clamber out of the truck. Rachel shakes her head, detouring to spend some time window-shopping at the Shop as she's not invited, already pulling a cigarette from her pocket. From the number of vehicles outside, it looks like we're one of the last to arrive. Luckily, most people aren't particularly bothered by things like that anymore – after all, most time-keeping devices have gone on a fritz. Inside, we move to our customary seats and I put my feet on the board table, half-closing my eyes as Richard and Mikito move to mingle. Even hindered by her incomplete English, Mikito's still more of a social butterfly than I am.

Underneath half-lidded eyes, I read lips, flicking from conversation to conversation as I dismiss idle gossip and pleasantries, my lips twisting in a half-smile. Yeah, I might not want to be here but there's no reason I can't learn something. This time around, I learn nothing of import before Fred and his entourage enters to bring the meeting to order.

***

"In conclusion, food stores continue to hover at the 2-day mark. While the hunters have been able to bring in higher number of animals due to their level increases, many of these animals are not as suitable for mass cooking. As per the Council's decision, we have canned and stored a fifth of the most recent harvest, which will provide a small vegetable surplus during the winter months, but our projections show that we will need to purchase a minimum of 8,000 Credits worth of supplements. I again must request that the Council earmark these funds," Battleaxe – Miranda Lafollet pronounces.

Fred thanks her for her presentation, pushing her request to another budget specific meeting while we continue the updates. The next Minion is shorter as he's not only purchased the ability to, but spent the time learning, how to manipulate the System screens to send information direct to us. He instead just highlights the information we need on the buildings. I tune him out and not just because he's nasally – I have learnt most of this in much more detail speaking with Roxley directly. We've purchased just over 30% of the land in Whitehorse as a group, with the parks-gardens and the community gardens taking up a major portion of that.

"Once again, I must insist that we purchase and upgrade the dam. We've been inspecting the dam for potential failures and while the spillway and emergency releases continue to function as designed, the potential for damage is significant. In addition, purchasing the Mana engine and upgrades required would provide us a consistent energy source which will be important during the winter," Minion concludes and I have to admit, he has a point.

Nic taps at his screen for a moment and then with a frustrated sigh, swipes it away and leans forward, "For those of us who weren't here, how much is that going to set us back?"

"350,000 Credits," drawls one of the other councilors – Norman Blockwell. He doesn't speak often, but when he does, most people listen. Nic chokes at the number, eyes widening further as Norman continues, "Just for the structure."

Fred raps his hand on the table, stopping any further discussion and nods to Jim. Jim stands, looks around and says, "We've got nearly three hundred hunters now, about half of them on rotating guard duty. Roxley has half of those on his payroll keeping an eye on the roadways. Two thirds of my group are in the low-teens in levels, the rest below that except for my three strike groups who are above level 20. 'Course that doesn't include the Circle, John's Group or the Brothers of the Wolf."

The Brothers grin and I swear, the two kids who represent them almost look like they are about to howl. Kid is the right term too since the entire group is in their late teens. I'm both extremely proud of the kids and rather perturbed at their inclusion – they are our first true success of the babysitting program but they are still kids. They've been throwing every Credit they've made into upgrading their equipment and themselves, which didn't sit well with Fred. So, he got them to contribute to the city by bribing them with a seat on the table.

The conversation drones on, going on about less important subjects. Non-combat characters are working on their levels and skills quite well and the stuff they've been producing has actually started getting good enough that our combat classers will use them directly. It's helping to keep some of the Credits we make in the local economy.

I tap my fingers on the table, trying to distract myself as they drone on and on. Fuck, but I hate this shit.

"And that is everything on the agenda," Fred smiles at all of us. "Great job everybody."

Thank god…

"The Raven's Circle would like to bring an expedition to Dawson City to the table again," Luthien speaks, flashing a smile at everyone around the table and I do my best to suppress a groan. An elbow by Richard to my side tells me I am not as successful as I thought. "Dawson City is the most likely location in the Yukon for a large group of survivors. We have abandoned them without access to the Shop for over a month now. There have been no supplies, no survivors who have traveled from there. If we are to help them, it has to be soon."

Luthien leans forward, her voice urgent with need, "The Circle is willing to risk the journey, but we can't do it alone. We need more volunteers, more supplies, more help. Are you willing to abandon them to their fate?"

When she finishes, the room erupts in discussion. I groan, burying my head in my hands as everyone has something to say. Fuck me sideways, we're not getting out of this room for hours.

***

My guess is just about correct as it's well past lunch before we finally exit the room. The Council is deadlocked, our resources spread thin but the call of a rescue tugging at heartstrings. I let Richard do the talking for us, since my

233

history with Luthien is well-known by now. Better to keep out of it, given we strongly oppose the idea. It's a 7-hour drive to Dawson City pre-System on a good day and there aren't any good days anymore.

We find Rachel sitting on the bed of her truck, working on a spell while waiting with one hand, an unlit cigarette in the other. Mikito, who snuck out the moment the Dawson City discussion broke out, is going through forms next to her. I pull a liquid meal from my inventory as I walk up, waving to our waiting passengers as I eat a quick lunch. Richard makes a face as he sees what I'm doing but does the same, rapping on the truck to get Rachel's attention. Where there's space, the trucks are loaded with non-System supplies, mostly excess food and clothing, though the vast majority of the supply run lie in the body of the passengers that join us. Using the System's trans-dimensional inventory option makes supplying the town significantly simpler than before. No more giant trucks making daily trips. Of course, it comes with the added danger of losing all the inventory stored if the individual dies, which is why they hire us.

"Constable," I nod to Gadsby who is engrossed in his conversation with fellow ex-RCMP member, Amelia. Gadsby has gone down the cybernetic route, a chrome left arm replacing a damaged limb rather than regenerating it and I have to admit, the look suits him. As I come close, they fall silent though what I lip-read is intriguing.

"... *not just me, Fred tried to convince Kevin and at last three others.*"

Gadsby smiles at me, offering his hand as I straddle Sabre. Outside of the party, I've been able to keep her full abilities a secret, at least as far as I know. You never know when having your personal mecha in your back pocket would be useful. "Good to have you on this run. Something was moving around Archer Lane, something about 30 feet long and blue. Looked like a weird lizard, snake hybrid with a horn coming out of its head. Gave us the shivers from the glimpses we saw."

I glance over to my team, Richard is already in the driver's seat and Mikito has taken her preferred place in the back with the huskies and his most recent acquisition, a foot-long pet turtle. Yeah, someone's pet turtle mutated and now breathes fire and Richard just had to tame it when we found it on one of our rescue runs. In the other truck, Rachel sits behind the wheel as one of Gadsby's men climbs in to play shotgun.

"We can handle it," I assure him and roll my neck in my helmet. I touch the radio for a moment and speak to everyone, "Usual routine everybody. I'll ride ahead, Richard you're next, then the trucks from Carcross. Rachel, you bring up the rear. We run when we can, we fight when we have to. I make the calls. Ali's in charge if I can't, then Mikito, Richard, Gadsby and Rachel. If we're all dead, the rest of you are fucked."

"Real inspiring boy-o," smirks Ali as he spins next to me in all his 2-foot glory. He gets a few snorts of laughter at his comments, which of course makes him preen. Unfortunately, a side effect of my increased levels is Ali's growing ability to interact with the world. He can stay visible without effort now and with a push, even physically affect the world. He's also got very, very limited access to his Affinity, which thus far he's mostly been using to play practical jokes with. Making a person blind after they get hit on the head in the middle of the fight is not funny, no matter how hard you laugh. Asshole.

Once I get everyone's acknowledgement, we roll out.

***

The trip to Carcross is pretty quiet at first. Regular hunting by Jim's teams have reduced the number of hostile monsters near the city significantly, so for the first 30 minutes, the drive is almost peaceful. When we hit the Cutoff, we make the customary stop-off at the fort to switch control around to give his people a little experience boost before I take it back.

The Hakarta – a race of mercenary space orcs - are still an anomaly, their original presence at the Cutoff a strange blip in the radar. It's just another thing to worry about, but since no one has attempted to take the Cutoff by force in the month I've had control of it, it's a concern for another day. Experience farming completed, I depart first to scout ahead. It's a 10-minute drive to where Gadsby's spotted his monster and I intend to take it slow.

***

Gadsby is correct, there is something in the woods. He was incorrect on the number though, there being a couple. I'm a good 300 hundred yards away, watching them through the scope in my helmet as they move around in a dip in the road. Considering the creatures have managed to fell power lines across the road in the time since Gadsby has come through, I can't decide if they are either sentient or just lucky.

Xu'dwg'hkkk Beast (Level 44)
HP: 2380/2380

Behind me, I can hear Richard pulling to a stop, the rest of the convoy a little further back. Mikito hops off the back the moment the truck stops, that disturbing smile already making an appearance. Her naginata levels against one and I nod absently, exhaling as I pull the trigger of my rifle. The flash and hit happen almost instantaneously, my target shrugging the beam off without seeming to be injured. I trigger another shot soon after with the same pitiful results but this time, I notice the way the energy seems to disperse around the skin, concentrating on the horn.

Shit. I throw myself aside a second before the creature returns fire, the shot disappearing off into the horizon due to the slight upward angle the creature has to shoot from. I drop the rifle into my inventory with practiced ease and start running to the side of the road, looking to split the two creatures' attention and take it away from Sabre. Fighting without her in mecha mode always sucks but I'm pretty sure we can handle it.

Richard spots the difficulty almost immediately and lets out a whistle, signaling Bella, Max and Shadow, the huskies, to join the fray even as the turtle – Elsa - trundles off the truck. I doubt Elsa is going to make it there in time, but she always tries. She's our heavy hitter if something charges us, though we do our best to ensure she isn't needed.

Bella and Shadow are clad in newly made bone-armor taken from a loot drop picked up by the Brothers. The entire armoring project is where Richard's funds have been focused in the last month. The bones have been shaped to fit the dogs, covering their body and the crown of their heads, gleaming a dull red. Whatever creature it was that the Brothers of the Wolf killed, it must have been a tough fight as the bones themselves are harder than steel but significantly lighter pound for pound.

Mikito is running at an angle to her target so that it can't get a good shot, occasionally switching directions. The moment it gets within 50 yards, Mikito changes direction again and sprints directly to it, activating her latest ability. A flicker of fire engulfs her and she accelerates, a fiery homing missile that slams into the creature at an angle and staggers it. She doesn't stop though, unleashing a flurry of blows with another skill that she calls the Thousand Cuts.

I don't have time to pay attention to her fight anymore since my opponent has charged up its horn again, using the leftover energy to send another sizzling blast to strike at me. This time, I don't get out of the way completely and catch a touch of it on my leg, causing muscles to clench in agony. I hit the ground and roll, crouched over with a hand splayed before me as the monster charges me with intent to gore.

A screech is all the creature has time to hear before Orel lands, smashing into the monster at an angle, throwing the creature's momentum entirely off even as claws dig into eyes. The Huskies arrive moments later, tearing into flesh and bone as the monster is distracted. Thankfully, the puppies haven't grown larger, though the constant hunting and leveling has given them new gifts. Bella bites and rips, her jaws encased in a metal that crushes through the monster's thick hide like it's nothing. Next to her, Max blurs as he jumps back to avoid a clawed foot, moving so fast that for a brief second, he almost seems to be in two places at once. Shadow is most disturbing of all, as its very shadow joins in on the attack, tearing into the monster's body and gulping down raw flesh into its dark throat. Leg recovered, I run in to join the fight, though really, I'm superfluous.

By the time Richard's animals and I are done killing our oversized lizard, Mikito is finished with hers and is cleaning her naginata, all calm and collected. I shake my head at that sight; once again deeply thankful she is on our side. I'm a jack-of-all trades with the ability to take a ton of punishment but she's just death on her feet if she can reach you.

We loot the body quickly but Ali warns us against eating the creature, one of the rare cases where eating it would be bad for us. I somehow don't think his advice includes Shadow's shadow. We shove the bodies aside and clear the road to complete the quest in Carcross. The town is as busy as it always is, walls fully built and reinforced with carefully spaced lookouts and gun posts. Inside, children play in the streets under the idle supervision of teenagers as the entire town is now a Safe Zone. You can guess how happy that made Roxley and the City Council in Whitehorse to learn, especially when people started asking to be moved there.

As we get ready to turn around after depositing the supplies, Elder Badger comes out. "John. We need a word."

***

Seated around another boardroom table with the ubiquitous bowls of meat stew and bannock, we listen to the scout's report on his findings. The room is now filled with maps, color-coded with various pins stuck through them and a giant white board with projects outlined. I glance at the maps, smiling slightly as I realize they are keeping track of which houses and subdivisions they've raided.

"Ali," I shoot a look over at my Spirit when the scout runs dry, waiting for his assessment.

"No idea boss," Ali states. "The way he reports it, it's probably a monster lair that hasn't become a dungeon yet. Leave it alone long enough though and it'll become a full dungeon."

There's more than one stifled groan, Gadsby's face drawing in a grim line.

"Ali, care to give more details on dungeons? The notes I have are rather short – 'Don't. Just don't' isn't particularly useful," I prod my Spirit for more information.

"That's pretty sound advice there boy-o," Ali points out before he flashes a pair of fingers up. "There are two kinds of dungeons really. You've got the natural ones – places where monsters congregate or just mutate into because of the extremely high Mana density. That's what it sounds like the scout found. The Canada Games Centre would be such a place if those Circle members didn't go into farm it so often. They're the easiest to deal with; normally the monsters aren't significantly more dangerous than the surrounding zone. Of course, if you leave them alone long enough, the monsters get more powerful and the Mana itself will warp the space. Always better to deal with them before they become full dungeons.

"The second are temporary dungeons. Those are dimensional holes in space connecting two high Mana areas together. Those generally aren't very stable, and don't always lead to dungeons. However, since most high Mana hot spots are in existing dungeons, it's a pretty good bet it's a dungeon behind the glowing blue portal of doom. Most smart people don't go in to those – since the locations are random, you never know what you'll find. Of course, that means there are about a hundred or so Guilds dedicated to finding and jumping down those rabbit holes," Ali spins a finger next to his head as he speaks before continuing. "Either way, temporary dungeons are bad because they start warping the areas around them as they shift the Mana flows around both locations significantly."

"Lastly, you have the System-created ones. You know how your entire world is a dumping ground for Mana for the galaxy? Well, on a smaller scale, System-created dungeons in a city work the same. Mana is drawn out from the surroundings and focused into the dungeon, forcefully speeding up mutations and breeding in the dungeon and creating occasional rifts. That reduces the total Mana flow in the city though which means that zones around the city lower too, eventually forcing bigger monsters out. System-created dungeons are weird. Since most dungeon owners are too frigging lazy to manage the day-to-day operations, they purchase dungeon cores to handle it and those cores, well, they make some truly insane decisions sometimes."

"You said two," Jason points out.

"Bite me, pimple face," Ali retorts.

"Children!" Jason's mum barks and the two fall silent, though not before Ali sticks his tongue out.

"John, I hate to ask this of you…" Andrea Badger starts and I look over at the old lady, actually look at her for once. She's tired, so very tired, and even with the rejuvenating properties of the System, she's old.

Quest Received – Clear the Caves

Clear the caves found by the scout and report back to the Council of Carcross.
Rewards: 10,000XP

I look at her and then at the group, getting nods of confirmation from everyone. Including Jason who isn't included and isn't going to be, considering the look his mum is giving me. It's one thing to take the kid out for a stroll in the woods, but another into an untested cave location against unknown monsters. I'm not that irresponsible.

Also, his mum scares me.

***

At night, we break up to catch some rest. Orel is sent off with a note to let Lana know that we're staying the night and we quickly set-up a large tent to crash in our usual spot near the river. The eagle disturbs me - nothing outwardly has changed but I could swear it's getting smarter.

It's not our first night away from Whitehorse and the System-purchased camping gear is much more convenient than anything we ever had as humans. Touch a button, you get a tent large enough to fit 6 normal sized humans or in our case, 4 humans and a turtle. The tent comes with internal heating controls, a humidifier and lighting.

The girls kick us out to get changed first and Richard and I manage to catch a few minutes alone. All around us, the town is quieting down as people get ready to sleep. In one stubborn corner of the camp, a small band entertains a few stragglers, but overall, most people are turning in. There might still be light in the Yukon at midnight, but most still need their eight hours sleep.

Richard waves to me, heading off to see if he can pick up another young lady and I sigh, watching him go. I guess we all have our ways of coping and he doesn't seem to be hurting anyone. Just a little secret I picked up from reading lips, but it seems he got himself chemically neutered in the Shop.

I watch him go for a moment before walking down to the water, lowering my bulk to the ground. One benefit of my high constitution and reconstructed genes – my sleep requirements have lowered drastically so unlike the others, I rarely sleep more than 4 hours a night. I can even make do on three hours without any major side effects, which leaves me a lot of time. Alone, I raise my hand and pull out my latest light reading material – *"A catalog of the types and peculiarities of System recognized classes by J.A. Ikyak"*.

Chapter 17

As we hike up the mountain early in the morning, the trucks left behind on the road, I can't help but listen to the conversations that my companions conduct as they catch up to me. Ali and Richard are talking about dungeons, delving into details that only the two of them could be interested in. Mikito and Rachel have paired up as well, the older woman taking the younger girl under her wing. It's good for Mikito, having someone she can look out for — it gives her another purpose that doesn't involve large-scale monster murder. She's not healed, not by a long shot, but the reckless abandon seems to have muted a bit since Rachel has become part of the team.

Thankfully, the map the scout drew was pretty accurate so finding the cave should be little trouble. I have to watch myself to ensure I don't outpace my friends, none of them having a Personal Assault Vehicle like me. Every once in a while, I bound ahead through the woods before stopping to wait for them to catch up, just enjoying the view while I wait. I don't worry about potential threats; Richard's pets are ranging out on all sides terrorizing the local wildlife. The only one that stays with him is Elsa, since she wouldn't be able to keep up otherwise.

Glacier capped mountains spread out around us, the snaking trail of the highway the only sign of civilization for miles. Summer in the Yukon has come and vibrant greenery assaults the eyes in the never-ending sunlight. In the distance, I spot the new lords of the sky — mutated storks, eagles and ravens are easy to recognize but scattered amongst them are more dangerous, exotic creatures that prey on them. Manticores, gryphons, a pair of snake-like creatures and in the far distance, what might be a drake.

"15 minutes," I answer Rachel's question to which she rolls her eyes.

"You said that twice before."

"15 minutes," I just reply and flash her an unseen grin, turning around and bounding up the mountain. Away from my companions, I continue to enjoy the scenery. So easy to forget how beautiful a land we live in with the constant threat of monsters and sudden, brutal death. I pop open my helmet to inhale the fresh pine scent and can't help but smile. Clear skies, beautiful scenery and mayhem in the future. What more could I ask for?

Thirty minutes later, the group finally makes it to the cave, Rachel having enough air in her lungs to curse me out further. I've been sensing the shift in Mana flows for a while, a subtle shift in the way the world now works. No surprise that Rachel noticed it well before me. The cave opening itself is innocuous, carved out of the limestone by glacier water and still wet. Shining a light attached to my arm via Sabre into the opening gives us little additional information, just a gaping maw of darkness that sends shivers through my body.

"You should put a few more points in Constitution," Mikito says while looking pointedly at the pair. "Also, stop smoking."

"Yes mum," Rachel answers before pulling out a cigarette.

"Ali, scout it out?" I gesture to the cave entrance, looking at the foreboding darkness with a grimace.

"You do know I can't see in the dark, right?" Ali raises his hand and waves it at the entrance, staring before he finally answers. "I'm not picking anyone up though, so they're definitely hiding."

Can't use the Quantum State Manipulator. It pulls me into a different plane, one that runs parallel to the world and doesn't let me interact with this world till I drop-off. That's great for running away or sneaking into areas, but when the cave is pitch black normally, it means that I'd be walking around in the dark. Night vision and Infrared on the helmet doesn't really help either, none of those cross the dimensional planes properly unlike normal light. No, I don't get why it's that way. Ali tried explaining it once, but the moment he started pulling out charts and equations I decided I didn't really need to know.

"Fine. Once Richard and Rachel get their breath back, we're going in all together. Usual formation - Ali in front, me, Mikito, Rachel then Richard. Richard – keep Elsa with you. We've got no clue about the size of the cave, so it's your call on the Huskies. Might be better to keep them all out here."

Richard nods at my words, pursing his lips in thought. The increased size of the Huskies is very advantageous in combat, but it does mean they find maneuvering in tight confines more difficult. Going into the cave with a single pony-sized puppy is going to be tough enough, three might be a bit much. I watch him silently debate his options before setting Bella and Max to guard and bringing Shadow along. Fair enough, I can deal with that.

I draw a deep breath once they are all ready, nodding to Ali and we step in. As we head in, the idle chitchat falls away and we all focus on moving as silently as possible. We're veterans of the apocalypse now, used to exploring our new world and killing the things that object, even if we do dumb things like check out monster lairs without backup. Unfortunately, calculated risk is the name of the game.

Ali floats ahead of us, glowing, as light from his body fills the cave as he taps into his Affinity. Behind him, I use secondary lights built into Sabre to provide additional illumination. At the back, both Rachel and Richard fish out chemical light sticks, tossing them along our path as we walk while Shadow ranges behind, marking his new territory with depressing regularity. A pony-sized dog comes with a pony-sized bladder.

One chamber to the next, Ali guides us without a word. Tension ratchets up as no attacks come and I find myself wanting something to come out to kill us. Another thing I never expected to be thinking.

When the attack comes, it comes from the side. The first blow smashes into Mikito, snapping her arm like a twig and throwing her into a nearby wall. I spin, sword flashing in the direction of Mikito's attacker. However, my sword passes right through the body of her assailant and I stumble slightly at the lack of impact. In that time, the creature reforms and punches me in the chest, armor deforming under pressure and my body is thrown back.

In the couple of seconds that the creature reforms properly, I catch a glimpse of it. Five feet tall, humanoid with two arms and legs, the creature is covered in purple fur, so dark it might as well be black in this dim light. Even fully reformed, shadows wreathe creatures and make it hard to see.

I hit the ground and roll, my sword falling to the ground before me. Mouth opening wide showing a double row of fangs, the creature lunges forward towards me. I'm already recalling the blade and get it up in time for the creature to impale itself on my blade, sword guard holding the creature just far enough away for it not to bite my face off.

As I begin to twist my blade, it dissipates into shadow again, disappearing entirely. I snarl, spinning around searching for it. In the corner, Mikito has staggered upright, naginata held in her uninjured hand while Richard waves his shotgun around, searching for a target as he covers our backs. Rachel is moving deeper into the cave, whispering a spell under her breath.

Ali zooms back from where he was, eyes wide as he shouts, "I can't track it!"

No shit. I figured out that much. I begin to move to my companions, chest aching from the single blow the creature landed, once again thankful for Sabre and the additional armor. Bloody hell, that thing was strong. As I near Mikito, I notice that her eyes aren't actually focusing properly, her entire body held up from sheer force of will and training.

I'm perfectly positioned to see the creature reappear behind her, a clawed hand arcing to separate her head from her body. I'm too far and too slow to do anything about it, only able to watch as Mikito's end comes in a graceful arc.

Shadow appears from the darkness, black coat and dull red bone armor blended into darkness as it rips into the creature, throwing its aim off just a little. The claw catches Mikito across the back of her neck, gouging out chunks of flesh in a spray of blood and dropping her to the ground. Even as Shadow worries the creature's leg, it begins to dissipate into the shadows again. A bad move as it screams as the husky's shadow rips into its incorporeal form with glee. Our attacker shimmers for a brief moment, then its corpse re-emerges into the light before us.

Shadow Aspected Crilik Shifter (Level 36)

HP: 0/370

I barely glance at the body as I finally reach Mikito, casting my only Healing spell immediately. Her voice reaching a crescendo, a flash of green originating from Rachel reaches out and illuminates the cave and three more of the creatures, who have been attracted to the noise on the opposite side of her.

Nature's Blessing Received

Effect: Increases regeneration rate by 23%

I stare at Mikito's still body, a hand already pulling a bandage from the inventory and slapping it across the open wound. The bandage spreads on impact, the pseudo-science mixture of human stem cells, Mana-infused plant webbing and high tech nanites working to stem the bleeding and fix the tear and failing. The flowing blood lessens but it doesn't stop. As I recall the three figures coming for us, the decision is easy. "Out!"

Richard nods, firing his modified, high-tech shotgun at where one of the creatures is. Light flashes as the shell arcs through the air, thankfully the firing itself is mostly quiet but the shell does no damage. Richard growls in annoyance, ratcheting a different shell as Elsa, laid down by his feet, trundles forward and opens her mouth. Fire erupts in a small, focused stream, which she plays across the entrance, drawing ragged screams from our assailants and filling the cave with heat and the smell of burnt guano and fur.

Ali spins around in the center of the room, eyes narrowing and his lips thinning as the glow surrounding him increases and increases again. Motes of light begin to break away from his body, floating through the room and lighting it up further, an intense look of concentration on the little Spirits olive face. In the light, the Crilik Shifters lose the cover of their shadows and are forced to materialize where Richard is able to shoot them. Dim fires from Elsa's original attack glow, the turtle breathing deeply as it recovers.

Spell cast, Rachel begins another, gesturing with her hands to pull earth from the ground to create temporary walls. All of this happens in moments, moments that I take to scoop up Mikito and bolt for the exit. A part of my mind idly notes that even gravely injured as she is, she has not lost grip of her naginata. Running, I notice my heal spell has come off cooldown and I cast it again, praying that it's enough.

I have to trust my friends to get out without my help even as the howls of more monsters joining the fight erupt behind me. I'm the only one who can save Mikito and I can't heal her and fight at the same time. Not when a single one of those monsters did this to us. I send a silent prayer that Richard and Rachel make it out just before I burst into the light.

***

Come on, come on, come on. I chant the words in my mind, a hand on Mikito's body as I heal her whenever I can do so. Such a useless spell, it barely edges her health up each time I use it and she's still losing blood, her health plummeting each second but I think, I hope, that I'm slowing down the bleeding. It's all I have right now though and when all you have is a hammer, everything looks like a nail. I'm hammering away as hard as I can while waiting for the rest of my companions to make it out.

A subjective hour later, I finally spot Rachel as she exits, clutching Elsa in her arms. A few moments later, Richard and then Shadow come into view, Richard moving backwards and sweeping his shotgun in front of him in practiced arcs. Nothing comes out of the shadows after him and he makes it all the way out into the sunshine. Only one person left...

"Where's Ali?" I ask the two as they reform around me, Rachel flicking her hands outwards to complete a spell. This time, vegetation bursts from the ground and encircles the entrance and I know the spell - Grasping Vines. I relax slightly when they appear, knowing that anything coming out now is going to be grabbed and held by the vines. At least until the Mana that Rachel imbued in the vines give out in a few hours.

"He disappeared a couple of minutes after you left John," Richard looks at me, concern etching his face. "One second he was all lit-up and backing the creatures off and then next, he just compressed and disappeared."

I blink, dumbfounded. No. There's no way Ali could die. He wasn't real, he was a Spirit. He couldn't be dead...

"John?" Rachel pushes me and I look up at her, realizing she's been calling my name for a bit. "Have you checked your Companion tab? Maybe he was just banished."

"Banished?" I blink at her, my mind trying to comprehend what she said. Finally, I nod slightly, grasping at the straw. Right. Companion tab. "Ummm…"

"You don't know how to access it?" Richard sounds incredulous, looking away from the cave again to stare at me.

"Ali normally handles that," I reply sheepishly.

"Just think about opening the Companion tab. Same with the Status Screen," Richard explains, looking down at Mikito. "After you heal her?"

Quickly, I bend down to cast another heal on Mikito, whispering an apology that she can't hear. The wound around her throat looks a lot better, no longer leaking blood around the bandage and her arm is no longer broken. She's probably out of the critical zone for now.

Following Richard's directions, I pull out the Companion tab and breathe a sigh of relief as it indicates that my Spirit Companion is banished currently. My eyes pop out a little bit at the cost of bringing him back though.

"He's fine. I don't have the Mana to recall him, but he's fine," I report to the two and some tension eases from their postures. I look back to the cave and frown. "Those things going to come out?"

"Not likely. They died real easy while they were lit up, but there's a bunch of them in there. I don't think they do well in the light," Rachel answers as she fumbles out a cigarette, only the shaking of her fingers showing how close things must have been.

"Right, well, let's get out of here anyway. Richard, we'll need the dogs to check for danger since Ali isn't here. Rachel, you good with playing rear guard?" I gesture down to Mikito to indicate my role in all this and after getting confirming nods, we hurry out of there. No reason to push our luck by hanging out.

***

"Crilik Shifters you say?" Gadsby replies, tapping metallic fingers on the table and frowning. I nod in confirmation and he grimaces, looking over at our unconscious party member. "They did that to her eh?"

I nod again in confirmation and the faces arrayed before me draw tight in concern. The members of the Council were all powerful with the exception of Elder Badger, the front-line team for the entirety of Carcross. Unfortunately, due to the concentration of strength in the Council, the rest of the combatants in Carcross were actually at a lower average level than what we saw among the dedicated hunters in Whitehorse.

"Don't worry, we'll finish the job," I tell them and they look up, surprise etched on their face. Once again, they look at Mikito and I just smile back at them confidently.

"If you are sure John," Andrea Badger says and I nod firmly.

"We'll need a few days to prepare, maybe more if what we need to buy is too expensive. If you don't mind, we'll stay overnight and let Mikito rest before we go back to Whitehorse."

Receiving their assent, I push back from the table as Richard meets my eyes, indicating he wants to talk. We head out, Rachel trailing along behind. Out of earshot, they wait for my explanation.

"It's okay. I have a plan," I grin at them and at their doubtful expressions, continue. "Give me a couple of days and I'll explain. Trust me, will you?"

Rachel's eyes narrow and Richard just snorts before letting the topic go.

***

"Jason," I nod to the man as I sit, legs propped up on a table as I read through my books. Jason frowns, glancing at the book briefly before taking a seat next to me. Mikito in the corner continues to sleep. Richard and Rachel have gone out to mingle with the others for the moment. My turn to keep an eye on sleeping beauty.

"John, about the cave," Jason starts and I sigh, waving the window away. I'm almost ready to pull Ali back but I'm tempted to let him stew there for a little longer. It's been nice and quiet without him.

"Not going to happen kid," I point a finger at him and continue. "Your mum would kill me."

Jason sighs and moves a hand to push non-existent glasses up his face before faltering, "She won't let me do anything without her around. If it wasn't for me, they wouldn't understand half this shit."

I nod in agreement at his words, letting the kid rant for a moment. He has a point, his knowledge of games and game mechanics certainly saved their asses early on.

Slumping in his chair, Jason looks me over again before saying, "I've been meaning to ask – what kind of build are you going for?"

"Huh?" I stare at the boy, waggling my finger for him to elaborate. Like talking to Ali.

"Build – you know, what are you trying to achieve? At first, I thought it was an Assassin-Rogue kind of thing, especially after our walk in the forest. But Rachel tells me you do a lot of fighting up front and actually get kicked around a lot and you've got that Healing spell, so I'm thinking Paladin-Tank now. On the other hand, she says you've been studying magic too," Jason says.

"Ah…" I tilt my head, looking him over once more, noting the still scrawny arms, the lack of a chest and the way he pulls himself in slightly. I recall the pitiful health score his Status bar had. Jason looks confused when I rub my forehead. "Let me guess. You're min-maxing your character right, putting all your points into Intelligence for a bigger Mana pool, some points into Willpower to control spells more finely and some into Perception to help cast them?"

Jason nods at that, puffing up proudly and I reach out and smack him on the top of his head very, very lightly. He staggers from the blow and I make a note to reduce strength even further the next time I feel the urge to do that, nostrils flaring as I cut him off by asking, "How much health did I take off you?"

"What?"

"Health, how much?"

"Ummm… 5 points?" Jason continues to rub his head, frowning.

"I was trying really hard not to hurt you and that's how much I did. And that's a significant portion for you," I point over to Mikito, continuing. "The creature that attacked us? The Shifter did more damage in one hit than you have life. You'd be so much red paste if you were in the cave with us."

Jason nods at the words, face set in stubborn refusal to get my point so far.

"What happens when you die in your games?" When silence greets my question, I prod him again with the same question.

"You restart," Jason finally relents and answers me.

"Yeah, no restart here. You can't min-max your stats in real life, Jason, not if you want to survive. There's no second chance here. If you want my guess why your mum isn't letting you out, it's because she knows you haven't gotten that into your head yet. Put your points into Constitution, build up some Strength and Agility. Hell, buy it from the Shop if you have to, but right now, you're a stiff breeze away from dying."

"What about you then? You throw yourself into crazy, stupid situations all the time," Jason retorts.

"Yeah, I do. We do," I correct myself after a moment. "Crazy and stupid is the kind of world we live in these days. You think I want to be out there? I just don't have a choice. If I stop, if I slow down, people die. If we don't keep pushing back the monsters, they keep building up and then we'll have a monster horde.

I draw a deep breath, pushing against the anger that rushes in. Damn kid. "Anyway, I didn't say don't do it, just don't treat it like a game. This world needs people like you, Jason, more than ever."

"So, go around white knighting because that's the right thing to do?" Jason shoots back, a teenager's cynicism in his voice.

"No. Just the correct thing," I say.

My reply just confuses the kid, which it should. How do you explain that's there's a difference between right and correct – that we make so many distinctions between good and bad, right and wrong but fail to see that some things just are. When the world just is, the choice stops being about right or wrong but about deciding to do the correct thing or not in a situation. It's a hard concept to grasp, and it's not as if I was ever good at it myself. I still struggle daily with the fact that I'm not hiding away at home but I've tried that and it never ends well.

Still, confusing him is enough to make Jason stop pushing back for a moment and I can see him slowly processing everything else we've spoken about. I can't help but wonder if I've done any good here though. Jason acted like this was a game because it was easier than the reality of our situation – a coping mechanism that helped him and his mum and Carcross survive. Taking it away might do more harm than good. I watch him sit in silence for a while and I push my doubts away, holding to the only truth that I know. What is, is.

***

Our quiet contemplation is disturbed by groaning from the corner as Mikito finally wakes. I am on my feet in a second and crossing over with a glass of water as I help her up. When her eyes finally open, she looks around in a panic for her weapon before relaxing at seeing it propped up next to her. She reaches for the weapon first, putting it right next to her before taking the proffered water.

"Welcome back, Mikito," I say. Behind, Jason takes it as his cue to leave.

Mikito drinks the water in silence, her head buried under the falls of her hair. After the Spiders, she just cut it short to get it out of the way but there's still enough to hide her. She stays in that position, head bent and slowly my ears pick up the sound of snuffling and I realize she's crying.

"Mikito?" I ask, moving to reach out to her and stopping, recalling she does not touch.

"So, close," she sobs again and pulls her knees up to her body, naginata cradled between her body as the sobs grow in intensity. I say nothing, just lending my support as she works through it. When she is ready, she sits up though she refuses to look at me. "Thank you."

"No need," I reply and then, deciding there is nothing to lose I ask, "Do you want to talk about it?"

She shakes her head and I sigh, leaning back on my heels to watch the tiny woman.

"I should be dead. Ken, he died for me. I asked to come. Here. We wanted a baby, a good luck baby. Good fortune. When System came, I got class. He gave up his for this." I look to the hand that clutches the naginata in a death grip and stay silent, letting her continue. "Ken knew my sofu, grandfather, trained me. Said I had to survive.

"I couldn't save him."

The last words are stark, a condemnation. I exhale, her raw grief a reminder of my own, "None of us can."

She looks up at me then, just a brief glance and then she looks down once more. "Failures. All of us."

I nod and we fall into silence for a time, caught up in our own dark thoughts. After a while, Mikito speaks softly, "Not easy. Hurts all the time. But, I do better."

I acknowledge her words with a smile and then stand, offering her a hand up which she hesitantly takes. "Come on, let's get some food into you. All that healing must have left you famished."

Mikito tilts her head at the last word and I quickly explain it as we leave to hunt down some food. And dessert. Seems today was the day of hard talks.

***

Hours later, when I'm alone, I stand on one unguarded corner of the wall.

Do You Wish to Resummon Your Spirit Companion?
Cost: 500 Mana
(Y/N)

I select the Yes mentally and I feel my Mana rush out of me in a wave, sending shivers through my body as the Mana collects to my left. It spins in a circle, glowing brighter and brighter before Ali returns, tapping his foot.

"You couldn't have waited another hour? I was just about done with America's Top Model, Season 5!" Ali grumbles, shaking his head.

"Fine, one second." I mentally select the Companion tab again, noting the option to banish him. It stays open for a brief second before it closes as Ali waves his hand up and down frantically.

"No, no, no. It's fine, it's fine. Tyra Banks will always be there," Ali comments quickly and spins around me, eyes unfocusing for a moment. "You guys all made it eh?"

"Yeah, we did," I add. "Thanks. I take it your little spell was too much for you eh?"

Ali grimaces and nods. "So, what are we going to do about the cave? Time to call it a day?"

"No. We'll be going back. I have a plan," I reply and watch as Ali dramatically shivers as I say those words. Yeah, yeah, laugh it up asshole. I missed you too.

"Come on, we've got a lot talk about," I gesture him over while the rest of my companions sleep. Truth be told, I have less of a plan and more of a concept and I'll need a lot more information to make this work. That starts with Ali.

Chapter 18

The next morning, the team is up by 7am. I guess sleep wasn't easy either, no matter how comfortable the bed is. I'd spent the night walking the perimeter before crashing, listening to the guards talk and chatting with Ali about what I intended to do. I didn't pick up much useful in terms of gossip, just low-level dissatisfaction with the ban on alcohol and the fast depleting stocks of cigarettes. If I was inclined to play trader or smuggler, carrying both on my regular runs would make me a decent profit. Instead, I just make note to look into the cost of a pack of cigarettes in the store. You never know when good bribe material might come in handy.

"Elder," I tilt my head to the old woman as she comes up to see us off. As late as I went to bed, she had been up later, catching up with paperwork and the toll is showing. Enhanced constitution or not, the woman needs rest. Unfortunately, it's not my place to say. "Need anything?"

She shakes her head, a tired smile crossing her face. "No, just seeing you off. You children be careful alright? It'll be lonely without you."

I smile politely, knowing what she means. The Circle is too busy grinding, venturing into more and more dangerous zones on the days they aren't helping out in Whitehorse. The Brotherhood has swung by Carcross once and promptly never returned. From what I hear, Ms. Badger took them to task for their lack of community spirit, which has resulted in them not returning. Guess teenagers, given a sense of power and freedom, aren't particularly fond of being told off like children. Then again, they joined the Whitehorse Council and are finally helping out with leveling the population, so maybe some good came of it. Either case, we're the only high-powered group that regularly makes trips in. Jim and his people swing by when they can, but they rarely have time with the food situation being what it is.

Leaving Carcross this time takes longer than normal. First, we have to pry the kids - and the not-so-suffering teenagers tasked with watching them - off the backs of the puppies, which always takes a while. Then we have to deal with the verbal fight that breaks out among the passengers who now want to move to Whitehorse over who gets to go first. Initially, when the supply runs started, we had a few decide they'd prefer living in the big city. Then, we had a small flow of people going the other way, when word got out that Carcross was an actual Safe Zone in its entirety. Now, word of the raid bosses has spread and people are running again, looking for safety in numbers.

Once all that is settled, we are finally ready to roll out, though more than one passenger complains about being stuffed amongst the puppies. Mikito just glares at them till they shut up as she's relegated to riding behind me today. Finally organized, we roll out.

***

Being overburdened with hanger-ons means we have to move slower, which means more chance encounters in the wilderness. Twice, we have to stop to deal with monsters that get too close for comfort. The first time, we have to keep Richard and company back since our opponents throw acid from their bodies. This time, Mikito even looks at me for acknowledgement before running into the middle of the pack while I work my rifle from a ditch in the side of the road. Mikito quite literally dances through the acid splashes, blade held together as she blurs at a dead sprint that'd make Usain Bolt look like a toddler. Once again, I can't help but wish for access to my Class Skills. The good news is that the creatures are squishy and when Mikito gets in between them, the fight is all but over. She's moving too fast for me to take a shot without the risk of hitting her, so I just sit back and leave her to it.

Our second run in is with a Troll and this time round, we're told to back off as Richard stalks out with the puppies in tow. What happens next is what I assume bear baiting looks like, with the occasional addition of a shotgun blast to the face. The fight is brutal with the puppies ripping chunks off the Troll faster than it can heal. Richard just smiles grimly as the puppies work. I guess we all have some unresolved issues.

Our passengers mostly cower and hide, though a few of the braver souls keep watch with their guns. I listen to one throw up and another sniff at the brutality, muttering about us being savages. That latter makes me want to walk over and bitch-slap the stupid blonde, but I breathe deeply and shove the anger down again.

As we close in on Whitehorse, Ali floats back to me and waggles his fingers in his sign for 'slow-down'. I do so, wondering what he picked up.

"So, John. You like Roxley right?" I nod. "And Xev's pretty cool too, even if it's a bit creepy, right?" I nod again. 'It' because Xev's reproduction method really, really doesn't come even close to the human dynamics.

"Ali…." I begin out loud so Mikito can listen in to both sides of this conversation.

"Right, so there's a group of non-human sentients at the gate in Whitehorse. They're here on invitation, so don't shoot them," Ali finishes and watches me for my reaction. I slow down even more, knowing Richard will follow suit once he catches up. Shit, non-human guests?

"They're here to settle under the invitation that Roxley set-up in the System," Ali explains and grimaces. "I'm guessing it's not going overly well with your people since there's quite a crowd of humans waiting for them."

"Shit," I frown and pull to a stop, well out of sight of the gate. I'm trying to work out my feelings about this, mostly, it's variations of 'oh shit'.

When the others catch up, I have Ali quickly explain the situation.

"What is he doing inviting people into our city?" Richard throws his hands up, and around us, the dogs bristle in reaction to his emotions.

"Pretty sure he thinks it's his city," I point out and shrug under Richard's glare. Just telling the truth there.

"Fuck. And you're okay with this?" Richard stares at me and at his question, both Rachel and Mikito turn their gazes on me. Mikito has gotten off the bike and is facing away from us, watching the treeline but at those words turns back to us.

"I sort-of figured we'd have alien guests sooner or later, though I'll admit, this is a bit earlier than I expected." Ever since Ali explained the reason for our world, it made sense that we'd get visitors. I just didn't really expect them till after the integration was complete, but I guess some people are more willing to jump than others.

Richard growls and points to Mikito, asking next; "And you?"

She considers, eyes tightening and then looking at her polearm before down again. At last, she looks at me and then back to Richard before she speaks, "I promised better. Lead, I follow."

"If you're going to ask me next, I don't care. Not as if anyone ever asks when they settle here anyway," Rachel speaks up, arms crossed over her body.

Richard opens his mouth and then shuts it, looking at Rachel and then the rest of us. Max moves over to Richard and he begins to stroke the dog on the head, the action visibly calming him down. "I'm not happy about this," he states.

"Yeah, I'm pretty sure most people aren't. Not as if we have a choice though," I point out and he nods at that. "So, overall we're good with this.

Question is, what do we want to do? We can head around, maybe skip around..."

"At this rate, it looks like someone might get shot," Ali says.

"What happens then?" I say.

"Then bad things happen. They are significantly higher level than the guards and if they get pushed..." Ali adds.

"Fuck..." I shake my head and look at the others. "Do we step in?"

Mikito doesn't answer, already having turned away to watch the treeline. Rachel just nods, and Richard grimaces a lot before giving a curt nod. Yeah, he's not happy. I roll my neck, trying to get the tension out that has suddenly appeared.

"Let's do this," I grumble and start the bike. I blink and Mikito's on the bike next to me, straddling again and I shake my head. Damn but that woman can move. "Ali, do you have anything useful to add?"

"Always. So, first thing – they're called Yerick. Or that's the closest you'll get anyway. They were integrated into the System 2,000 years ago and their planet is nearly on the opposite side of the Council's lands. Unfortunately, they weren't very advanced when they were integrated like you humans, so they've mostly been relegated to being the lowest class of workers – Adventurers," Ali begins talking, looking ahead to where we are and information only he can see. "Looks like they're going to be a mix though, crafters and Adventurers with some kids."

I nod, taking the curves down the hill as we begin to approach the city proper. I tap my helmet, letting it retract and feeling the wind on my hair. Damn but I need a haircut.

"One last thing, you guys are probably just going to call them minotaurs," Ali says.

Considering he drops that note a second before I finally catch sight of the scene, I make a mental note to kick his ass. A bit of warning would help – seeing a crowd of thirty or so bull-headed, horned creatures with the ripped, humanoid bodies carrying rifles and swords is enough to give me a shiver. The Yerick are facing the twelve-foot reinforced concrete wall, standing in a group right in front of the gates and watching the guards who are posted there warily. The wall itself is really just an extra high vantage point, the Mana shield behind it is the real source of defense. Physical defenses like walls really only work against the most basic of creatures, what with most monsters able to punch their way through concrete without effort.

On closer inspection, I note that Roxley's guards are between the minotaurs and the wall and are facing in to the human guards. Behind the wall, I can hear the unruly crowd that Ali mentioned, though so far, no one has started a chant.

The minotaurs are extremely well trained, the moment I come around the corner, one of their lookouts at the back barks a warning and suddenly we've got guns being raised and swords drawn. Even as I hit the brakes, Mikito is hopping off and running to the side of me with naginata held next to her. Behind the wall I can see humans beginning to aim their guns. All it's going to take is a spark and everyone's going to start shooting.

Shit!

"STOP!" The shouted command washes over all of us and for a brief moment, my body locks up. I shove against the mental command, forcing past it and feel it give way beneath my will.

Mental Influence Resisted

All around me, I see people frozen in mid-motion. I know that voice though and I get off the bike, leaving my weapon alone. As I move, I note that I'm not the only one able to resist the command.

Capstan Ulrick (Level 7 Yerick Flame Warrior, First Fist)
HP: 2100/2100

My eyes bulge out slightly when I spot his health. Christ-on-a-pogo stick. Capstan towers over even his own people by a good foot, putting his total height including horns at just under ten feet. He's holding a rifle in one hand that by human terms would be a crew-mounted weapon with three barrels on it in gleaming black, and on his back is an axe. He's wearing a simple jumpsuit like us but I do note the variable shield pack on his hip. The Yerick's eyes glow red and nostrils are flaring as it looks between me and the walls, caution so clear in its every movement that I can read it over the species barrier.

I wonder if his Level is a bug or something? In fact, why is only a quarter of the Status Bars on the minotaurs showing? I look over to Ali and realize he's frozen too by the command and I can't help but consider if I can buy Roxley's skill.

As if summoned, Roxley jumps over the wall and lands on the opposite side, startling Capstan. The minotaur is well trained though, he doesn't just start shooting, as Roxley doesn't do anything more dangerous than smooth his robes down. Capstan and I both spend a moment to stare at the pretty, pretty Elf with his marble skin, pointy ears, black hair and golden robes before we both begin to speak.

"Harglexasss Roxley," or at least that's what I hear.

"Roxley!" I stride forwards, keeping my hands well away from the pistol strapped to my thigh.

Roxley raises his hands up, forestalling our words as he turns to speak to everyone, black eyes glowing with an inner light. "The first person to shoot dies by my hand. The person who shoots after that condemns the group he is with to death as well."

Like a weight that's suddenly lifted off, I feel the pressure in my mind release. More than one individual staggers, the kids among the minotaurs bawling their eyes out though worried parents don't move to comfort them beyond a single free hand. I spot at least one guard leaning over the wall and throwing up as control is released. I can't tell what my team is doing behind me, I just hope they keep to what we agreed on.

Roxley beckons Capstan to him and as I begin to approach, he holds a finger up to me admonishing my actions. Fine. I'll let them talk. Lip-reading doesn't help either since they aren't talking English or any human language. It doesn't take them long before the two break away, Capstan walking to the Yerick and speaking to his group, while Roxley turns to us, voice like iron; "These are my guests, they will be treated as such. Harm caused to them will be as though harm is caused to me and so you'll be punished in the same way."

Oh boy. I've picked up a few things from Roxley and guest rights are pretty big in the Galactic Core. It's one of the only ways any civilized conversation can be had between such a disparate group as the Council members and so it's vigorously enforced. It's what got us into trouble in the first place - the envoy expected some minimum level of guest rights and instead, it got shot, captured and then dissected. Alive.

At Roxley's command, the gates open and his own guards move to flank and escort the Yerick in. I turn to Roxley to speak with him and he shakes his head again, mouthing 'tonight' before leaving to join the group. As the initial after-effects of his command leeches away, his more regular presence exerts himself. Even the guards who should be watching for danger are throwing quick glances at the Elf and the humans are mostly just staring at the pretty, pretty Elf. It's no wonder he doesn't make a lot of public appearances.

Fine. Tonight. Not my fault my traitorous, gluttonous stomach wonders what will be served for dinner.

***

By the time we get in, reporting in to the Council about the dungeon would be problematic at the very least. I can just guess that they'll want to drag us into an 'emergency session' which involves talking for hours in circles, so instead I get Richard and Ali to go and calm them down. Ali, because the little bugger actually has relevant information, and Richard, because he can actually charm the pants off anybody if he put his mind to it. I can see him give me his 'we're going to talk later look' but he follows my lead for now. Hopefully, Richard can keep the Council from doing anything really stupid.

Mikito and Rachel get sent off to do the same thing with the hunters that gathered at the gate attempting to bar it, with orders to ensure they don't cause trouble. Last I saw, Mikito was organizing the hunters into a spontaneous hunting party. Crude, but effective.

Me? I go shopping right after I drop Sabre off at Xev's.

The Biology of the Crilik Shifter (100 Credits)

I make the purchase and information floods into me. I'm looking for some specific details in this and it's a simple matter to locate and confirm. Great, next...

Carcross Wet Caves (#12356) Layout (25,000 Credits)

Jesus that's expensive. I wonder if it's because it's a known monster lair. I frown at the screen and the Fox sidles up to me, offering me a toothy grin. "Perhaps I can be of assistance, sir?"

Oh, I know the assistance he wants. Every single Credit that I have and without Ali here, I'm a bit leery of dealing with it. Still, no harm asking, "I need to work out the layout of this location but it costs too much to buy it."

"Ah, but we do have a significant number of mapping accessories," the Fox grins and waves his hand. "Now, you're not looking for something passive that will add to your map currently, correct? So, we must look for active options. Does the sir have a preference for biological, spiritual or artificial methods?"

"Don't care really, show me the best."

"Budget?"

I grunt, picking through my mind what I have left. I'd need at least 10,000 Credits for the rest of the equipment I have in mind, which doesn't leave me with much. Then again, I might be able to get a loan from the group, so... "Let's go with a maximum of 12,000 Credits,"

"Tight," the Fox looks displeased for a moment before it raises its hand and starts waving.

Wil-o-wisp Spirit (Modified)

This nature Spirit has been modified to accept basic commands and is able to update a map with locations it has visited.

Cost: 12,000 Credits

Hunii Dragonfly Drone (Scouting Type IV)

This dragonfly drone comes equipped with multiple visual and audio recording options and can update 3D landscaping maps.

Operating time: 2 Hours

Cost: 5,000 Credits

"Why the big difference in cost?" I enquire, staring at the two.

"The Wil-o-wisps are a contracted companion, much like Ali, and have the additional benefit of being extremely difficult to damage. The drones are more versatile but much more fragile," the Fox answers promptly.

"The wisps, are they sentient?" I can just imagine having 2 Ali's chattering at me all through the day.

"Mildly. Along the lines of a rat pet you humans have," the Fox continues. "Though I would not recommend keeping this one summoned constantly. Unlike Ali, it will drain your Mana continuously."

"There more options?"

"Of course, sir," the Fox doesn't even frown when I ask, pulling up other information. Twenty minutes later, I have to admit, he's probably picked the best options. Biological entities generally have to come back to report on what they see, not having an option to inform me directly and adding a direct connection is way too expensive and brings its own host of issues. When it comes to Spirits, anything smarter than the Wil-o-wisp ends up being too expensive and unable to map. The drones have the better array of options, but most just become variations of one another with minor changes in operating hours, structure and locomotion methods. The only other option is to upgrade Sabre herself, adding a more powerful sonar and radar mapping option, but that would use a precious hardpoint.

I make note of the two options and start digging into the shop for the tools that I'll need. Since Foxy is so useful, I let him know the outlines of the plan and we get to work, putting together my shopping cart. I'll need Ali to take a look at this later once he's free, but best to get as much done as possible.

***

When I get out of the Shop, it's mid-afternoon and there just so happens to be a group of human guards waiting outside. Considering the minotaurs are currently housed in the same building, I'm not buying the coincidence.

"Amelia," I can't help the disapproval in my voice as I stare at her and her friends. Most are guards like her, though I'm surprised that's it mostly women, especially considering the gender inequality we see among the guards and hunters in general. From the corner of my eye, I watch a pair of cats slink out behind me, sending shivers down my spine. Whitehorse isn't much of a cat town, and I'm glad. Mana warped cats are just frightening – something about the way they look at me reminds me that they are just a little way off from going completely feral.

Amelia smiles at me when she first spots me and then looks confused at my tone of voice. It takes a moment for her to clue in before she waves her hand, "No, no. Nothing like that. We're here to help. Keep an eye on things, you know."

"Ah," I nod slightly, still puzzled by the mix. Whatever, not my business. "Good I guess. Roxley's serious about the entire guest thing."

Amelia's lips twist as she continues, "Yes. We understand what it's like to be judged for being different."

I nod slightly, glad that some people have sense. I won't kill them if they don't kill us. "Manbun running class still?"

"Aiden," Amelia replies, her voice stressing the name, her tone disapproving, "is running class today, yes."

"Thanks!" I wave goodbye to her. Might as well get some training in since I've got a few hours before dinner.

***

"Breathe in and extend your arms to the heavens, open yourself to the world. Be one with it. Accept the Universe into your soul," Aiden chants as he walks around the class, guiding hands tapping and adjusting us. "Relax, let your hands fall to the earth and fall back on your heels. Stretch into downward dog. Hold and breathe. Feel the way the world moves with you."

Today's class is yoga. Aiden has a lot of methods for gaining ability in Mana manipulation - most of it cribbed from bad translations of Asian philosophy – but considering it works for him and those he teaches, I really can't complain. Much.

Mana manipulation or more specifically, progressing the skill, is all about learning to visualize that force that surrounds us and changes everything. Understanding that force is kind of like threading an elephant through a needle, not possible without significant adjustments in our worldview, though. Manbun's method is no better or worse than Rachel's envisioning of her ancestral spirits – the elephant still isn't in one piece. In some ways, it's very similar to how Ali trains me to access my Elemental Affinity of electromagnetic force, though as he is quick to point out, one is artificial, the other, natural.

So, here I am, doing warrior pose in the middle of the day trying to connect with Mana by moving. I have to admit, this particular class might not be for me, though that just might be as much due to certain lycra-clad distractions. Don't judge – I've got a much higher Constitution, streamlined genes and haven't been laid in months.

After class, most of the other students' cluster around Manbun, talking to him about how great the class was and how they felt closer to being connected. I take the moment to wipe the yoga mat down when a hand falls on my arm. I don't really think about it, just grabbing and turning, putting the arm into lock even as I stand. The soft gasp by the brunette whose arm I had grabbed is not without a little pain, so I let go.

"Sorry. Habit," I reply and at her smile, return it. Light brown hair in a ponytail, liquid brown eyes under long, curving eyelashes and a cute button nose look back up at me. I notice she doesn't step back even though I've let her go, and can't help but admire the tight stomach in the yoga top and pants ensemble she wears. She's so close to me I can smell her, a somewhat heady combination even mingled with her sweat.

"Not at all," she replies and her voice is like sweet taffy. "Did you enjoy class?"

"Truthfully, this didn't work for me. Though it is looking up," I say.

"John, isn't it?" she says.

"Yeah…" I look above her head and realize Ali isn't around, updating her Status bar for me. Damn it.

Misreading my hesitation, or at least the cause of it, she replies. "Karen."

"Well, it's nice meeting you Karen," I reply, neither one of us moving. She's so close; I can feel the heat rising off her body. Or maybe it's me that's getting hot.

"Well, John, my friends and I have to go wash up in the river. Perhaps I'll see you soon. I'm staying at Selkirk for now," she smiles slightly at me and turns, walking away but not before letting a hand trail along my chest as she does so.

"Yeah..." I blink, watching her move off to join her friends and do a surreptitious check to make sure I'm not drooling when I finish rolling up my mat.

Chapter 19

It's late by the time I get home, though I take a moment to admire the house in the evening sun. We've managed to divert a little of our funds to the house, adding a new eight-foot-tall wall with lookout towers on either end that elevate it to a good twelve-feet. While physical walls aren't the most useful things these days, even I could leap them at a standstill, it was better than nothing.

The separate garage has been purchased and turned into a workshop for automotive maintenance. Richard's taken an interest in that, working with Chris on the trucks. Unfortunately, we still have to buy Mana engines and Mana batteries from the Shop, but when Chris isn't working on our trucks, he's upgrading vehicles for others, which gives us a separate and small income stream.

Power for all this is now provided by a residential Mana engine and battery combo that lights up the house and the spotlights we have situated along the walls. Reinforced security doors and windows are now installed throughout the house too, giving us a little extra security if we are ever attacked and even the walls are upgraded to Galactic standards.

As I walk in, I can hear the voices of more of our constant guests. Since we have one of the only places with power in town, we've also become the go-to hangout location for many kids, especially since Lana looted a 72" TV for the living room. I pause at the doorway, just listening to the happy, contented voices as they chat while an episode of Firefly plays in the background. I close my eyes for a time, leaning against the doorjamb and let the noise and smell of home wash over me. I can't make their world better, can't make it what it was before, but at least, for a little bit, I can give them a place that is safe.

When I open my eyes, Lana is leaning on the staircase opposite the door, watching me with a small smile on her face. I feel my face go blank, caught for a moment but that just makes her smile wider, still not saying a word. I return her violet gaze before breaking eye contact, letting my eyes roam over the redhead's form. Images of Karen flash into mind as I compare her to Lana, finding no fault in either. Lana's dressed casual as usual, just a simple grey top and jeans which she pulls off with aplomb.

"Done?" she flashes me a mischievous look and I realize I'm looking a lot more than I should.

"Yeah…" I shake my head and she snorts, coming the rest of the way down.

"Dinner will be done in a bit but you need a shower," Lana saunters past me to the kitchen, and I swear, she puts a little extra wiggle into her hips as she does. As she leaves, she calls out behind her. "No chocolate for the kids!"

I grin, waiting for a moment for her to exit before I walk into the living room. The kids, on seeing me, crowd around and I wink at the teenagers as I pull out a handful of mini-Toblerones from my inventory and drop them into waiting hands. Good deed of the day done, I take the stairs to my place, heading around the corner to my suite. Unlike the rest of the house, nothing has changed much down here. I've barely been back to make any changes really – which sadly includes my sheets. I really need to change those sheets.

Once again making a promise to myself to get laundry done, I get into the shower, turning it all the way to freezing as images of Lana/ Karen on those sheets cross my mind again.

Once I'm done, I head to the kitchen and realize the rest of the party has finally made their way out of their respective engagements. I plop down in a seat but shake my head as Lana begins to stand up, "Got a dinner with Roxley later."

Lana just nods, sitting back down before pointing to Richard, "Carcross?"

"Right, so the City Council is perfectly happy for us to deal with the issue at Carcross. No arguments there at all, though…"

"I've got a plan, I think," I flash him another reassuring smile and Richard rolls his eyes. "Though, we need to be smarter. I know we've all got the first aid bandages already, but if things go bad again, we might need something more immediate. So, two things. We hit up Sally's and get some of her best potions for emergency use for everybody. In addition, we should just get the rest of you guys Healing spells. Rachel – maybe a more powerful one for you?"

Rachel nods, eyebrows furrowing in thought. Her buff was powerful and it tapped into her specialization, but it wasn't instantaneous or anything close to it. Richard scratches at his beard, still unused to having it and adds, "I'd like to look into some spells for myself too. Perhaps something that benefits everyone."

"Okay, well, no real rush. I've got an idea about how we're going to deal with the dungeon anyway," I continue before gesturing back to Richard. "What's the feeling about the Yerick?"

"The minotaurs?" Richard replies

"Don't," I shake my head and as he begins to bristle, I point to the hovering Ali. "He told me Orcs were waiting for me and then I got shot at by beam rifles and grenades. Nearly cost me my life. These aren't Greek legends or mindless beasts. The Yerick are a sentient race – aliens if you will. Better to name properly and think about them right."

Rachel looks startled by my words and Richard nods slightly, eyebrows crinkling as he digests that piece of information. Lana just smiles and Mikito… Mikito just keeps eating, every movement precise and contained, as always.

"As I was saying, the Yerick aren't a welcome addition. But the Council won't take any official action and are spreading the word to keep out of their way, but this entire thing is rubbing them the wrong way. Especially this declaration of the mino – the Yerick – being guests," Richard continues.

"Three days. That's how long it lasts," I point out and then look over to Ali for further clarification.

"Like I told the Council, the Yerick have three days to come to an agreement with Roxley. At the end of the time, they either leave or they become residents like you guys," Ali clarifies and I nod, filing that information away.

"Three days or not, people aren't happy with a whole community of aliens just appearing," Richard stresses.

"Happy or not, I don't think they are leaving if they are bringing children," Lana says and at Rachel's look, smiles. "Everyone is talking about it. I understand the kids are actually quite cute."

Mikito nods firmly at that and even Richard has to shrug his shoulders. Okay, maybe sending cute Yerick kids out as ambassadors might work. Maybe something for later, I shudder to think what they'd do if one of their kids got hurt. Or ours. "Rachel?"

The young lady just shrugs, looking at me and I have to repeat my question.

"What? Mikito and I rode the guys we had till they were falling over from exhaustion, then we got them up and ran them more into whatever monsters we could find. They won't be up for doing anything tonight, but..." she shrugs her shoulders again. "They didn't like Roxley and they especially didn't like that thing he did or the fact that the 'cattle' are coming to take their land."

"How bad is it?" I push her, watching her and Mikito's reactions.

"Bad. Stupid is as stupid does you know. I even heard one say Canada was for real Canadians," she almost snarls at that one, continuing. "Made sure Mikito was in range to hear that. He ended up eating dirt. A lot."

I nod and rub at my temples, thinking. Richard interrupts me before I can put together anything useful.

"You sure we are on the right side of this John? It doesn't sit right with me, letting them just come in. We've fought and bled to keep the monsters out and now, we're what, asking them to be our neighbors?" Richard says.

"What would you suggest?" I turn to the man, making sure there is no challenge in my tone.

"Well…," Richard opens his mouth and then shuts it. He's smart enough to work through the options if he thinks about it. We can't make Roxley rescind his offer, we can't fight them and even if we did, so what? The next bunch is just around the corner. As his brows furrow further, Lana reaches over and squeezes his hand and Richard huffs out. "I hate this. It feels like we're just giving up, giving up Earth and Whitehorse and just saying, it's over."

Mikito looks up, finishing chewing before she adds, "We aren't giving up. But we already failed. The world has changed."

"It might not be all bad," I point out and Richard raises an eyebrow. "We know things are going to get worse. Their leader was a Level 7 Advanced Class if I'm not mistaken," Ali nods and I continue, "so they're going to be one heck of a helping hand. Paw. Whatever."

That pronouncement just leaves the group in stunned silence for a time. A Level 7 Advanced Class puts him at around level 57 - except it doesn't work in a linear fashion that way. Each level is harder and harder to get and Advanced Class levels are even harder. I let them stew on it a bit before I turn to Lana.

"I know, John. I'll do what I can, talk to the people I know but…" Lana shrugs and I nod my head again. Don't expect miracles. Got it. Richard who seemed to have rolled with the punches of this world has gotten his pants in a twist over the Yerick. How much work is it going to be with the rest of the population?

Skill Acquired

Manipulation (Level 1)

Everyone wants their own way. You're just better at getting it than some others.

I flick a look over to Ali when the screen pops up and he raises both hands, palm up. I hate this. I really do. I'd worked so hard to stay out of this, to keep things casual and friendly in the group, a modicum of respect between all of us. I didn't want to be a leader, not really, but the world never asks what we want, it just is. I hated the pressure, the fact that I was the one who always had to be thinking, considering, planning. I just wanted to go back to my room, to hide in it but instead I've got to fight, kill, loot.

I sigh and push away from the table, standing up. "I've got to go. We'll need to get the spells and gear from the Shop tomorrow. Xev will have Sabre fixed by tomorrow morning and has promised to drop it off here when it's done. Theoretically, we could try again tomorrow. Though I'm not sure leaving is the best idea."

There are nods from all around. We could leave Whitehorse and the shit storm that's coming and go kill things, but it might blow up in our face by the time we get back. On the other hand, leaving the monster lair alone isn't a great option either.

"Off to see your boyfriend then?" Lana suddenly asks me, her voice too light and relaxed.

"Roxley isn't my boyfriend, Lana," I reply immediately, frowning at the rather weird direction this conversation has taken.

"Uh huh. Late night dinners, long talks and 'private training sessions' all sound like dates to me," she teases and I roll my eyes. Richard's lips twitch slightly and Rachel looks between the two of us, rolling her eyes.

Oh, I think I see. Still, a little devil in me pops up and before I can think better of it, I reply, "Why, jealous?"

"Mmm…" she puts a finger to her lips before she continues, her voice suddenly turning serious. "Maybe?"

I pause, brain coming to a stuttering stop as she says that, lost in the implications. We've been flirting for a month now, kind of dancing around the entire issue and this is the first time anything has ever been said out loud. My brain restarts when peals of bright, bubbly laughter rise up from her chest. I shake my head, feeling somewhat put-off as she continues, "Oh god, your face…"

Damn it. I fell for it, hook line and sinker. I can't help but acknowledge she's won this round. As I turn away again, she crosses the distance to place a hand on my arm to stop me. Her hands are soft and warm and this close, I can smell the soap she wears and just the hint of her beneath it. "John, I'm sorry. You deserve your happiness, we all do."

"I'm not dating Roxley!" I say again.

"And that's a good thing. You'd make a horrible boyfriend right now," Lana points out, that soft smile back on her lips.

"Worse husband," Mikito adds from her corner of the dining table, not even pausing as she cuts up her steak.

Lana nods in confirmation to Mikito's addition, eyes crinkling in amusement. "Definitely that too. So, go play with your boy for now, we'll be here."

I growl, glaring at the two women. Richard just keeps his head buried, slicing a piece off his steak with great care, though at least Rachel has the grace to look as confused as I am. What the hell makes me a bad boyfriend? I stomp off with my rifle and it's only my increased Perception that lets me hear Richard - that traitor – finally speak before everyone breaks out into laughter. "His face!"

***

Dinner at Roxley's is always a formal affair. A small, ball-like creature serves us our dishes and rolls away with speed, cooking with gusto and experience. The dishes are amazing - each time I eat here, the dishes are new and exciting, an artistic masterpiece that comes with its own history lesson. Most important is the dessert, this time from the Orion region of space – a sweet bread-like recipe that we dip in a red sauce.

Talk at the table is always limited to general topics, Earth or Galactic Council history, the state of the world, even how the System works. We never speak of the personal or business stuff itself – topics such as those are considered crass at a Dark Elf's dinner table. Or more correctly, a Truinnar's dinner table. Fascinating group, from what Roxley has told me. Unbridled ambition combined with ruthless morality and a dedication to the deal.

When dinner is done, I push away from the table and follow Roxley as we retire to his study. It's where we go to rest and digest and where the 'work' of these meetings get done. Once we leave the dining hall, Ali pops back into existence next to me, returning from having his own conversation with Roxley's Companion.

"The Yerick," Roxley begins, glass of blue liquid held in his hand. I have a cup of coffee in mine. "Will be staying. There are still some minor matters to be settled, but the First Fist Ulrick and I have come to an agreement on all substantial matters."

I grunt, leaning forwards and wait for him to elaborate on that if he will. I doubt it though.

"The Yerick will be purchasing a series of buildings in the East along Fourth Street. They will be opening a number of shops when they do so, including another Armorer and a Weaponsmith along with some sundry goods production," Roxley says. "Mostly though, they will be doing what the Yerick do best – Adventuring.

"How much trouble will your Council give me?"

"One. Not my Council. I'm just one member and really, we're there as a single vote," I repeat for the hundredth time. "Two, officially none. Three, stupid people are stupid."

Roxley nods slowly, tilting his head to the side. "You expect some will act against the Yerick?"

"Didn't some try with Xev?"

"Yes. I decided not to look into it at that time."

"Best to do that again," I reply and wave downwards to where the Yerick are. "If you can keep them here till guest rights are removed, the Yerick probably can deal with the problem makers themselves."

"And you want me to stay out of it," Roxley raises an eyebrow and I open my hands.

"Getting you involved just complicates matters. When you side with the Yerick, they'll resent you, which means the Council gets more flack for working with you. If you stay out of it, it's just a bunch of idiots being idiots. That, the Council can handle," I reply and don't add the 'I hope' I tack on to the sentence in my head.

"Very well," Roxley nods and I relax slightly. Working with Roxley is somewhat easier than the Council since his motives are relatively clear, at least in the short-term. Grow Whitehorse and make it a powerful base to work from. Everything else flows from that single objective.

"Now, you had something to report?" Roxley just continues to smile, looking at me over the rim of his glass and I feel a wash of emotion once again staring at him. Damn, but he's hot.

I deal with the new visitors first, listing their names and numbers and watch the quest completion notifications pop-up. Fewer than I expected actually, significantly fewer.

"Ali?"

"About two-thirds of those you brought back came from Whitehorse initially. Looks like the quest isn't updating for those," Ali replies in my mind.

That dealt with, I explain the reason for their return – the monster lair. I keep the description of the events brief and to the point, flicking a map over at Roxley's request.

"And you went in," Roxley states.

"Yes," I nod and Roxley rubs his head, looking at Ali.

"Your Companion did not advise against it?"

"No," I shake my head and he nods again.

"You play a dangerous game Spirit," he locks eyes with Ali, voice cold. "The rules may be loose, but they are not that loose."

Ali smirks and just floats in the air and I watch the by-play for a moment before I just ask, "Explanation. One of you two."

"I will leave the Spirit to it," Roxley waves his hand, dismissing the topic. Past experience has shown that he won't budge on that, so I just make a note to follow up with Ali. Realizing I have no more business to discuss, Roxley smiles and waves to a door.

I narrow my eyes, knowing that's the wrong door. You have to admit; the man is persistent and direct.

"No, not tonight," I stand, shaking my head and walking to the foyer exit. Roxley's eyebrow rises and I jerk a thumb at Ali. "I've got a conversation to finish."

Roxley nods slightly, for a moment a look of fleeting sadness crosses his face and I just want to kiss it away. I push it aside with a thought and keep walking. I told Lana the truth – Roxley and I aren't like that. As much as I want to, as much fun as it could be, I can't trust anything to do with him. Not the feelings I have, not his motivations, not even my own.

***

"So, Ali, talk," we're by the river, the sun finally dipping below the horizon. Still enough sunlight to see by so I'm not surprised that there are a few Farmers still working in the park-farm on my way over. I watch the water lap at the riverbanks and wait.

"How come they cancelled Baywatch but kept Law & Order? I mean, it's the same thing – the same stories told over and over again but one has women in swimsuits and the other, well, lawyers," Ali says. I don't answer directly, instead pulling up the Companion menu and hovering a finger over the 'Dismiss' button.

"Alright, alright. Goblins-arse, I really wish you hadn't found that," Ali mutters and then shrugs. "Roxley's just concerned that I'm pushing you too hard."

I look to the Spirit for a moment, putting things together in my mind before speaking, "The lair. You weren't supposed to let us go at all right."

"Yup. Monster lairs are dangerous. Monsters often fight harder than they would because that's their home, you know. Generally, you really shouldn't be entering dungeons or lairs of your level, especially without your Class Skills," Ali says.

"So, stay away from Level 14 creatures?" I ask incredulously.

"28. Or close to it at least – the maths gets fuzzy with your perk," Ali waggles his hand in the air, making shadow puppets in the water as he floats. "Sabre makes a difference and your pals do too."

"And you didn't say anything," I point out, watching the Spirit contemplatively. I should feel something – anger, betrayal, annoyance, but all I have is a comforting numbness. Too soon maybe to react, or just another pile of shit to watch out for.

"I don't like wasting my breath," Ali replies and floats over to me. "You annoyed a Salamander when you were Level 4. Fought a Boss more than double your level – your real level. You're practicing the Honor Guards techniques by yourself, without instruction. And those are just the highlights of the stupid reel."

"So, what? Let me do stupid things anyway? Let me drag my friends to their death because I don't know when I'm out-classed?" Oh. I'm not numb - I'm just so angry I've come out the other side.

"I've tried, you've refused. You fight when you should run, run when you should fight. You're unpredictable because you don't even know what you want. One day, you're hiding from the world, the next you're on Sabre riding out to meet monsters. You get your ass kicked, you get back up and fight. People ask you to lead, you run away. You say you want to hide but every chance, you're out there fighting," Ali states quickly, rapid fire.

"I..."

"No, let me finish. Our first conversation, you asked me to find a way for you to survive, to get out of the Park. Right after that, you also asked me for something that would let you stand up to anything, to kick its ass in the future. You didn't ask me for a transportation method out, you didn't ask for a spaceship, you didn't even ask for Credits. You asked for the power to kick ass," Ali points a finger at me. "You keep going, spinning around and around, and you expect me to know what the hell you want? Fuck that."

Shit.

I pause and just look at my actions for once, everything that I've done, all the small choices I've made. "Shit…"

"Exactly. Get your damn head out of your ass and tell me what you want to do and I'll help. That's my job. Till then, I'll provide you the best advice I can, but don't fucking ask me to read your mind."

I nod, staring away from him at the river. Fuck. He's right, of course he's right. I just, I can't… I shudder, hands clasping before me. I can't deal with this, I can't. But I can't go on like this either. "Ali, I'm sorry."

Ali shakes his head at that, spinning around and then sighs, floating back to me. "I've been jerking you around too. I've been pushing you, to get tougher, to get harder. You need it, needed it. The System, it's not kind, not to people in Dungeon Worlds. It gets worse before it gets better."

"I know," my answer is a whisper, shivering. I know. Damn it, but I know. I saw the things in Kluane, I know how out-leveled we are. I still remember the bones. I just can't… "Help me, please."

"Of course," his lips twist slightly, Ali floating back down to eye-level. "That's what I'm here for."

I find myself flicking him the ghost of a smile before nodding, shivering in the cold as I stare into the river. My mind shifts and skitters, trying to find purchase as my emotions roil beneath me. "Ali, please, no more half-truths, no more hiding shit or playing mysterious guru. I need you to be straight with me, even if you don't think it's worth it."

"Fine. On that note – reconsider your stance on Roxley," Ali says.

"What?" I frown and then my eyes narrow. "You just want to watch."

"Yes, but also, he's a Truinnar noble – out of favor perhaps, but still a noble. His favor could open doors for us in the future," Ali states matter-of-factedly.

"Sleep with him to get my way?" I can't help but frown at that.

Ali shrugs again, "What do you think he'll be doing to you? Anyway, you're so backed up, I swear, I can see it coming out of your ears."

"I do not need advice on my love life from you," I state, quite seriously and the rage under my voice clamps Ali's mouth shut. Good. I turn back to the water, keeping my hands clasped as I work to get my emotions back under control.

***

An hour later, I find myself knocking on a door. When she comes out, I can tell she's been sleeping but her smile breaks out when she sees me.

"Hi! I didn't expect to see you so soon," she whispers, voice low as we try to avoid waking up anyone else.

"Care to go for a walk?" I murmur, gesturing away and she pauses for a moment before nodding, ducking back in to grab her coat.

Ali was right. It has been too long. Karen steps out, sneaking around the bodies that make up the school, clutching her thin robe to a tight body and somehow having brushed her brown hair in the few seconds since I've seen her. I smile slightly, enjoying the sight and the lack of complications here as I take her hand and lead her to the water.

Chapter 20

"Morning!" I greet everyone at the breakfast table. What I get is chilly silence from Lana, an uncomfortable look from Richard and Rachel's snort. Richard's latest conquest takes one look at the situation, gives him a quick kiss and heads out, swaying a bountiful ass on the way out.

"Ohayō Baka," is Mikito's reply as she turns to me, placing her bowl of rice down.

"You know, I know what that means," I point out, frowning at her. She just turns back to her breakfast and I look at the group.

"What?" Shit, were the Yerick that much of an issue? I thought we had talked it out yesterday.

Lana stands up, dumping her plate in the sink and walks out, never once saying a word to me. I open my mouth then shut it, before looking to the others. "Richard…?"

"Nope. Not a chance," Richard holds his hands up and looks to Rachel. "You good to hit the Shop?"

She nods at that, standing up and they repeat the plate dumping action. As she walks past me, Rachel whispers under her breath, "Jerk".

I'm just left standing there, dumb-founded. What the hell? "Mikito?"

"Baka," she just replies and concentrates on her food while I puzzle it out. Fine, this sounded personal. The only thing that I did that could have been personal was Karen – but really? Lana pretty much told me to go get laid, so what the hell? I don't get women. I really, really, don't.

As I finish working it out, I realize Mikito's gone and left the kitchen, leaving me with the dishes. Now that's just mean.

***

With my team having dispersed to do their own thing, I find myself with nothing to do. At least, nothing that I want to do but someone has to. I'm not exactly sure when I became the diplomat for the god damn human race in Whitehorse, but well, here I am. Waiting to see Capstan to have a chat with him while Ali, back in his invisible mode at my request, does handstands.

The door opens and Capstan walks in and I realize what the higher ceilings and wider doorframe of Roxley's base are for. When you deal with a wide variety of beings, you make certain concessions to architecture. I wonder how long it'll take us to figure that one out. Up close, Capstan is even bigger and more imposing, his movements having that feral grace that you see in large cats. He carries no obvious weapons though he continues to wear his simple dark brown bodysuit with armor plates. It's expensive armor – lighter, stronger and easier to replace than the ones we bought.

He studies me at the same time, eyes flicking over my form and up above me before he speaks, voice rumbling like a series of rocks ground together, "Greetings of the morning to you Redeemer of the Dead John Lee."

"*Ali, does he have a System Companion too?*" I think to Ali, putting on a closed lip smile to the minotaur. No baring teeth – that might be bad.

"*It's First Fist Ulrick, and probably not. Adventuring families often purchase the Class Skill Observe from the Shop for their children when they can,*" Ali answers.

"Good Morning First Fist Ulrick," I parrot and then blink, realizing what just happened "You speak English?"

"Yes," Capstan continues and then stops, patiently waiting.

"So…" I look at him and then brace myself, deciding to just say what I came here to say, "Look, you probably guessed, but there are people who aren't thrilled with your presence. Especially in such large numbers."

"Yes," Capstan says again.

"I believe Roxley's asked you to keep your people indoors till you aren't his guests anymore, but I wanted to add, it might be an idea for your people to move together in pairs. Well, not you obviously," I add, "but, those who aren't able to defend themselves."

"You are threatening us?" Capstan rumbles and I hold my hand up. Capstan growls and I pause, freezing in space as I realize that might not go over well. Right, cultural differences.

"No, not me. Warning, not threatening. It's…" I frown, then continue "look, idiots are idiots. I don't, the City Council, doesn't have control over everyone. Not the way we work, so some of those idiots, well, they might do something stupid. I'd like it if that stupid thing didn't end up with anybody dead."

"You are asking that we not kill our attackers?" Capstan rumbles again and standing next to him, I realize I can smell the musky tang that I've come to associate with livestock.

"Well, put that way, probably?" I say. "It'll make your life more difficult and probably mine."

"You are a leader here," Capstan says.

"Yes. And no. I have an Adventuring Party and we're one of the highest leveled, so I've got some influence but I'm not in the chain of command," I state bluntly. No reason to lie here and if he knows the truth, hopefully, he won't expect miracles.

Capstan copies my nod, the motion jerky and unnatural on the creature.

"System-bought language skills often come with body language knowledge too," Ali says helpfully next to me. *"Also, if you didn't guess, he's amused."*

"Amused? How the hell is he amused?" I squint at the large Yerick and still can't see how Ali is getting amused from the giant brown, fur covered boulder in front of me.

"Check his tail. Also, he's tapped his hand on his leg thrice," Ali replies as the same time Capstan says, "We will not kill humans if we can Redeemer."

"Thanks. Do you mind me asking what your plans are?" I say.

"If the stars will it, we will settle and build. A Dungeon World is a lucrative world and if Lord Roxley allows us to do so, we will Adventure and earn the blessings of the System," Capstan answers again, his hand splaying at the start of what he said.

"Ah…" I frown, thinking and then shrug. If we've got to have them here, then we might as well have them on our side. "Once you're settled, talk to me? Might be able to give you a few directions about what's out there."

"That will be done, Redeemer," Capstan does his jerky head nod thing again and Ali to my side snorts.

"Well, I guess that is it. I'm sure you and Roxley still have more to discuss," I automatically offer my hand and then wince, already beginning to withdraw. However, Capstan does not react to it with aggression this time and so I let it hang out there where he stares at it before reaching out to clasp it, engulfing my entire hand and half of my arm in his. Then he squeezes.

Son-of-a-bitch! He crushes down on my hand and I reflexively squeeze back, both of us locked in a sudden contest of strength. Of course, he's got the advantage considering I'm squeezing only a tiny portion of his body, but he'd win anyway. I can feel bones creak and muscles begin to mush and anger flares in me, my lips curling in a full snarl. Capstan just returns my gaze, no trace of anger or bloodlust in there. Just as I begin to get ready to curse him out and stab him, he lets go and steps back.

"May we see the dawn again together, Redeemer," Capstan rumbles and I glare at him.

"Ali, tell me that Alpha-male bullshit is part of their culture," I think furiously at my Companion. I came here to keep things peaceful, not start the fight myself.

"You should be happy, he thought you were tough enough to test to see who has a bigger dick. Which, by the way, he does," Ali pauses and continues. *"Literally. Yerick are famed for it actually. The occasional Yerick that gets into the business does really well for himself."*

I've already tuned Ali out after the first few words for the most part, a skill I've learnt a while ago, "Goodbye Capstan."

I then walk out, chanting the minor Healing spell in my mind as I leave. Mana infuses my bones, knitting things together and smoothing out crushed muscles, *"Ali, why the hell did he feel the need to test me?"*

"Uh, you told him you were one of the leaders. Also, if you've forgotten, you've got two titles, an Advanced Class and more levels than him. At least from what he could read," Ali shrugs. "Not his fault you cheat."

Put that way, it makes sense but… "This is going to happen a lot, isn't it?"

"Yup. Get stronger faster boy-o," Ali notes grimly and I sigh.

Fuck. As if I needed another reason to run around getting shot at.

***

It's been ages since I've done this, gone hunting by myself. As much as I like the team, there's a liberating feeling about being out here alone without having to worry about where people are and how they are doing. No need to worry about their inability to run away or sneak up on enemies, just me and the shadows.

I'm over an hour and a half from Whitehorse, deep in the forests and up a mountain after taking a pair of backtrails that came off the highway. I doubt a single other human has been down this way since the System turned on, the roads so badly damaged and washed out that I'd switched to armor mode to traverse it.

Such a strange thing, sneaking around with Sabre in armor mode. It should be a lot harder than it is, sliding from shadow to shadow without disturbing a leaf and yet, more than once, I manage to locate my prey and kill it with a single shot or strike without it ever noticing me. If I had to guess, it's the damn System adjusting reality, pulling shadows closer, making the steps I place softer and lighter.

The forest around me is quiet and strange, the typical Yukon alpine forest of spruce, willow and fir trees having mutated, some growing spikes, others gaining a new sheen to their bark. I accidentally brush against a tree that was once a paper birch and set the contact point on fire. The fire dies away after a moment, leaving the tree unharmed and me with a thundering heart. In addition to the mutated trees, additional fast-growing vines drape across the area between trees. The vines are dotted with bright red flowers, some already fruiting with a fleshy, reddish-yellow oval fruit. I've taken a few of the flowers and fruit, figuring that at the least Sally might know what they are. Thus far, she's been less than enthused with the various flora and fauna available in the Yukon natively. Of course, there's always hope that the mutated variety might be of greater use.

It's the silence that gets me, the lack of birds or other animals - a sign that something nasty is out there. It has been like this for the last half-hour but whatever it is, I hadn't come across signs of it until now. And what a sign it is.

"Earth elemental," Ali confirms and I eye the ground before me. The earth isn't just torn up, it looks churned – as if the ground had pulled itself apart and then was dropped by a very large, angry toddler. Shattered and uprooted trees give a clear indication of the elemental's path and for a moment, I almost think of going back. Almost.

It's an hour of fast moving to catch up to the elemental, only slowing down once I'm close. I gently pull myself up the top of the hill, sticking my head above it to see the creature continuing its journey. Finding it would have been a little faster if it didn't randomly just move around, though now that I look at it, I wonder if it was so random.

Thirty feet long and twenty feet wide at a guess, the elemental moves on six legs along the ground with a head that is reminiscent of a toddler-made sculpture of a lizard. As it moves, the earth churns up around in a reverse waterfall before falling away behind it, the gold it's sifting for sticking to its body. My jaw drops as I stare at the creature, already, half its body is plated in gold from the bottom up.

"System's balls – that's not an Earth Elemental, that's a Metal Elemental!" Ali says next to me as he stares at it. Even as he spots the creature, the status bar fills in.

Metal Elemental (Level 43)
HP: 2470/2470

As if the creature can hear Ali, it cranes its neck around and then slowly lumbers around. My eyes widen and then I look at the Spirit who suddenly looks sheepish.

"Shit boy-o, forgot they can see me. Best get killing," Ali points and starts floating upwards and out of range of the creature.

I don't have to be asked twice, cursing the little Spirit as I bring my rifle to bear. I depress the trigger and am rewarded by the flash of the beam striking it, flakes of gold burning off. I continue firing, grinning slightly even as the creature begins to pick up steam. 300 meters when a creature is 30 feet long isn't that far at all, but I'm not worried.

"Oh, John, the QSM won't work either. Elementals are like Spirits, we exist in multiple dimensions at the same time," Ali calls out from above and I curse him again as I throw myself to the side, attempting to roll away from it. The elemental clips me as I unsuccessfully get out of the way, sending me spinning through a series of trees before I come to a standstill. Vertigo takes me for a moment and I can feel the bruises coming already but nothing major seems broken.

I look up, the creature slowing down from its charge and beginning to turn, which lets me open fire. Slow on the turns eh? I grin and start running in a circle, opening fire as I go and dodging around trees when I can and on a few occasions, just going through them. I'm careful not to do that too often though — some of these trees have mutated enough that I probably would bounce right off. Stupid, damn System. There's no reason why, if I can bench press a tank that I can't jump through a tree — even if the tree itself can hold, its roots should tear out from the earth. Then again, under the influence of Mana and the System, straight Newtonian physics has long ago taken a bow and exited stage left. Some things just don't make sense.

Running and shooting is easy, and I chip away at the creature's health for long minutes even as it pulls more metal towards it, regenerating the damage. I'm winning the damage game until my rifle does a distressing beep and I realize I'm out of charges. I move to reload and realize I've already done it once. Oh shit…

I keep jogging as I slap the rifle back into its resting slot above my shoulder and try to decide what to do next, eyeing the monstrosity's health. Only half down and that's with me using both Mana batteries. I could possibly outrun the creature, though a glance at Sabre's battery indicates I'm taxing it too. Fighting the creature without Sabre would be suicide, so I can hope to run and risk getting caught when I am out of power or I can fight it now. Really, who am I kidding?

A savage grin tearing my face apart, I rush it. Right then, quadruped with a big, wide body. The play here is simple – get close, get on top and stab at it from above till it dies. I rush the elemental, going straight for its face and as it goes for a bite, I jump and use its head to vault myself upwards onto its back. At the apex of my jump, I call forth my sword and lead the attack with it, slamming into the earth and metal body of the creature. I feel the sword bite in deep and then the body shudders, the sword snapping in my grip. That was a first in a while – as I leveled, so had my weapon and its durability and sharpness had increased considerably.

I grin, crouched with a leg splayed out behind me and a hand on its body, as I call forth my sword again. Just as I am about to plunge the blade, a spike made of gold forms from the body, impaling my back thigh. It's only a last-minute jerk of my body that stops another spike from piercing my torso and I scream into my helmet as I swing at the spike that skewers me, shattering it.

Another second as I roll away, spikes jutting out from the creature's body as it continues its unconventional attack. I kick off with my good foot, sending me spinning blindly into the trees and coming to a rest a good 40 feet away, a thick gouge in the earth marking my landing site.

Pushing past the pain, I grab the golden spike and pull it out of my leg and slap it against my helmet. A moment later, a potion appears in my hand from my inventory and I'm chugging it down before casting a quick Healing spell. Already, the wound in my leg is closing up and I'm able to stand to face the charging creature. As it lunges to me again, I jump directly at it and to the left, twisting myself around so that I slide on my back on the ground. I lash out with my sword as I do so, chipping at the gold of the creature's body and managing to carve a chunk of gold off.

On my feet, I back off as quickly as I can even as the elemental spins to me as I begin casting Lightning Strike, struggling not to sneeze from the dust that the creature has kicked up. The Mana pulls from my body as the chant runs through my mind, a hand held up forth before me. The casting takes too long and I trigger another jump backwards as I dodge around a spike. As I land, the spell nears completion and Ali flies down next to me, putting his hand on mine and connecting us further, willing a touch of his own Elemental Affinity into the bolt of lightning as it exits my body.

Power rushes out of me, super-charged by Ali, and the cackling electricity slams into the creature, shocking it still. The elemental writhes as the charge runs through it, conducted directly into its core and super-heating the metal. Gold heats up and begins to melt, dropping from the body onto the ground as the elemental loses control over the metal. I focus, pouring everything that I have into the spell, my Mana dropping like a waterfall. With Ali directly connected to me, and lending his aid, I can feel the electrons ripping free in the air. The elemental is locked in pain, unable to move to attack me, as its health drops at a precarious rate just like my Mana. This is going to be close.

Eleven seconds and then I drop, Mana drained entirely from my body. My head feels like it's been filled with wool and I can't focus properly, eyesight fading in and out. I find myself slumping down and forcing breaths through my body, wondering why there's a little part of me screaming and shouting that I should be doing something more important. I shut it away and I fall backwards, looking up at the clear blue sky.

I'm not sure how long I'm out but when I wake up, Ali is hovering over me playing cards. I groan, slowly shifting up to look around. Where the elemental was, a slagheap of gold and earth stands. Crap – I fainted in the middle of a fight.

"How long was I out for?" I try to stand up, my head spinning and I find myself sitting down again when I regain control.

"About 20 minutes. Drink your Mana potion, it'll help," Ali continues to play his cards, the game nothing that I recognize. A spread of seven piles with cards laid out in a fan-shape, Ali occasionally moving one card from one pile to another or dealing a new card from the deck in his hand.

I don't argue, following his directions. My hand hesitates between the cheaper or more expensive one and my inner miser makes me pull the cheap potion and down it. The relief is immediate, the wooziness dropping to a manageable level. Right, first thing first – loot. I'm sure Ali will tell me if there's any danger, not that I'm in any condition to deal with more trouble. I don't even look at the loot I get, grabbing and dumping it into my inventory as I struggle not to throw up.

"Ali, map this for me will you. We'll want to get the body later," I eye the fused golden body of the elemental and a part of me does a little dance at the sheer amount of gold there is. Then again, is gold worth anything anymore?

Glumly, I consider the fact that gold might just be worthless before I push the thoughts aside. Something for later. I look to Ali who sees that I'm mostly done and he waggles his fingers again.

Lightning Strike Enhanced!

You have combined Lightning Strike with your Spirit Companion's Elemental Affinity to empower the spell. Description updated.

Lightning Strike

Effect: Call forth the power of the gods, casting lightning. Lightning strike may affect additional targets depending on proximity, charge and other conductive materials on-hand. Does 100 points of electrical damage.

Lightning Strike may be continuously channeled to increase damage for 10 additional damage per second.

Cost: 75 Mana.

Continuous cast cost: 5 Mana / second

Lightning Strike may be enhanced by using the Elemental Affinity of Electromagnetic Force. Damage increased by 20% per level of affinity.

Mana Withdrawal

You are suffering from severe Mana withdrawal.

Effect: -80% recovery rates. -80% to all stats. Inability to cast spells till withdrawal effects are over.

Duration: Withdrawal effects will reduce by 1% for every 1% of Mana regained

Metal Elemental (Level 43) Slain

+7000 XP

Seriously, no level up? I look at the experience marker and grimace. Trying to level an Advanced Class sucks. I push the thought away again, worrying about something I can't change isn't particularly useful.

"Why was the elemental so much harder to kill? I mean, we kicked the ass of the troll with ease and the elemental isn't that much higher," I ask.

"Mikito had worn it down a bunch – even if it was regenerating, getting your ass kicked around takes a toll. Also, this was a bad match. Beam energy weapons don't work as well, and well, your biggest hitter only really worked because I was around," Ali shrugs and continues. "Metal elementals are tough against physical attackers and you don't have access to your class skills to bypass its armor. Frankly, if you didn't have Sabre on, you'd be dead. Then again, that's not new either."

I nod and groan, a throbbing pain in my leg making itself known as I come down from my adrenaline high. It'll heal soon enough, but till then, I'm just going to have to suffer. Can't even cast anything with the Mana withdrawal going-on. Definitely time to call it a day.

***

"Mr. Lee," I am flagged down as I drive into Whitehorse, head still pounding a little. I groan, seeing that it's Fred and Minion but pull over. Playing diplomat sucks, but if making sure we don't start a war in our own city is the result, I can suck it up like a big boy. I can't help the little bit of anger, of resentment, that creeps into my voice though.

"Fred, M…" I pause and then look at his name, "Eric."

Eric – Minion's – eyes narrow but he does not say anything. Fred smiles, waiting for me to clamber off my bike before he speaks. "I hear you have spoken with Lord Roxley and the minotaurs?"

"Yerick. I've spoken with the Yerick and Roxley, yes," I answer.

"Tell me, what did you learn?" Fred smiles ingratiatingly, leaning forward to come into my space just a little.

I shiver, feeling the need to wash as he smiles at me. "Not much. The Yerick are Adventurers mostly, some craftsmen. They'll be joining us at Roxley's invitation and will be buying buildings from the Shop. That should get us closer to the Safe Zone mark, help us stabilize the city more"

I watch Fred as I speak, hoping the news about the buildings will make him happy. I know there's a lot of pressure to get us to that 80% mark, but the cost of doing so is staggering – especially when you consider our needs for the future. We're only at 40% but even that is helping to stabilize the number of spawnings already. "The rest, well, I figure someone like you or Miranda would be more appropriate to discuss with them. I'm sure the Yerick would be happy to talk with you about how they fit into our little community."

I'm laying it on a little thick, but I can see Fred grab at the sentence and run with it. "Yes, we'll need to talk about the contributions they can provide and maybe they could join the business association."

"Of course," I nod blandly, already mentally checking out. To my side, Minion's eyes narrow and his fists clench as Fred blathers on more to himself about how to integrate this new community in our city.

"Evening then, gentlemen." I smile and get on my bike, heading to see Xev. Thank god it was only armor plating this time, should be a pretty quick fix. I wave to her, drop the bike off and take the offer to be dropped off via tandem bike. All I want is my bed and peace and quiet. Just for a few hours. I really need to make sure never to drain myself like that again.

Chapter 21

Breakfast the next day is more civil, everyone seeming to have settled down. Lana doesn't serve me like she normally does, but no one is giving me the cold shoulder either. However, conversation is stilted, long pauses breaking up conversational gambits. Most, since Mikito continues to quietly eat her rice without participating as usual.

As we finish, I tap the table to get everyone's attention. When they look at me, I say, "Today's day 3 of the guest rights. The Yerick have said they'll keep indoors till tomorrow, so that leaves us a day of peace. I think we should try the cave today."

Richard and the others look at each other before he sits forward, staring at me. "What's this brilliant plan?"

I grin, waving Ali over and together we outline what we know and what we plan. When we are done, the group sit there in silence, Richard scratching at his beard and frowning, Lana with a slight quirky smile on her lips, Mikito calm and collected and Rachel smirking.

"Man, that's kind of broken, isn't it?" Rachel replies, shaking her head as she spins an unlit cigarette around her finger.

I flash her a grin, shrugging, "If it works, sure. We'll need help though."

Rachel wrinkles her nose and then nods, "I know just the people."

The group slowly nods and we quickly assign the last of the tasks we need to do. As I head towards the door, Lana grabs my arm and says. "Sorry about yesterday."

"What was it about?" I prod her, wanting confirmation about what I've guessed. I'm dense but not stupid.

"Nothing important. Not right now. You just make sure to bring them back okay," her eyes flicking over to her younger brother betraying which one she really means. I know, she likes us all but it's her brother. I don't blame her.

"I'll be the last one out," I promise her and she lets go of me. Alright then, time to go kill something. At the thought, I can feel the slow thrum of anticipation run through me. Yes, definitely time to kill some monsters.

***

I squat outside the cave, a couple of hours ahead of the rest of the crew. They are headed into Carcross first before joining me. Me, I've got to get the initial part of the plan going – scouting out the cave. Ali pointed out to me that while the Wil-o-wisp might be interesting, it wasn't exactly subtle in its presence and the Shadow-aspected Crilik shifters could kill it. Instead, we compromised by purchasing a bigger Mana battery for the drone and a second one just in case. Expensive, but it's not as if I have a better choice.

Ali's watching the doorway, actually paying attention since he can't automatically scan for monsters while I watch the drone map the caves. I keep it high and near the ceilings, running in infrared vision and letting out low-level radar pings, enough to create 3D maps of the area it travels through. Hooked into Sabre, the cave renders in exquisite detail in my helmet visor. Best of all, the Crilik shifters don't have a clue.

The cave system isn't that big, not really. Just over half-a-kilometer long with about five main caverns. The Crilik move about too much for me to get an accurate count, but at a rough guess, I'm looking at just above 40 of the shifters, including a nasty looking Alpha that is nearly double the size of the next largest shifter. The Alpha prowls the last few caves, and after a time I notice that there are some shifters that are smaller than the others, half-again the size in some cases. Right, monster lair.

When the team arrives, they come with extra help. Both Jason and Mike have been added to the team, though they've been sworn to secrecy about Sabre for now. At this point, I'm seriously wondering why I bother with it but it's habit by now. Rachel moves to the cave entrance the moment we arrive, hands raised as she begins to pull stone from the earth to form walls and a ceiling around the entrance. Richard walks forwards, the Huskies ranging out beside him even as Elsa is dropped down next to him. Above, Orel watches from a perch right above me. Richard lets loose with a series of flares, lighting up the front cave fully and then settles in to keep an eye for the Shifters.

Mikito and Jason get to work, felling trees with blade and magic in quick order before slicing them into pieces that are less cumbersome for Gadsby to carry. Gadsby, grinning, carries logs about double his size on his shoulders with ease, bouncing into the cave and stacking them up just like you would if you were making a campfire.

By this time, I've brought the drone back to the second cave and am watching the shifters. They prowl the edges of the light, waiting for us to move in but don't take further action. No surprise there, the compendium indicated they weren't the smartest creatures in the world, mostly ambush hunters. Since we aren't moving deep into their territory, they are willing to wait and watch our strange actions.

Superhuman strength and speed means that the preparations are completed really quickly and I gesture for Mikito and Richard to come to me. They take the sensor data I have and while the others wait, we spread out over the mountainside. This is the tricky part – we want to block off enough airways to reduce airflow, but not too much or else we'll just kill the fire completely. Ali and I figure about half should do it, or at least we hope so. Not as if either of us are arsonists or firefighters. The insta-cement pouches we pull from inventory work fast and set within moments of application, filling our respective holes within moments of application.

By the time we're back, the entrance has a nice overhang and is enclosed with stone with only a single wide opening left. Richard and Elsa start the ball rolling, moving deeper to get in range before Elsa begins to breathe, flames licking at the wet logs till Elsa has to stop. We pull them back and Jason takes over, sending wind in a steady roar to fan the flames and more importantly, create the smoke we need. I wish I knew what was going on inside the cave, but I've already recalled the drone to keep it from getting damaged. However, the howls that start emanating from inside let us know that the Crilik aren't happy.

There's little more to do, Gadsby, Mikito and I are the front-line at the cave entrance while the flames roar, wet tinder super-heated by the turtle creating quite a bit of smoke and blocking lines of sight. We catch sight of something moving behind the flames, snarling at the fire before it disappears behind smoke and shadows and then there's silence.

Now we just wait, as smoke continues to build in the cave system, forcing the creatures to choose to die from asphyxiation or run through the flames to meet us out here. Of course, half-a-kilometer of caves would take a while to fill with smoke fully, so Gadsby has the enjoyable task of hauling the extra wood we chopped and adding it as necessary.

"You know, this just feels wrong," mutters Gadsby during one particular long stretch of waiting and Jason nods in agreement.

Jason falls silent for a moment, letting the wind from his spell die down as he watches to see how the fire is going. Spotting an area that has not lit, he calls forth a spear of flame and throws it, the spear erupting and setting the logs on fire. Jason turns to me then, hand absently pawing a pair of glasses that are no longer there, "Not a game right."

"No, not at all," I reply and narrow my eyes, trying to spot the monsters. No game, just our fucked-up lives. This could take a while, but we've got the time, the wood and the discipline to wait.

The first sign of trouble comes after a few hours, a trio of Crilik panicking and rushing us. The first takes a shot to the head from my rifle and drops, the second slips and thrashes in the flames and the third is met by Mikito and her blade and loses its head. An hour later, we get a series of notifications that more Crilik have perished.

Then nothing, as time drags on. Gadsby heads away to grab more wood when the fire begins to die down and that's when the remaining Crilik charge us. Stripped of their main advantage in combat by the fires, strength and stamina sapped by the carbon dioxide poisoning they've been going through, the fight is a massacre. It doesn't stop them from charging though.

I launch a Lighting Strike in, joined by a more powerful and impressive attack of the same form by Jason and the bolts dance between the bodies, jumping from creature to creature and forcing more than one to fall into the fire. Rachel flicks her hands, stone spears launching from the ground to impale other monsters that make it through the first magical barrage. Behind us, Richard works his shotgun as they close to his range, targeting those in the lead. They lose more than half their numbers in this way and then are forced to funnel to where Mikito and I wait, blades drawn to end this. Gadsby rushes back to join us and Mikito meets the Boss herself, polearm dancing in strikes that keep the creature off-balance and on the defense. I occasionally slip aside, letting a Crilik out so that the Huskies can grab it and savage the creature while I fight the others. Next to me, Gadsby smashes his opponents into paste with an armored metal fist and a truncheon.

As I said, it's a massacre. Already damaged from the run through the fire and carbon dioxide poisoning and stripped of their greatest weapon, they are no match for us. When the fight is over, we're left panting but victorious over the bodies. We grin at each, and then as a group, we begin to go over the notices we've been given.

Quest Complete!
You have cleared the Carcross Cave of Crilik Shifters!
10,000 XP Awarded. Reputation increase in the village of Carcross.

Level Up! * 2
You have reached Level 16 as an Erethran Honor Guard. Stat Points automatically distributed. You have 18 Free Attribute Points to distribute.
Class Skills Unlocked

I scream with joy, breaking out into an impromptu dance. Fucking finally! I can't help but grin, ignoring the shocked looks everyone else is giving me. I needed just one more damn level and I get 2! Allocating a few additional points to my Charisma stat and I'm good to go.

"Problem, John?" Gadsby asks, not looking directly at me and scanning the surroundings.

"No, I just got my Class Skills," I grin widely.

"No need to scream like a little girl you know, we all got levels," Jason replies, grumbling as he rubs the ear nearest to me.

"No, you don't understand. I just got my Class Skills unlocked. Finally," I can't help but bounce a bit on my feet, no longer feeling the need to hide that particular lack.

"What?" Richard turns around and stares at me and I realize most everyone else is as well. "How the fuck have you been keeping up with us without your skills? I just thought you were dumping them all into physical stats like your Constitution." Mikito nods firmly at that and Jason just stares at me, mouth open.

"Nope, just haven't had access to them yet," I chuckle evilly, rubbing my hands together in thought. Oooh, the things I could do.

"Broken. You're a fucking broken character," mutters Jason.

"Don't give the boy-o too big a head. He'd be dead a dozen times over without the Mech. Or me," Ali points out, smirking at me and I nod in acknowledgement. Fair enough, being able to spot, hide and run away from creatures that truly out-classed me was a huge advantage.

"Are we all going to get locked out of our Class Skills if we get an Advanced one?" Rachel chimes in to the conversation around the cigarette in her lips, staring at me.

Ali tackles this one immediately, "Nope, sugarplum here is special. Don't worry about it."

Rachel nods and Mikito points back into the cave with her naginata. "Work. Dance later."

The others nod, shooting me curious glances but she is right. Time to get to work. They begin looting the corpses on the outside while Rachel and Jason work to cool the cave down sufficiently for me to head in. Even in Sabre, I'm not exactly looking forward to the walk.

Chapter 22

After we've sorted things out, I'm seated at the back of the truck, working on my Status Screen.

Points allocated to Charisma

Class Skills unlocked
8 Class Skills Available to be Distributed. Would you like to do so?

Would I? I feel a thrill shoot through me and I can't help but grin widely. Gadsby is riding Sabre with permission as I get busy poking at the details, calling up information on the Class Skills. It's not as if I don't have a rough idea about them, not from the information I've already purchased, and the hours of video footage in my mind. However, when I pull up the Class Skills box, there's another tab right next to it – Basic Skills.

"Ali, what are these basic skills? They unlock at the same time?" I page over to them immediately and grimace, flicking through the pages at a rush since the sheer volume is staggering. Power Blow, Sprint, First Aid, Mana Dart, Poison, Elemental Imbue. When I pull up the information though, I'm less than impressed.

Power Blow
Effect: Physical attack deals 20% more base damage
Cost: 25 Mana

Sprint
Effect: User is able to move at a run 5% faster
Cost: 10 Mana/ second

Elemental Imbue

Effect: Imbue your weapon with an elemental effect of choice. Choice must be made upon purchase and may not be changed. +10 Elemental Damage

Cost: 30 Mana/ Second

"Not really, you could have bought them before," Ali turns to me, hands on his hips as he points. "I blocked them so you couldn't see it, because, well, they are shit. It's what they catch you with and keeps you power-downed. Just a little bit of a boost, but never good enough to really challenge the patient, the smart or the knowledgeable."

I twitch at his words, hands wanting to reach out and strangle the little Spirit. Instead, I pull a chocolate bar from my inventory and eat it, focusing on the now. He's not wrong – but this magic rabbit trick thing he's doing is getting old. I force myself to breathe, thoughts thrumming with anger, *"We just talked about you keeping secrets from me."*

Ali pauses, looking me up and down and then his face twitches. It does something I've never seen it do before, and for a moment, I can't figure it out. When I do, I realize it's the closest thing to remorse I've seen on his face. Then he speaks, "Yeah, you're right."

"Say again?" I prod him.

"You're right I said. I'm sorry, we agreed to tell the truth. I'd just been keeping this one for so long, I forgot," Ali replies and I grunt, anger still simmering but under control. I'm not happy, but at least he apologized and done is done.

I tab back to my Class Skills and finish up the chocolate, focusing on reading now. I'm not sure I'll be making all my choices immediately, but knowing what I have to work with is important.

The Honor Guard Class Skills are broken into three separate tracks, with skills above each track a pre-requisite to more powerful skills beneath. Each track aided the Guard in their regular duties as bodyguards, champions and of course, shock troops for the army.

Erethran Honor Guard Skills

The first track focused on the Honor Guard's soulbound weapons, enhancing the potential and damage of each weapon. As I understood it, the options varied in this track slightly depending on the weapon soulbound. Mana Imbue added Mana damage to the weapon which bypassed all resistances, Blade Strike extended the range of my weapon. Thousand Blades created extra copies of my soulbound weapon for use and Army of One combined all the above into a massive attack.

The second track allowed the Guard to be effective bodyguards. Two are One shared the damage a target received with the Guard while the Body's Resolve increased regeneration rates, letting the Guard take more damage. Soul Shield allowed the Guard to manifest a shield while Sanctum created a location that stopped all attacks for a short period of time.

The third track involved their ability to move and hit. Thousand Steps was a movement buff, Altered Space gave them enhanced inventory storage abilities, while Blink Step was a short-range, line-of-sight teleportation ability. Perhaps the most interesting power was Portal – this allowed the Guard to link two locations. Get a single Guard with Portal in your backlines and he could drop an army on you. Or a nuke.

Shield Transference enhanced Soul Shield, allowing users to absorb a portion of any attack to the Shield in order to enhance their own soulbound weapons. Greater detection allowed the Guard an awareness ability, much like Ali's, while Body Swap let the Guard swap places with pre-determined targets, no matter the distance.

Unfortunately, as I prod the skills I realize that some of them are still locked. Looks like at least for now, the first two levels are the only one's unlocked, until I hit Level 30. It's only at Level 40 that I'd unlock the last tier, but even with that, I've got a ton of things to play with. I could just pick up a single level in everything and enhance a single other skill but that might be a touch too simplistic. After all, I'm not entirely sure I need Greater Detection since I have Ali already for one. And ranged attacks with the sword seem interesting, but I've got guns for those.

Decisions, decisions, decisions. As I stare at the information, I idly pull out another chocolate bar and chew on it, ignoring the conversations around me. I'll definitely need to talk to Ali about this at some point.

***

When we get back to Carcross, I put away the information. The guards at the gate nod to us, waving us through and we find Mrs. O'Keefe on gate duty by sheer coincidence. Another guard has hurried into the meeting hall and the Elder makes her way out slowly. Gadsby gives her the thumbs up and she relaxes and then straightens as if a great load is taken off her.

I hop down, smiling slightly as Jason does his best blasé teenager impression for his mum, while bouncing on his toes slightly. His need to play it cool is obviously warring with his need to tell the story of what we did. Richard just smiles at Mrs. O'Keefe who gives him a quick smile of gratitude back before she turns to her son, guiding him away.

There's still time to get back if we wish, but at Elder Badger's and Gadsby's insistence, we decide to call it a day. For everyone else but the guards on the wall, the evening fast turns into a celebration, food and drink coming out in large quantities. An unlucky moose becomes the center of the celebration, its 20-foot body the feature of the evening.

The night comes on us fast, and I spot even Mikito relaxing slightly through the night, sitting and chatting with a few other melee weapon users. They seem to be comparing weapons and techniques, animatedly discussing moves from their body gestures. Rachel has disappeared into one of the motel's rooms, dragging along Jason and I idly wonder if it's romance or knowledge or a little of both that is being shared. As for Richard, well, as usual, he's the star of the show with people clustered around him, listening to him talk. From the looks the pair of women who sit at his feet have given him, I'm pretty sure he won't be sleeping alone tonight.

Me? I ghost around the edges, doing my best to blend in to the crowd. I watch them laugh and smile and I wonder why. We destroyed a lair, killed a few monsters but we're a fucking Dungeon World. It's just one of a thousand, ten thousand, that are going to crop up and we can't stamp them all out. Then again, just because I don't feel the party doesn't mean they shouldn't enjoy it. So, I stay hidden, blending in. I do so well that I even get a minor notification.

Skill Acquired

Camouflage (Level 1)
It takes skill to disappear in a crowd.

After a while, I realize I can't even give a damn to put up a face for them all anymore. I head out, leaving Sabre and my team mates behind, sneaking out past the guards while dumping points into my Class Skills. There are a few things I definitely want, the rest can wait. A single point first, into a few areas.

Class Skills Acquired

Mana Imbue (Level 1)

Soulbound weapon now permanently imbued with Mana to deal more damage on each hit. +10 Base Damage (Mana). Will ignore armor and resistances. Mana regeneration reduced by 5 Mana per minute permanently.

Class Skills Acquired

Blade Strike (Level 1)

By projecting additional Mana and stamina into a strike, the Erethran Honor Guard's Soulbound weapon may project a strike up to 10 feet away.

Cost: 40 Stamina + 40 Mana

Class Skills Acquired

Thousand Steps (Level 1)

Movement speed for the Honor Guard and allies are increased by 5% while skill is active. This ability is stackable with other movement related skills.

Cost: 20 Stamina + 20 Mana per minute

Class Skills Acquired

Altered Space (Level 1)

The Honor Guard now has access to an extra-dimensional storage location of ten feet cubed. Items stored must be touched to be willed in and may not include living creatures or items currently affected by aura's that are not the Honor Guard's. Mana regeneration reduced by 5 Mana per minute permanently.

I'll stick close to the town and keep quiet, but there's no better way to test my new Class Skills than on a live opponent.

"Ali, the Thousand Steps skill. Doesn't seem that great to me," I converse with the invisible Spirit who is working hard on looking out for threats. The night is the time for stealth predators and even though his higher-level means he can pick out more of them, we're still under-leveled for this region. At least in terms of actual levels, which unfortunately dictate Ali's abilities.

"It's stackable and effects your vehicles boy-o. Think about what a platoon, each with a single use of that, is like. Additional points widen the range, too and increases the speed bonus. There are movement specialists in the Guard whose main job is to help get the Guard where they need to be," Ali replies and I nod slowly. So, not as useful for me but I wonder what the interaction is going to be like with Mikito's own speed skills. She's frightening enough as it stands.

My first victim of the night is a slow-moving, dark shelled creature that resembles a turtle, if the turtle had spikes in its shell and two heads. I ghost up next to it and cut down fast, beheading the first head with a snick. The second retreats and the spikes flash out, forcing me to dodge. When I step back in to attack, I'm surprised that the blows it catches even on its shell seem to do damage, leaving deep gouges in the armor. Fighting the creature is strange, I have to watch out for its second head as it comes in and out but at the same time, any of its spikes can thrust out at any moment. After the first few passes, I begin to target the spikes themselves as they rotate out, chopping them off with the blade before I finally boot the creature hard enough to make it flip over. Unfortunately, without its spikes to push it up again, its stuck and its ending comes fast. The moment it dies, I loot it and then stick the entire corpse in my Altered Space.

That done, I take a moment to actually take a look at my sword again. Now this was more like it.

Tier II Sword (Soulbound Personal Weapon of an Erethran Honor Guard)

Base Damage: 63

Durability: N/A (Personal Weapon)

Special Abilities: +10 Mana Damage, Blade Strike

Hunting down the next creature takes a while as it seems even the monsters around here have begun to grow wary of the town. My next target actually finds me, swooping down from the trees and nearly tearing my eyes out. If I hadn't been wearing my helmet, it would have. As its first strike fails to get a proper hold of my head, the owl takes wing and I get my chance to test out Blade Strike.

The quick draw and focused explosive strike leaves me tired as Mana rushes through the blade, filling it and extending the slash in a diagonal across the sky. It mostly misses the Owl, only a small section of the strike clipping a wing but it's enough to send it flipping through the air to land awkwardly on the ground. I stride forward, triggering my ability again and again as I get the timing of the activation down. It doesn't take long to reduce the poor creature to mangled pieces of meat, which is good because I can feel the strain the Strike takes on me. Definitely not a skill to be used too often. Exhaling, I stretch and loot the body, leaving the mangled remains behind this time. Not much eating there for sure.

Satisfied, I head back to Carcross. As little sleep as I need, I do need some. Sneaking back in isn't much harder than leaving, neither the ditch or the wall a huge obstacle. They definitely need more defenses. Once inside, I flick my hand up, calling access to my Status screen as I dump a few points into Perception and Luck, leaving 5 more for use later when I need a boost. That done, I finally call up my Status screen.

Status Screen			
Name	John Lee	Class	Erethran Honor Guard
Race	Human (Male)	Level	16
Titles			
Monster's Bane, Redeemer of the Dead			
Health	790	Stamina	790
Mana	630		
Status			
Normal			
Attributes			
Strength	52	Agility	74
Constitution	79	Perception	30
Intelligence	63	Willpower	63
Charisma	16	Luck	15
Skills			
Stealth	6	Wilderness Survival	4
Unarmed Combat	6	Knife Proficiency	5
Athletics	5	Observe	5
Cooking	1	Sense Danger	5
Jury-rigging	2	Explosives	1
Blade Mastery	7	PAV Combatics	5

Energy Rifles	5	Meditation	5
Mana Manipulation	2	Energy Pistols	3
Dissembling	3	Erethran Blade Mastery	1
Lip Reading	2	Manipulation	1
Camouflage	1		
Class Skills			
Mana Blade	1	Blade Strike	1
Thousand Steps	1	Altered Space	1
Spells			
Improved Minor Healing (I)			
Improved Mana Dart (I)			
Enhanced Lightning Strike			
Perks			
Spirit Companion	Level 16	Prodigy (Subterfuge)	N/A

Chapter 23

The next morning, I'm seated on Sabre and waiting for everyone to get up. I'm still riding the high of getting my Class Skills and I just can't wait to go out again. It feels like I've finally been let loose, and if I had my say I'd be out hunting monsters to really test myself. Instead, I've got to wait for the team and of course, the usual traffic that needs us to bring them along. I can't help but feel a little resentful – it's not even as though we're getting any experience from this.

I force myself to calm down again, going back over my Status sheet and my remaining Class Skill points. The increase in damage from Mana Imbue was amazing, though the reduction in regeneration rates from it and Altered Space could be worrisome if I ever started using magic more. Before I selected it, I could regenerate my entire pool in 10 minutes, which considering most fights took less than a minute to finish was quite pointless to worry about. On the other hand, in a longer battle, I'm sure that kind of regeneration rate could be important, though that's why the Guard didn't rely on magic entirely either. The System might make high-tech weaponry somewhat less useful than you'd think, but it still was a powerful equalizer.

On the other hand, while neither of the first couple of levels were that interesting to me, the Soul Shield Class Skill was certainly tempting. Being able to project a shield was a powerful ability in any fight. That meant I'd have to put the points in for the preceding skills at some point. Of course, I could just hold off on spending the points till I reached the requisite levels, though that might take a while. Better probably to use it now and get the benefits immediately. Decisions, decisions, decisions.

When the convoy is ready to roll out, I finally pull myself away from my thoughts, having only paid the barest of attention to what is going on around me. The road, however, isn't the place to be thinking deep thoughts. Around towns, the levels range between 10 to 20 these days, at least for the first few kilometers. It's only a few kilometers out that the range starts heading up, hitting as much as 50 before dropping again. Unfortunately, this world isn't a game and while monsters have their preferred hunting grounds, there is nothing stopping them from moving to a new location and we've run into higher-level monsters in weird locations before. As a group, we could take anything below level 60 if it's alone but we've got hanger-ons.

All that said and done, it's still no surprise then that the journey into Whitehorse is pretty quiet. I make sure to collect the bodies of the monsters we do encounter into my Altered Space, winking at the party as I do so. I do have to leave the weird half-reptile, half-bird creature on the ground though since it's just too big to fit. Somehow, it makes sense that the first sign of trouble comes at the gates. A pair of Roxley's guards are waiting and I've been around them enough to know what happy looks like on a Truinnar and they aren't.

"Adventurer Lee. Lord Roxley wishes a word with you. Immediately," the first guard speaks even before I come to a stop as the gate rolls aside. My eyes narrow but I follow, waving the others off as they start to enter as well. This should be interesting.

"Adventurer Lee," Roxley speaks as soon as I arrive. My eyes sweep to the right, clocking Capstan and another Yerick and then I turn back to Roxley, my heart speeding up slightly but not for a good reason. Something's up, and I definitely don't like it.

"Lord Roxley, First Fist Capstan;" I greet the two that I know and look towards the third but get no reply. Okay…

"We have a few questions for you, Adventurer. A few days ago, we spoke about the Yerick's plans. I understand you spoke with the First Fist soon after to confirm this information," Roxley says, his voice cool and authoritative.

"Sort of, I spoke with you certainly. And then I spoke with the First Fist about potential problems," I answer, eyes narrowing. Ali, floating next to me is silent.

"Tell me, why did you do so?" Roxley continues in that same tone and I look over to Capstan, noting he hasn't moved at all.

"I was trying to make sure nothing bad happened. I'm getting a feeling something did."

"Really, and you spoke with no one about their plans for buying property in the city?" Roxley says.

"I might have told my team," I reply and then pause, remembering something. "And Fred. And Minion… ummm… Eric."

"Did you plan for that information to be used against the Yerick?" says Roxley and I note the other Yerick is watching me really closely.

"No, and I'm done now. I've answered that question a dozen different ways and now I'd like to know what the hell is going on," I reply, glaring at them.

In answer, the other Yerick turns and speaks to Capstan.

"He's saying you're telling the truth," Ali says to me in my mind and I shoot him a look. *"New ability, I've got access to the common languages and dialects in the System now."*

I nod and keep my face bland, watching the three as they exchange looks before Capstan gives Roxley a small nod. Once he does, Roxley says, "The buildings, all the buildings the Yerick purchased were burnt down early this morning. As you were the only one we spoke to about their plans, we are forced to presume the leak came from you. And the results, whether intentional or not, are from your actions."

I blink and then look at them, a hand coming up. "Look, I didn't…"

"It does not matter what you intended, Adventurer Lee. Your actions are what are judged here, and your actions brought about great loss to the Yerick. And myself. That you did not intend the results is perhaps just as bad," Roxley shakes his head and waves his hand, dismissing me.

I stare at him and then at Capstan who has not said a word to me this entire time. I can feel the rage building in me, at being so casually dismissed, for the way they are acting. I can feel the anger at being treated like this for just trying to help, but I keep control because they are right. I fucked up. I thought I knew what I was doing but I didn't.

Stupid, stupid, stupid John. Never really good at anything important.

I walk out of the building, not even bothering to go to the Shop. I swing Sabre to Fourth Street and it takes barely five minutes to get to the burnt-out husks of the buildings that take up the entire street the Yerick purchased. I look at the burnt ashes still smoldering slightly and I wonder how they managed to keep it contained, managed to stop it from spreading throughout the city.

"Nice, isn't it?" a voice comes from behind me and I turn around, seeing Minion lounging against a lamppost.

"What?" I reply.

"Looks like someone decided the minotaurs shouldn't get what we humans built for free," replies Minion, smirking.

I find myself snarling, crossing the distance in a blink. I don't think he was expecting me to move so fast, but then again, he hasn't ever seen one of us let loose either. I want to grab him, but I stop myself, getting right in his face while I snarl, "You! You did this didn't you!"

"Me, what would I do?" Minion smirks, not backing down. "I wouldn't dare do anything like this. I'm just a minion."

I growl at him but force the anger back, hands trembling slightly with contained rage. I make myself step away, and Minion's smirk grows wider.

"You look so unhappy. Did your Elf-lover tell you off? Did your pet monsters not like you anymore?" he taunts, waving his hand out to the fires. "Perhaps they are beginning to understand that the real humans don't want them here."

"John," Ali begins but I tune the asshole out.

"Shut up Minion. Now," my eyes narrow and my fists clench as I work to keep my anger tamped down.

"I guess it's no surprise human women like Luthien turn you down, what with you being a - urk!" One second I'm a step away from him, my hands by my side and the next I have him by the throat and he's smashed against the wall of the building behind him, crushed against it. A small part of me holds back, just enough so that he doesn't die immediately, "Shut Up. All I want to know is who did this."

"Fuck you, monster lover," Minion grates out beneath my hand and I start closing my grip, choking him out. I watch his face turn purple, rage tinting my vision while I smile. I watch as he claws at my armored hand, kicking at me feebly. I watch as his struggles weaken as he begins to die and I smile.

The blow that catches my outstretched arm catches me by surprise. I stagger back, hand opening by reflex to release and then Mikito is in front of me, naginata between us. She is crouched low, watching me like she watches the monsters.

"John!" Richard shouts, and I realize he's been shouting at me for minutes now. He's panting, the Huskies spread out before him in a defensive formation, all of them baring their fangs at me. Behind, Rachel has her hands raised, ready to cast a spell.

"What?" I grate out, anger still threatening to spill out as I massage my arm.

"You were killing him!" Richard says, his voice shaky.

I look at the slumped over, vomiting Minion and the anger flares again. I take a half step unconsciously towards the body and Mikito shifts to block me, leveling the naginata at me.

"John, you need to calm down. You can't do this," Richard says, his voice low and soothing, trying to calm me down.

Mental Influence Resisted

Son-of-a-bitch is trying to charm me, to calm me. Fuck that. I almost take a step to him, I actually do, before I can stop myself. The Huskies are all growling at me and Rachel looks pale and so scared she's about to throw up. I can feel the anger in me, a hair's breadth from being unleashed and I look between them all, all my friends staring at me as if I'm the monster. I snarl, grabbing hold of what is left of my self-control and go to Sabre in silence. I need to kill something, and there's nothing in town that I can kill. Or should kill at least.

Two in the morning and I can already see the glimmers of light on the horizon. Faint now, though I know in a few weeks' time it will be as bright as day even at this hour. The guards do not stop me as I drive into town, though they watch me with care. I understand their hesitation; it's why I am making the trip now.

Three days now, I've done this, coming in late at night to sell my earnings to the Shop and then visit the nocturnal Xev. There, it provides me with the quick fixes that I need for Sabre and takes a look at the remains that I bring, helping to make arrangements for the pieces that it does not want.

Three days while I live in the fort by myself, hunting and killing, letting the anger cool. I'm tense, waiting for the other shoe to drop, but I know it's better for me not to be in town. Not to be around directly, at least for a bit. A lot of things have changed but trying to kill a man for calling you names isn't exactly civilized behavior. I was just so angry at him, at Roxley and Capstan, at the idiots who started the fire.

I draw a deep breath and exhale, forcing myself to focus. Xev's first - no reason to go to the Shop, my inventory is now large enough to store a few days' worth of loot. Unfortunately, my Altered Space storage isn't that large and thus the nightly visits.

The doors to Xev's parking lot are open and I swing in, the doors swinging shut behind me. I step out, looking around me as Ali floats beside me, staring intensely at a screen only he can see. If I had to guess, it's probably more reality TV. I don't understand his addiction, but it keeps him occupied, which is all that I need.

"Xev," I greet the mechanic, turning to where it lurks in the shadows above me. An angry chitter lets me know it dislikes being found out, again. I then turn to the other visitors, raising an eyebrow slightly, my voice cooling a touch. "Amelia. Lieutenant Vir."

"John," the ex-Constable smiles at me, running a hand through her short-cut blonde hair in absent thought. Amelia has filled out further, wide in the shoulders and stocky. She moves with a lithe grace that belies her bulk and with her new bulk are new levels. "I see you know Lieutenant Vir."

"By sight," I acknowledge, having spotted the Lieutenant in Roxley's presence a number of times.

"I'd like to talk to you about the Yerick and the buildings," Amelia continues to smile at me, though she has crossed to stand closer to me. Only a small hand-span away from reaching out to touch me, in fact. Instincts honed in combat tell me hers and Vir's positioning to my left are not by accident. They're treating me like a potential threat. "Lord Roxley has requested I aid in the investigation due to my previous career."

I nod slightly, flicking a glance at Vir and then back to her, keeping my voice level. A little resentment flickers, burns away at my control but I keep it tamped down. "Ask away, I have nothing to hide. If Xev doesn't mind."

Xev scurries down and prods me to get off Sabre, rolling the mecha into its shop while I turn to the two. What follows is a pleasant interrogation, one filled with all kinds of cordiality but it's an interrogation nonetheless. She is good though, honing in on any hesitation or dissembling on my part to clarify things, pulling out details about my meetings with Roxley, Capstan, Fred and Minion and my conversations with my party with consummate ease. She even asks about my last confrontation with Minion. She takes notes constantly on a little paper notebook, Vir standing behind her and silently observing our interactions.

"Well, that should be it. Thank you, John. I hesitate to ask, but you will be around will you not?" Amelia says and I shrug.

"For now. The hunting is good and Xev's the only mechanic who can fix Sabre for a few hundred miles," I reply.

"And you're staying at...?" she continues, jotting my affirmation.

"The fort. Carcross crossing," I answer and she smiles again, closing the notebook with a snap.

"Problems with the party?" she tilts her head, quirking her lips and inviting me to spill.

"The interview isn't over boy-o," Ali sends to me, even as he continues to stare at his screen, acting as if he's ignoring us entirely and probably not fooling anyone.

"I'm enjoying the peace. It's been interesting hunting alone again," I reply, smiling back at her, though the smile is strained. All politeness, no warmth. I've not talked to my party, not discussed what happened. I think they need time and I surely do. Time to resolve how I felt, or didn't feel, about nearly killing Minion. That was perhaps the worst part – that I still couldn't bring myself to regret what I did. What difference was there in killing a human or monster? I've killed sentient creatures before, I've killed non-sentient creatures, they are all just grist for the mill of blood and experience. Yet, I should feel bad about it, shouldn't I? Bad about killing someone for just calling me names. Which really is what it amounts to right now - I don't have real proof that he was the perpetrator. At least I know I feel somewhat ashamed at almost attacking the party.

Amelia is staring at me as I think, before jerking her head to Vir and the two turn to leave together. "Well, we'll find you if we have any more questions."

"Of course," I reply and watch her go. A good woman, trying to do an impossible job. I'm glad Roxley pulled her in, it'll make finding the parties responsible a little easier. Though I guess they could just ask the System – everything is for sale in the Shop after all. Maybe they even have and all this is just a show, a way of appeasing the humans that a proper investigation is being done.

Either way, that's not my problem. Not anymore. I watch them leave and when they are gone, only then do I turn to the last set of shadows and call out, "You can come out now."

Sally chuckles, walking out from where she has been hiding. "Damn, how'd you find me?"

"I have my ways," I smirk. Truthfully, it was Ali. As he grows in strength, even lower level Stealth methods are falling to his scans. "What's this about?"

"Xev tells me you've been bringing it the bodies of your kills. I thought I might come and look for myself. It knows a bit about alchemy, but really," she shrugs and I nod, walking to the waiting platform. I pull the bodies out, depositing them on the platform in quick order and arranging them for the Alchemist. Sally pulls a knife from her inventory, prodding and pulling at the new bodies and dissecting them with quick, precise motions. She pulls and sets aside various organs and body parts as she goes, muttering to herself as she works.

"How are things? With the humans?" I ask curiously, normally our interactions are brief and to the point at her store.

She pulls her head out from the gullet of a particularly big, scaled kill to call out, "Tense. Very tense. Someone tried to firebomb Xev's place this morning, but the shop's upgraded so they failed. No one's bothered me but I'm next to the Centre so it'd take someone really dumb to try something. Now, if you don't mind…"

I leave her to it and find a seat, propping my feet up and waiting, pulling a chocolate bar from my inventory while I wait. An hour later, she emerges covered in blood and guts and flicks a hand to send me an itemized list of what she wants to buy and for how much. I eye it for a second and then send Ali to dicker with her. As if I'd know the price of a pair of Lizard balls. As I watch them, my eyes drift shut and I let them. I'll just rest my eyes for a moment.

***

When I open them again, Sabre is right beside me, nice and shiny and the gate doors are open, trucks driving in to pick up the meat. Jim is there, nodding to me as I slowly stand up and stretch.

"Jim," I greet him and he grunts, looking me up and down before he walks over, only the slight pause at the beginning betraying his hesitation.

"John," he offers his hand and I take it.

"How are you doing?" I ask him, looking the man over. He's raised a few levels since we last spoke and he looks fitter, though his shoulders are curved in more and he looks even more tired than before.

"Good," he replies and I raise an eyebrow. He looks me over and shrugs, "I'm good. Haven't lost anyone in three days now."

I nod slowly, "Yeah, the monsters are stabilizing a bit, though the changes continue."

He grunts, spitting to the side as I mention that, "Changes. Lots of those. Can't recognize some of the trails anymore, can't even recognize some of the land. About two kilometers from here, we found a new lake."

When he mentions that I can hear the sadness in his voice. I look at him then and he smiles at me wryly, shaking his head. No use complaining, I guess, but I can see how the land changing can be hard for the First Nations. How do you deal with the land you grew up on, that your ancestors grew up on, changing under your very feet, transforming into something you can't recognize? How do you deal with the fact that there's nothing you can do about it? Then again, perhaps I'm being too patronizing – it's not as if the dams, the National Parks or the lack of land claims haven't done the same.

Truthfully, I have no answer to his concerns. In the end, we just stand and watch the rest of his team load up the last of the bodies to be sent for processing. He looks at me once more, opens his mouth to say something then closes it before walking away. I guess neither one of us has anything useful to say to one another.

***

"John," Richard is seated on the porch of the fort as I pull up, petting Shadow as the other puppies' gambol around the yard.

"Richard," I look around, not seeing any of the others.

"I'm alone," he spots my actions and waves me over to a seat. I groan as I put the kickstand down, getting off the mecha. Stupid brain – still thinking I should hurt when my health is all fixed up already.

"What's this about?" I enquire as I walk over, slinging the rifle I took from Sabre over my shoulder.

"Minion. The Council, well, they wanted me to talk to you," Richard shifts uncomfortably and I nod slightly. No surprise – nearly killing someone was bound to have some ramifications. "This isn't, well, this is what they agreed on. In the majority."

I almost want to ask how he voted but I push it aside. That kind of answer could end a friendship and we're on shaky ground as it is, "Go on. Promise not to kill the messenger."

Richard glares at me, obviously not finding the joke funny. "They aren't going to press charges," I snort at that though Richard continues without stopping, "but you're no longer welcome as a member of the Council. They also, well, they'd also like you to leave but…"

"But they don't have the right or ability to enforce it. And Roxley probably doesn't give a damn," I finish for him. Sure, we had a jail, but considering most of those held there weren't particularly dangerous before the System change, the ones who survived the initial massacre had been returned to the populace. We didn't have the resources to staff it and frankly, I'm not going to jail peacefully if they tried that shit.

"The matter hasn't been brought to Roxley's attention, as far as we know. He hasn't said anything to us at least," Richard replies and I nod. As I said, he probably doesn't give a damn.

"And you guys?"

"The group, we're divided. We know why you did it, but John…" Richard looks up from stroking Shadow, speaking firmly. "You scared us. That anger, that rage, we've seen it before out there. We thought you had it under control but you tried to kill a man. And I could swear you were about to kill us."

I smile grimly and I then tell him the truth, "I almost did."

Richard's hand that has been stroking Shadow stops for a moment at my revelation before he continues to pet her. I can't help but notice that the other pets have all focused on me, surrounding me without a sound. "So, you don't trust me anymore?"

"We do, we trust you. We just, don't trust your… anger." Richard struggles and I laugh, shaking my head and wave him away. "We…"

"Forget it man, I get it. Don't worry about it," I cut him off, pointing to his truck and dismissing him with a flick of my hand. "Better this way anyway."

"John…" Richard opens his mouth and I wave him away again, suddenly tired. Fuck this and fuck emotions.

"You guys take care alright?" I get up and walk into the fort, shutting the door behind me and walking to the bathroom. I need food then some sleep. Then it'll be time to kill things again. It's for the best really. This way, I need only focus on one thing – getting stronger.

Chapter 24

I step out of my shower, reveling in the feeling of being clean for the first time in a few days. I stretch, shifting my weight forward before walking into my room to look for something to wear. That's when I remember that nothing I own fits me now.

"John?" Lana comes around the corner, red hair leading the way as she leans around the doorway and smiles when she sees it's actually me. As always, it's like someone turned on the sun, colors brightening when she comes in and smiles.

"Lana," I nod to her and reach out to my inventory, pulling it open to grab the clothing I bought from the Shop. I really have to remember to buy some casual clothing soon – under-armor while comfortable isn't exactly relaxing.

"Sorry, I didn't mean to disturb you," she looks me over again before she turns away. "I'll be upstairs."

I sigh, really not wanting to have that conversation. It's why I chose to come mid-day to the house when I figured the group would be out doing their thing. Still, now that I'm here, I won't run. I get dressed then come upstairs to find Lana nursing a cup of coffee and another waiting for me.

"Thanks," I say as I sip on it.

"How are you doing, John? We've been worried about you," Lana states, peering at me as if she could read my mind if she tried hard enough.

"I'm fine," I answer her automatically.

"Really?"

"Yeah, I am," I begin to get irritated, wondering why she's pushing the matter.

"John, it's okay to be angry. It's okay to be upset you know."

"I'm fine," I say again, stressing the words.

"So, Richard tells me you're staying at the crossing?" Lana asks, looking me over again with those blue eyes.

"Yeah, I am," I say. "Pass the word on to Richard, will you? Let the Council know, I'm not accepting visitors anymore. Not without an appointment and payment."

She frowns, puzzling through my meaning before she gets it. No more free experience taking the fort away from me and then giving it back, "Why?"

"It's my home now. I don't want strangers tramping through it unannounced," I explain.

"You intend to stay there then?"

"Yes. It's a lot closer to level appropriate hunting grounds," I sip my coffee, looking at her over the rim.

"You know, you're not the first," Lana states, swirling the cup before her.

"Mmmm?"

"You're a classic case. Full of anger and resentment with the world, unable to process what has happened so you've just turned it into anger and more anger. Now, when it starts getting too much, you pull away from everyone who cares about you," she shakes her head, red hair swishing around her face and smiles sadly. "You're not the first, even if you have been more constructive than most others."

I swallow the last of the coffee, the heat burning its way down my throat as I stand up. "I'm fine, Lana. Drop it."

"No. No, you're not. You tried to kill a man because you were angry and now, rather than deal with your loss of control, you're running," Lana moves to touch me and I shrink away, dropping the cup on the table. Lana stops moving immediately, staring at me.

"I didn't intend to kill him. If I wanted him dead, he would be." I spit out, my voice trembling. "I just wanted, I wanted..." him to stop. To shut up. To go away. I wanted it to burn in the thousand hells for all it did. I just wanted it to stop. I can feel the fragile set of controls I've managed to put in place begin to creak, begin to give way.

"You don't even know do you?" Lana whispers softly, pity in her eyes now.

I walk out then. I don't have an answer for her, I don't think I have an answer for myself. If I stay here any longer, I think I might just hurt her to make her stop looking at me like that.

***

"John…" Ali starts and I hold a finger up to the Spirit.

"Not a word, not a word or else I'll dump your ass back in the Spirit world and leave it there," I snarl, getting on Sabre and heading out. I need to kill something. I barely slowdown at the guard post, gunning through as I head South.

"Find me something to kill. A lot of somethings," I grate out, eyes burning as I push the bike.

"Right, ummm…" Ali floats beside me, flicking his hand around and then suddenly a small map shows up in front of me, just translucent enough for me to see through. I see the blinking dot that is me and a whole series of others.

Blood. Violence. Death.

It's so simple when I'm fighting, when I'm in the midst of kicking ass. I feel the mutated wolf bite into my shoulder, teeth tearing into the flesh beneath and I grab hold of it with my other hand, ripping it free. The wolf growls and I throw it into a tree, calling forth my blade and channeling Mana to send a wave of force outwards. The blow cuts it into half and I glance at the small puncture holes in my shirt, watching as the wounds begin to close.

"More," I whisper, walking further in. Behind me, Sabre sits unused. "More Ali. Find me something tougher. Something harder."

"No John. Put Sabre on and we'll talk, but this is stupid," Ali floats in front of me, arms crossed. "This isn't even training anymore, this is suicide."

"I ordered you to do it," I hiss, raising my hand.

"No."

I flick my hand outwards, calling forth the Companion screen and then dismiss the still defiant Spirit. Fine then. I'll find them myself. I drop points into Two are One, The Body's Resolve and finally Greater Detection, ignoring the notifications about the skills. I watch as a small mini-map flares into life in the top right, small colored dots indicating monsters. I concentrate and the grey, green and blue ones disappear, leaving it blank. Frustrated, I focus and the blue ones reappear and then I start jogging as clouds gather overhead and the first signs of rain start appearing.

Fine. If there aren't any greater threats around, I'll just kill my way to one.

***

Blood.

I slide my sword in the lizard's neck, ripping outwards and blood flies. I feel another bite into my leg, but the feeling is remote, the pain a shadow of what it should be. I kill it with a flick of my hand, sword appearing and disappearing, a head torn off.

Pain.

The stone bear lands a paw on my shoulder, throwing me into the air and gouging out a chunk of flesh. The creature is chipped and shattered, stone

335

flesh carved from its limbs and chest smashed in by pommel strikes. I roll and come up on my feet, free hand rising as Mana darts smash into the body, tearing chunks of stone from its chest. The bear staggers, the last dart finding its heart and it falls, dead. I watch it crumble, just another wet boulder in the rain.

Death.

The horn pierces my stomach, the creature lifting and throwing me with the same motion. I finish my attack as it does so, sliding my blade into the back of its skull as I land, driving all the breath from my body. I struggle to pull forth a stamina potion, to cast a Healing spell but that cold, empty place that I've existed in, finally crumbles.

Blood. Pain. Death.

Blood rushes from my open wounds mixing with the rain, countless hours of running from one battle to another, pushing pain aside and laying death around me. Blood runs and pain overwhelms me and death comes but at least the anger is gone, the emotions gone. Just a nice, floating emptiness with old voices from the past.

"Is that it? Is that all you can say? How can you be so cold?" Luthien, the last night before I leave when I tell her to get out, when I tell her we're over.

Cold. Yes, that's me. My body is shivering, cold from the blood loss as I stare up into the sky, watching the lights shift. There's nothing more for me to do, nothing I can do.

"We're all failures," Mikito now.

Yes, but I failed a long time ago. I've never been good enough, smart enough, tough enough. Always the loser, always the outsider.

"81%! So stupid! How are you going to be a doctor with such marks! Get me the cane. Maybe you'll learn this time." another voice, my father's this time.

I learnt. I learn that it's never enough, nothing is ever enough. You just keep going, just keep trying, just keep running and you don't look back, not ever.

"You tried to kill a man because you were angry and now, rather than deal with your loss of control, you're running," Lana. Beautiful Lana who told me I'm not good enough for her. She's right though, I never was good enough for anybody.

It doesn't matter, doesn't matter at all. The pain has receded and I can't feel my body much anymore, can't feel the rain hitting my face. I've run as far as I can, done all I can. I feel my eyes drift close and I smile. Maybe I can rest now.

Chapter 25

I wake up and pain comes with it, pain from my numerous wounds. I gasp, drawing a deep shuddering breath as pain eats at me, enveloping my mind. I can't think, not really and so I pull a potion out, drinking it down and feeling it take effect, Mana coursing through my body and stitching wounds close, replacing lost blood. I should be dead, I was bleeding out and I should be dead.

Memories of blood-soaked hours, of killing and killing and killing in an attempt to run away from my memories, my feelings, my failures come back to me. Sadness catches me, grips me and I curl up, wondering why I can't even do this properly.

Stupid, stupid, stupid.

I feel tears leaking out and I rub at them, refusing to cry. I don't cry. I never cry. You don't ever let them see you cry, not ever. Like everything else in my life, I fail. I sit there, amidst a clearing filled with the dead and I cry. For my father that I'll never meet and tell off again to his face, for the millions that have died, for a world destroyed. For myself and all the times I've never been good enough.

The sun begins to set by the time I wake up again, the dead congealing and rotting around me. My wounds are closed and I'm healed - in body, if not mind. I roll a bit and a soft gasp makes me look up and I realize that I'm not alone.

"John," Lana bends down, offering me her hand and I blink, staring at her.

"How are you here? Why?"

"Ali contacted me before you dismissed him, before you got out of range. Told me you were out of control. I couldn't find anyone else so..." she waves her around and I see she's brought her pets with her, all of them.

I look around and shiver, realizing how far I've come. Hours of running and fighting has taken me far away from Whitehorse into zones that I have no right to be in, nor should she. "You shouldn't have come."

"You shouldn't have run," Lana points out and I feel that coil of anger rise up again. I try to fight it but I don't have to. It gutters and dies, my body, my soul too tired right now.

"This, I..." I try to find the words and fail.

"It's okay, you don't have to say anything. Not right now," she waves to her animals and they come up to her. "We should leave anyway, it's getting late."

I nod slowly and then turn to survey the small clearing I'm in. I walk along the bodies of the monsters I've killed, spotting the monstrous horned Alpha that I fought and loot it before dropping the body into storage.

My hand hovers for a moment before I sigh, waving and recalling the little monster. Ali reappears, foot tapping and arms crossed in front of me, glaring. Before he can speak, I raise a finger, "Not a word, Ali. You've done stupid shit too."

"..."

"Right, we should head back. Plot me the best way back will you," I instruct Ali and then flick a glance to my side.

"Can do. We picking up the Loot on the way?" I give a nod, no reason to waste it after all. "Though you might want to head this way," a blue arrow appears, "first. There's a stream there, might help to wash your face. Baby."

Strangely enough, it's comforting the teasing. No anger, though I do send him a warning glare that reminds him not to push it. I change directions, following his arrow as Lana falls in behind us and exchanges greetings with Ali, her pets staying close by. I sigh, pulling up my notifications while we move. With Ali back, I know I don't have to wade through the idiotic mess so I pull up the good ones.

Class Skill Acquired

Two are One (Level 1)

Effect: Transfer 10% of all damage from Target to Self

Cost: 5 Mana per second

Class Skill Acquired

The Body's Resolve (Level 1)

Effect: Increase natural health regeneration by 10%. On-going health status effects reduced by 20%. Mana regeneration reduced by 5 Mana per minute permanently.

"Well, that explains that…" Luck. Pure luck that I had to choose Body's Resolve to acquire Greater Detection. It was the only reason that I can think of that I had survived the giant hole in my stomach, the bleeding stopping before I died out while my body regenerated the damage. Pure frigging luck.

Finding the stream, I wash my face and arms, cleaning off the blood that I can get at before finally giving up. I'm going to have to replace the entire damn skinsuit armor, it's so torn up I might as well be naked. When I stand I notice Lana isn't watching the woods, but me, and I give her a tired grin. She smiles again before looking aside.

Cleaned up, I get back on track and head for the nearest body while flicking through my other notifications.

Class Skill Acquired

Greater Detection (Level 1)

Effect: User may now detect System creatures up to 1 kilometer away. General information about strength level is provided on detection. Stealth Skills, Class Skills and ambient Mana density will influence the effectiveness of this skill. Mana regeneration reduced by 5 Mana per minute permanently.

"Ali, did I just reduce my total Mana regeneration by 20 points?" I grimace, doing the math quickly. Mana regeneration is based off my Willpower, so I'd just reduced my entire regeneration rate by a third. Put another way, it'd take nearly half again as long to fill my Mana tank, nearly fifteen minutes. In a fight, that's forever. I guess I know where some of my saved points are going when I get my next level up.

"Impressive," Lana murmurs as we come to the next body and I nod slowly. How the hell did I get that body up there? And that body is in two parts – it looks like I tore the poor thing into two with my bare hands. Well, marveling at the death and chaos isn't getting me anywhere. I get back to looting, jumping up first and then going for the torn apart bodies.

Class Skill Learnt – Frenzy

Due to repeated actions, you have learnt a Class Skill outside of your class.

Effect: When activated, pain is reduced by 80%, damage increased by 30%, stamina regeneration rate increased by 20%. Mana regeneration rate decreased by 10%

Frenzy will not deactivate until all enemies have been slain. User may not retreat while Frenzy is active.

"Okay, now that's just trolling me," I mutter staring at the next blurb as I walk through the forest towards my next kill site. Still, a skill is a skill and at least this one didn't have an on-going cost. One last notification then.

Level Up!

You have reached Level 17 as an Erethran Honor Guard. Stat Points automatically distributed. You have 8 Free Attribute Points and 1 Class Skill Point to distribute.

Right, dumping 5 into Willpower immediately then. I guess going on a rampage was good for one thing. I smile grimly to myself, coming up to the next corpse. Ah shit.

"I'm out of space," I point out as I stare at the corpse of the bear.

"Let me take a look," Ali disappears for a second and then suddenly bodies start getting dumped out from my Altered Space through a floating doorway, the grunting Spirit appearing behind the last dumped body. "Right, those are crap. Grab the bear."

"That's so weird," mutters Lana as she watches the bodies just appear out of thin air.

Having the Spirit pays for itself once more since I still don't have a clear grasp of what everything is worth. Too damn much to learn and not enough time. As I think about it, I can feel the tightening in my chest, the sudden pressure as I think of all the things I need, I want to do.

I stop, closing my eyes and force myself to breathe. Just a few seconds, just a few moments to still my mind. One step at a time. That's all I can do. That's all I've ever been able to do. Don't worry about the future or the past, just focus on the present.

I feel a hand close on mine, gripping it tight and squeezing and I open my eyes to meet Lana's. She smiles at me and I nod slowly, forcing a breath out. Right then. One step at a time and the first step is to get the rest of these bodies and back to Sabre. At a nod from Lana, I start jogging.

In.

Out.

In.

Out.

I exhale, seated in the middle of the fort, meditating. It's noon already, the sun shining down on me as I sit in my bedroom. I slept like the dead when I got back, and I'm dirty, smelly and bloody but for a moment, I feel more like myself. Lana tried to get me to go back to the house but I refused. There's a talk there that needs to be finished, but I need this time alone.

In the calm that meditating gives me, I slowly prod at my feelings, slowly test them out. Rage of course, always that. So much anger – at my father, at the bullies from childhood, at Luthien, the System, the monsters, myself, the list goes on and on. It's cooler now, but it's still there, just this churning sea of anger that colors all my emotions. Not repressed or compartmentalized like I thought, more like dammed with all the boxes of my other emotions floating in it. Except the dam is broken and leaking.

Next emotion - grief. For a mother that I never really knew, a sister that I loved, a world that was. It's a gut punch that refuses to stop hurting, to go away, always gnawing at my control. Resentment, at Ali for using me, at the Council for never saying thank you, at the citizens for just lying back and letting the world roll over them. Pressure, to do something, to save people, to prove that I'm not a failure to myself or to my father. Fear of a System that wants to kill me, that I'm not doing enough, that the next fight is my last. Frustration that I didn't choose right, that there's not enough time, not enough money. So many emotions, so few of them good.

I sit there and open the boxes that I've shoved away, finding time to let myself feel, let myself watch and note before letting them get boxed away again, a little lessened perhaps. It's a waste of a day, sitting here and feeling them, thinking about them, but I don't have a choice. I guess that's resentment again, for the wasted time doing this, for taking a moment to take care of myself. Anger for thinking that I'm not worth it...

I draw a deep breath, exhale and repeat, forcing myself to find that dispassionate peace again as I get derailed. Not the first time it has happened, probably not the last time it'll happen. I've put this off too long, pushing myself because there wasn't anyone else, but that's not true either, is it. Pushing myself because that's what I do.

Not right now though, no more judging, no more worrying – just do what needs to be done. I'll deal with the world later. Right now, this is about me and finally, finally coming to terms. What is, is. And that includes me.

The End

Before the System arrived on Earth, life was rather different for many in the Galaxy.

Sign up for my newsletter to read more about Lord Roxley in the short story *Debts & Dances*.

www.mylifemytao.com/my-book-series/the-system-apocalypse/debts-and-dances/

Author's Note

If you enjoyed reading the book, please do leave a review and rating. Not only is it a big ego boost, it also helps sales and convinces me to write more in the series!

Continue with John's adventures as they deal with the changes the System brings to Earth in:

- Redeemer of the Dead (Book 2 of the System Apocalypse)
  www.starlitpublishing.com/products/redeemer-of-the-dead

About the Author

Tao Wong is a Canadian author based in Toronto who is best known for his System Apocalypse post-apocalyptic LitRPG series and A Thousand Li, a Chinese xianxia fantasy series. His work has been released in audio, paperback, hardcover and ebook formats and translated into German, Spanish, Portuguese, Russian and other languages. He was shortlisted for the UK Kindle Storyteller award in 2021 for his work, A Thousand Li: the Second Sect. When he's not writing and working, he's practicing martial arts, reading and dreaming up new worlds.

Tao became a full-time author in 2019 and is a member of the Science Fiction and Fantasy Writers of America (SFWA) and Novelists Inc.

For updates on the series and other books written by Tao Wong (and special one-shot stories), please visit the author's website:

http://www.mylifemytao.com

To support Tao directly, please go to my Patreon account:

- https://www.patreon.com/taowong

For more great information about LitRPG series, check out the Facebook groups:

- LitRPG Society
https://www.facebook.com/groups/LitRPGsociety/
- LitRPG Books
https://www.facebook.com/groups/LitRPG.books/

Subscribe to Tao's mailing list on his website to receive exclusive access to short stories in the Thousand Li and System Apocalypse universes!

About the Publisher

Starlit Publishing is wholly owned and operated by Tao Wong. It is a science fiction and fantasy publisher focused on the LitRPG & cultivation genres. Their focus is on promoting new, upcoming authors in the genre whose writing challenges the existing stereotypes while giving a rip-roaring good read.

For more information on Starlit Publishing, visit their website: https://www.starlitpublishing.com/

Join Starlit Publishing's mailing list to learn of new, exciting authors and book releases.

System Apocalypse: Australia

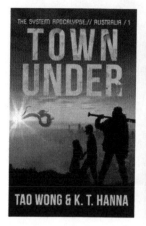  

What's worse than Australian wildlife? *Mutated* Australian wildlife.

The System Apocalypse has come to Australia, altering native organisms and importing even more menacing creatures to the most dangerous continent on Earth. For Kira Kent, plant biologist, the System arrives while she's pulling an all nighter at work with her pair of kids in tow.

Now, instead of mundane parental concerns like childcare and paying the bills, she's got to figure out how to survive a world where already deadly flora and fauna have grown even more perilous - all while dealing with the minutiae of the System's pesky blue screens and Levels and somehow putting together a community of survivors to forge a safe zone to shelter her son and daughter.

It almost makes her miss the PTA fundraising sales. *Almost.*

Read more of the System Apocalypse: Australia series

www.starlitpublishing.com/collections/system-apocalypse-australia

System Apocalypse: Relentless

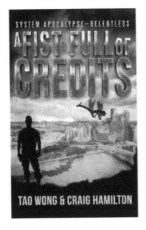 

Bail bondsman. Veteran. Survivor.

Hal Mason's still going to find surviving the System Apocalypse challenging.

While bringing in his latest fugitive, Hal's payday is interrupted by the translucent blue boxes that herald Earth's introduction to the System - a galaxy spanning wave of structured mystical energy that destroys all electronics and bestows game-like abilities upon mankind.

With society breaking down and mutating wildlife rampaging through the city of Pittsburgh, those who remain will sacrifice anything for a chance at earning their next Level. As bodies fall and civilization crumbles, Hal finds himself asking what price is his humanity. Are the Credits worth his hands being ever more stained with blood?

Or does he press on - relentless?

Read more of System Apocalypse: Relentless
www.starlitpublishing.com/collections/system-apocalypse-relentless

Glossary

Erethran Honor Guard Skill Tree

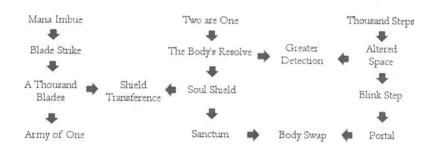

John's Skills

Two are One (Level 1)

Effect: Transfer 10% of all damage from Target to Self

Cost: 5 Mana per second

The Body's Resolve (Level 1)

Effect: Increase natural health regeneration by 10%. On-going health status effects reduced by 20%. Mana regeneration reduced by 5 Mana per minute permanently.

Greater Detection (Level 1)

Effect: User may now detect System creatures up to 1 kilometer away. General information about strength level is provided on detection. Stealth Skills, Class Skills and ambient Mana density will influence the effectiveness of this skill. Mana regeneration reduced by 5 Mana per minute permanently.

Frenzy (Level 1)

Due to repeated actions, you have learnt a Class Skill outside of your class.

Effect: When activated, pain is reduced by 80%, damage increased by 30%, stamina regeneration rate increased by 20%. Mana regeneration rate decreased by 10%

Frenzy will not deactivate until all enemies have been slain. User may not retreat while Frenzy is active.

Mana Imbue (Level 1)

Soulbound weapon now permanently imbued with Mana to deal more damage on each hit. +10 Base Damage (Mana). Will ignore armor and resistances. Mana regeneration reduced by 5 Mana per minute permanently.

Blade Strike (Level 1)

By projecting additional Mana and stamina into a strike, the Erethran Honor Guard's Soulbound weapon may project a strike up to 10 feet away.

Cost: 40 Stamina + 40 Mana

Thousand Steps (Level 1)

Movement speed for the Honor Guard and allies are increased by 5% while skill is active. This ability is stackable with other movement related skills.

Cost: 20 Stamina + 20 Mana per minute

Altered Space (Level 1)

The Honor Guard now has access to an extra-dimensional storage location of ten feet cubed. Items stored must be touched to be willed in and may not include living creatures or items currently affected by aura's that are not the

Honor Guard's. Mana regeneration reduced by 5 Mana per minute permanently.

Spells

Improved Minor Healing (I)

Effect: Heals 25 Health per casting. Target must be in contact during healing. Cooldown 60 seconds.

Cost: 15 Mana

Enhanced Lightning Strike

Effect: Call forth the power of the gods, casting lightning. Lightning strike may affect additional targets depending on proximity, charge and other conductive materials on-hand. Does 100 points of electrical damage.

Lightning Strike may be continuously channeled to increase damage for 10 additional damage per second.

Cost: 75 Mana.

Continuous cast cost: 5 Mana / second

Lightning Strike may be enhanced by using the Elemental Affinity of Electromagnetic Force. Damage increased by 20% per level of affinity.

Improved Mana Dart (I)

Effect: Creates a dart out of pure Mana, which can be directed to damage a target. Does 15 damage. Cooldown 10 seconds

Cost: 25 Mana

Equipment

Silversmith Mark II Beam Pistol (Upgradeable)

Base Damage: 18

Battery Capacity: 24/24

Recharge Rate: 2 per hour per GMU

Cost: 1,400 Credits

Omnitron III Class II Personal Assault Vehicle (Sabre)

Core: Class II Omnitron Mana Engine

CPU: Class D Xylik Core CPU

Armor Rating: Tier IV

Hard Points: 4 (1 Used for Quantum State Manipulator Integrator)

Soft Points: 3 (1 Used for Neural Link)

Requires: Neural Link for Advanced Configuration

Battery Capacity: 120/120

Attribute Bonuses: +20 Strength, +7 Agility, +10 Perception

Tier IV Neural Link

Neural link may support up to 5 connections.

Current connections: Omnitron III Class II Personal Assault Vehicle

Software Installed: Rich'lki Firewall Class IV, Omnitron III Class IV Controller

Ferlix Type II Twinned-Beam Rifle (Modified)

Base Damage: 57

Battery Capacity: 17/17

Recharge rate: 1 per hour per GMU (currently 12)

Tier II Sword (Soulbound Personal Weapon of an Erethran Honor Guard)

Base Damage: 63

Durability: N/A (Personal Weapon)

Special Abilities: +10 Mana Damage, Blade Strike

Preview for Redeemer of the Dead
Book 2 of The System Apocalypse

Chapter 1

"This is a bad idea." Ali, my two-foot-tall Spirit Companion floats next to me, staring at the cave entrance cut into the river canyon's side.

I crouch, glacial water flowing past my armored legs, summer sun highlighting the emerald greens and clear blues of the river. "Of course. What exactly in the last four months has been a good idea? Taunting a Salamander? Hunting a Drake? Clearing a monster lair? Ever since the damn System came into place, it's all been one bad idea after the next. It's just a question of how bad we want to make it."

I check the readings from Sabre, my Personal Assault Vehicle (PAV). Normal humans would just call it powered armor, or maybe a mecha. After all, a half-hour ago it was a bike. I got it nearly at the start when the System, the over-arching mechanism put into place by the Galactic Council, came into being. According to them, since "Mana" had finally reached significant levels on Earth, the System could now be put in place. Along with the System and Mana saturation came the destruction of all our electronics and the mutation of Earth's ecosystem and spawning of monsters from lore. Cue the Apocalypse as civilization fell.

In the end, what Ali and I are arguing about is the blue floating System window dominating my vision.

Dungeon Located!

Warning! The current dungeon has not been categorized at this time due to System limitations. All XP rewards are doubled. Successful completion of the dungeon by a System-registered individual will generate increased rewards.

"You said it. These kinds of rewards can be quite good." I stare into the darkness and heft my armored right arm, where I recently integrated a projectile weapon. While I love my beam rifle, good old solid projectile weaponry has certain advantages, including the option of using multiple ammo types to suit the situation.

"Still a bad idea, boy-o. Could be a bunch of really high-level monsters in there," Ali says as he spins around in agitation.

"Yeah, yeah. Then we run. We still have a full charge on the QSM."

The Quantum State Manipulator, or QSM, is one of the first toys I acquired when the System kicked into play four months ago, bringing an apocalypse to Earth and shutting down all our higher-end electronics. When activated, the QSM phases me into another dimension, which makes it incredibly useful for running away. It has drawbacks, including a long recharge time and a short use period, as well as allowing high energy states— read explosions—to pass through, but it's saved my life more times than I care to count.

"Fine, fine. Light her up," Ali mutters and I grin, pointing the barrel down the cave entrance.

I cycle the ammunition in the barrel then open fire, embedding three glowing light sources into the cave walls. I learned my lesson about going into a dark cave a month ago. Even if Sabre and my helmet give me enhanced low-light vision, it's still a better idea to light things up.

The cave entrance shows me nothing new, but better to be cautious. I launch one of my drones to check things out, sending it to the ceiling to scan for potential threats, before I send it deeper and lock it in place a couple dozen meters ahead of me. Once that's done, I walk in while shrinking the feed enough that I can watch it and my surroundings at the same time. I keep an eye on the mini-map that my Spirit and my Skill Greater Detection updates even as I do my best to stay hidden. I'm a pretty good sneak, if I do say so myself, though announcing myself with a bunch of lights probably takes away from the surprise factor. Can't win it all.

The first cave I find has nothing more dangerous than some mutated fungus. Fungi. Whatever. It shoots out spores that are probably poisonous, but I'm in a fully sealed armored suit with an independent oxygen supply so John 1, Dungeon 0. Sweat runs down my back as I walk farther in—cold sweat that even the environmental controls in Sabre can't fix. Fear courses through me, but along with it comes excitement.

Yeah, I'm screwed up in the head. I was before this started, and now I'm probably even more twisted. I actually like this—risking my life, dancing along the knife's edge of danger. It wakes me up, thrills me in a way that nothing else ever has, and I'll admit I take risks no one else would. That moment when everything tilts, when I could live or die, is when I finally feel truly alive. No more walls, no more compartmentalized and contained emotions, just moments of perfect control amidst the chaos.

Crazy. Told you.

"Picking up two. Nope. Three," Ali mutters.

A moment later, I feel them myself. Damn, even now he's better than I am. Then again, if the Spirit wasn't, I'd feel as though I wasn't getting my money's worth. Not that I pay him—not exactly, at least. He's a Perk I gained for being in the wrong place at the wrong time, and the System pays for his upkeep. If it didn't, I'd have slowed my Mana regeneration down even further and I've got enough Skills that do that already.

I send a slew of new commands to the drone, launching it toward a higher point in the ceiling to check out the new threats while I lay down more light orbs. I wonder what I'll find this time?

The answer is ugly, ugly monsters. Quadrupedal creatures with faces like a mutated rat's, spiked bodies, and whip-like tails that drip with acid. The creatures are dark green with blotches of black across their bodies, providing them an effective camouflage in the darkness of the cave.

Kongorad (Level 28)
HP: 480/480
Status Effects: None

I watch them for a few minutes in my feed, the creatures not noticing the drone. They don't do much beyond strolling around in curious circles in the cave ahead of me, occasionally bumping into each other and play fighting. After I've watched them long enough, I sneak in and launch a single light orb into the cave.

As they startle, twisting to stare at the orb, I take the opportunity to put a few rounds into them. I've staggered the rounds in the loading chamber, so I shoot high explosive, armor piercing, and normal in order. I then put a single round into each of my opponents. The high explosive projectile blows up the spine of the targeted Kongorad, the armor piercing drills all the way through, and my normal round smashes into but doesn't pierce the monster I targeted. Armor piercing it is.

Even as I make the adjustments to my ammo lineup, the surviving Kongorads are returning fire with their barbed spines. I duck behind a nearby outcropping, but the launched spines move so fast and cover such a wide area, I get caught by a few. They drill through the nearby walls, the outcropping, and my armor with ease, carrying their Mana-imbued barbed poison into my body. I grunt at the notification that lets me know I've been poisoned. There is no pain though, just a comforting numbness that slowly spreads.

A light chime lets me know the gun is ready, and I twist around the corner of the outcropping to open fire, concentrating on slamming three bullets into one monster. Each bullet smashes through its body, splattering blood around it before I duck back behind the measly cover provided by the rock. Thankfully, after drilling through all the rock, the spines can't completely penetrate my armor.

"Can't touch this," Ali chants and literally dances as he floats in front of the Kongorad attempting to kill him. He might be visible, but he's not corporeal, which means he's a very good distraction.

Grinning in my helmet, I charge the distracted Kongorad and slice down with the sword I conjure into my hand. My personal weapon might not look like much, but with my Advanced Class skills, I cut through the monster's head with ease, killing it.

Level 28 monsters are a cakewalk for me. While my own Level might be a measly 23, because I have an Advanced Class, my "true" level is about double that. *About*, since as Ali points out, the math gets fuzzy. Jumping directly to an Advanced Class without a Basic Class has given me a bunch of side benefits, including a higher resistance to most effects—like poison.

Monsters dead, I scan for any further surprises before slowly sinking down. My body shudders slightly as it fights off the poison, heat washing over the numbness. I lick my lips, tasting the salt from my sweat while I wait for the effects to go away. It doesn't take long at all, then I'm standing, walking over to the bodies, and putting the System-generated loot into my inventory before dropping the bodies into my Altered Space. The Altered Space Skill creates a dimensional pocket I can store objects in, a nifty little

Class Skill that lets me store more loot and corpses than most parties can as a whole.

Right, that wasn't so bad. If that's all I'm facing, this should be simple.

***

"Ali, this cave seems huge," I mutter, kicking the latest victim off my blade. I've been down here for a good hour, walking through caves and killing Kongorads, and there is no way this canyon holds such an extensive cave system. It makes no physical sense. If I'm going to be walking around here for much longer, I better get started recharging my beam rifle, since I've switched to using it as my primary ranged weapon.

"Dungeon," Ali answers.

"That isn't an answer."

"Yes, it is. The System designated this a dungeon, so it altered the physical space. It's now bigger on the inside." Ali pauses, awaiting a reaction. When he gets none, he mutters, "Goddamn muggle."

"I think I liked it better when you were watching reality TV," I grumble while walking the cave.

Normally my Skill gives me more of a heads-up about potential problems, but the increased Mana density in this dungeon is screwing with my Skill, reducing my ability to scan for threats to a bare ten meters. Ali's got it better, but it still means we have to move carefully.

The bat drops from the ceiling and I sense it just a moment before it hits. I twist, spinning around and conjuring my sword as I cut the Noxious Bat in two. Not its real name, but after my first encounter and a quick briefing, I had to turn off my oxygen tank. They're extremely good at hiding, but they smell like the seven heavens—so much so that even through the environmental filtering, my best method of locating them is my sense of smell. Of course, considering how powerful the environmental filtering is supposed to be, the fact that I can even smell them makes no sense. Then again, it doesn't have to make sense if the System decides to break the rules. Again.

I loot the Noxious Bat's corpse but don't stick the body in my Altered Space, not wanting to contaminate my other goods. Then again, I'm not entirely sure the Bat would contaminate things. I have a theory that the System breaks many of the rules of physics because it's trying to balance technology, magic, and skills. So if it gives a monster an environmental advantage, it wants that to mean something. Thus, the System breaks other rules to make it work. On the other hand, I can punch through walls without breaking the ground while doing so, so I'll take the occasional weirdness. Not that I have a choice. The System is the System.

After another half hour of walking, I finally come to the end of the first floor. And I say floor since I find a straight chute going down, leading to what I can only assume is another level. Arse.

"How many floors do Dungeons have?" I frown. I'm confident, but if I'm looking at a dozen...

"How long's the Ether Serpent's tail?"

I point the gun down, firing another light orb, then call back my first drone so it can recharge while I send my second down. Hopefully it's only these two floors—I only have two drones and their batteries take forever to recharge.

✳✳✳

Down, down, down we go. Wherever we go, that's where we kill. That doesn't work, does it? Fine, you put together a rhyme while fighting off spine monsters in packs. Here, I'll wait. Actually, no, I won't, because I'm fighting Kongorads.

Ducking low, I grab a Kongorad and pick it up, power armor assisting the lift, and I use the creature to block the spines from its friends. I poke my rifle barrel around the twitching body, using the camera mounted on the barrel to target and fire. As I hear a distressed beep, I send the rifle back into my inventory and throw my improvised shield, following it to the last of the still-living monsters, which I stab in the head.

Monsters dead, I squat as my head swims, my body shuddering as it fights off the poison and gives me back full control of my body. Casting a Minor Heal helps a little, so I do it again.

The second level is taking forever. The Kongorads move in larger packs down here and they have a friend, a tripedal creature that skitters along the ground and releases beams of light that I have to dodge. Luckily, they aren't that common, but between dealing with increasing amounts of poison and greater swarms, I've been having to take longer and longer breaks between each encounter.

"John, you sure you can do this?" Ali asks again.

I nod firmly, slowly standing and rotating my shoulders and knees as I check how far I've recovered. I check my projectile ammunition next, noting I'm down to less than two dozen armor piercing bullets. I queue up high explosives next, but I never bought that many of them—I'm a bit of a cheapskate and high explosive rounds are expensive. I kind of regret cheaping out now. Just another thing to lay at my father's door.

Tackling these monsters head-on isn't going to work. I need to think of a new idea or pull back. I frown as another shudder crosses through me. I can't snipe the monsters—I don't have the line of sights. The monsters work in packs, so trying to drag them out to kill one by one doesn't seem to work. So…

***

"This is degrading!" Ali grouses.

I chuckle, looking over the cavern I've altered. If I can't kill them one by one, I'll pull them into a kill zone and force them to fight me in smaller numbers. I've torn down some stalagmites and stalactites and piled them up to create a bottleneck by using some of the insta-cement grenades I carry these days. On the improvised wall, I've got a small perch that has a little extra padding to slow down spines, enough that I can shoot at the monsters in relative safety. I've also added light orbs as far as I can see to give me as much visibility as possible. After that, well, it's all up to Ali to play bait.

"Yeah, yeah, suck it up, buttercup." I grin, leaning back and checking the map again.

"Asshole." Ali heads toward the nearest group on the map, fully visible and glowing ever so slightly.

The kill zone works almost too well—pulling monsters to a fixed position and firing on them as they near me ensures I take out one or two before the swarm arrives. After that, most initially try a long-range duel. When that fails, they charge the opening I've left. It's so tight that the monsters have to scramble and push to get through it, giving me more than enough time to whittle them down. The monsters are so blindly aggressive and stupid, they keep coming because they've got just that little chance to end me.

After each group, Ali gives me a few minutes to rest and loot before we start the process again. Each break takes longer as he searches farther and farther afield, drawing the monsters to me. The T'kichik are the most difficult, since they actually understand a bit about cover and sniping at long-range. Unfortunately for them, I can use magic and I'm more than happy to spam my Improved Mana Dart (II) at them till they fall over and die.

I almost feel bad for the Kongorad Alpha when Ali finally locates it. It comes rushing forward, flanked by its guards, and I greet them with a pair of plasma grenades, one after the other. The explosions rip apart most of my improvised walls, but between the grenades and my Lightning Strike spell, the guards are so much crispy meat. Facing the Alpha, who's just a bigger version of the Kongorads, after that is simple. Outside of the numbness in my body that slows me down and makes me feel as though I'm running through water, killing it isn't difficult at all. I just have to keep ducking, cutting, and shooting the monster till it falls over. When I'm done, I finally get what I'm looking for.

Congratulations! Dungeon Cleared
+5,000 XP

First Clear Bonus
Having cleared the dungeon for the first time, you have been rewarded an additional +5,000XP +1,000 Credits. Bonus for being the first explorer +5,000 XP +5,000 Credits.

Ingles Canyon Dungeon classified as Level 20+ and above

Damn. That was a good haul. That's a huge experience increase, especially at my level. Between the two bonuses, I'm nearly halfway to a new level. I loot the last body and drop it into my Altered Space.

Pursing my lips, I consider the room around me. I always knew we'd be facing more and more dungeons—after all, we are designated a "Dungeon World" by the Galactic Council and System. Having finally run one, I'm thinking these will be a real problem. Running something that's half my "real" level has me nearly out of ammo, tired, and just a little nauseated. Overall, I think it's time to call it a day and head home. Home is good.

Follow John and Ali's continued Adventures in
Redeemer of the Dead (Book 2 of the System Apocalypse)
www.starlitpublishing.com/products/redeemer-of-the-dead

Preview for Adventures on Brad: A Healer's Gift

Chapter 1

"Daniel Chai. Miner. I'm here to join the Adventurer's Guild." Answering the guard's questions, Daniel looks across the 10-foot wooden wall that separates the dungeon town of Karlak from the wilderness behind him before letting his placid brown gaze rest upon the guard and his pike once more.

The fair-haired guard, clad in a simple leather tunic and wool pants, stares at Daniel, waving his hand to summon Daniel's status screen to confirm the truth of his words. The guard reads over the information before he gestures for Daniel and his employer to enter. With a flick of the wagon's reins, Atrieus, who has sat beside Daniel during and undergone the process just moments ago himself, sets the wagon rolling.

"I turn off to the right here, boy. You okay with being paid now?" Atrieus grunts at Daniel, a hand absently coming up to scratch at his matted beard.

For a moment, Daniel is irritated but he quickly dismisses the emotion. At twenty-one, Daniel is well past the age when the term boy is appropriate, but as Atrieus has watched him grow up working the mines since he was an actual child, another thousand protests at the term are unlikely to change the old man's mind. Instead, Daniel just answers politely, "That's fine. Thank you."

"Damn waste, boy. You sure you want to do this?" Atrieus growls out, digging through the bag at his feet to pull out a small coin-laden cloth purse to hand over to Daniel.

In answering, Daniel just shakes his head, accepting his wages and waving goodbye to his temporary employer as he hops down from the ore-laden wagon. Daniel has no desire to retread that conversation either, one that has happened in many forms these past few weeks of travel. Reaching behind before the wagon leaves, he grabs his backpack and his only weapon, a 20-pound sledgehammer. Heavy as it is, Daniel carries it with little effort, muscles from years spent working the mines flexing.

After parting with Atrieus, Daniel starts off to the town center and the Adventurer's Guild, enjoying the feel of the brisk late autumn air. Home to barely more than a few thousand people, Karlak is a small town with only a single Beginner's Dungeon of ten floors. Like most dungeon towns, Karlak has grown out of the need to serve the Adventurers who bring in the majority of the town's income, and so, the entire town splays outwards from the Guild and the Dungeon entrance.

As Daniel walks deeper into town, buildings shift from simple wood to stone, prosperity showcased in architecture and materials. Around him, townsfolk weave through traffic with casual ease, most dressed in plain woolen tunics and dresses. For a town, Karlak is quite uniform in its race profile, only on occasion does Daniel spot a figure that is not human, with Beastkin the most common minority. The growth of the town has stabilized in the last few years, its presence near the contested border between Brad and the Orc nations a significant dampening factor in immigration. On the other hand, the Dungeon that provides the main source of income for the town has been around for over twenty years, and is well-mapped with a well-known and well-balanced mix of monsters, ensuring a constant stream of new hopeful Adventurers.

The latest of these hopefuls walks down the street, drawing more than a few glances his way. All new Adventurers are a potential source of income for the town, and many of the townsfolk are making quick assessments of the likelihood of his survival. His impressive musculature is a point in his favor but most quickly downgrade his chances of being a true earner. Hair so brown that it is almost black, the broad-shouldered newcomer is only 5'8" tall and human, his stature and race creating a significant disadvantage that the youngster will need to overcome.

That smells good… Daniel twists his head, searching for the aroma's origin as his stomach wakes to remind him that his last meal was early that morning. Spotting the roadside stall that has awakened his hunger, he picks up his pace before a sickening crunch followed by a chorus of screams draws his attention.

Just behind him, a child lies on the ground, his body damaged after being hit by a speeding cart. An errant wind, a loosely held flower and a hurried attempt to catch his gift are all that was required for this tragedy to happen. Unable to stop, the cart's wheels have first pushed and then rolled over the child. The child's caretaker finishes her dash out from the alleyway, a moment of distraction now twisting her face with shock and regret.

Daniel is moving without conscious thought; his worldly goods dropped behind him as he dashes to the small, crushed body. His eyes narrow as he draws upon a portion of his Gift and assesses the damage as he touches the slightly twitching body.

Shattered collarbone, crushed ribcage and heart, severe bleeding in chest cavity and stomach. Hairline cracks in the spine, a minor concussion, and a broken arm. The damage jumps out to him as he touches the child, information pouring through his mind as he catalogs and instinctively understands both the natural state of the child's body and the damage done. Information continues to flow, though he dismisses most of it from his mind. A slightly lower quantity of blood than normal, previous damage to the tendon in his ankle still a week away from healing, improper placement of the hip socket….

Even as the information comes to him, Daniel speaks familiar words, "I'm a healer. Please let me do what I can."

From the viewpoint of the child's caretaker, what Daniel does next is nothing short of miraculous. The child's caretaker is an experienced Adventurer and is well-versed in the forms of healing magic available in the world. Nothing short of a Greater Blessing by a senior priest could have saved her nephew, and yet the stranger, without uttering a single word or calling on a God, is healing her nephew before her eyes. Bones knit, lungs inflate, and the bleeding stops within minutes. All there is to indicate that anything is even happening is the gentlest of glows coming from Daniel's hands which surround his small patient. As the glow fades, the boy's eyes open and he draws his first conscious breath before proceeding to scream and cry into his aunt's arms.

Clutching her nephew and rocking the child, the blonde-haired Adventurer looks over to Daniel who's slumped over, breathing heavily, and mouths her gratitude. Daniel just nods weakly, slowly regaining a sense of himself after the use of his Gift. As always, there is a price to pay. This time, only a half-a-day of his past - memories and lessons learnt during a fight with an overgrown badger that blocked the ore-wagons way and conversations with Atrieus - are sacrificed to his Gift.

Around Daniel, the watching crowd and the cart driver gawk at the miraculous healing; the gossip mill among the townsfolk will have new grist tonight. A good Samaritan carries over Daniel's dropped items, patting him on his back in congratulations before he leaves to finish his own errands for the day. The Samaritan's actions break the spell, with others crowding around and thanking Daniel and murmuring congratulations and consolations to the blonde-haired Adventurer, who still clutches her nephew to her chest.

Eventually, the child calms, and the crowd disperses as Daniel's attempts to make them leave finally make a dent. Work done, he stands with a groan and bends to pick up his pack and hammer but is stopped from leaving by a hand on his arm.

"Thank you." Her voice is soft, cultured and feminine, a sharp contrast to her bearing and appearance. Short-cut yellow hair, an aquiline nose, and piercing blue eyes rest upon a face that many would call striking. The adventurer holds herself with a martial air, a hand unconsciously resting on her sword hilt, the shape of her toned and firm body easily seen under the loose cut blouse she wears. "My name is Mary Lavie, and this is Charles."

"Daniel Chai." He smiles at the boy, impulsively reaching out to ruffle the child's hair, "You'll watch yourself running out into the road next time, right?"

The boy nods slightly, his face hidden in Mary's pants. He peeks out with his own pair of blue eyes around her pant leg before burying his face once more. In the child's mind, he will still feel the breaking and the healing, a stark contrast of experiences that will, thankfully, fade in the coming hours.

As Daniel sways slightly, the Gift always taking a little of his own strength to fuel, Mary queries, "Are you okay?"

"Yes. Just a little tired and hungry. I'll be fine after a meal."

A smile brightens Mary's face, and she gestures down the road, "My sister runs the Spinning Top, just down this way. She'll want to thank you too."

For a moment, Daniel considers refusing, but he reconsiders quickly, remembering the weight of his purse. Even the payment from Atrieus is insufficient to truly fatten it out, especially with his expected expenses in the next few days. He nods gratefully in acceptance and Mary smiles, her blue eyes sparkling at his acceptance.

"This way."

Read more of the completed series Adventures on Brad

www.starlitpublishing.com/collections/adventures-on-brad

Made in the USA
Columbia, SC
05 August 2024

39513162R00202